ALSO BY MIGUEL SYJUCO

Ilustrado

I

WAS THE

PRESIDENT'S

MISTRESS!!

* **I** *

WAS THE PRESIDENT'S MISTRESS!!

MIGUEL SYJUCO

FARRAR, STRAUS AND GIROUX NEW YORK

Farrar, Straus and Giroux
120 Broadway, New York 10271

Printed in the United States of America
First edition, 2022

Library of Congress Cataloging-in-Publication Data
Names: Syjuco, Miguel, 1976– author.
Title: I was the president's mistress!! / Miguel Syjuco.
Description: First edition. | New York : Farrar, Straus and Giroux, 2022.
Identifiers: LCCN 2021053878 | ISBN 9780374174057 (hardcover)
Subjects: LCGFT: Novels.
Classification: LCC PR9550.9.S96 I4 2022 | DDC 823/.92—dc23/eng/20211105
LC record available at https://lccn.loc.gov/2021053878

International Edition ISBN: 978-0-374-60757-9

Our books may be purchased in bulk for promotional, educational, or business
use. Please contact your local bookseller or the Macmillan Corporate and
Premium Sales Department at 1-800-221-7945, extension 5442, or by email at
MacmillanSpecialMarkets@macmillan.com.

www.fsgbooks.com
www.twitter.com/fsgbooks · www.facebook.com/fsgbooks

10 9 8 7 6 5 4 3 2 1

I
WAS THE
President's Mistress!!

THE CELEBRITY
TELL-ALL MEMOIR

BY VITA NOVA
(with Miguel Syjuco)

Acclaim for Vita Nova's

I Was the President's Mistress!!

"Finally: the explosive exposé! Singer, dancer, movie star, philanthropist, former paramour to the most powerful man in the realm, the tragic Vita Nova puzzled together an uncompromising life lived with too many compromises . . . Beneath sundered bodice and heaving breasts beat a heart bolder than any beast's on the skin of this earth—but to bare, on the temple's steps, the truths of society's malignant cancer, Vita had to touch the untouchable, and offer mankind the ultimate sacrifice: herself. That she did, like a kamikaze bomb blast."
—Furio Almondo, author of *Broadsides: The Collected Columns*

!!

"A scandalous . . . kaleidoscopic . . . five-star . . . steaming . . . cannonade . . . of brazen fabulism . . . and amalgamated ratfuckery."
—Ambassador K. Sisboy Pansen, former host of *Heds & Tales*

!!

"I spy a certain determined darling . . .
turning our country inside out, like dirty laundry . . .
South is now North, West follows East . . . in this love letter to baduy."
—Kitschy Katigbak, columnist, The One-Eyed Woman

!!

"The bridges are ablaze!
And the powerful reign from behind locked doors.
Within this unfinished labyrinth: a book of keys."
—Crispin Salvador, author of *Ilustrado*

To my fans, my lovers, my haters, but especially to my Mama.
—VITA NOVA

For Clinton, Bryan, and Carlos, whom we lost too soon.
But most of all for Emma, whom I found, finally, forever.
—MIGUEL SYJUCO

Content Warning

This volume contains personalities expressing references to ableism, abortion, addiction, alcoholism, animal cruelty, anti-Semitism, blades, body-shaming, bullying, cancer, cults, death of a prominent character, deceased family members, depression, domestic abuse, eating disorders, foul language, genocide, gruesome descriptions, guns, hate speech, homophobia, incarceration, infertility, infidelity, injustice, intolerance, Islamophobia, kidnapping/abduction, mental illness, miscarriage, misogyny, murder, nonconsensual sexual activity, oppression, pedophilia, police brutality, prostitution, racist language and depictions, religious extremism, religious shaming, sexual assault, slavery and human trafficking, slut-shaming, suicide, torture, transphobia, vigilantes, violence, war, workplace harassment, xenophobia, and other content that may disturb some readers.

Specific to the Philippine context, this volume may contain opinions subjectively construed as expounding and proclaiming doctrines openly contrary to public morals; glorifying criminals and condoning crimes; serving to satisfy the market for violence, lust, and pornography; offending race and religion; tending to abet traffic in and use of prohibited drugs; and standing contrary to law, public order, morals, and good customs, established policies, lawful orders, decrees, and edicts.

This volume may also contain fair comment on matters of public interest misinterpreted by certain individuals as malicious imputations of crimes, vices, or defects, real or imaginary, or acts, omissions, conditions, statuses, or circumstances tending to cause the dishonor, discredit, or contempt of natural and juridical persons, or to blacken the memory of one who is dead.

We acknowledge that words—along with ideas, images, facts, and fictions—can be weapons just as they can be tools. This volume engages in discourse on vital subjects that elicit all manner of human emotions and may therefore be confronting. We expressly state that the perspectives contained herein are entirely those of the personalities presented and are neither those of their interlocutor nor those of the publisher.

Publisher's Note

On the afternoon before the bombing, an email was sent to us
that included, as attachments, twenty-four voice recordings.

Versions of questionable veracity have since circulated
on the internet before being repeatedly taken down.

We have therefore decided it is in the public's interest
for us to publish everything. At the time of printing,
the raw MPEG-4 audio files could still be accessed here:
https://www.iwasthepresidentsmistress.com.
(Use of a virtual private network is strongly advised.)

For complete transparency, we have printed all twenty-four
interviews verbatim, translated into English from the
vernacular only where necessary for wider accessibility.

It is our responsibility to publish these materials unabridged.
It is yours to make sense of them.

from: Miguel Syjuco ███████████████
to: ███████████████
date: 11 Dec, 13:43
subject: Update
Dear ████,

Happy holidays, old man! Hope your new bride kept you cozy during the blizzard. (Congrats again!) Been seeing photos on Facebook; I miss Manhattan mornings after snowfall--a world away from the decidedly exotic tropical craziness of the Pearl of the Orient (here, the Christmas season begins in August & our elections are an endless fiesta).

Am jammed in traffic en route to the storied Plaza Miranda, for VN's final rally before polls open tomorrow.

I tried your advice, but she's typically stubborn. I've explained journalistic responsibility, ad nauseam, yet she won't budge on my interviewing her other friends or colleagues. I'll give it one last college try after my closing powwow with her tomorrow (luck may yet be a lady, if VN's in a victorious mood).

Meantime: am lobbing over what I've thus far. (See zip file attached.) Early: to give your poor fact-checkers a fighting chance, ere our deadline looms.

So here's 12 (of 13) with VN. & another 12 (in total) from:

President Fernando V. Estregan;
Former Press Secretary and Special Assistant to the President Kingsley Belli;
Deepak Roy (who's now in Canada);
Leader of the Opposition, Senator Nuredin Bansamoro;
Bishop Verdolagas Baccante, OP;
Steve "DJ RedCentre" Robert;
Governor Rolex Aguirre;
Petty Officer Second Class LeTrel Dyson, USN (Retired);
The journalist Furio Almondo;
Narciso Odyseo "Cat" Jang-Salvador IV;
Juan Miguel "One-Mig" Sontua;
Basilio "Loy" Bonifacio, whom I finished interviewing in jail moments ago.

One more to go with VN, post-elections. More anon.
Best, Miguel

PROVERBS 31:25

Vita Nova Transcript: 1 of 13.

(26:31.41—VN1.M4A)

I know you're wondering—yes, it's true: his birdie *is* thick, as he's always saying, but like a thumb is to a finger, and hard to find beneath the paunch and hair that make a nest for it to rest on its two eggs—or *repose*, if metaphor's more politically correct re: the pitutoys of powerful men. His is bigger than you'd guess, smaller than he thinks—and would prove his downfall, obviously. On his lap I'd lay my head and talk to it: Hello there, little sir, you look noble, endearing—why do you quiver with such rage? At attention it resembled a speechifying Mussolini, like in the photos in the biographies the president left by the toilet in my CR. Did you know that we spend a life's total of ninety days on the can? He admired men so great we know them by their initials: JFK, LKY, FDR—the kind you'd never imagine on a porcelain throne—though most of all he respected Hitler, the brilliant and tragic, he said, whose one name was enough. But it was in my lover's that I believed truly, coz he believed in me, and let me lead. Between two fingers I'd make little FVE march, and dance, and sing the national anthem—falsetto, vibrato—and peck it on the head, declaring: ♫ *Viva il Duce!* ♫ When the president laughed he looked like his dashing old self from the Technicolor screen. "Vita," he'd whisper, "my life"—touching my face with fingers smelling of Marlboros and Brylcreem, caressing my closed eyes like a blind lover wishing a final farewell. And I'd sing: ♫ *Viva President Fernando Valdes Estregan!* ♫

(Lighter click. Exhalation)

Sorry—TMI? Just thought you'd want me to start at the most intimate. Guys are the biggest gossips, don't deny. Coz knowledge is power. Time the world knew every juicy detail—especially *my* side, instead of all that cyberbullying by the Nandotards, with their fake news: that I'm a tool of the Liberty Party, that I'm the lesbian lover of the lady senator Lucy Lontok, that we're all in cahoots, adding oil to her old corruption accusations, orchestrating this impeachment together, because of course. I've never claimed to be the sharpest tool in the shed, but we all know I'm the shiniest—and that triggers them. Li'l ol' me and my twenty-point-two million Instagram followers. If politics is showbiz for ugly people, then in politics my imperial beauty will change the motherlovin' world. In a couple of weeks I, oh, you know, *testify*. And from the closet the skeletons will sashay. So keep that recorder pointed my way, coz here we go: Vita Nova, hashtag-no-filter. Welcome to her celebrity tell-all memoir. Our setting: a sweating, heaving country, where the future's always promised, and men act like boys, and women are punished for not putting up with it. The time: ever now. The plot: a lost lass rises from the ashes; a desperate assassin brandishes a pistol; a government is set to fall to a scandal everyone calls Sexy-Sexygate. Among the players: a flawed dreamer who boxed and acted his way to the presidency; his Koran-toting nemesis in the Senate; a horny bishop; a cowboy turned warlord; an American naval officer offering a way out; a washed-up reporter redeemed by one last scoop; a poor little rich boy dying with his dynasty; and, of course, a high school sweetheart gone cray from decades of disappointment. Juicy enough for you? It's got legs, right? Viewer discretion *is* advised. TBH, our nation's dramedy started long before the lady senator Lontok pushed this latest impeachment, and even super before Mister President Nando caught me recording his conversations—about withdrawing police protection from certain troublesome you-know-whos. In fact, we could say it started thirtysomething years ago, when my father abandoned my pregnant mother and gave the world a new heroine for me to emulate. But history will write that the real unraveling started the first day of this month, on what the media's dubbed Sizzle Saturday, the hottest date ever recorded, at the launch of my expanded Mustard Seed Foundation, in a covered basketball court slash multipurpose town hall in my old hood in Angeles—city of angels!—with Nando deciding it was too hot to wear his bulletproof vest, because anyway the crowd consisted mostly of battered women—"And what harm can they do?"

he said, in that way I actually once found attractive. About men like him, Mama had warned me—but my beshie Jojie says I have a father complex, coz Daddy Dearest was actually Daddy Deadest. (And beshies know besh.) According to Jojie's proven wisdom—from the University of Life and reality TV—I tend to romanticize my father's absence, which makes me fall for dangerous dudes. But that afternoon, when my first love, Loy, stepped through the audience to point that shining pistol, and the presidential guard piled on Nando—leaving me and Loy the last ones standing among the cowering crowd—the first thought I thought was, maybe Jojie's right, maybe I *should* rethink my terrible taste in men. Coz obviously.

(Laughter)

Then came the Fart that Shook the Nation. When Furio—good ol' Furio, back in my life and back on the beat—when Furio encouraged me to use my responsibility as a social media influencer to bust that story wide open, and connected me to his old colleagues in mainstream media, and put me in touch with you to help ghostwrite my autobiography, there was no way for the president, and his Estregan's Everlasting Supporters, to put this Pandora back in her box. Those 'Tards were always too baduy—as in, capital B-A-D-U-Y, which spells: totally tacky to death. Like, who thought it would be so fetch to adopt the same initials as the Estregan Elimination Squads? Shameless, kinda; baduy, totally. And aren't they all just überfugly? I was never one of them—they rode his coattails. Me, I actually loved the guy. Since before this presidential term, before even his first one he got ousted from, and way before he was even mayor. Loved him since those Betamax tapes my mother brought home from Tita Henny's corner store slash beauty parlor slash video rental shop. Tita Henny was such a fan, back since Nando's boxing days, which I'm too young to remember, naturellement. Back when Henny, the local entrepreneuse, was still Henry the regional welterweight champion, which I only discovered after being sent out to pay for her taxi one afternoon—she came to lunch, all in a huff of tattooed eyebrows raised like pleas to heaven, "Horribly insulted!" she declared, by the cabbie, who I found, head back and snoring, in the driver's seat, a red bump on his forehead expanding like in the cartoons. That was my mother's BFF—towering Tita Henny, her huge hugs all lavender,

baby powder, and batik muumuu. "Hello, dear . . . ," she'd say, dabbing
her brow with a lacy handkerchief, her voice a sultry baritone, just like
this: "help me carry these to my shop"—bags of sample sachets of hair
dye (Provençal Violet, Terra-Cotta Warrior, Angel's Gold), which she'd
take the bus to the city for every week. To me her ropy arms and mon-
umental knuckles were normal, just who she was. At least until RJ,
our neighborhood ngongo—since no community's complete without a
harelipped rumormonger; just saying—till he pointed at the knocked-
out taxi driver and whispered in my ear, deadnaming Tita Henny, like
an inside joke, though to me it was more like a superhero's origin story.
Apparently everyone knew, and nobody cared, coz why should they?

(Muffled)

Sorry—lapel mic almost fell. So, Tita Henny: such a fan of the great
Nando Estregan that she'd send Mama home under tottering stacks of
Betamax tapes, after my mother rescued a junked player from the U.S.
air base, where she worked in the canteen, and fixed it with her trusty
Swiss Army knife, though the tracking was always annoying, fuzzing
out at the best parts like the most unfun video game ever. (No Nintendo
for me, just dirty tape heads.) Watching together became our ritual,
after dinner, when I'd clean the table so Mama could roll out the fabric she was cutting—she dressed all the women in the neighborhood,
to pay for the materials for my pageant gowns. Yup—I went all the
way to runner-up in the regional Snow White Lightening Soap's Little
Queencess finals. So anyways, our first Nando Estregan movie, my
gateway drug, was, of course, *A Pocketful of Bullets*—because: classic—
then *Robbing Hood*, then *The Copabanana Republic*—still my fave out of
all his musicals. Oh, em, gee, could Nando ever mambo, which makes
sense: his boxing nickname was Sweet Mr. Suavé. Eventually, when I
was old enough, he went from childhood idol to teenage crush, thanks
to that trilogy that made him everyone's avenging guardian angel: *My
Brother's Keeper*; *My Brother, Cain*; and *Dear Brother, Dead Brother*. Not
only did Nando produce them, with his championship winnings, he
did his own stunts and sang his own songs. Hubba-hubba, right? As
Tita Henny always said: Talent is the most attractive talent. You know
that famous duet Nando did with Winkee, the iconic unano action
star—now the party-list congressman for the Midgets' Alliance of the

Philippines? You must've caught their viral vid last year—ancient ar-
chival footage on d'YouTubes—Frankenstein and Igor out to see the
world, duetting: ♪ *With a big heart walk tall. No matter if you're small . . .* ♪
That's Nando's real voice—a capella, no auto-tuner. Quite the crooner,
despite his pronounciations. Sweet Mr. Suavé, the southpaw gangster
with a castrato tenor's wounded soul. No way would I get in the way of
him singing "My Way" at karaoke; rumor has it he's killed three men
for singing it ahead of him, which people say happens in the Philippines with that song—don't know why, it's just a song, and anyways
nobody sings it better than me (forget bel canto, I can belt-o). Seriously,
the motherlovin' best: ♪ *I do it my way . . .* ♪ But that's the thing with
urban legends: people love believing them, and Nando's made him
mayor of Korpus Kristi—the famous left hook turned infamous iron
fist, prowling the moonless streets on his vintage Lambretta, appre-
hending sex manyaks who surrender the instant they recognize his
signature wristbands, his unlit cigar, his broken-nosed backlit profile,
as he pulls up under a stuttering streetlight and approaches with a fa-
therly sigh and shake of the head. Who cares whether it's true. Which
brings us back to his penis—want to know his nickname for it? Yes,
nickname. Surely yours must have one—but please don't tell, we're
not there yet, and never will be, thanks. Don't know why men nickname their privates; mine doesn't have her own name, she just *is*. But
his was Rabbi Tickle. As in: "Don't you dare wake Rabbi Tickle!" And:
"Here comes Rabbi Tickle, out to get you!" Yes, Rabbi Tickle—I don't
know why, since both he and it are Asian and not remotely Jewish.
Probably from his favorite joke, about the inventor of circumcision—
the Hasidic surgeon, Doctor Katzurkackov. Chaboom!

(Laughter)

Puns: the beating heart of Filipino humor—coz life's too hard for complicated jokes. Unless, of course, it's a cosmic one. When everything
went down on Sizzle Saturday, when the presidential guards wrestled Loy to the floor, in that instant of silence which felt like forever,
I looked at Loy, then I looked at Nando, as he pushed himself up from
his own pile of bodyguards—staggering to his feet, still holding the
huge golden scissors, untangling himself from the red, yellow, and
royal blue ribbons he was supposed to cut. Somehow, right then and

there, my life having flashed before my eyes—from my first love to possibly my last—I realized I had to make my choice: betray poor Nando or betray our poor nation. Coz our years together, I'd convinced myself I could make up for his sins, in my role as his latest lover—well, technically, no longer latest, but still his fave—compensating for him, and his good intentions that went bad. So while others Zoom-schooled or made sourdough, I spent my pandemic adapting my philanthropic projects: psychosocial counseling teams (for families of drug-war victims); online training for girls in my shelters (to sew and sell masks and other PPEs); and even one of those community pantries to help the hungry during EWANQ lockdown (which I had to close when the EES started red-tagging them, which was kind of a turning point for me, honestly)—all that, work I'm mighty proud of; not to mention my latest hit album and three blockbuster movies after the world opened up again. But that morning, on Sizzle Saturday, in that covered basketball court, something clicked. I didn't feel guilty anymore about making secret recordings, and I wasn't afraid anymore of getting caught. Which is probably why I did get caught, come to think of it. Everything happens for a reason. That afternoon, after we got home, Nando wanted to console me. I was hiding in bed, in the dark (an amethyst on my third-eye chakra), not answering when anyone knocked, and he was so concerned he unlocked the door and let himself in—never mind that it's my house, he gave it to me, my name's on the deed. I hated that, the lack of privacy—my entry fee to his inner circle—his fawning flunkies and crony crones lingering like an underage gang outside a liquor store: the chinless wonder Uranus Jupiter Kayatanimo-Uy, once House Speaker, currently sports commissioner; Senate houseboy Bingo Bobot, who looks like a stubbed toe; General Rustom "Rusty" Batlog, once leg-humping police director, now ejaculating solon; and spokesperson Hari Pukeh, the anti-human rights former human rights lawyer; plus Bang Rebolvar, the actor turned senator turned detained alleged plunderer turned senator; and Bingbong Changco, of the Changco brothers media empire, one of our country's preeminent thieves. Oh, and Kingsley Belli, obviously, which was hella awks, since he was forever around—press secretary and special assistant to the president (aka Lucky Lackey Numero Uno). Despite being the one to introduce us, he never got over my moving on with Nando—though come on, seriously, me and King went out for like literally two seconds—and on some level he must understand. Nobody's as ambitious as he is. He might look dumb—the way his steely eyes gaze longingly at each other—but actually he's smart, relatively. Once a noble journalist, according to Furio (they used to be close). Eventually he'll even be Senator Kingsley Belli—mark my words.

(Knuckles rap the table)

Watch what happens at the impeachment next week, when he's called to testify. So anyways, that afternoon of Sizzle Saturday, I just wanted to be left alone, without Nando beside my bed, mansplaining why it was unlikely that an old, made-in-the-Philippines revolver—at that distance of twelve meters, with a compromised shooting stance, on a day with more than sixty percent humidity, with the chaos of panicking women, and the sunlight in the shooter's eyes, and bodyguards forming a human shield on a stage four feet above the ground—no way it could hit its target, much less prove fatal, because yadda yadda yadda . . . Nando can be such an Orion, if you know what I mean. But there he was, ignoring my protests, his dominance his love language, opening my bedroom lamps, declaring: "That son of a whore will hang in the plaza till he stops kicking." Then, with his signature smile: "I eat assassination attempts for breakfast . . ." Then, seated by my side: "And fart bullets the rest of the day." Coz fart humor between lovers never fails, right?—unless it's truly over, and you're dug in and aiming at each other across an ever-widening bed, emptied of gas and filled with resentment, till death do you fart. Which is how I finally knew, then and there, that we really were kaput. Even if I appreciated his effort, sweetly playing the clown to make me feel better, the way he does for those he loves, which of course the public never sees, though we're all familiar with his famous flatulence—the definition of impunity: his trumpet of macho defiance, his trombone of honest authenticity, his stamp of humanity that he unashamedly unleashes in cabinet meetings, press conferences, campaign events, getting into the car, state dinners, leaving elevators, because, gods darn it, you hypocritical sons of Bs, he's OG, a working-class savior, toughened by the streets, in touch with his inner self, including, especially, his gas. For that, Germany had Hitler, but we have him, as Nando once said, and his happiness to slaughter three-point-two million druggies (sorry, suspected drug users) to save our country from perdition. That's his word, *perdition*. The savior who could care less what you think of his baggy jeans and suspenders under his barong with rolled up sleeves, who picks his ears to hear you better, and mines his nose, and flicks any findings behind him—a man's man, and a bona fide ladies' lover, too, as he's always quick to say, treasuring women, protecting women from themselves, placing women on the mantelpiece—for all to admire their beauty and shine. His gas must be a side effect of the painkillers he's addicted to, for his colorectal cancer, though it's in remission, coz even tumors ain't tough enough to deflate the great Fernando V. Estregan, the Louis Armstrong of flatulence, boasting such a repertoire—some just punctuation, others with personality: the thunderclap, the wilting rosebud, the razz, the stutter, the silent but violent, the punctured trike muffler, the concerning squish (which brings up another bit of Tita Henny wisdom: "Never trust a fart"—a lesson, she said, you need only learn once).

(Burst of simulated flatulence)

Now the one that would shake our nation had quite a story to tell, with a beginning, middle, and end; a heinous crime against humanity, launching Nando and I into silly laughter, like old times, till we were rolling on top of the bed, shaking it so much that the Scotch Tape on this little digital recording thingamajig under my box spring gave way, and this little recording digital thingamajig fell on the floor with a plasticky clack, and this little digital thingamajig recording rolled out in front of us, its red light blinking like a siren in slo-mo, for dramatic effect. Nando released me from his embrace and sat up and sighed that sigh your mom will sigh to let you know she's disappointed in you for doing what you did—disappointed, but not really surprised. Typical Virgo. He could hardly look at me. That's when I shoved him aside and split in like literally two seconds—grabbing the recorder, my phone, my stuff, fleeing into the night. And that's how I found myself at Furio's front door, not knowing where else to go, not knowing what to do, knowing only that the one secure place was where I'd always been safest: in full view of the world. By next morning, we released the first recording, the nation now shookt, and Nur and Lucy's struggling impeachment effort suddenly saved, starting us all down this cray road that's scary AF, if I'm honest—and I can only be honest; it's the only way I know. Honestly, all those years, I never believed the accusations. Fake news, I thought—like the rumors his opponents threw at him when he was mayor of Korpus Kristi. And yeah, okay, sure, we all saw the footage of that kid, Albeo Cruz, returning to his seminary, grabbed by cops just minutes past EWANQ curfew—the neighbor livestreaming the shooting on Facebook. But Nando didn't order that, so why would he need to threaten the dead kid's mom? A president's immune from prosecution. And how could he not hate on my idol, Rita Rajah, who took up that case for free, and was also the one who investigated Nando's children some years ago, as human rights commissioner? But for Fernando to suspend the mother's police security, in this age of corrupt ninja cops and drive-by scalawags, to scare her into silence—I mean, seriously? That's not the man I love. Loved. Though in fairness, people never understood the toll it took on him, not having enough power to fix things. If he went all bleeding heart, the Commies would take over, and the Abu Sayyad would take more heads—like what's probably gonna happen to that Aussie and his American husband, hijacked while sailing in the North. Our country is so broken, and honestly this impeachment by lady senator Lucy Lontok was at first just another attempt to stop Nando's new Constitutional Assembly from revising our Constitution— just leverage to save her father from his corruption charges. The Liberty Party, led by former president Respeto Reyes, is so afraid a new Constitution will freeze them out forever—the *chilling effects* of Estreganism, they call it. Those Fuchsias never got over Nando winning this second term after being ousted, in the fourth People Power Revolution— which, tada!, the Liberty Party orchestrated. Look it up; it's true. Tons of YouTube videos . . .

(Inaudible)

Are you serious right now? Maybe you should also have a mic, to listen later to what you're saying. Like, really, what did the Fuchsias accomplish during Reyes's six years? Our country was a hot mess. Our renowned runaway economy only benefiting the rich—the rest of us locked in traffic, corruption, hostage crises, terrorism, families shattered and shipped around the world. Reyes's clowning glory was impeaching Arriola Makapal Glorioso, all because, as chief justice, she led the Supreme Court in acquitting Nando that time he was ousted and jailed, for plunder—the same old, same old allegations they're now accusing him of again: this time, hidden bank accounts and trunkloads of Château Pétrus flowing into the wee hours at mah-jongg, gambling away our resources with the Chinese ambassador. Fligga, please— I thought—fliggas just green with jelly. But I had to know. You know? So one night, in my house, when Nando and his lackeys went again into the bedroom to discuss, I'm cleaning up in the kitchen—by myself, coz privacy's priceless and maids are hassle—when I get a total brain wave: Why not just prove that my faith in him's not misguided? Just record a few conversations to confirm my truth's the truth? Bishop Baccante—formerly my spiritual advisor, before he got all creepy gentlemanyak—he once told me the surest way to affirm our faith is to journey through doubt. So I grabbed my recorder, which I use for song ideas, and is actually like the one you're using—voice-activated's handy, right?—and I taped it under the box spring. Since it was *my* bedroom, since I hated how Nando and his men would go inside with their shoes—ugh!—and sit on my bed wearing their outside clothes— so gross!—as if they're white people who don't know any better—and Kingsley would give me the eye—crookedly, of course—and shut the door, and lock me out, of *my* bedroom, in *my* house. Guess they'd never read *A Room of One's Own*. Like, why must the world act as if it's impossible for a mistress to be a feminist? You know, at first, that was the toughest thing about mistresshood—there were no role models or self-help manuals about such love. No stars to help you navigate that tumultuous ocean. It's unfair, honestly. In everyone's first romances, when we're lovesick teens, there are rom-coms and ballads to guide us from heartache to heartbreak. Of my twelve "relationships," quote unquote, the most conventional were the most comforting. You knew what to expect. But a mistress—as common as it is, as understandable as it can be—hers is less a life of dependence than independence. Believe it or don't. Being second—or third, or fourth—means you're often alone, which also means you're more free. But it takes time to understand that. And love's about timing. As Dr. Deepak Chopra writes:

"Whatever relationships you have attracted in your life at this moment are precisely the ones you need in your life at this moment. There is a hidden meaning behind all events, and this hidden meaning is serving your own evolution." I think about that a lot, actually—especially my first love, Loy. So many years after. ♫ *First cut is the deepest . . .* ♫ I gave him all of my heart, I guess, coz he promised me a better life—away from Angeles City, my mother's expectations, and the uncertainty that comes with not winning the birth lottery. Romance is all about making plans, right? Especially if your suitor's a real macho gwapito—with quiet intensity, and hair like jagged obsidian—valiantly offering to save me. I remember, like yesterday: him climbing through my window, during yet another brownout, soaking wet and dripping bits of plastic garbage from the canal, asking—with his surrendering smile— asking me to run away. And I'm standing there like I'd dreamt of the future and it's now coming true. All like: "Yes"—no question, no hesitation. Kissing him in the dimming light and telling him to hurry back, and not be seen. Then cue packing montage: rushing out of my school uniform, filling my bag, stealing my mother's Swiss Army knife, unsticking photos from my wall and leaving one on her pillow—of me and her at the main gate of the air base where she worked, where my father had flown away from—so that she'll never forget me, and always understand why I had to go. Without looking back, I rush out into the silver hour—pass Tita Henny's salon, pass the local canteen, pass the familiar houses with lanterns flickering on, pass the roaming vendor singing out his snacks, pass our parish church, pass the kids playing one last round of patintero, pass Joe's corner store, then turn and down the road there's Loy, slouching in the driver's seat of a stolen taxi. Quickly, quietly, we drive off, a boxing Nando bobblehead figure nodding his approval from the dashboard, me and Loy checking behind us, past the line of stuffed animals in the rear window, just in case. Heading forward, of course, to our future. ♫ *Coz tramps like us, baby, we were born to run . . .* ♫ And just as we're leaving our neighborhood, soon as the streets become unfamiliar, right when the electricity comes back to cheers in the houses, a motorcycle shrieks around a corner, with two guys in full helmets—one pointing at us, drawing a gun from his jacket. I see him. So does Loy, and our car jumps to go faster, and faster, the world blurring, streetlights streaking, corners coming then bending, stuffed animals flying everywhere, dogs on the street jolting out of the way, the Nando bobblehead suddenly headless, the crucifix stretching this way then that way from the rearview mirror—and in that mirror, the motorcycle's headlight getting closer and closer, and up ahead a stoplight so red and an intersection so busy with cars and buses and gaps closing and opening and closing that I grab Loy's hand and I look at him and he looks at me like I'm the last good thing he'll ever see and far behind a siren screams and a cop car's lights flash the world blue, then red, then blue, the motorcycle's headlight bigger and bigger till it's almost hot on my neck and up ahead the gaps close and open and close and I hold my breath and shut my eyes . . .

(Silence)

After a lifetime, I opened them again, and there was Loy, at the front of the crowd of women, on that fateful sizzling afternoon, the hottest on record—as if all I'd ever lived had flashed before me and all I'd seen was what could have been. It felt like that, but I knew it wasn't. I couldn't help but smile. I was glad he'd see how far I've come, standing in front of huge Styrofoam letters covered in glitter, spelling my name. He steps out of the crowd just as Nando mambos across the stage towards the ribbons. That scar on Loy's cheek, that was from me, when he told me he was leaving for the Middle East, and I slapped him with our engagement ring in the palm of my hand, before the first time he changed his mind, then changed it again coz he had to go make a living somehow. Years later, that scar was how I recognized him—like I'd been engraved into who we'll always be—and from across that crowded distance he gazes straight at me, raising his arm like pointing a finger—then I see the gun, and everyone sees the gun, and the world falls down, and for an endless instant the gun is all there is—silent, heavy, like a bell waiting to be rung. But for some reason it never was. I don't know why.

(Silence)

I don't know why. So, um—that's all. Let's continue next time.

(Pause)

Please?

President Fernando V. Estregan Transcript.

(32:43.69—FVE.M4A)

Son of a whore, the Lord is my shepherd, and all this I shall fix . . . six months, promise . . . to one year . . . time is of the elements . . . while they are thinking there I am blind to their scheming . . . I will tell you about blindness . . . all this politics nothing more than weather, weather changing with the wind. What can I do? I am a simple man only, simply keeping my promises . . . You sure you don't care for cigar? Cuban . . . world's best, sent by my fan, Raúl. We can smoke here inside, but if I catch you outside I will make you eat it there . . . Do not doubt me, I always mean what I say . . . except when I am joking . . . Go, prove me a liar, I will resign . . . I swear, on my presidential oath, I will stand from this desk and walk from this palace back to Korpus Kristi . . . Jet Ski between islands . . . Son of a whore, I am sick and tired of all the naysayers who do nothing but say nay. Let them impeach . . . they are barking up the wrong dog . . . Why should I be afraid? Fear cannot . . . I will never cower . . . I'm no squealing, limp-wristed bading . . . my solemn duties . . . but of course I will duck from a gun pointing at you there from the crowd . . . that is mute and academic. Tell Death to come, I will box him there . . . take his blade for myself . . . Son of a whore . . . it is true, that morning I had a premonition . . . in retro-flect, premonitions feel like fear . . . but fear is a lie . . . still you must enter the ring to see if fear is worthy of controlling you. Goddammit, always they threaten . . . This lady vice president, Hope Virdsinsia . . . getting into my nerves . . . controlling, controlling there like a nanny chasing, chasing there with a bottle of baby powder, to stop what you are building and take you out of the night air . . . fucking Fuchsias . . . pushing, pushing another fishing expedition . . . let them subpoena more tempting bait. Ask yourself, why are oligarchs against reform? All you Richie Riches . . . all you Lupases, Alayas, Pagilitans, Salvadors . . . if you were to break the law and save yourselves by selling your businesses to individuals who happen to support me . . . Why am I to blame for your ruination? Son of a whore . . . oligarchs funding . . . I am certain . . . my intelligence sources . . . I can share with you a matrix . . . funding there that lady senator, daughter of Filimon, what's her name . . . Abbie? Nancie? . . . No . . . Lucy, yes, Lucy Lontok, protecting her father . . . good girl, family corrupt as anything, but loyal like daughters should be . . . like my daughter, Farrah, serving effectively as mayor of Korpus Kristi . . . Goddammit, I should have shot that Filimon . . . when he was mayor . . . that itchy city . . . And also his son, plundering the coffers to build his city hall parking lot . . . They are using Vita . . . she is hijacked, this court of kangaroos . . . but you cannot teach old tricks to new dogs . . . Why should I testify? I am not blind to their trap . . . All politically motivated bullshit! Human rights . . . bullshit . . . allow my right as a human there in the witness stand . . . I will spill the milk, if worse comes to shove. Let my attorney place me under scrutiny . . . due process . . . Attorney Warden Cantuteh, waddling and ugly, but effective . . . the gays always are, to compensate . . . this is only true. And Madame Arriola Makapal Glorioso . . . of all our current twenty-two Deputy Speakers . . . When Respeto Reyes impeached her as Supreme Court chief justice . . . she profited from the Fertilizer Fund, so he says . . . She, Madame, knows something or two about fighting wrongful impeachments. With all our nation's predicaments . . . the Abu Sayyad will behead those two foreign badingalings! . . . Communist cadres will put their feet up in your kitchen! . . . Watch out, there will be chaos . . . a no-win-win situation, this coup against the democratic will of the Filipino peoples . . . I am launching an investigation into those behind this impeachment. I insult them in public and they refuse to reply . . . proof they are guilty . . . My old friend Rolex . . . to save his own neck, what song will he not sing? Whatever you say so, son of a whore . . . saying illegal gambling . . . son of a whore . . . saying I sold us to China . . . Don't me, son of a whore . . . He sold the Chinese entire islands to mine in his province . . . to build their naval bases there in the West Philippine Sea . . . Ever since he boxed that cow he thinks himself a god. Do not throw stones or I will throw your glass house on your head! And that Furio Almondo . . . another red journalist aiding and abetting Communists . . . let that fiction novelist tell it to my face, I'll box his Pinocchio nose . . . The most corrupt are most noisy in shouting corruption . . . like when you hide your infidelity from one of your women yet suspect her first of being unfaithful. Don't you dare shake your head, pretending you Richie Riches don't know what I am talking about . . . Goddammit, let the accusations come. Eat your hat out . . . what do I care? The Lord knows all . . . Impeachment reflects only the will of your opponents. But the will of the people . . . have you seen the opinion polls? I never fought alone in the ring . . . our nation feeling every blow I received. They want someone like them, who gets up and shakes off yesterday's defeat . . . They gave me the largest majority in history . . . what does that mean? They understand me. I agreed to run for an extra term . . . what does that mean? I understand them . . . the ones who voted me out of my palatial cell and back into this moldy palace for an unprecedented second term . . . I keep my promises: free healthcare, subsidized education, military pensions, the corruption in the coconut levy finally rooted out, rice smugglers shitting their Jockey shorts so scared they are . . . Also six million people lifted out of poverty, and all the infrastructure projects of our Win! Win! Win! program . . . funded by bringing Chinese with money to spend . . . regulated gambling . . . That is why my pal Rolex . . . son of a whore . . . he is angry that his illegal gambling revenues are gone with the wind . . . If the Americans took it, he would be complaining, complaining about the G.I. Joes . . . it so happens it is the Chinese . . . he is complaining, complaining there about the Chinese. The future . . . the Chinese . . . the Americans are the past, dictating, dictating there . . . Tell me, why will I accept someone who dictates to me what I should be doing? Go to hell . . . I have enough ladies in my life. This is my own country. Theirs is a mess . . . in Chicago, you cannot even walk at night outside. Tell me, when you go to Chicago, can you walk at night outside? Even here in Manila, when you walk at night outside, nobody bothers you . . . not like Chicago. Do not doubt me, it is true. America is like that crazy mistress not treating you well but also not letting you go . . . threatening there to ruin your life by threatening to ruin her own. They massacred our people . . . ever since one hundred years ago . . . still today they are saying to us what to do. Tell them to come here, I will box their faces . . . son of a . . .

(Unintelligible)

. . . the only goddamn thing I cannot condone, self-righteousness . . . America, what a mess! . . . A house divided upon itself cannot understand . . . our Asian values, especially. American workers, acting always as individuals, arrogantly believing in their own excellence. Chinese workers, acting as one . . . It is Reyes's fault . . . I have always said ladies and retards are too emotional to be president . . . do not doubt me . . . it is neurology . . . Reyes did not stop those hardworking Chinamen from building in our waters in the first places . . . Shall I start World War Three? Over little islands? . . . Go enlist, I will send you first . . . After I became president again . . . this unprecedented second term . . . tell me, how shall I oust those Chinamen? Order Filipinos to certain death? . . . Armed with what? . . . A piece of paper from the corrupt United Nations, not suitable even to wipe your shitty asshole . . . too rough. America treating us like that old mistress, good for nothing except fond memories . . . talking, talking there about promises made when her hand was squeezing your pititing . . . Americans . . . their gun massacres . . . their drugs—oh my God! My God, I hate drugs! Son of a . . .

(Unintelligible)

. . . the one thing I refuse to condone is drugs . . . to bring our country to perdition . . . the youth of our . . . over my dead body, son of a whore! . . . I shall kill anyone threatening the youth of our nation . . . my one commandment . . . What is that harm reduction the bleeding hearts talk about there? Syringes and shabu smoking kits, places to conduct their pot sessions . . . you give all that to the addicts? Bullshit! Do you give your money to a gambling addict to go place a bet? Son of a whore . . . give first your asshole there to the badafs . . . you'll be whistling a different tune, from both ends . . . You bleeding hearts, go adopt your beloved addicts to your homes. You drug cuddlers . . . you want to give shelter, food, medicines . . . yet law-abiding Filipinos receiving nothing? Bullshit! Smoking there your drugs on street corners . . . expecting handouts from society . . . for rendering our communities unsafe? Is that justice? Son of a whore . . . they call me strongman, as if that is not better than weak man . . . Respeto Reyes, what a mess I inherited . . . what did he do six years as president? Not even a girlfriend! . . . Under him . . . Abu Sayyad, drugs, Communists, releasing criminals . . . tell that closet mongoloid to come here already, I will box his ears . . . To refuse to act is worse than all those in my government who do not act holy but act for me, for our country . . . son of a . . .

(Unintelligible)

. . . the one fucking thing I will not condone is hypocrisy . . . These starfruits in Congress are not the boss of me . . . son of a whore, only the Filipino peoples are the boss of me . . . Still they try . . . those Porky Pigs . . . as if I am their puppet anymore . . . Aguirre, Villa, Gordion, all the rest . . . saying I am ill . . . saying TKO . . . you want me to die? Pray harder, you badingbat starfruits! Fuck you! The feeling is actual. So long licking my asshole . . . shifting now their technique . . . I enjoyed more when it was sweet and tender . . . how sharp the tongue of hypocrisy! You want again the Liberty Party? Reyes arrested powerful politicians he saw as a threat, I released them to serve the people . . . I clear the streets of criminals, Reyes freed them back into communities they victimized. Prevert Losojos, for example . . . who raped a thirteen-year-old girl . . . similar to that congressman . . . Romeo something? . . . An ironic name, no? . . . The one who raped an eleven-year-old girl . . . had a tennis court in prison . . . served only eleven of his one-hundred-thirty-two years . . . released by the president with the fake boobs, all for his political support . . . Always that way, do not doubt me . . . Too many oligarchs with power . . . too many scalawag cops wanting power . . . too many courts wanting and powerless . . . jails bursting with suspects awaiting conviction. Until we reform our criminal justice system, we do whatever we must to keep our children safe. When Reyes placed me into the prison . . . after that false prophet Brother Martin . . . son of a whore . . . he threw me into the bus . . . ending my first presidential term . . . I served my time . . . that almost-mongoloid Reyes pardoning me to avert his own impeachment by my allies. But in prison I discovered their shenanigans . . . the drug trade run from their sacred positions in power . . . Reyes . . . the power-clawing Rita Rajah . . . all the rest . . . Goddammit, that woman should be committed, not loose to commit her craziness . . . but her doctors say it is cancer . . .

What can I do? . . . I am not a cruel man . . . In Korpus Kristi, even dogs have rights . . . Believe you me, there will be divine justice. That bitch Rajah hiding now behind the relatives of that seminarian, Albeo Cruz . . . as if I commanded the ninja cops who shot him during the Enhanced Widespread Ancillary Quarantine . . . A woman's best weapon is using somebody else . . . I told the police, do not abuse your badge . . . those bad eggs must face due process. I never told anyone to murder . . . Do not put words into my mouth, I will put my fist there in yours . . . I said only, do your duty . . . if criminals fight back, defend yourself . . . your fellow officers, your innocent public . . . shoot to kill, because why will you let them shoot you? Do not depend on our hospitals . . . our prettiest nurses are all abroad . . . The ivory soap badingbats in their towers, saying to the world I killed twenty thousand, thirty thousand addicts . . . Except for isolated incidents with ninja cops, twenty thousand, thirty thousand fought back . . . legitimate police operations . . . If you are not guilty, why fight back? How many hundreds of thousands of drug personalities did I make surrender since assuming office? Son of a whore, reforms take . . . time and tide wait for no slow man—

(Inaudible)

Do not interrupt! Our appointment is almost finished already, but you will have time for your questions there . . . and if you want my job, I will step down, happily, this every second . . . for more energy with my families . . . the Church permits up to sixteen wives . . . four richer, four poorer, four better, four worse . . . sixteen! I am a laggard . . . no summer chicken anymore . . . Why will I serve an ungrateful country? Already my women are fighting, fighting over my dead body . . . let them fight, so I will always be king . . . But I made a solemn oath . . . six million addicts in this country . . . son of a whore . . . if they continue to destroy the youth of our nation . . . six million I will shoot . . . Goddammit! . . . If that is the only thing I accomplishment. My brother Felix owns a funeral home . . . I will make him richer . . . You bleeding hearts . . . human rights, what about human wrongs? . . . Caring so much about the lives of criminals, what about the lives of their victims? Don't me, son of a whore! Never did I say to anyone to shoot Bansamoro . . . I said our esteemed Opposition leader is so arrogant one day someone will shoot him . . . someone, I don't know who . . . Why am I always to blame? With Bansamoro's divided loyalties, our country will be divided . . . Sharia law, to chop your skinny pititing if you fall in love and put it somewhere by accident . . . Sharia, to force our women to cover their beauty . . . I will not allow it, goddammit! Always I am protecting rights of women . . . look at my laws I passed . . . equality for all, especially the weak . . . "Of course not, Mr. President," he was telling to my face, only six months ago . . . shaking, shaking there my hand after my State of the Nation speech. "We must never allow our country to be filled with hate" . . . that Muslim Commie Christ-hating cocksucker . . . let him defend it there in Plaza Miranda . . . I hereby challenge that badingaling to a televised debate. Go announce it there on your social media . . . Are we not divided now, more than ever? He and that girl senator Lontok . . . if their impeachment succeeds, our country's best assets will be hidden under burkas . . . why will tourists come all this way? What will the husbands look at here? Sunsets and tiny monkeys? The Communist cadres . . . if they are not neutralized, they will curl their filthy toes on this very desk . . . If the cat is away the mouse is alone . . . who will protect our nation from another disgruntled Fuchsia taking there a pistol to attempt assassination of its guardians? That Loy Bonifacio . . . son of a . . .

(Unintelligible)

. . . the only thing a person should never condone is blind faith . . . badingbat Catholic bishops there in their dresses . . . like that one who tried to touch me when I was a student . . . Now they fight the death penalty, even for assassins too incompetent to be allowed to live . . . Those bishops who stole my first term . . . they grabbed their revenge, their coins of silver . . . all because I signed the Reproductive Rights Bill into law . . . Ousting me there the first time . . . Now they want . . . with that Bishop Baccante . . . the one who looks like the frog from *Star Wars* . . . they will oust me a second time? Grabbing again for power . . . preaching, preaching there against the drug war . . . Thou shalt not kill, they say . . . Son of a whore, to be pro–death penalty is to be pro-life . . . that is what Padre Laverno preaches . . . say no to drugs, say yes to Jesus . . . My spiritual advisor, the anointed son of God, in the Kingdom of Faith in Christ . . . Laverno Kidohboy's religion is from our country, relevant to our concerns . . . Do not tell me to follow orders from some badingaling in his castle there in Rome . . . fat on centuries of conquest . . . That is why I trust military men . . . generals appointed to the Ministry of Customs, Ministry of Corrections, the peace process with the Communists . . . they follow orders because they give orders . . . Loyal to our Constitution . . . not that Church there in Rome . . . not Western values like a god to countries who do not know ours one bit . . . If the military asks, I shall resign . . . I want to go home . . . I am tired of the traffic and pollution of Imperial Manila . . . Let me be frank, I serve because Vice President Hope Virdsinsia is not strong . . . our country will be led to perdition . . . Maybe I should call a snap election . . . my daughter, Farrah, can carry on my work . . . with Junior . . . He knows what our country needs . . . the hard decisions made by his father . . . why I appointed him head of the Department of Interior and Local Developmental Organizing . . . Son of a whore, I am tired of my judgment being doubted . . . The Lord Jesus did not come to bring peace, but a sword . . . that is in the Bible . . . peace achieved through our Savior's almighty power . . . God knows Judas not pay. God knows I am no dictator, but a fighter, against oligarchs and imperialists . . . Why dictator, if I am democratically elected? Why, because I will not resign over bullshit criticism? Bullshit! . . . From the bishops to their lambs . . . from the Senate to the seas . . . bullshit stinks . . . son of a . . . am I expected to . . .

(Unintelligible)

Hoy! Are you falling asleep? Pay attention to me or I will box your head there! I am your fucking president, goddammit . . . Tell me frankly, am I expected to condone bullshit? . . . The problem with your asshole being licked, it becomes enjoyable . . . Let them dig deep for their impeachment . . . So be it, I will resign . . . Let them make gold from this kingdom of bullshit . . . Bureaucrats in government CRs, four times a day brushing away the taste of what they must swallow . . . Secretaries with isopropyl alcohol in top drawers, washing hands of all the dirty deeds they perform for others . . . Take my job! I dare you . . . your back will be stabbed the moment you step inside the door . . . all of them the same . . . Axel "Money" Villa, for example . . . his lady congressman wife, Sinta . . . the nation's wealthiest property developers . . . So I name their daughter ministress of development . . . conflict of interest be damned, our people deserve expertise . . . There are so many rats to join the impeachment! . . . Senator T. T. Gordion, that ultimate Porky Pig . . . with more fat than hair. At least the media are consistent . . . always fake . . . they shall never forgive the No Spoilers Act, the Anti-Cybersex Law . . . they do not care about our children, victimized by white perverts on computers in Norwegia . . . the media enjoying learning on Facebook the plot twist finale of the show everyone is watching but you cannot watch, you are there at your second job . . . They say freedom of speech? What bullshit are they saying there? What about responsible speech, son of a whore . . . do you shout fire in a crowded theater? Son of a whore, everybody can still speak whatever bullshit . . . no law against stupidity . . . Take your Western values and go out of here . . . EU . . . fuck you! . . . Go to hell . . . come get me, you International Criminal Court . . . I will box you there in the balls . . . My country . . . I do not go to Brussels to tell you how to govern yours . . . Only to the Filipino peoples do I answer . . . a simple Filipino . . . not always right . . . once I thought I was wrong, but it turned out I was right . . . Regrets, I have a few . . . but then again, too few to mention . . . Why do you smile? My way . . . my proposed Constitutional Assembly . . . it would have reformed . . . fixed this overcomplexicated model inherited from our American colonizers . . . A new Constitution . . . autonomy for the leaders of every region . . . establish a parliament . . . impose federalism . . . greater regional responsibility . . . sink or swim. Let me be frank, nobody enjoys discipline . . . weakness is too great a temptation, believe you me . . . The only time I was arrested . . . a beautiful girl in my school . . . voted official muse of our basketball team . . . very short shorts, God-given boobs . . . Milky Way . . . her nickname, an endearment we boys gave . . . In the room practicing her cheers alone and oh my God I knew I had to touch her or else I would . . . so beautiful I would die if I did not touch her . . . that is how truly beautiful . . . you should have seen . . . nose like a Spanish girl raised by nuns, fair skin . . . with a very loud scream. I told her stop, stop that noise there or I will not be interested anymore . . . I hope I am not offending you with my joking . . . this is how men like me speak . . . of the people . . . with big dreams . . . that woke everyone, from the bottom, from behind . . . no breeding, no dynasty, no political machinery . . . only these fists and this heartbreaking face and the guidance of Jesus Christ, my Lord and Savior. They accuse . . . for saying my mind . . . for drinking and gambling . . . for loving too many women . . . like all men on the streets, not like you Richie Riches who refuse to share . . . Let us start with you, that Panerai watch . . . how beautiful . . . a family of eight can be fed six years . . . should you give it? Can I force you? Of course not . . . Why should you give it . . . a gift from your daddy. You see? The problem of every president, where to begin . . . We cannot impose the violence of the Communists . . . Oh my God, I hate . . . son of a . . .

(Unintelligible)

. . . only thing I cannot condone is Communism . . . This world cannot be equal . . . even if we give everything . . . Outside my cell they always changed my guards . . . I am too charismatic . . . but one young officer, he told to me about his friend . . . the only way he can tell his story . . . The wife, he said, she goes to work in South Korea . . . not a domestic helper, she is beautiful . . . a magical voice . . . in Seoul she works as a singer. Like our millions of heroic Overseas Filipino Workers, building the world's pyramids . . . Every week calling . . . life is good . . . until one day she stops, but the remittances still coming . . . The husband, he is worried, but what can you do? One day, he receives a call . . . his wife . . . crying, confessing . . . she married an old Korean farmer . . . for a year already, but now she is in jail . . . stealing from the Korean's account, to send home here to her family . . . The young man telling me, he said his friend doesn't know what to do . . . our consulate in Incheon doing all they can . . . like with all our OFWs . . . but a large fine, years to pay. His friend, he said to me, the husband begins taking bribes . . . what else can you do? His fellow officers before always teased him, Mr. Clean . . . but now what can he do? This should be a scandal . . . it is a scandal it is not . . . How can I accept that I am powerless to protect those I am sworn to protect? My guard, he was crying . . . I gave him money . . . they accuse me of bribing . . . how can that be a crime, doing the right thing? The Lord always tests the imperfect vessel. You think I do not see? Son of a whore, I know what it is to be blind . . . to see only with your heart . . . As a boy, waking up, opening my eyes . . . only nine, maybe ten, still no hair on my bird . . . Waking up blind . . . in the beginning, all fear . . . terrible . . . thinking nobody can ever love you, with your useless eyes . . . a burden to your family . . . but suddenly, beside you there, an angel with a sweet voice, telling you what you long to hear . . . a protector to guide you . . . suddenly poking, poking there against your thigh his hard pititing . . . Nyehhh! I tell you, to be homosexual is worse than animal . . . even animals do not do these ungodly things . . . That is why, trust only what you can feel . . . For a year I suffered . . . my parents giving attention . . . my brothers and sisters, very jealous . . . ten of us children . . . running there between the tombs, they left me . . . taking bets with neighbors if I could feel with my fingers who was who . . . laughing . . . I wanted to run away . . . but what could I do? . . . My universe, already different . . . even time, different . . . my dreams, very different . . . only a boy but already wishing to not be a burden. When you are blind you see many things clearly . . . there in the cemetery, the coughing of my father waking us . . . a stonemason . . . coming home, covered . . . like a statue of those ancient Greeks . . . One night . . . like falling, I awoke . . . my sight returned, a miracle! . . . More terrifying even than when I became blind. My mother . . . I saw her praying in the candlelight . . . son of a whore, I thought she was the Virgin Mary. Imagine? . . . When I told her, I saw her crying . . . she dragged me, I couldn't walk . . . outside, my father was there, in the fluorescent lantern, washing dust from his body . . . water white like milk, my eyes telling me it was blood. Even your eyes can fool you . . . After, I would close them . . . listening, to the world . . . touching, the tools of my father . . . love songs, vibrating on the little radio of my mother . . . my hand in the rice sack, counting every grain. As a boxer . . . son of a whore, how scared I was! Each punch could loosen the wires behind my eyes. But what could I do? Choices are for you Richie Riches . . . I thought maybe not so bad to return to that darkness . . . at least everything is sure. I closed my eyes and touched Vita's nose . . . cheeks, temples . . . long hair, like warm water in my hand . . . she sang to me something she created in that moment . . . I touched her face . . . so beautiful . . . I knew everything she would try to take . . . but her stupidity, I did not expect . . . son of a . . .

(Unintelligible)

. . . one thing I shall never condone, disloyalty . . . A bitch on the street even knows not to bite the hand that feeds . . . Do not mistake me, I am not angry with Vita . . . only love can break a heart . . . Too much light makes you blind . . . Goddammit, who am I to question a miracle? But I was blind but now I see, the Bible says . . . How can I not stare, at all the beautiful ladies there? . . . The Lord blessed me . . . I see a beauty, how can I not sing to her something sweet? . . . ♩ *You are the light of my world, a half of this heart is mine . . .* ♩ Son of a whore, do not begrudge me the joy of providing . . . Tootsi, my scared one . . . Gaia, my ambitious one . . . Pasha, my dreamer . . . My wife, Jiloizapet, my rock . . . she is always right, even when she is wrong . . . She tells me, Nanding, do this . . . I say, Yes, yes, sweetie pie, of course, what else can I do to make you happy? She tells me, Nanding, do not trust that son of a bitch . . . When I don't listen I always regret. She told me, "Nanding, do not trust Vita, I do not like what I see." But I am looking only with my thick pititing there . . . blinded by the sincerity of Vita's lies . . . I understand her . . . I also tell the truth even when I am lying . . . But you must never be a holier than thou . . . she was not loyal . . . I may not always be faithful, but always I am loyal . . . sometimes to lie is the most loyal thing . . . When your mother wants to act, give her praise and roles in all your movies . . . but if a bastard puts in his newspaper that Lassie the dog acts better than she, I will stab you there in your buttocks . . . son of a . . .

(Unintelligible)

. . . disrespect, the only thing I will never condone . . . that alleged journalist had it coming . . . So I increased the libel laws . . . To protect the truth . . . Who will you believe there? Me or all the liars? . . . I tell them, do not abuse your rights . . . Only you Richie Riches can protect your loved ones? Bullshit! . . . Even when your family does not deserve, you must provide . . . My father died, I was eleven years old . . . we had only each other . . . Felicia, me, Ford, Frankie, Filomena, Fritz, Fe, Freddie, Famela, and Bong . . . my parents ran out of *F* names. How hard I tried . . . my father, every day before leaving for work, he went around . . . putting his hand on our heads, one by one . . . "You're in charge" . . . whispering only in my ear . . . "Do everything you are sup-posed to do" . . . He died. I did everything . . . stole . . . begged . . . sold scrap . . . Only lacking was I become a gigolo . . . good I didn't . . . if I became rich I would not have learned how to struggle . . . When I was thirteen, I met the syndicate . . . the trainer Darwin, who tormented us until we were angry enough to win . . . no gloves, in the room there behind the bar . . . boxing, boxing your best friends you live with . . . friends you trust . . . friends you study to learn their weaknesses . . . so you are the one able to eat tonight . . . not the one on the floor, convulsing . . . the men who were cheering your name now throwing their tickets at your body . . . You are born in the cemetery, you die in the cemetery. But God granted me lessons to make me free . . . pain is a lie . . . victory teaches you nothing . . . you are safest when confronting your fears . . . strength is not how hard your punch, strength is standing after you have fallen . . . Lessons from my trainer, John C. Evans . . . American, from Ohio . . . the great one, when he is finally ready . . . Only this year Fritz told me our father whispered the same reminder to all of us. "You're in charge. Do what you're supposed to do." But our broken world . . . how do we fix it? Son of a whore, the bleeding-heart naysayers hindering my efforts . . . They call it a dynasty . . . Why dynasty? Because I provide? My loved ones' only sin, being trustworthy . . . my brother Fritz, my chief of staff . . . Ford spearheading the Anti-Crime Organization of the President . . . my wife, the Commission on Workers' and Women's Affairs . . . my sons and my bulldog daughter, Farrah, caring for Korpus Kristi . . . The only loyalty I trust: your faith in what I can give you . . . A wise man knows, never count your chickens in one basket . . . Kingsley will testify, in my defense . . . this, I know . . . I try to matchmake him with Farrah, but who knows what sort of person she likes . . . My allies, our brightest political stars . . . Bingo Bobot, Uranus Jupiter Kayatanimo-Uy, Rusty Batlog . . . Ambassador K. Sisboy Pansen . . . Attorney General Jehusepat Caldera, with his no-nonsense crater face . . . They understand . . . Even Kingsley, he found me there . . . that chair you are sitting . . . fitting my pititing inside his girlfriend Vita . . . he understood . . . every erection at my age, manna from heaven . . . do not dare refuse what the Lord gives! . . . Do not doubt, I will give all that is deserved . . . If you abide the law, why are you afraid? . . . This drug epidemic . . . even one year is too little . . . Goddammit, how deep is the rot! . . . ninja cops, narco mayors, all the scalawags . . . I have so many matrixes . . . spiders' webs of corruption . . . But you cannot be the spider if you are made to be the fly . . . a fiasco from the beginning. I do all I can to fix, but what can I do with not enough power? . . . I am tired already . . . I admit to you, I miss walking late at night in Vita's little house . . . catching my breath, after she is satisfied already . . . you know women . . . you do not strike me as a badingbat . . . In the darkness there, double-checking the front door, the oven, the stove . . . a man's greatest pleasure, keeping loved ones safe . . . When I first took my oath of office . . . there in that field where our ancestors died for your liberty . . . my hand on the Bible, vowing . . . uphold this, uphold that . . . I knew I could not allow Filipinos to live in fear anymore. I looked out . . . the ocean of people, my face on their chests, in their hearts . . . I knew even God chose between love and power . . . casting down his most trusted, most beloved . . . there to rule in hell. Believe you me, boy, one day you shall see . . . That hot Saturday with Vita, I saw . . . I felt . . . like something important you forgot . . . there in the assassin's face . . . my entire life: my father's cough against the gravestones . . . men's shouts for blood . . . raising my fist, always the underdog . . . my mother cleaning my wounds . . . my oaths there facing the Filipino peoples . . . smell of dust and polish of this ancient Palace . . . entering with my Jiloizapet, our children running to open all the doors to our future . . . I saw there, in his gun . . . that instant . . . there is a time for everything . . . a time to be calm . . . to be silent . . . a time to be poignant . . . to be subdued . . . a time to be vicious . . . that is life . . . now it is time for . . . Goddammit, they want a fight? Son of a whore, why did they pick a fighter? That is all I want to say first . . . Ops! I see my sexytary there, signaling again behind you . . . only two minutes left, she says . . . another meeting. Time, the only thing a person must condone. Goddammit, I am tired . . . all of this . . . but what can I do? Go ahead . . . now, ask . . . tell to me your first question there.

Vita Nova Transcript: 2 of 13.

(23:11.32—VN2.M4A)

Previously, on House of 'Tards: Governor Rolex Aguirre lifts the hand of his rival, Fernando V. Estregan, declaring to the crowd "the second coming of your savior!" Supporters in red weep for joy outside the reelected president's campaign HQ. Bodies in slums wrapped in duct tape wear signs saying "I'm a pusher, don't follow me." A beaming Police General Rusty Batlog unveils his seven-foot fuzzy-mascot twin while shackled drug suspects behind him turn from the cameras. The Dictator's waxy corpse is led from the family's air-conned mausoleum to the national Cemetery of Heroes, Junior smiling from the head of the procession. Newspaper front pages fill with grainy satellite images of Chinese navy forces on islands in the West Philippine Sea. President Estregan signs the No Spoilers and Cyberporn Act and throws the pen to the Palace press pool, nobody catching it. Respeto Reyes, Filimon Lontok, and Rita Rajah are led out in handcuffs from their offices. Hordes of Chinese workers smoke outside new buildings where they work as online casino dealers. And Press Secretary and Special Assistant Kingsley Belli takes my hand to introduce me to his boss after I sing happy birthday at the president's sixty-fourth. The rest, as they say, is *his* story. Poor Kingsley's really backed himself into a corner now.

(Inaudible)

Testify? I doubt he will. Mr. Loyal never seemed to mind me with Nando, which says a lot about his sense of duty, and sorta feels almost admirable. Probably why I didn't give up on him, either, those six months we were together—which were unforgettably forgettable, like our lovemaking, as poetic as haiku: short, unsatisfying, but intriguing enough you'll try just one more. It was a dark and stormy afternoon, when we met, in the whisky bar at the Mandarin Oriental. I'd go fiddle with their baby grand on slow days and sing whatever I wanted—coz sometimes only sad songs can make you feel better. My scotch was on the rocks, just like my career, the manager was an admirer, and after that disaster abroad with Deepak, I needed some booze and admiration. So I'm half staring at the tan line from my engagement ring, fingers stumbling through a Chet Baker song, when Kingsley's reflection in the window startles me. He's in an armchair at the back, like a tombstone, staring like a mourner, in a fedora with a not-quite-jaunty feather, and I trip over the keys, pretending I meant to. Of course he saunters over, stiffly, tells me I should smile more, makes a joke about my favorite color being blue, and somehow anyway we end up sitting together, since we're already sharing a drink they call loneliness. By our fourth Lagavulin I'm convinced he's the most rational man I'd ever meet, which was attractive, after all the idealists in my life. And he didn't open up like most men do when interested, oversharing as if caring. Not him, no way. I found out only later, from his old frenemy Furio—they were cub reporters together, back in the day—that Kingsley started as a student radical, long before he was editor of *The Bullet*, a universe away from becoming Fernando's spin doctor and Lucky Lackey Numero Uno. He'd even ran off to live with the Communists in the mountains, composing poems on banana leaves about the proletariat, and three decades later he's exactly the person he wanted to overthrow. I know, right? I was intrigued by his contradictions, his wounded defiance—don't you kinda envy unapologetic people?

(Inaudible)

Like *love him* love him? I mean, I loved that we talked books. And music. And whiskey. And hated on love. And he always made me laugh, except when he tried too hard—like with his moldy oldies that probably kill with the toupee-and-pearls bold-faced left-to-rights: about his being a master debater, and a cunning linguist, and a vigorous packer, who can't wait to turn sixty-nine. What's prettier than roses on your piano? Tulips on my organ—classic Kingsley, with his expensive designer Dirty-Old-Man chic, slick as a DOM salamander, his pubes dyed black, and his plethora of unexpected hats. Like, okay, boomer. But don't get me wrong, he's kinda brilliant—the mastermind behind Fernando's radio fireside chats, and YouTube explainer videos, and the Win! Win! Win! infrastructure initiative, and the text-message jokes—compiled into that booklet, *Estreganisms*—that had everybody snickering on their toilets while Fernando squeezed endearingly into their hearts, fresh from prison and back towards the Palace. Only Kingsley could engineer an unprecedented second-term presidency—who cares about the Constitution, coz anyways it's broken? Hella clever; totally dastardly. But to me Kingsley was sweet, his sweetness charmingly cynical of its own sweetness, his lovingness meant for me alone: snarky, corny, cajoling—am I saying that right?—cajoling, drunk messaging me from Palace parties he hated, or begging me to let the secret of our relationship out—so that he could, he said, "shout it from the rooftops!" Besides, I'm a pushover for any guy who dances me, and Kingsley was just wow—♫ *simply the best, better than all the rest* ♫—fetching me for our first date, when he hands me a box, which, shake shake shake, reveals glittering LaDucas—mysteriously in my size, with three-inch heels and traditional T-strap—then leads me from the car down the stairs at Where Else?, grabbing my purse, bowling it into our reserved booth, whisking me onto the dance floor for a perfect tango—estilo milonguero, at that. My panties nearly dropped, I gots to admit, as the room watched him push and pull and spin me like a scandal urgently needing to be finessed. And there's real joy in watching ugly people be happy—his lizardly face beaming as I whisper coquettishly: "Did you know a tango's a sad thought danced?" Without missing a beat he replies: "Did you know a tango's lovemaking with your clothes on?" Oh em gawsh! Only thing cheesier was me falling for that. So baduy!

(Clap)

Besides, who doesn't love being a dream come true? Kingsley confessing that he used to watch me—"religiously," his word—every Tuesday night, at 8:30 p.m., on that dance show I hosted—remember that?—*Smooth Moves*, sponsored by the foremost tea that promotes regularity—way before I hit the big time—pre-Sexy-Sexy Dance craze, and he liked me since then? How could I not crush on him? Paunchy, pushing sixty, disowned by his son, his marriage annulled and void—as Nando would say. Nicknamed RoboCop, for how he swivels stiffly to face his former colleagues in the Palace press corpse, shooting down questions like they're rampaging shabu addicts. But with me, Kingsley was a secret surprise—lithe with his wit and light on his toes, with a taste for K-pop videos before they were fetch, and a flair for the dramatic, which we'd share like a big bowl of bingsu—a fluffy guilty pleasure that makes your day so much better. When he brought me home after that first night dancing, and kissed me by my front door, desperately, then gently, his mouth plundering mine and tasting of masculinity—peated scotch and menthol lights—and he turns stiffly to go—like: kthanksbye—my face like, are you serious right now?, his footsteps down the hallway fading—that's when I understood that Kingsley always knows what he's doing, exactly. The game was ahand, and it's a game I love playing. That's something the Estreganettes never got: that love may be a game, but games are supposed to be fun, for both winners and losers—that's why they're called games. But them girls ain't playin'—on Wednesdays they wear pink, and pink was never my color. See them attacking me online? Tootsi, the sancti-mommious momfluencer with the mind of a Venus and body of a bodhisattva—always gloating, in her stupid statement necklaces, about her Trevi Mansion (till it became Corruption Paper Trail Exhibit A); in Nando's eyes, her unvaccinated son now makes her alpha cougar, despite the kid's growing resemblance, every day, to her hunky body-guard manther. And then there's Gaia, blessed less with looks than with an expensive flat iron (hashtag just saying), with her flowy flowery sundresses, and show dogs, and dressage, and semiregular Twitter feuds. And last but not not the least, there's Pashmina, the Fil-Am thirst trap from Dirty City, who swapped her striving dignity as a risqué dancer for the rabid influence of an EES blogger—ever since Nando got her preg-o she's like her Exploited College Girls clip, circa 2011, wasn't last year's top-trending on Pornhub Phils. I'm against slut-shaming, obviously, but quelle double standard, right? Pasha gets a pass while Baraka Vousfils and the rest of the Estregan's Everlasting Supporters crucify Rita Rajah for the video that's so obviously not her with some Black dude in a motel in America. Fligga, please! There's a reason Dr. Rajah's my idol, her verses ruling all my vision boards, ever since I discovered her poetry collection, (Fe)males, in Furio's library a lifetime ago. And that title poem! "What is the atomic weight of woman / ele-mental / high-valence / yet like all equally / rust-unresistant . . ." I was so thrilled when me and her became Facebook friends, then Messenger pen pals, when I was fighting Bishop Baccante over the Reproductive Rights Bill—Rita teaching me a ton about the world, and who I can be in it. She actually warned me about Kingsley, her ex, but never judged me for not listening.

(Inaudible)

I know, right? How could she run with Junior as her veep, last presi-dential election? I'll always wonder, but I won't judge—single mom, stage-four cancer . . . And I'd like to think she felt *someone* had to stop Fernando from winning. Besides, now's her perfect final act of re-demption: helping Muslim senator Nur and lady senator Lucy remove him through impeachment—which the EES, of course, dismiss as partisan. Which is, like, duh: that's how democracy works—who else is gonna dig up your dirt if not your opponents? That's why Nur ac-cepted Nando's debate challenge, and we're all awaiting the president's reply. Now if only Kingsley could see testifying tomorrow as *his* chance to step up, to redeem himself.

(Lighter click. Exhalation)

So anyways, post–first date: it didn't take me long to turn the tables, which he loved. Salsa night, ballroom night, some cha-cha, some sass, a kiss or two in the shadows interrupted by my breathless doubts—coz nothing excites a man quite like the words "we *really* shouldn't be doing this." Pretty soon he was begging me to move in with him. As if. Sorry—was that cruel? It's just I never wanted us to fall into the quotidian—flossing yellow globs onto the mirror, wearing ratty T-shirts as pajamas, retreating to whichever side is yours to plug your phone in. No, I wanted to revel in the kilig factor, the joy of baduy, the crash of privacies, the delicious awkwardness of the new and never anything more. Wanted him to see himself being happy, using his tall-tale telling for good, finally. His stories about his life and job so elabo-rately sob-worthy he had me laughing till I was literally crying all over our extra-garlic-and-cheese Shakey's—his storytelling's all that, and a side of mojo potatoes. And I loved making that sad old Eeyore smile—coz there's no greater power than bringing joy to someone's life (says Eleanor Roosevelt, one of my sheroes). Though even joy can be selfish, and with Kingsley I always knew what's what. When you're using each other you don't want to be the one who gets more used. That lesson I learned long ago, those months after Loy split for the Middle East, me just seventeen, suddenly alone—♫ *just a small-town girl, living in a lonely world* ♫—on a midnight train bound for nowhere, all my courage just my fear of looking backwards, and my dream of teachers' college disappearing as quick as the stack of sketchy cash Loy left me. I had hella few options and running home to Mama wasn't one of them—coz we'll admit tons to our parents, but never to repeating their mistakes. That's when the universe taught me a hard lesson, then gave me a second chance to use what I learned. Oh, twists of fate!—they're so twisted. Discovered in the mall, twice, the first time almost leading to my perdition. Just as I'm going store to store, sowing my last few biodatas, this totally random bading exploding into a fan-girl squeal like I'm already famous. And that's how I met Khrys—"With a statuesque *K*," he says, "and demure *H*"—who links an arm with mine and whisks me to a café to present me to his boss with a flamboyant "tada!" And that's how I met the notorious Mussolina "Mona" Angbabat, a butchy young future-TERF polishing off her fifth bottle of Red Horse Beer in the middle of the day. All of us getting our start through her "The Face of the Year" contest—a hella brilliant, totally rigged affair designed to rope Mona a fresh stable of talent. As you know, Khrys rose quick and fell even quicker, in that scandal where he molested male models on tape to fluff them up for their tighty-whitey practice shoots. And Mona, as everyone knows, bulked up to being the most rabid political loyalist shmoney can buy, her coke habit and date-rape drugs protected by the powerful people she sucks up to. My own career, and its downs and ups, began that afternoon when they bought me churros con chocolate in Dulcinea, leaning in to sugar the deal and pour on cue: "You'll win for sure!" "Just show up!" "Imagine the contracts!" "Easy money!" "But you'll have to work hard!" To which Khrys scoffed: "Please, babes, just look at her!" Who was I to turn down any of that? Especially without any other options. I know now I always had my wits, but the world forces upon us this notion that a woman's primary value is her looks, and when you're young—este, younger—it's easy to think you're a blooming genius for making bank off it. Not that it was easy: all the hours training under demanding Khrys and his certificate of completion for a course at John Robert Powers. And all the VTRs: pretending to devour a bowl of ramen, or flirt with the imaginary cutie-pie bartender, or whip that hair flip that sells gazillions of gallons of shampoo slash conditioner the world over. And all those countless go-sees: waiting rooms packed with girls checking you like they've discovered poop going cloudy in a public toilet. The Face of the Year contest was a scripted telenovela, and the other models were okay with it, except of course the girl I replaced as the anointed one, who either didn't get the memo or believed she could pose her way back into the judges' hearts—poor thing. That's how I realized that the shame of my being a half-breed mongrel came from its unearned power—everyone so mean to me it suddenly felt fair that I was predestined to win. But I won't lie, it was exciting. The pageant training Mama gave me so naive after Khrys taught us how walk, how to smile, how to execute professional choreography: first position, head pivot turns, three-quarter spins. Catwalk, hands on hips. And the grunge, which is good for jeans. And the crossover, for formfitting collections. And the Clydesdale, for super-high fashion. Getting home exhausted—but in my pension house, in my room not long enough for four strides, I practiced each technique till I owned it. And nailed Khrys's signature combo: the basic, strike the fade, rock back, then pivot. Wanna see? Just like this.

(Footsteps. Laughter)

So fire; such baduy. The hard work making my coronation feel like actual victory as I strode down the stage in the central atrium of Galleria mall—upper floors crowded with eyes, faces, shopping bags, ice-cream cones—feeling hella self-conscious, like a Christian in the Colosseum, "don't trip don't trip don't trip" strutting through my mind, the plastic crown threatening to slide off my coif, and my roses still with thorns that honestly hurt, but not enough to turn my big smile fake. I was going to be a star! And the gigs came quick. You know how it is in this city—when it rains, it floods. My debut as a promo girl at the unfortunately acronymed Metro International Literary Fair—tottering in heels, shivering in skimpy dress, clutching a cardboard box containing a paella pan and heavy hardcover book, with a sash draped across my cleavage declaring: *Olé! 101 Delicioso Recipes of Sunny Spain*. Then came the back-to-school catalogs, department-store fashion shows, and a regional print campaign for armpit whitener. (Like, why regional, right?) Eventually working as an official Beverage Beauty for Carlsberg, which probably isn't the best beer in the world. And chasing people around Faces Discotheque with a tray of Quick Shags—Kahlúa, Baileys, and Midori melon liqueur shots, which nobody wanted a second time even if they were free. Till finally I snagged my first dramatic role, in a karaoke video for the Korean market—me bidding my sweetheart farewell at the bus station as he goes off to war, Céline Dion accompanying our silent evocations.

(Chair scrapes. Heels clack)
♫ Near, far, wherever you are, I believe that the heart does go on . . . ♫
(Chair scrapes. Seatback shifts)

That iconic flute intro—stirs my soul till this day. But when I turned eighteen, Mona started pressuring me "to make decisions like an adult," she said, which meant the path towards being a boldstar. What a decision to face alone! I lit so many candles in Quiapo Church, talking for hours to Mama Mary, before somehow it popped into my head that beauty is one of God's blessings, and blessings are given for a reason. That's how I ended up the calendar girl for Great Wall Trading Hardware Corp, busting out of overalls for January, smudged strategically with grease for December, with various tools covering my privates for the months in between. Getting my biggest paycheck ever but never seeing a centavo. At that point I'd been living in Mona's guest room, and she creatively calculated rent, commission, and fees "for previous services rendered," she said. But still I stayed, because she scared me. Even doing a couple more risqué gigs: go-go dancing in pekpek shorts for two episodes of *Ready! Set! Go!*, and a walk-on part in *Savage Hearts*—the new maid from the province, half-raped by the master of the house. Mona afterwards pressuring me towards a real boldstar role, talking up my debt of gratitude, dangling big bucks for a feature film: *Taste Her Pineapple 2: Beyond Taboo Island*. So I . . . I mean, I respect other women's decisions to own their sexuality, but never felt comfortable needing to; *want* and *need* are such subtle opposites. Plus this was during that trend when love scenes focused on hip pumping—like what would my mama think? So I told Mona no and she threatened to spread the nip-slip pics from my calendar shoot—the first time anyone weaponized my own body against me. I tossed and turned, worrying till morning, then ditched her—like grabbed my purse and split, abandoning my stuff in her guest room. Even back then I wouldn't be threatened, and I've got heels higher than her moral standards. Should've stolen something, though, coz I left with nothing to my name—but why let her think we're no different? In the pension house I moved to, my roommate, Mariclaire, heard me crying into my pillow and kept offering to intro me to her boss, who was looking for a guest relations officer, "with a pleasing personality," she said. "Massaging only," she promised, "unless you want more." All day, all night, all week I was thinking—what I'd give up and what I'd gain—and I wandered the mall with my last stack of biodatas, browsing things I couldn't buy, watching retouched matronas served by eager salesgirls bullied by wrinkled managers. Sometimes temptation isn't about pleasure at all. But just when I needed saving from myself, someone up there heard my prayers. And in the video arcade, still sweating from a *Dance Dance Revolution* throw-down, right after I met One-Mig Sontua—who'd eventually be my second boyfriend—I was discovered, tada!, one last time, by Boy Balagtas, überagent to stars, not starlets. I owe that badaf my life. He's the one who got me those gigs I became known for—including hostess with the mostest every Tuesday at 8:30 p.m., on *Smooth Moves*, which Kingsley would watch, religiously. Poor old Eeyore. I used to tell myself he's just the classic Gemini—but truth is, Kingsley isn't of two minds. He's not good; he's not evil. He just quit trying to tell the difference. Now the nation waits to see which side he'll choose—in a heckuva who-shot-J.R. cliff-hanger. Maybe what we were saying earlier is true, about duty, and why he gave me up. But if he does testify tomorrow, it won't be about pride, or love, or right versus wrong. That's not Kingsley. That's why I fell for him. And that's why I left him for the president.

Kingsley Belli Transcript.

(51:40.02—kingsleybelli.M4A)

My answer to your first question: Next, please.

(Inaudible)

Isn't this interview about Vita? Next you'll be asking: Is Manila burning? Am I to reply as did General Dietrich von Choltitz, Hitler's military governor of Paris: "Jawohl, mein Führer, all is clear and burning good"? Bear in mind it was his lie, not the truth, that saved Paris. No, I do not think this is the end of Fernando V. Estregan. That's my honest answer to what you're pussyfooting around. It may not prove true, but it will not mean I've lied. This impeachment is a partisan putsch. The Fuchsias' narrative to justify subverting the will of the Filipino majority. Courting chaos that may last a generation. It's easier to fool people than to convince them that they've been fooled. You've seen that meme? Attributed to Mark Twain, all over the internet. No proof, however, exists that the esteemed American uttered those words. "How easy it is to make people believe a lie," he did write, in his autobiography, "and how hard it is to undo that work again." That insight of his persisting today through someone's paraphrase—a lie, if you will, to make his truth ring truer.

(Inaudible)

Sure, man. Of course you think it matters. That's noble. Naive. And predictable. I, too, at your age, armed myself with truth and threw myself toward Goliaths. However, my weapons were not memes, Facebook, and snark; we hurled our voices, bodies, bombs at the armored riot squads, the Special Police Intelligence Force, the tanks bearing down on our barricades. Meaning our incendiary projectiles for the Dictator himself, his Iron Buttercunt, their bastard daughter, and feckless cokehead son—as we'd convinced ourselves they were. Committed heart and soul, all creativity and pluck. Ours were not the desperate, rag-stuffed flaming jugs of Generalissimo Franco's Spanish Nationalists. Fascism's so prosaic and we Filipinos tend to fight poetically, subversive as all metaphor. In that Winter War of 1939, Vyacheslav Molotov claimed that his Soviet bombers were only dropping aid supplies. To the old Bolshevik's "breadbaskets" the Finns responded with their "Molotov cocktails." That's how we partied at your age, daddy-o, armed with the university library, not the internet, our weapons steeped in history, science, and the truths of literature—not anonymity, Wikipedia, and cognitive bias.

(Inaudible)

I'm glad you ask. Mine were the bomb, as you kids say. Alcohol alone burns too quickly. Gasoline on your fingers and matches in your pocket were all the proof the SPIFs needed to leave you dead by a roadside at dawn. The trick's in the mixture: the fluid viscous, the fire smoky. Not the size of the explosion, but how well it sticks. Mine were made with gasoline, kerosene, tar, potassium chloride from my chemistry class, capped and sealed in empties of San Miguel Pale Pilsen, which we drank like soldiers through their final night together. The brown bottles concealed the long rags snaking inside, and outside we taped windproof storm matches, as the Finns did. On the bottoms we wrote our slogans in Pentel pen—dedications to our fiery poems. And we hid it all in plain sight. The Spiffies were on alert for slinking cadres, not some hep cat with a transistor radio blaring the Juan de la Cruz Band from his vest pocket, the front rack of his ratty Vespa bearing nothing more than rattling cases of beer for a party. Just a hippie pacifist trying to get through the totally hassle protests, man—our libations later passed hand to hand to the front, with postage-stamp-sized sandpaper to light the match that would burst the bomb once the glass broke on its target. No telltale lighter or stinky fingers to betray you as anything more than a mild-mannered student exercising your constitutional right to peacefully protest. It was intoxicating, joining our voices in chants we all knew, fighting what we thought was the good fight. I remember one protest, after the bombing of the Liberty Party's rally in Plaza Miranda. Standing fearlessly on the bridge to the Palace, behind farmers who lay down before an approaching armored column. In my hand, a bottle, solid as a club, the sulfur of the match like something that could get you high. In my first act of violence I arched my arm in silent answer to the barking bullhorn and clanking tanks. My bottle a bright smash in the treads of the first one and the old T-shirt going round and round, in flames, deeper and deeper until something ignited in the vehicle's belly and the whole column gnashed to a halt. Man, I felt like Jesus walking on water. Incredulous, righteous, invincible; then I ran like hell before anyone knew I was a fraud.

(Chuckling)

That's why I dig Vita's bombshell explosions. Her clandestine record-ings remind me of the tapes made by the Dictator's own lovey-dovey, which plunged him into hot water with the wily Iron Buttercunt, who used his infidelity to demand he share power with her. At rallies we'd play those recordings on the university PA system, all the glory of his grunting intimacy, inane pillow talk, and crooning love songs crack-ing smiles among even the soldiers in the phalanx we faced. Every joke is a tiny revolution, wrote Orwell—and he was right. Vita's petit guignol may yet oust some mole kings from their mountain kingdoms. Maybe even me. Never once did she deign to include me in her Insta-gram posts, yet there I am, my voice on her recordings, among a cast of characters elbowing each other to lay gifts at our dear leader's feet. What's damning, though, to my mind, wasn't President Estregan's de-cision to withdraw police support from certain individuals who'd long expressed hostility toward our dutiful officers of the law. Nor was it his plans to jail certain Opposition politicians for engaging in the cor-ruption for which they themselves had once jailed their predecessors. And to say that our discussions of Rolex Aguirre's illegal gambling was evidence of collusion is tantamount to saying an undercover detective is complicit in the crime being investigated. No, that hotsipatootsie's recordings are simply sandpaper on a storm match, for the gunk the Opposition insurgents are now using to tar and feather our most pop-ular president ever. Vita's role is to sex up a lie—the fake news fueling the Liberty Party. That's the irony. We built the machine that's trans-forming her from ditzy jiggler to democracy Jeanne d'Arc. Everyone blames me for first instrumentalizing all those websites, blogs, and social media influencers now tacking their jibs to this new prevailing wind. Should I apologize for understanding this wired world and preparing my boss for its unique demands? His YouTube chats. His book of Estreganisms. All the memes with pull quotes, bullet points, infographics. Hashtags to create solidarity like the slogans we used against the Dictator. Explainer videos simplifying complex issues so that every Filipino can participate in the solution. I built the nerve center of five hundred operatives who crafted our message to share with those who'd benefit from listening. I trained them to engage in civil discourse with dissenters to expose the hypocrisy and bankruptcy of their woke arguments. All that grew organically into a grassroots movement beyond anything I ever dreamed. Columnists committed their pens. Like Bobby Tubul, who's fluffed virtually every president he could get his lips on. Joined by even relatively well-regarded journalists, like K. Sisboy Pansen, who's vaulted from respect inherited from daddy to his own plum ambassadorship at the EU. Minor bloggers and aspiring socmed influencers, like Paz Panot and Baraka Vousfils, rode the wave to become major, major players, in their circles. Ad agencies and media companies threw together news platforms and even replica websites of international media giants, to write updates, satire, and fan fiction supporting the People's Champ, Nando for the Needy, the man who declared that Change Is Here. Vital work we needed to do to enable the Filipino people to select a strong leader who can finally give us all we need. For there are no tyrants where there are no slaves. You see, I had witnessed, under the Dictator, and the decades since, how easily our vital institutions can be hijacked. When the mainstream media is run by oligarchs and their partisans, we can no longer trust it. When they make it so we cannot know what's true, we empower leaders who will tell us what to believe. When we discover to be false what those leaders say, our human nature takes that as proof of the superiority of that master strategist in a political arena where only manipulation can get things done. For if he is deft enough to fool us, he is worthy enough for us to follow. That is how a mere mortal becomes a nation's father, savior, führer, king—whose jokes and idiosyncracies have us laughing at the absurdity of it all. That is simply how the machine works. I merely worked to drive that toward good.

(Inaudible)

Of course you'd say that. Propaganda is routinely disparaged as deliberate disinformation wielded by devious ne'er-do-wells. But what if we used it to provide deliberate information? To arm people with the truth? To give them the means to participate? A public trust, so they'll not be fooled by those who don't have our best interests at heart: the power-drunk editors, thought leaders, gatekeepers, rent seekers, and all the other herpetic establishment nimrods clinging white-knuckled to their slipping grip on power. Their legalistic Plan B—to oust President Fernando Estregan and install Vice President Hope Virdsinsia—that is nothing more than rape without lubricant. To keep it arousing, Vita's now their centerfold. A juicy little ambuscade who but titters and tactically parts her legs to have everyone lapping it up. I did, face first and eager to please. She sat tickling the ivories in an empty whisky bar, singing songs as if just for me. Because what's more beguiling than a rose at a piano? Tulips on an organ. That fact, she knows well. Yet she'll remain a mere pawn, despite her queenly aspirations, unable to inch herself to the other end without anyone noticing. Her revelatory recordings may be authentic, though they're simply a meme paraphrased from someone else's age-old idea. The starfruits in Congress, as Fernando calls them, interpret his age and ailments as the bell beginning the battle royale. History repeating. Many great leaders hid weakness that fueled their strength. Julius Caesar had cluster headaches. Franklin Delano Roosevelt had polio. The Dictator, when his lupus hit, released footage of himself shadowboxing shirtless on the beach, the archetypical proto-Filipino from our mythology: Malakas—strong, in our parlance. Matched only by his mate, Maganda—in our language, meaning beauti—

(Inaudible)

Oh, you understand Tagalog? My apologies. I thought you were a foreigner. Therefore I'm sure you see Vita assuming the role of Maganda, ever-honeyed of voice, whose strength is her apparent weakness, especially compared to the brutishness of Malakas. We shall see who wins. I once gave Vita a postcard that she loved so much she taped it to her mirror, alongside old Post-its with the names of places she longs to visit—Italy, Hong Kong, Japan. On this postcard, a quote by Simone de Beauvoir. "On ne naît pas femme, on le devient." One is not born woman, one becomes—

(Inaudible)

Oh, you parlez-vous français aussi? Je m'excuse. What I mean to say is that petite chienne's become quite a force. Our nation's walking-talking embodiment of our over-acting teleserye melodramas, all tragedy and hope and buzzwords and metaphor waxing poetic about mysteries and human frailty. I'm man enough to offer admiration, however deservedly grudging. She hooked me with her wisdom accrued from the *Sun Tzu for Dummies* book beside her toilet in her comfort room, and reeled me in with the illustrated *Kama Sutra* open casually facedown on her coffee table when she invited me up for a nightcap. Even I'm not immune to a depressed beauty breathlessly singing "Milord"; squealing, "I love that it tastes so funny!" of triple-wood Laphroaig, when I introduced her to single malts, and two weeks later she's shamelessly holding court on terroir and peatiness to a circle of drooling admirers at a reception I brought her to in the Australian embassy. What a joy to watch, especially when she didn't know she was being watched. In those moments, I admired her most—the unadulterated adultress, which sounds like one of her beloved romance novels, but it's true. I'd come home from work and peek from my front door as she sat on my couch, bathed in TV light, legs folded like switchblades, hand holding up the remote control like a magic wand projecting the scene in front of her. She'd match the narrators' accents when commenting back at her nature shows. In the morning when I'd leave for work she'd shuffle out in her Garfield-head slippers and cat pajamas, her face creased by the pillowcase as if God had just pushed her from the mold He made her from before breaking it across His knee. I was so intrigued by her daily transformation in front of her mirror and ring light, into whom she thought she should be. How could I resist such a fantasy? She'd call me at work to sing the first two lines of a baduy love song, setting me up to reply with the rest. Boy did I ever. Soon I was parasailing at Subic. Or blindfolded on a trip to that mountainside spa half an hour from where I once lived as a Communist. I guiltily laid myself beside her on the terrace to be massaged like a Wagyu cow, my malaise later floating up, up, and away with my erection, as she emerged from the bubbles of our private jacuzzi wearing only a grin. I once warned her about Fernando: Never grab a knife by its blade. I say the same to you about her. She can shift who she is, to flourish in any situation. The grateful giver for her fans. The ice witch against other females. The sassy queen around that walking Adam's apple, Jojie Paganda. The relentless pro for that pockmarked charlatan, Boy Balagtas. The woketivist swinging statistics, as if they're the whole story. And the orphan girl when it's just you and her. Even that name—"Vita Nova"—she says it's real, but it reeks of a plan. She was back hardly a few weeks after her fizzled engagement abroad, yet I'd been widely warned about that sockdologizing man-trap. And I became the punchline, taking my upstairs seat at the slaughter and—bang! But other than that, Mrs. Lincoln, how was the play?

(Inaudible)

No, that's a fair question. Why will I deny? Vita made me jealous. Even RoboCop was part human. She orchestrated it as my brilliant idea to have her sing at the president's birthday party. I introduced them proudly, then saw the way she offered her hand, how she laughed and smiled. I brought her home after and fucked her like a broken toy, then stopped answering her calls. I knew. Now she has my old comrade, Furio Almondo, once again licking between her toes. The Malakas who will save the Maganda from the clutches of an evil king whom she selflessly seeks to topple. Furio was always such a fool. Both he and my ex-wife, Rita, are true believers still, with their pitiful, infantilizing illusions. I outgrew mine decades ago. There was nothing radical about our armed struggle—merely another tryst with merely another dictator in merely another poor country in Asia, Africa, Latin America. We took to the hills like sexy messiahs, horny with answers, uniformed in ideology, barefoot on our native soil, enamored with our own body odor, and young beneath the ancient sky. When the Spiffies captured me I even fancied it was the strongman who'd ordered it personally, or his lunatic first lady, and my blood boiled those two years in that overstuffed detention center, until one day I realized neither despot nor diva knew I existed. Oh, what a blow, when it dawned on me that it was my comrades, our uptrodden and innocent countrymen, who'd stolen my youth. Like Samson in shock at his shorn locks in Delilah's hands. And oh, daddy-o, you should've seen my hair back then, proud as a lion's mane, as I strutted across campus, the bottoms of my pants so belled that each step almost clanged my arrival. Far out, man, a real free radical. The sharpened tip of the spear that was our vanguard. I look back with embarrassment at all those hours we spent strategizing, oozing revolutionary truisms, misquoting Mao in our parents' kitchens while upstairs they slumbered off their day's hard toil.

(Inaudible)

I knew Furio from high school. We'd sit at the back during mass, making up bawdy lyrics to the liturgical songs. After a few tokes in the parking lot, he could rattle off a scathing limerick or sacrilegious villanelle. I liked him the way you do someone you envy. After we graduated, I went to the public university, he stayed with the Jesuits, though we worked together as student leaders, despite our differences. He found me too radical. I found him chickenshit. I urged him to come when I took up armed struggle in the mountains, but he loved being a rebel with a cause, and that cause was the chickababes. Why else sport a beret and carefully unkempt facial hair? Why be a revolutionary if not to lead a beer-garden putsch against convent-school oppression? Look at him preening now, as if he's consequential.

(Inaudible)

Rita? There's another one taken in by Vita's vulnerability—the incestuousness of our society never ceases to amaze. I met Rita in the detention center, of course. I was nineteen and had been in the mountains for eleven months, where I was perpetually soggy in the rainy season and chapped in the dry, practicing ambushes, proselytizing village to village, training the peasants so that they could train others and together we could free our country of all that ailed it. I would vilify in my head the fantasies I still wanted—the sports car, the private-college magandas, the fine liquor of the imperialists—wrestling with my convictions like a seminarian smacking into puberty. When I received word that my mother was fighting her cancer I defied my commander, he of the hairy mole he cultivated as a testament to his fecund authenticity. I went home and my mother thought I was a ghost. I remember wondering how she'd become so short. I embraced her and held her head against my chest and her hair came away like a wild animal leaping to bite me. I was so shocked I dropped the wig on the floor and knelt to pick it up, crumpling around her knees. The problem remained that I still believed in the cause. As luck had it, while I luxuriated in a hot shower, two SPIFs knocked on our front door and my mother answered. I heard her voice when I turned off the water. She was raising it, like she never did, even with her students. "I told you nincompoops last time," she yelled, "my son's not here. Why do want him?" One Spiffy replied, "Sedition." My mother asked what that meant. The other Spiffy said, "Sedition is . . . ah—just sedition, ma'am." I could've heeded her warning and fled through my bedroom window and over the rooftops. Instead, I dressed forthwith and went to the door, hands held high like an idiot.

(Inaudible)

I was taken to the Police Intelligence Command. For questioning. Where I found out that the commanding oxymorons didn't even know I'd been away. I was just another name on a list of dangerous nobodies. They remanded me to a detention center where my fear gave way to the pleasure of seeing old friends. Two weeks became two years, spent writing and talking, and talking about each other's writing. It was the boredom that eroded my convictions, like in that soixante-huitard slogan: l'ennui est contre-révolutionnaire. Then Rita appeared one day, gliding searchingly between the bunks. She was new, younger than me, and had a soul filled with sampaguitas. Student, poet, sloganeer who could recite from the Bible, *The Red Book*, and Audre Lorde without pausing for breath, which she often did after a few swigs of moonshine, to our great applause. Rita, with Jung in her head, Marx between her legs, and a chest puffed with pride at shaming her loyalist parents who were friendly with the Iron Buttercunt. Man, were we a hot item! She'd mistaken me for a grizzled veteran and true believer—why would I selfishly disavow such comforting bourgeois illusion? Both of us were released as part of the New Decade Amnesty and her family tried to keep us apart. Love and hatred have always fueled history's rebels, and Rita and I were blissful in our discontent. That kept me believing.

(Inaudible)

Exactly, that's when I entered journalism. In the footsteps of my father, the managing editor with famous principles, who never allowed me to work at his paper. That's when I finally broke with my old comrade Furio—after I applied at *The Sun*, where he worked. I'd gone to his condo to ask for help, with a bottle of his beloved brandy. We drank like brothers through the night. Later that week, he came to my parents' house to tell me his editor wanted a bribe for the position. I told him my money would take a few days. Furio looked at his hands. "I'm sorry," he said, shaking his head like in pain. "I'm not going to be party to a bribe." We didn't speak after that. He knew my mother was ill and I needed that job. When I finally found a position at *The Bullet*, there was Furio backbiting me to all our friends, saying I sold my soul to a tabloid. As if he and I didn't used to speak loudly in buses and jeepneys, knowing that gossip was the best way to spread word of a protest. As if he didn't know that sex and crime are the racy book jackets for the larger narrative, because plot points promise all readers both purpose and resolution in a world that gives neither. We must expose life for liberty, Don Quixote said. Though where did that get us? While Rita tilted at organizing women in communities, to create democratic spaces wherever they safely could, I strove to make *The Bullet* the people's paper. Rita gave birth to our son, Trotski, nine months and three days to the night our incontinent strongman hid diamonds in his diapers and fled the country into the arms of the Gipper. Everything changed for me. Had I not become a father, had that dictatorial parasite and his family held on, I'd most likely remain a fellow traveler like Furio. Rita and I would probably still be together, despite her disdain for the work I did—the stories about uncles raping nieces, celebrity rifts, orgies in gated subdivisions, and underhanded basketball trades—while she manned society's barricades doing consequential quelque chose. But with the Dictator's ouster my fervor was pointless, while my comrades remained shortchanged by our cause's success and continued to dream even after the alarm clock blared. I would finally lose any lingering faith, years later, when I gazed upon the Soviet Union from a stranger's window in West Berlin. A poetic transformation into disillusion. I had grown so sick of being judged by Rita that I accepted a fellowship for journalists, in Paris, knowing she'd see it for what it was. She always said I've a propensity for surrender, and I thought, therefore, that France would be fitting. Besides, if the capital of European Enlightenment had served Ho Chi Minh well, why not me?

(Inaudible)

We were seven reporters, from developing countries, though I skipped the workshops and team-building to browse the book stalls by the river, or to gaze at transplanted frescoes and anonymous masterpieces till the museums closed. I'd wander jet-lagged through crepuscular gardens and squares, my footsteps behind like history itself. One particular night I swam in cafés and bars and crackling vermouths, and lurched through blackened doorways and starlit courtyards, pursuing distant jazz like a lifeline, as jazz often is, and I danced alone in a vast ballroom that became a street that staggered beneath a procession of overcoats and suitcases, which I chased the way your fingers do a loose thread to its end. There was a station, and a door that slid away, into which I hurled myself simply because I'd always wanted to, falling into a blur of smoke, five faces, flashing towns, and my intermittent reflection, borders and badges like bad dreams, till somehow an interminable thud pushed me onto a rain-polished platform, breakfast and tobacco huge and hectoring in my mind. The hour bled with that silver we don't get here in the tropics and I followed a man's directions to a wall that funneled me toward Checkpoint Charlie and the vast distance it overlooked. On the other shore, silhouettes paced and stood in the mist within their yellow halos that grew as the sky tarnished deeper, and it hit me that dawn was actually dusk. A young woman with an umbrella crossed the street and gestured for a light, offering a cigarette, my matches dying one after the other in the quickening rain as we laughed and huddled nearer, finding commonality in mangled French. We arrived at her block, at what was once a family's mansion, its stairs so worn in their middle they looked defeated. I felt closer to her than I had to Rita for a long time. The ceilings slanted in her small flat and the pong of cat urine poked beneath the liturgical vanilla of Papier d'Arménie. When she took off her plastic rain bonnet I saw that she wasn't young at all. Her fingers brushed the water from my hair, then led me to the bedroom. She pulled back a lacy curtain and the floodlights and parallel walls and death strip in between looked just like a movie set. She said the people on the other side called it the Anti-Fascist Protection Rampart. In the distance, it curved in such a way that I could see the opposite face. I'm not hopeful enough to be a mystical man, but when I saw the murals on our side, and the blank gray of the other, I thought of the Giottos in the Louvre, the pharaonic steles, the graffiti in its rebellious colors here at home protesting injustices or obscurity. Now it might seem obvious, but in those times things were still closed; ignorance, not overabundance, was still the heart of propaganda. I rushed back into the rain, seared by that image of the blankness of Communism's walls. The vivid paintings on this side following me like images in a zoetrope. I took the next train back and the earliest flight home.

(Inaudible)

Let's not be sappy. I wasn't a new man. But doubt, with its many shades and hues, had taken root. I'd no longer allow myself to see the world in black and white. I tried again with Rita but let her go gently when she wanted. I took up tango. I found purpose at *The Bullet* and eventually made editor in chief. I taught Trotski the electric guitar. I was done with the fatigue of piety and my comrades' brutality toward those who questioned. You'll give your life to the struggle, but will you also sacrifice your soul? And what of your family? "You want to love everyone equally," E. M. Forster wrote, "and that's worse than impossible—it's wrong." I didn't stop fighting, I merely stopped losing. In hindsight, our government was indeed dictatorial, and had been for twenty years strong; however, it was also right about us—we really were dangerous; as dangerous as the Reds today, who need to be neutralized. We'd left the government little choice but to fight back.

(Inaudible)

I do understand the heartbreak. I shared that pain. Communism was the last great belief in something transformative. But Rita, Furio, all of them remain fueled by the righteous anger of the unsuccessful martyr. Doesn't a wise man put his money on whoever's leading? My old comrades still form their evidence to suit their beliefs, while I can only form my beliefs to suit the evidence. America and its capitalism may have lost me that spring of '68, at My Lai, but they won me back in the autumn of '89, on the road to Wenceslas Square, when I filled the front page of *The Bullet* with images of Czech students and reporters being beaten by the thugs of the National Security Corps. Between then and now, I've thought long and hard about what freedom means and how easily our commitment to it can become tyranny. My doddering fellow travelers continue to boil the minds of university students in a fermenting borscht, seasoned with the glory of their well-intentioned failures. As if they've not wasted their own lives. Or become the petite bourgeoisie they once despised, complicit in supporting the landed oligarchs of the Liberty Party. Even los hermanos Castro's Cohibas have gone from apparatchiks to plutocrats, smoked now by Wall Street capitalists and our own aspirational President Estregan. I refuse to let pinkos inculcate a new generation into their woketivist cult that rejects incremental change, that works to impeach, and cancel, and shake each other's cocks in congratulations, convinced that our history should be rebooted. Because that worked brilliantly in Cambodia, n'est-ce pas? Oh, daddy-o, we deserve the leaders we choose. Suffering the bad ones is part of our education in how to choose better ones. Or a step toward ourselves becoming the leaders we need. For fuck's sake, man, revolutionaries are so predictable. Where is the valor of living by your convictions if your convictions are wrong? They criticize Estregan for his manners, his drug war, his wary response to the pandemic, as if other countries didn't have it worse. I'm fairly certain it was Rita's influence as Vita's cyber-mentor that led to the president's betrayal. Though tell me, what leader doesn't have flaws? What about Reyes, after Rolex Aguirre implicated FVE that first time, seizing power at the end of the last book? Reyes, with the rise of the Abu Sayyad and spread of shabu in our communities? Reyes, who jailed all those politicians in the Pork Barrel Scandal and replaced them with his friends who weren't much better? Reyes, who with his left hand bumbled the tour-bus hostage crisis and with his right hand released recidivists before they were rehabilitated? The irony is that Estregan was among those he released, allowing his eventual resurgence. Our decades of democracy since the dictatorship: What did they get us? Decades of too much democracy, with corrupt, weak leaders, and progress benefiting only the few. I saw this, when I worked as spokesman for Arriola Makapal Glorioso, whom

Reyes ousted as chief justice and arrested at the airport as she sought medical treatment abroad for the traumas of his injustice. I established the *Keep It Real* blog to provide a platform for those who spoke the truth about the Reyes administration. It was the foundation of all I've built since.

(Inaudible)

That's patently unfair; I'm no yes-man. President Estregan may have deputized me to debate Bansamoro in his stead, but that doesn't mean I agree with all of his policies. On China, for example, I never agreed with compromising our sovereignty for loans, investment, arms, or vaccines. I wanted him, however, to succeed in his overall vision for our future. We always have a choice, but why choose treason when you can help build a new nation? It had become so bad. Twenty percent of our annual GDP lost to graft and corruption. Forty-five percent of government expenditure wasted, daily, on kickbacks. Corruption thrives when temptation meets tolerance, and man, are we Pinoys a tolerant people. We accept graft however much we resent corruption—the former understandable, the latter unforgivable. If someone were to pay five million to Customs Head Nicolas Faelyor to do what he *is* supposed to do—say, quickly release a shipment of kitchenware—that would be graft, a levy for a service in a country where most of us are underpaid. But if someone were to pay five million to Jack-Jack Bolero, of the livestock ministry, to do something he's *not* supposed to do—say, skim the coffers and deliver substandard fertilizer to poor farmers—that is, in part, what we would call corruption; robbing you, me, the breeders, the farmers, colleagues in the civil service, congressmen who established the Fertilizer Fund, and every taxpayer and child, present and future. Both graft and corruption are wrong, but one of them we take more personally. We may never respect the thief who shares, but you'll always despise the thief who doesn't. And despise we did, that unrespectable Respeto Reyes, and the presidents before him. Those rulers who fooled us into accepting the unacceptable. Who made slaves of the millions of Filipinos they exported abroad, calling them heroes for their remittances. Once you accept such absurdities—to misquote Voltaire—the more willing you are to commit atrocities. Such as attempting to assassinate the president, like that Fuchsia OFW Loy Bonifacio and his

jaundiced perception of the fighter who works to save him. But with
Fernando V. Estregan, what we see is what we get. Usually, heroes are
so normal they're ugly, and very flawed. Can we fault him? Do we fault
the blinded fool who believes the moaning of a whore? Satan was always the Bible's most interesting character. Still, I did not expect that
night in the Palace, when I knocked on the door of the president's office, and opened it because I thought I heard his snoring. A shaft of
light swung across the darkness like a spotlight, and there she was,
bent over, red panties stretched between her ankles, bosoms poured
onto the desk beside a stapler and an overturned mug spilling pens
and a small Philippine flag. Behind Vita was Estregan, with his barong
open over his belly and his famous cowlick flopping on his forehead,
which he kept pushing back slowly as if all his pleasure derived from
it. Vita was chirping and growling the way she does—as you'll find out
eventually, when she needs you—like a starved hound in an incubator
filled with hatchlings. I should've left but I couldn't. I cleared my throat,
like in the movies, to ruin it for them. The son of a whore didn't stop.
He smiled and went faster. Vita looked at me and the spell broke and I
could move. I shut the door and went to sit in my office. All that time
I told myself that you can't blame a hungry man for eating the food
placed in front of him. Now I unexpectedly find my plate tantalizingly
full. To be or not to be, now that is the question. Whether 'tis nobler to
suffer the slings and arrows at tomorrow's testimony, or to take arms
against a sea of troubles, and, by being silent, continue them. The way
the two of them looked at me—like I was nothing. I warn you, in your
task as her new spokesman: Making others willingly repeat lies is the
height of power. Willingly repeating someone else's lies is the height
of powerlessness. I think of Vita and her postcard with the quote about
becoming a woman, and I think of my own favorite Beauvoir meme:
"If you live long enough, you'll see that every victory turns into a defeat." At the impeachment tomorrow, when I suffer the subpoena and
answer the question from our nascent führers—Is Paris burning?—it
may strike some as heroism. Or hubris. Or self-preservation. Inevitably,
however, it's always much more prosaic.

Vita Nova Transcript: 3 of 13.

(33:48.02—VN3.M4A)

True story: Pashmina Shaw's been filmed giving BJs to dildos, when she was starting her career as a sex guru—google it. So that ratchet basic better back the frak off, coz I will grab a leash and walk her. She's just jelly coz I got like ten times the Instagram followers as her, coz they're there for me—not like her five million on Facebook, who only follow for her troll-farm articles and reposts. Seriously. All week, anticipating my testimony, she's been throwing mad shade, digging through my past relationships—with Rolex, with Nur . . . Check your head, girl—a supertyphoon's coming, thousands evacuating, but this morning she's using her platform to threaten me with some supposed molly-sex vid from my ex-not-even-boyfriend, Red, that scenester I hooked up with for like literally milliseconds, way back when it was safe to party. If he's holding anything, it wasn't made with consent. The jerk's got revenge porn written all over him—you know the type. Oh, you *know him* know him? Condolence.

(Lighter click. Exhalation)

The EES are hella desperate—see Baraka's blog—after Kingsley's testimony last week, and mine in a few days, and Rolex's later today, which will probs be the bombshell everybody's talking about. He's effed Nando so often in their bromance they're like that couple always breaking up and you don't believe their tears anymore. The Nandotards are revolting—in both senses of the word. All like: This impeachment is an unconstitutional coup meant to invalidate the lawfully elected choice of the Filipino majority. Cue resting bitch face. Their strategy's now to discredit and cancel any threat, and their main target's the veep, of course. Coz if Nando's out, Hope's in, and the rest of the Fuchsias are back, ♫ *from outer space* ♫—with, a, vengeance! But seriously, leave her daughter alone, right? Kid gets a scholarship to M.I.T., coz she's wicked smart, but they claim it was bribery, bought by taxpayer money, plundered by the Liberty Party, during the Reyes administration. No limit to how low they'll stoop. Poor kid had to deactivate her social media. So pardon my rudeness—gotta keep checking mine, to see if I'm also being deluged in new and nasty ways.

(Inaudible)

I wouldn't say *scared*. After Sizzle Saturday, and fleeing Nando, I feel I can take on anything. It *is* kinda tempting—I won't lie: just peace out, for an extended vacay, till everything blows over. Safari in Botswana— three months in the Okavango Delta, which apparently is magical. But running always looks like guilt, and I've no guilt to run from. So it's on, like Donkey Kong. Or better yet, *Street Fighter.* Ready? Fight! Good versus evil. Fire fighting fire. The famous against the infamous. But that's the funny thing, right? Fame, infamy—such a fine line between the two most people can't tell the diff. I myself once thought that either one was all I needed to be secure, and therefore happy. When you're young, and wise with innocence, with nowhere to fall but up, being discovered in the mall literally seems like prayers answered. Especially when I should've been getting out there with my biodatas, instead of losing myself in the video arcade. But cheap thrills are the best—that's why they're called cheap thrills. And *Dance Dance Revolution* was my addiction. It had just come out and I was dancing away the money Loy left me, stomping on pink and blue arrows for hours upon that little stage. Perfect! Perfect! Perfect!—that's what the machine declared, exactly what a person needs to hear sometimes. Perfect combos up to a million before I'd miss a step. Lights. Music. A gathering crowd—and suddenly this guy steps out of it, all cocky in the way only cute skinny guys can be. "Duel?" says he, stepping onto the stage beside me. And I'm like: Try to keep up, punk. So we take our places and swipe our cards. "Lady's choice," says he, and I pick my fave: Mitsu-O!'s "Make It Better"—in maniac mode, naturellement. And the beat kicks in—Tack! Tack! Tacka-tack-tack! And we're waiting, bobbing our heads with our avatars' (he's cool-cat Disco, all bell-bottoms and 'fro; I'm raver Jenny, pekpek shorts and platform boots), and the electric piano slides in, funky as a Friday night—and the vocals preach—"Got no money? . . . Talk to my dream! . . ."—and arrows pour up the screen as the game's afoot: step, step, stomp—lights washing over us—stomp, stomp, step—the crowds both real and virtual cheering our rocketing scores. Perfect! Perfect! Combo! Perfect! I gotta say, the cocky punk was keeping up—though he's more tech (like, perfection at all costs) while I'm more freestyle (just riding the feels)—and right when I'm dissing him in my head, he suddenly twists like backwards to hit the pads with his hands and spins up like a starting top, smiling smugly—and the chorus girls sing: "Yeah! Yeah! Yeah!"—and he shouts over them: "What's your name?" And I reply with a spinning killer twenty-move combo— knocking him off his rhythm as our scores soar higher—and the chorus girls sing: "Yeah! Yeah! Yeah!" And then it's over, the crowd's cheering, both of us huffing and puffing, the game declaring: "You're a dancing machine!" Everyone checking the scores as they blur then stop: over forty-nine million each, with him up just over a thou—so close! "Guess that makes me champ," says he. And I'm like: Who says that was for the title? And he's like: "Who says you got a title to defend?" And so I'm storming away, parting the crowd like the Red Sea as he follows like a righteous Egyptian offering a second chance, which of course makes me slip faster down the crowded escalator as he's dodging alongside down the stairs till he's stuck in a knot of scowling shoppers. And just as I'm about to disappear into the crowd, he shouts over their heads: "Tomorrow! Same time! Same place! . . ." And just as I'm about gone, he adds those three words I most love to hate: ". . . if you dare!"

(Fingers snap three times. Laughter)

So comes tomorrow, same time, same place, and he's leaning against the *DDR* machine like it's his fresh-waxed Trans Am outside the Tastee-Freez. We swipe our cards without a what's up and take our places as a crowd circles. The game begins. By the end, we're so breathless with laughter we don't even check the score. "I'm Juan Miguel," says he. I'm Fendi, I reply—I don't know why, but that's how I knew I liked him. Suddenly, a voice booms: "Perfect! Perfect! What a combo!" And a man as wide as he is tall wraps his baby bingo arms around our shoulders and steers us through the crowd, whispering in our ears. "I'm Boy Balagtas. And I'm going to teach you how to be famous."

And boy, did Boy deliver. Never once saying the words "promo girl." Nor ever uttering "fashion show" and "the mall" in the same breath. Along came print ads, TV commercials, recording contracts, sleeper-hit movies, even nationwide tri-media campaigns. We became part of Boy's huge family: Vits and One-Mig, as we were dubbed, our generation's ultimate love team, as you might recall—a true-to-lie story that couldn't last. But through hard work, my lucky star soared onwards and upwards, while I fell in love, again and again, as one does, next with Cat, then Furio, LeTrel, Rolex, Nur, and Deepak . . .

(Inaudible)

Actually, no—why would you need to interview any? Bad enough you suggested charting my story through my years with them. I'm grateful for those times, but I won't let their gaze define me, or take credit for my growth while I was becoming more of who I am. On ne naît pas femme, on le devient. Right? So I took on bigger and bigger challenges: Channel Eight's Petronas Weather Fairy, then Levi's 501 Crush of the Country, then lead singer of the Hell o' Kitties (before Sanrio's copyright lawyers killed our punk career), finally hitting my one-time big-time with the Sexy-Sexy—that wish-upon-a-star, household-name success that everyone and their grandmother was dancing and singing to. ♫ *Ooo, Mr. Sexy-Sexy! He makes the weather right. Keeps me cool all day, makes me hot at night. Thanks to him, I'll be alright. Ooo, my sexy, sexy. My Mr. Sexy-Sexy. I dance this dance for you. Eight, seven, six, five, four, three, and two.* ♪ By the count of one came the predictable scandals: the camel-toe incident, Bishop Baccante's boycott, the fatalities at my comeback concert, Nur publicly dumping me right after. By that point, obscurity sounded peachy. So when Deepak entered stage left, in the self-help section of a bookshop, I was dying to run away. And we did, of course, because it was that kind of love: Me and Deepak Jonathan Roy, alias Paki, or Deep, then DJ, then Too-Pak, then Pak-Man, and even Pak-*Yow!*—in the end known by his new friends as Deepaflex. I'm not kidding—names he eventually used, first with irony, then fake irony. We ended under the worst circumstances: returned diamond, airport tears, second and third thoughts among duty-free perfumes, Longchamp bags, giant Toblerones. But our start was so unlikely not even Nostradamus could've predicted what Deepak would mean to me—the dream of every Pinoy: a Great Escape (from the noise, pollution, traffic, people, fear). It all began after I'd paid my debts—you know, the settlement, after my supposed-comeback concert. I was finally venturing into public again, in the self-improvement section of Fully Booked, beside this stranger I hardly noticed, our tilted heads browsing towards each other. I'm picking up Dr. Chopra's latest when I hear my neighbor's sudden ujjayi breath. "Hey, um, wow," says he, "that dude has my name!" I half smile and completely move away, worried he's a stan. Couple minutes later, he's beside me again, swallowing loudly. "Self-help's funny," says he. "If you can actually help yourself, why read a book by someone else?" And so I turn, ready with my bye-Felicia look, but the guy's so nervous—like walking a tightrope for the first time. And cute—his smile like it's ashamed of its brightness. With these lush eyelashes under thick glasses—like Venus flytraps in bell jars. And me the fly; caught. But he looks down, deflates, and mutters, "My bad, this book, jeez, *The Game*, it says, meeting beautiful women, a guy should, jeez, my bad," and turns to rush away. So I'm like: Bet the book also says don't give up! That's when he pivots, face red as the pope's shoes, swallowing again, and takes a deep breath. "My name's Deepak Jonathan Roy," says he. "Pleasure to make your acquaintance." Offering his hand, which feels like a dead fish. "What's *your* name?" he insists, and I'm like rolling my eyes and wiping my hand on my jeans, telling him that if he wants to impress a lady he should start by being honest. His face going like the smiley emoji with the S mouth. "Honestly," he says, "I don't know who you are. But I'd really like to." And that was my fresh start—as *his* Vita; no one else's. His first start—as someone's man; *mine*. Coz we all want our romances to be kilig clichés and gigil surprises, and Deepak was all that—and free Cinnabon samples at the mall. My first younger boyfriend, though totally an old soul. Finishing his thesis, in business management, double-majoring in graphic design, and he knew *so* much about the world, without really knowing it—but not like some dum-dum Orion, not at all. How I loved Deepak's spirit, his mind. How we traded trivia, like kisses, or slaps. How we challenged each other. At first he had more books than friends, knew more dead composers than pop songs, and always wore loose shirts to hide his chubbiness. Just like one of these shut pistachios you ignored in this can . . .

(Tinny rattling)

At first. And what an adorbs love noob. He said our first date was a non-date, and took me ice-skating, cracking me up by trying a hella awkward hockey-stop—which he kept repeating till it wasn't funny. (Which is actually funny, in retroflect.) On our second non-date, we went to a Bollywood movie, then the mall to get Dippin' Dots, and he hid behind a post and pretended to be Saif Ali Khan—poking his head out from left, then right, serenading me with "My Dil Goes Mmmm." Our third non-date was a poetry reading at Sanctum and he kept encouraging me to share the poems hiding in my purse, and I kept ordering cocktails for him to sip, trying to teach him how to drink, and I ended up drunkenly seeing how many toothpicks would stay in his curls if he shook his head. Our fourth non-date, he cooked at my place, sorta: nachos with jalapeños and cheddar (spread evenly on every chip!)—and we sat cross-legged at the coffee table and watched that week's *Oh-Em-Gee!*, holding hands for the first time. I loved how lush his palms were and how slowly he was taking things. Three months later, he made it official, asking to be boyfriend-girlfriend with a love note sealed in red wax stamped with a curlicue *D*. At his graduation, I met his family, and his parents hardly spoke to me at dinner and ate all the skin of the Peking duck. Every time I turned the lazy susan Mrs. Roy spun it the opposite way—but his brother, Ram, and his wife, Sharmila, were nice, like all embarrassed relatives. Alone in the car afterwards, Deepak insisted everyone would love me when they knew me like he did. "It's a test," said he. "Dedication always beats tradition." But I knew better, coz of what I'd gone through with One-Mig's fam, though at least they had the excuse of a tragedy. So my friends didn't like Deepak either—just to be fair. They're both usually so empathic— Boy with his balding and fab turbans, Jojie with her fight for acceptance in the semipro wakeboarding circles she loves—but you know how we Pinoys are. Jojie like: "He's just too . . . you know." Which I knew. And Boy positively agasp when I brought Deepak down the red carpet at the Golden Durian Awards. "What do you have against underwear models?" he whispered. "You're killing your career!"—as if it wasn't already smooshed beneath the scandals. But when they mocked his "moobs" and held their noses, making vroom-vroom noises whenever he called—nicknaming him "Mr. Five-Six," after the Indian loan sharks on motorcycles—that's when I quit hanging with them. Deepak asked why and I made the mistake of being honest. That didn't go down so well. So with the world against us—as it always is in great loves—how could we not fall madly? Deepak was so . . . Deepak: quietly talented, timidly driven. His world so far from mine I felt free. Thing with fame is the public persona eats into your private personality, but with Deepak I could be finally me. Or maybe that just happened while I happened to be with him. I don't know. But I even started planning to go to college with the payoff from the ferry company for my mother's death. And Deepak started changing, too—at first for the better. He'd asked for my help, honest about his insecurities, and I learned that a person's strength can be seen in how they accept their vulnerability. Most lie about it—like Fernando with his penalties, or Nur with his aloofness, or Cat's self-destruction, or Kingsley's affection, so insecure it turned spiteful . . .

(Inaudible)

Sorry—Kingsley said *what*? Hold on, you interviewed him? Him and the president? Are you serious right now? This is *my* book. But hold up—Kingsley actually said that? As if! I mean, fine, I'm not gonna lie—he did walk in while I was in an intimate uttanasana, but it wasn't like I wanted him to. It was a nightmare! Kingsley busting through the door so unexpectedly I can only stare up at him, hoping he'll see how sorry I am. Fernando shifting me over to open a desk drawer, then tossing him a bundle of money. Kingsley gazing at me sadly before he splits, and I want to stop, of course, to run after him—or even to just stop. You know? But what was I gonna do? It would've been pointless. So I chose to let go. That's satori, right? Actually, come to think of it, fine, whatever—interview whoever the heck you want, with your alleged journalistic responsibility. Didn't your last book celebrate the lives of lost men? This one's different. Let them run their mouths. You boys go incriminate yourselves. This story's mine. You're only here to help me tell it. I choose to trust you.

(Sigh)

Letting go. Like when Deepak and me suited up for skydiving—after he graduated, after his laser eye surgery, after a fire was uncovered in those baby-browns and he'd dropped twenty pounds—suddenly hungry for life. And I accepted. Deepak coming home from Krav Maga classes, bloody-lipped, bruised, and smiling, feeling studly in his Axe deo-cologne and aspirational Ferrari gear: jacket, sneakers, money clip fat with small bills. I'd tell him: Deepababy, slow down! Take it one manly thing at a time! Trying to talk sense into him by saying he couldn't skydive without me—which is how I found myself high in the sky, squeezing out of that tiny plane without a door, following the directions of this grizzled American Vietnam vet above the former U.S. air base. "No deaths in almost four years!" he assured, during our class that morning. But nothing prepares you for climbing out of a perfectly functioning plane—the wind like stepping into a waterfall as you grab the strut and stand on the wheel. Nothing, except your entire life, and the weight of all those things you want to let go of: trauma, control, unfinished business, memories of Wile E. Coyote's chute releasing pots and pans—the junk of your existence. And all you've got to do is open your hands. Empty them of who you were. That's how I feel these days, you know?—so single I'm singular, for the first time since probably ever—unburdened by anything that doesn't spark joy. That's why, go ahead—interview my twelve apostles. They'll each try to change your mind, but at some point you'll need to take a stance and say: this is what I believe is true, and right, and my role in this. Because you know the world can't stand a free woman. It makes her pay; takes her story, all she earns, because it can. Like my house—a seizable asset, they're saying, bought by Fernando with public funds. Both Furio and Boy telling me: just let go. Coz anyways I'm the Comeback Kid—♫ *And when you've got nothing, you've got nothing to lose* . . . ♫ Invisible, right? With no secrets to conceal. Just don't look down or you'll get vertigo.

(Lighter click. Exhalation)

So when Deepak's family closed their factory here and moved abroad, I closed my eyes and jumped, following him a month later. Coz I'd passed up my chance to get out before, with LeTrel. But this time with Deepak felt right—coz certain shades of limelight just ruin a gal's complexion.

And he'd wooed me with promises of privacy, and the aurora borealis, and dogsledding, and French-language courses. A totally new start, said he. I remember I couldn't stop looking past the wing at the new river far below, as silver as you imagine cold is, the island city furred with dark colors and the mountain at its heart like a torch—all orange, yellows, reds. Deepak surprising me at the airport with flowers and a faux-hawk. He was embracing change, and getting seriously swole—as in, gay-guy buff. In the taxi he warmed my hands in his and taught me useful French phrases—which I tried out till we were giggling. And I couldn't stop taking pictures: of the trees, of the stone buildings with roofs trimmed in gargoyle green, of a sixteen-wheeler truck with winged mooses painted on its mudguards. When we got out by our condo, Deepak held up an umbrella and it bloomed red, but I stepped out from under. I'd never felt rain in such a mist, or seen my breath before. I inhaled the scent of leaves on the sidewalk—ashy, like green being burned—and when I kicked them their ghosts stained the concrete. Deepak pulling me into the solitude of our umbrella and kissing me. We looked up at the windows of our new home. A light was on. Inside, I kept running around, cooing at the high ceilings, Noguchi table, and fridge that made ice-chips. At the Tempur-Pedic mattress, walk-in closet, floor-to-ceiling windows. Deepababy, I cried, we can't afford this! He kissed me again. I tried to run my fingers through his hair but his gel repelled them. Outside, a cloud of birds frolicked in the sky, chased by their shadows. "Those are starlings," my nerdmeister explained. "They change direction together." Thing is, those honeymoon weeks made it easy to overlook the way Deepak was changing. We'd go sightseeing, or to the supermarket, which I love—the museum of everyday anthropology—to marvel at all the strange snacks, expensive artisanal essentials, and bottled water from around the world. (Water, from around the world!) I didn't notice Deepak loading our cart with Mutant Mass, Builders Bars, and more bananas than a gorilla could handle—at least not till we bumped into a barista he knew from a nearby café. "Yo, Deepaflex," the guy said. "How's it hangin'?" Deepak replying: "Long and hard and full of juice, bro." And I was like, Whaaat? Then I was like, *Deepaflex?* I know, right? Apparently, his trainer called him that once, and he took to it like a doofus to popularity. "Aren't we always trying to self-edit to perfection?" he told me in the car. "You can just call me DF." More like WTF—right? Always such a neo-maxi-zoom-dweebie, but that's why I loved him. The guy who once showed me the nostril-spray applicator for his migraine meds, like it was some James Bond device. The guy who took me camping to watch the Perseid meteor shower, all excited over Venus, Jupiter, and Aldebaran lining up that year with a crescent moon. Same guy who whimpered when clouds blew in just as we reached the hilltop, and nearly cried when it poured just before we finished pitching camp. Though the rain on our tent later sounded like applause, as we first consummated our love—what better way for a geeky kid to pop his cherry? *That* was the Deepak I knew. Not the one literally flexing all over his Instagram, whose new fave color was camo, and did push-ups during commercial breaks, even stretching before making love. I mean, he did look amazing. It was a sincere turn-on watching us in the mirror beside our bed, me looking at him looking at himself. And it was so great how he no longer nursed his Diet 7-Up by the bar as I danced with our friends—but why was he suddenly buying kamikaze shots for everyone, then tearing off his shirt, buttons flying everywhere, scream-singing the latest trance anthem? In *The Seven Habits of Highly Effective People*, Stephen Covey says: "People can't live with change if there's not a changeless core inside them." Yup.

(Phone vibrates)

Hold on—sorry, gotta check . . . still nothing on social media, I'm good. Anyways—autumn faded and I couldn't understand why Deepak still hadn't brought me to see his parents. But I was keeping busy, with my classes—French, soapmaking, pol sci, poetry—and enjoying my first melancholy of winter's hurried days and endless nights. I remember the moment I first saw snow—studying late, by the window, surprised by movement beneath the streetlamp like dying moths. Wanting to rush out but not wanting to miss a second of the world fading to white. Then three young Hasidic men trailed footprints into the empty intersection, stopping to face each other, like about to argue, before linking arms to dance in a circle, legs kicking jauntily, coats flapping like the black flags of notes in a song only they could hear. Kept me smiling for days. Usually, my classes finished earlier than Deepak's work and

I'd take long walks before meeting him for our daily random activity, the cold nipply and the wind on your eyeballs like Listerine. That winter—our happiest memories. My first toboggan ride, snuggled in his arms and legs. And hikes up the mountain, to hot chocolate. And my terrifying debut on skis, which pulled like resentful spouses with a wishbone, wishing different things. And lying on our backs in the snow, counting abandoned nests in the trees, branches like cracks in the white sky. Deepak had become my life; I loved it.

(Inaudible)

Actually, I did try to make friends. But one time I introduced him to my classmates and overheard some of them from inside a CR stall—they'd nicknamed him Apples, coz he walked like he held one in each armpit. I blamed them, of course. But I began to wonder if his family even knew about me. I'd ask him but he'd swoop me in his arms, gaze into my eyes, and tell me just how wonderful he was to me.

(Inaudible)

Absolutely right—it felt wrong. Worse than when I was Rolex's mistress—at least he had a reason. So I was tempted to show up at the Roy family office and say hi, all simple, but kept thinking of Rule Twenty-Two in Jullie Yap Daza's book, *Etiquette for Mistresses*: "Resist the urge to be found out." I'm no drama-mama. But when he started borrowing money and never paid me back, even after buying himself a turntable, I told him my favorite quote from Oprah: "Lots of people want to ride with you in the limo, but what you want is someone who will take the bus with you when the limo breaks down." Which went over his head. And you should've heard him when I considered going home for a month, to make some money—by then I'd made up with Boy, who kept offering modeling gigs. Deepak all like: "Didn't you say privacy was your new superpower?" And: "No money in the world's worth that safety." Disguising his fear as love—I realize now. But not then. Thing is, all the regular jobs I applied for needed French. Et mon français est trop limité. Eventually we stopped doing our daily random activity and I moped at home, battling the mean reds and blaming Mercury retrograde. The farthest I'd go out into the brutal cold was downstairs, to roam the aisles of the Pharmaprix for surprise reductions on toilet paper, toothpaste, and the delicious and miraculous Gas-X—basically just waiting for Deepak to get home so we could watch *Toddlers and Tiaras* on TLC while eating the dinner I overcooked. Dolla to make ya holla, Honey Boo Boo! Clearly, spring couldn't have come soon enough, and I started my walks again, hoping for hope in newness. One time I went down to the river to see the ice cracking—you could hear it blocks away—and it so reminded me of childhood, and the pink bag Mama sewed for my marbles—cat's eyes, green ghosts, brass bottles, glimmers, clacking together when I poured them on the road in front of our house—the recollection so strong I cried on a street corner till someone called the cops. Fascinating—huh?—how memories with a world between them can tie a life together, making it almost manageable. Did you know elephants are born with their ancestors' migratory maps etched into their minds? Bet that's just like homesick feels. No wonder they've got such long faces. Seriously though, in fairness to Deepak, it wasn't all bad, even towards the end. I'm no martyr. There *was* lots to love. The Neil Diamond Christmas concert for my birthday. Make-up sex. Waking face-to-face, sharing the dreams we each had, finding ways to weave them into one. And laundry day, the warm cotton embracing us back as we carried the sheets to our bed, making it together as intimate as messing it up, almost. Or our monthly Costco run—wholesale couples therapy: walking in, reaching blindly for each other's fingers, thinking, Yes, we *do* need a paper shredder, electronic piano, and twelve-pack of canned air—yes, our life *is* that big. And how I loved our random drives into the great wide spaces that expanded the further we went. And the daily foreign language that surrounded us and kept us two outsiders together. Most of all I miss how Deepak adored me. I've kept every drawing—every memory of him taking a page, a pencil, and some moment when I didn't catch him gazing, to transform me into a warrior princess in a chain-mail bikini (wielding a chipped broadsword atop a hill of skulls), or a cyborg who needs to be taught the pleasures of being human, or a slave in polar bear furs (prized for being the one who finally tamed the half-orc barbarian king, he said). I should've probably known better, but I didn't. Sometimes it's just nice being someone's fantasy, if you don't think about it too much. "Madam," he'd say, offering me his arm as we set out into the day with the rest of the city, drunk with spring fever—sidewalks suddenly bare, calves finally naked, black snow tinkling into gutters. How he always carried a pocket pack of Kleenex, for my killer hay fever and forgetfulness. Now I can laugh at our stupid fights. Now.

(Inaudible)

Like naming our Wi-Fi network—I wanted Bergman's "Silence, action!" and he wanted "More cowbell." Ask him—since you nobly insist on interviewing them—ask about the personalized action figure I ordered for Christmas. It looked exactly like him and talked when you pushed a button on its back. Deepak got so mad. And I felt bad, kinda. But people change—what can you do? Love is patient, love is kind . . . it is not self-seeking . . . it keeps no record of wrongs. I accepted his manscaping and the way he wore his jeans low to show off the skulls or ganja leaves on his boxers. Even making his protein shakes, since he got queasy breaking bananas for the blender—he thought they sound like poop when it gets cut from your bum. And I was there at every competition, applying his layers of Preparation H, Jan Tana Competition Color, and Muscle Sheen Posing Gel. Never once poking fun at his purple velvet banana-hammock. But I drew the line at his sudden habit of precision spitting, and should've done an intervention when our sexy and playful texts were replaced by the likes of "recycling tomorrow!" or "fyi dishes in machine are clean." When the fights came, every week, then every day, and he stopped using his boyfriend voice . . . I should've known. But summer. With its sky-blue optimism and green horizons. The humidity making me homesick, but everything else so magical: the luscious stink of roofs being tarred, the ding-ding of the roaming knife sharpener's van, the tick-tick of bicycle gears as hipsters would come and go talking of Chromeo. Deepak trying again, joining my walks, tucking catnip in our socks for the kittehs in the alleys to follow as we ventured towards fresh Fairmount bagels. On festival nights we'd sit on the steps at the Place des Arts, my head against his shoulder, watching kids frolic in the fountains. That's probably when I thought having children might not be so bad. Anyways. At other times it seemed like the only reason we stayed together was because our books and CDs were so mixed up. We called it quits so often I finally got off the pill, as a symbol to myself of finality. We made up, though, as usual, and of course, you know, it was inevitable, it happened. I cried in our CR. Then got dinner ready for when he'd get home.

(Silence)

(Inaudible)

Yeah. Yes. But no, no way—imagine if I told him. I literally threw the test out the window.

(Pause)

And, like, a week later, we fought and broke up, so, yeah, good thing I didn't tell him. I made the appointment by myself; it was going to be a long three weeks. It was just . . . he was *still* making excuses for not telling his parents about me. That's when I threatened to leave—this time meaning it. He's on the bed—boxers inside out, coz I stopped doing his laundry—saying he has to think—and I'm looking at him like: really?, *you're* the one who has to think? So I tell him: Guess I have my answer. Next day, while he's at work, I pack my bags and leave—for Mexico City, to stay with my friend from home, Tinky, who'd just moved for her new husband. On the flight I can't sleep. The stars scattered above, roads and farms below like constellations, towns entire galaxies. Lightning on the black horizon like a great war on the frontiers of the known universe. Violence can be beautiful from a distance, sometimes—like sighing wistfully over old heartbreak. I'm so cold in my seat it's like I'm out on the wing. Alone, having been given everything in the world except what I need from him. The next night, Deepak shows up in the wee hours and Tinky doesn't want me to open the front door. What a scene, in the yard, the fool shouting as porch lights go on up and down the street. "I don't need no limo!" he yells, hiccuping drunk on mini booze bottles from the flight over. "I'll ride, hic, the bus with you!" Only in the movies is that cute and I open the door just to shut him up, coz you don't mess with sleeping Mexicans. He gets on both knees and opens a small box—and there it is. "Please," says he, "please do me the honor, hic, of being Mrs. DF Roy." Me looking down at my beautiful lost man, remembering that day so long ago, the parachute a rainbow above as I floated to the ground, Deepak tearing off his helmet as he ran across the field—all adrenaline and love, both of us—falling into each other's arms. If we could defy gravity together we could defy anything. So I tell him: I'm sorry, baby, I won't be Mrs. DF Roy—his face falling, like this, look, like this—but I'd love to be Mrs. *Deepak* Roy. I know, right? Baduy, to the max! In the plane the next morning, I keep holding my ring to the window to catch the light. Sometimes you love someone so much you'll accept uncertainty. But when we transferred planes in Los Angeles he had some customs trouble with the TSA tyrants—because 'Murica—and his reaction freaked me out. That's when I changed my mind about telling him. And, anyway, the day before my appointment, the decision was made when my spotting became bleeding and didn't stop till it was over.

(Silence)

Sorry. Just need to check my phone . . . Oh, my, gosh—look: all over Facebook. This video. I can't. The Aussie and his American husband . . . begging—see? Gods, those terrorists, Abu Sayyad, their orange jumpsuits—the stuff of nightmares. I just can't watch that. Our poor country. Somebody's gotta do something. Maybe I should run for president—I got more social media followers than Nando got votes last election. Would you vote for me? Joking aside, though, this impeachment, everything else, it's gonna get worse before it gets better—right? Always that way. Sometimes. So, yeah, me and Deepak, at the end—at this big music festival with a killer lineup: New Order, Florence and the Machine, Arcade Fire, Turbo Goth, the Ineptaneli Cockup, Seona Dancing, Snoop Dogg (who was still Snoop Lion at the time). The two of us out by the porta-potties smoking the medical marijuana he'd get for his migraines. I hadn't gotten high since Red—coz I get paranoid when my life's not stable, especially with sativa—but at that point I was like, whatever. We're laxing in this Astroturfy chillout area on a hill overlooking the stages, putting our arms around each other, snapping selfies. Music, grass, Lark and Moon filters, a clear summer night—what more could young love need? Later, we're holding hands, pushing through the crowd to the front, for Arcade Fire, Deepak's fave. I'm trying to memorize his calluses. The musicians come on and everyone cheers and holds up phones. I don't want the night to end. Deepak starts hooting, shouting, whistling again and again. That infectious joy that always made me so happy. The band got into their set and Deepak got into his groove and kept going, yelling and yahooing. And going.

And going. And I looked at my husband-to-be, the man I'd ran away with for supposedly the last time in my life, his shouting and the music and everything else washing over me, while a voice is singing about hope and pain. Deepak screaming, "It's gonna get filthy!" The voice telling me that in some light they could look the same. Deepak scream-ing, "It's gonna drop!" ♬ *Oh God, well look at you now . . .* ♬ "Filthy!" ♬ *You lost it, but you don't know how . . .* ♬ But I knew. All I needed to know. Couple weeks later, we're at the airport, nodding our goodbyes across the X-ray machines.

Deepak Roy Transcript.

(26:17.44—deepak.M4A)

A new chapter begins, eh? Tomorrow the movers come. Then I put my parental units on a plane. This weekend me and my bro hand over the keys to our childhood home. To a Chinese family. Mainlanders. Nuff said.

(Inaudible)

Hey, no prob, guy. I'm happy to talk. Did Vita mention anything about wanting to see me? She knows I'm leaving, right? Getting out, right after the typhoon, before they probably eventually declare martial law, if the president's actually still alive. I caught Vita on TV today, at the impeachment. Her testimony was badass, but see how she's being attacked online? So much for the security of privacy she had when we were together. For reals, bro, she should mic-drop and bounce. Live long and prosper. So what did you two kids talk about? No, come on, I can take it.

(Inaudible)

She said that? Seriously? She basically literally tends to exaggerate *all* the time. That Deepaflex thing was a joke. The fellas at the gym being schmucks and it stuck for like a week and half a day. Vita never got irony. She was always falling for satirical articles on Facebook. Like how U.S. Customs caught Senator Bang Rebolvar smuggling wads of cash in his pec implants. Or that Senator Enrile is actually a remote-control cadaver. Vita believes, that's her superpower. She believed in me, and I used to be such a hoser. I should've hopped on a plane and come back here to chase her. Totally. But who knows what the ladies actually want, eh? Like with sex—is that her trembling or trying not to laugh? Are you pushing her limits or disrespecting her? Will she give her consent and regret it later? How can us guys ever tell? Girls aren't the only ones vulnerable. I'm not even being sexist. Like, it's tough even with your guy friends. When you see each other after a while, you hug, right? But how long's a while? A month? Couple of weeks? A week? Maybe it's never. Maybe all the fellas are just politely hugging you back but you're actually known as that huggy friend everyone thinks is homo? Hells tough, I tell you. I just have to say, it's actually Vita's fault. She said *I* changed. *I* became a douche. Except *she* was the one encouraging me. Said she wasn't changing me, just helping me improve. At first she's like, "Just come to the gym to keep me company." Then she's like, "It'll help your lower back," since I'm a gamer with chronic issues. When I started dropping weight, she was always telling me I'm sexy, feeling my muscles. It only became a thing when I stopped doing it for her. When I discovered that exercise is taking pride in yourself. Owning your limits. If you can do six you can do eight. If you can do eight you can do ten. I mentioned *once* that lifting's meditative, the burn's sanctifying, and she goes and orders me this personalized talking action figure for Christmas, which totally doesn't look at all sort of like me. Press a button and it says shit like, "Super-sets!" and "I need protein!" Seriously, let me celebrate, eh?

(Inaudible)

Dude, my childhood was hell: braces, headgear, papal aspirations. When I was like twelve, I was changing my shirt when my pops walked into my room to scold me about some mess in the kitchen and he stopped midsentence, spun around, and shouted from the top of the stairs for my moms. "Padmini! Deepak has breasts! Big breasts! You must do something!" Everyone in the house heard. Everyone. My brother in the rec room. His basketball team playing Famicom. Their girlfriends in the kitchen who'd been baking cookies with me. My nickname in two exclusive Christian schools—two! One boys' school, one girls'—became BB. That didn't stand for basketball. My moms put me on a diet and I'd smuggle chocolate bars into bed. My pops constantly criticized me for being vain. My teenage years were all camouflage and over-compensation: books and the Bible, slouching and loose T-shirts with decals on the front. The medical term is gynecomastia. It's glandu-lar. And common. Up to sixty percent of men struggle with it at some point in their lives. Most get lipo, but I beat it through discipline. And avoiding soy. My body fat's down to like eight percent, so pardon me for wanting to see what it feels like to be the opposite of who I always was. Vita said my competitions made me douchey. Far as I know, douchebags aren't self aware. I could stop being douchey anytime I wanted. And I did. Obviously. She's a great gal, but she knows how to hurt a guy. It's just that she's so easily hurt herself. After she broke off our engagement we still messaged like every day—stuff I caught on 4chan and lolcat memes she'd love—until one day she was ready to move on and started seen-zoning me. I was like, are you serious? I'm just being true to my feelings and she pulls that? She just didn't want to do the work. So addicted to her phone, but the only time we ever video Skyped was for her to tell me about that Kingsley dude. She wanted me to hear it from her, she said—except I'm pretty sure it was just passive-aggressive retaliation for my Instagram posts slugging GG at the club with the ladies, as if *I* was at fault for getting back into the game. She's just a hurtaphobe. Spinarama with her heart. Did you see at the impeachment, right after that Kingsley schmuck gave his testimony? Vita wouldn't even look at him sideways. I know her.

(Inaudible)

Impeachment's crazy, eh? Estregan's *so* not gonna testify, despite all that Kingsley keener revealed—suddenly a hero, even if he used to be spokesman for the Armpiturangutans, those guys who massacred like fifty people or something. Twelve years later, we're now supposed to forgive and forget and thank him for testifying about Estregan's sketchy meetings with the Chinese ambassador, Lan Chao Dao? I'm not really political, but even I believe China devised the armies of trolls and hackers for Estregan and Junior. There's just basically shit-all we can do. China grabbed our islands. China smuggled in tons of shabu. Literally hundreds of thousands of Chinese have infested the country. Real estate prices and organized crime rates have skyrocketed.

(Inaudible)

I don't know, guy. Respectfully, I disagree. It's not racist if it's true. We should be allowed to talk about it. You're right, it's their government that sucks, except that doesn't explain why Mainlanders can't queue up, and don't wash their hair, and are grinding the rhino into extinction.

I just have to say, nothing ruins a luxury brand like Chinese people in Louis Vuitton or Prada. Seriously, no matter how much money or power they have, in the eyes of the world, China will never be in style. Hashtag China baduy. Oh, shit, dude—dude! Dude, write that down. We have to make that a thing. Hashtag China baduy. Choice. Totally. I'm not political at all, but after that Kingsley dweeb's testimony, the military probably won't put up with Estregan selling us out to China. I got a lot of friends who like him, but they're basically murderers for condoning what he's done. Good riddance, I have to say. That's not even out of jealousy. I wasn't jealous, just sad. Just grossed out at the thought of Estregan touching her. At first I didn't believe it. Found out one night when I was up late, hitting my bong, as one does. Checking for new photos of her on Google Images, as one does. Like any dude on Facebook, with the girls who got away, or the ones you never got. You click their beach holiday albums. Download their bikini shots into a special folder before they change their minds. Try to ignore the balding husband. Pretend that's not her baby. Celebrate that she isn't—or is, actually—fat, depending on how she treated you, eh? Scrolling through all the folders and years you never got to share with her. Just cuz you're too sad to go to bed. You do that, too, bro. Be real. That's when I found out. On Vita's Wikipedia page. At the bottom of all the typical info: career, filmography, discography, philanthropy, assorted scandals. "Vita Nova is the latest mistress of President Estregan." No citation. I was like, whaaat? I blamed the world, of course, not her. Figured it was the sort of sick slander the butt-hurt ass-hats always dish whenever beautiful women make it in a man's world. I literally registered onto Wikipedia, read their whole tutorial on how to edit, then went back to her page to delete that line. Set phasers to kill. Expunged the shit out of it. Totally. Even tracked down the anonymous editor, to sign his email up for tranny porn newsletters. I stared at Vita's entry for ages. Why would somebody say that about her? Vita with that fat fuck? I'd just as soon kiss a Wookiee. I logged on again and even added to her entry: "Ms. Nova's detractors habitually spread specious rumors out of jealousy, such as linking her romantically with the corrupt Fernando V. Estregan." Yippee-ki-yay, motherfucker. My chaotic-good alignment put to noble use. In the morning, someone totally different had changed it back. Again, I was like, whaaat? Then I googled her and him and literally wanted to upchuck. It was all over the celebrity news sites. One interview, in *The Bullet*, had a pic of Vita smiling with him at the front door of the house he got her, with her quoted in the caption: "The sexiest part of Fernando is his hands." Dude. Seriously. For basically a month I fell endlessly through a dark place. In the land of Mordor, where shadows lie. Literally wrestling the Balrog. That's when I realized I should've saved her and not been such a schmuck. Should've married her the way we dreamed. Alfresco in San Sebastián, with pintxos and txakoli and everybody dancing barefoot on the grass to her wedding playlist. "Bizarre Love Triangle." "Buttercup." "Bongga ka 'day." "Badaf Forever." Maybe by now she's learned her lesson. Come on, guy, tell her for me: I'm splitting next week, she can come with. This turd-reich's totally going to declare martial law, especially with the Liberty Party calling for more protests tomorrow. She's done her part and doesn't have to be guilty anymore about bailing. Nothing wrong with wanting to raise a family where you see your taxes at work, and can walk the streets without fear. It's only like every Pinoy's wet dream: a simple life. Simple enough to get bored again—remember that? When you were a kid and could read for hours, everything, even books that confounded you, back when you felt comfortable not understanding everything, and didn't need to have all the answers. No Filipino longs for complications. We've had enough. The ones who criticize you for leaving are just the ones who are stuck. Nobody wants to lose it like that Loy Bonifacio OFW dude, driven nuts by jealousy. Nobody wants to lose their heads like those two homos probably will.

(Inaudible)

No way, bro. It breaks my heart, leaving. It's just . . . it's not guilt, just sadness. Really profound sadness. This'll always be my home. I was born here. I grew up here, mostly. Bet I speak Tagalog better than you. I had to, managing the factory floor. I'm totally a product of this city's organized chaos. The traffic, the everyday injustices, the inequality— all that taught me which values really matter. How to spend my time, whom to protect, what to work toward. It's just there's more stable countries from which to manufacture shit. That's our business, making everything, from toothpicks to battleships. It's just here the throwaway costs too much. Dude, all it buys you is access—to basics: permits, materials, contracts, protection, all on top of official taxes that just line the pockets of people like Reyes, Estregan, and the rest. It's just that no matter what, I'm Pinoy. I got the passport to prove it. People of Indian descent have been here for centuries. Before the Americans and the Spanish. An old minority, fifty-thou-strong. Always seen as outsiders. At some point leaving's just wisdom, not betrayal. When the Brits surrendered the Philippines in the 1700s, sepoys deserted and made a life here, just to be free. When my grandparents came from Hyderabad, during Partition, they wanted that same thing. The cost is that me and my brother are foreigners in an India that doesn't even exist anymore. And to our kids, the Philippines will be foreign, too. It's just that my pops doesn't want his family living in fear. That's why he diversified during the dictatorship and we lived in Montreal, even if he had to go back and forth every other month. After the Dictator fled, we came home. This will always be home. It's just that now we're forced to start again. In Quebec. Which isn't all that different, eh? The most corrupt province in North America. Roads just as bad as ours. Except at least drug suspects don't turn up mummified in duct tape. And there's universal healthcare. And four seasons—almost winter, winter, still winter, and construction. Vita loved living there, I'm pretty sure. Even if I stupidly made us poor. It was the best year of our lives, I think. Simpler times. Seeking that boredom. She did her French lessons and kept such a clean home for us. She even sorted my vinyl by genre, then alphabetized them. Who knew I had so much ABBA? Even if I neglected her toward the end, she always made me dinner. She loved walking and we'd just wander. Vita appreciates everything. I love that about her. She'll stop to pet every dog. Browse every charming shop. Explore every pretty laneway. Smell every flower. We'd split a sandwich from Timmy's and picnic on the museum steps and watch the immigrant families. "Aww!" she'd say, at the dad in sandals and T-shirt tucked into his shorts. And his wife clutching her shoulder bag like she's threatening thieves with her biceps. And their two brown kids in matching Habs jerseys and flashing running shoes, sucking down freezies. Dude, I miss her. I know. Pathetic. I'm fully cognizant. I even got this clip of her mumbling in her sleep, stretching suddenly the way she does, limbs trembling like all electrified. We were supposed to grow old together. I love who she's becoming. Less crazy than in her twenties, not freaking out yet about her forties. You know what I mean, eh? Sometimes when she was sleeping she'd go very still and I'd panic and check if she was breathing.

(Inaudible)

That's not it at all, bro. I wasn't ashamed, I was . . . Look, my folks had no problem with Vita. It was my brother, Ram, who made me doubt. He was always so nice to her but in private he'd tell me, "Vita's just too different. She'll never fit in. Don't do that to her." I was protecting her from them. I just know that once she mellows we'll probably end up together. My family just wants to see me happy. My parentals secretly envy love marriages. Cuz theirs was arranged—my pops actually wanted to marry this Gujju girl but my grandparents thought she was too modern. My folks left their religion, language, and caste to settle here; the only zealotry they keep, as perpetual immigrants, is for assimilation. You should see them with their romantic comedies, especially my pops. Hugh Grant to him is like Bollywood is to white people. They're perversely proud to complain that us kids don't know how to speak Sindhi. Nothing could make them happier than me snagging some white girl from Westmount with folks who are devout Tories and have exotic names like Jim and Vicky. Ram was the one who was all up in tradition, ever since he took Hindi as a freshman and had a revelation during his gap year while footboarding to the Kumbh Mela. The little enthu cutlet returned wanting a three-day desi wedding with all the curry colors and fluoro saris and kurtas. The only thing more wack is I actually listened to him. It's just that Ram pretty much raised me. He and our yaya Subingita, since our folks were always away. He told me: "Vita's the kind of girl you have fun with, and that's okay. Nobody needs a wife who was mistress to a governor and got sexually abused by a priest. Our parents sacrificed too much." It's just he never understood what I'm willing to sacrifice. Vita and I can start again, doesn't matter when or where. If at first you don't succeed, call it version one-point-oh. We'll find a new city to love then hate together. Canada's a great place. The real equalizer. Look at Subingita's kids. My old yaya's doing awesome. Growing up, she cleaned, cooked, laundered, sewed, bathed us, disciplined us, picked up dog shit, manned the leaf blower, cleared the eavestroughs, and helped us with our homework. My second mother. I'd slip down to her room in the basement and she'd show me again how to make that little house and subtract for the remainder. My pops paid her third-world rates—seventy-five dollars a month, which she could've made in a day working in a hotel. She just refused to leave me and Ram. When we moved back here, she stayed and worked her way up to supervising all the chambermaids at the Pan Pacific hotel. Her two kids literally ended up in the same school me and Ram went to. Now on scholarships at McGill. Subingita's got her pension, house, two cars, a van, and a totally choice barbecue. Last time I was back, at my folk's place, she brought over some of her famous ribs, but my moms still treats her like the bumpkin who washed her feet in the toilet. *So* obvious who's the lesser woman, eh? Don't quote me on that. Seriously.

(Inaudible)

Thanks, bro. I have to admit, Vita reminds me a bit of both of them. My moms and my yaya. You know when I knew Vita was, you know, the one? When I saw how she judged the Miss Philippines-Montreal pageant. There were six contestants, the sweetest things, old enough to drive, too young to drink. All dieted, exercised, plucked, and practiced, in gowns funded by summer jobs and resentful godparents. I saw when the two finalists sang their talent segments, and one was a natural and knew it, and the other couldn't sing but gave it her all. Guess which one Vita championed, eh? Sitting there with like seven other judges, her score card sticking out like a streaker at a quidditch match. That night I went online and maxed out my Mastercard on a ring. My brother's wife, Sharmila, secretly helped me choose. She was thrilled for me. When I think of what she and Ram went through, I get so angry about what Vita did. She didn't even tell me until after. Did she mention that to you?

(Inaudible)

Seriously? A miscarriage? That's literally what she said? *So* not true. She just decided. Like I had no say. We fought real bad and that's why she bounced. I didn't think I could ever forgive her. Who the fuck gave her the right to choose without me? Like, there was Ram

and Sharmila, seeing special doctors, getting him looser gotchies, finally going to India and navigating this etch-a-sketch world of adoption. They handed over ten Gs to this womp rat of a fixer who counted
out little piles in front of them, distributing it all along the process,
for this paperwork or for that stamp. Just to get the baby they always
wanted—my nephew, Krishna, who's fricking rad. Except my moms
says she can't love him as much since he's not blood. Vita knew all that
and she still didn't consult me. I was really angry, for a really long time.
Took me a while to realize that's just who she is. I don't mean that
badly, like she's some murderer or something. I don't believe that. She
just thinks courage is doing anything to achieve your dreams. I guess
I respect that. It's just she doesn't have to be afraid with me, not anymore. Just like with her dad. Always so scared that if she let him into
her life he'd leave again if she couldn't forgive him fast enough. Did she
tell you why she left me?

(Inaudible)

Really? That's what she said? That's like literally a lie. After Mexico
we had a stopover in LAX and those TSA thugs basically racially pro-
filed me. I'm not even Arab. We only flew American Airlines because
they're the cheapest cuz they suck ass. Their itinerary obliged us to
change planes. Why would I want to enter that dangerous country of
entitled, bigoted yahoos, who are always generalizing about people?
We weren't even exiting the international terminal and still had to
retrieve our luggage, recheck it, be fingerprinted and photographed.
Then, dude, I got strip-searched.

(Inaudible)

Dude, as in blue latex gloves and a hairy wrist up my crack. Taken to
a room without windows for hours. Dude, I had to choose between
unlocking my phone, to let them perv through my selfies and artistic
nudes of Vita, or having the whole thing confiscated. I basically had no
choice. Seriously, I didn't have a meltdown. I literally had every reason
to be upset. You'd be, too, eh? Vita obviously doesn't remember it properly. She's just oversensitive about confrontation. That's why I forgive
her always being so tempestuous. We all do things we wish we could
control-zed away. And I've studied evolutionary biology. Women are
just built differently from us. Physically, mentally, hormonally. I don't

want to be an Orion here, it's just science. But women are stronger in other ways. Like in childbirth. There's scientific reasons their pain threshold's much higher. Like the man flu is really just a bad cold but us dudes are like, oh my god, I'm fricking dying here, eh? It's not women's fault things are unequal, but it's not my fault, either. Just because there's historical biases and inequalities against women doesn't mean biases and inequalities aren't happening now against us men. Seriously, we should be allowed to talk about that. I'm sure you know what it's like. Like men don't face discrimination, eh? We face it all the time, obviously, but we can't talk about it because of how men before us acted. I'm not saying that just cuz I'm threatened. Seriously, I'm a Sindhi who doesn't know India and grew up in the Philippines and migrated to Francophone North America with brown skin and a Filipino passport. I know what discrimination feels like. I recognize it when it happens and I see it happening to me all the time, basically just because I'm a cis male. But that's society. It's inherently unequal. There are roles that I just can't enter as a man. Like I can't be a midwife, for all sorts of good reasons. Equity's a totally noble goal, but nature gives us roles. All humans should have the same rights, but, like, for example, don't adults still have to protect children? From like alcohol, tobacco, pornography, and bad decisions? If kids screw up, you don't put them in adult prison. So what's wrong with women and men being treated different? Equality on every level is a myth, because everyone's not fundamentally the same. Like beauty—it's unequal and pretty much arbitrary in society's primitive conception. But the lucky ones, who are perceived to be beautiful, they never really appreciate their advantage. And they sure as shit don't act responsibly with it. That's what makes the world so lonely for so many of us. All that oversharing on Instagram, the pornography of other people's lives. That's why I'm against promiscuity. I have to say, it should be just one person for every person. Nothing radical about saying that. When did being traditional become intolerant? What about some tolerance for my views, eh? What's wrong with wanting to get married and stay married? With respecting our separate roles as husband and wife? Seriously, something's wrong about a world with so much loneliness. Some people have to try so much harder than others. Like when I was twelve, I decided one day that everything would be different. Vita knows this story. How I wasn't just chubby, I was chubby *and* asthmatic. Inhaler, emergency ID bracelet, the whole shebang. Always dead last in PE class. But after everyone started calling me BB, I told myself the day had come to take my life into my own hands. Mr. G, our PE teacher, had us running track and I got it into my head that it was just mind over matter. He blew the whistle and I took off like Barry Allen. For the first time in my life, I was passing everyone. Dude, it was amazing. Wind on my face. Cool O_2 in my lungs. Legs pumping against the track. My classmates stunned as I blurred by and ran in first place. And then, halfway around the track, the freshness in my chest became like fire. The guys I'd passed passed me. I could hardly breathe. I felt like I was going to die. Guys told me to move aside. The guys I'd passed, who'd passed me once, passed me one more time. I stumbled across the finish line, glad to not be dead last. The other fat kid in class crossed soon after me. Just as I was walking to the locker room, Mr. G shouted: "Deepak! Get your butt back here! This is the eight-hundred-meter. One more round, buddy." That last lap, I walked by myself. Even the teacher didn't bother waiting. When the list was tacked up in the hallway I was relieved I wasn't given a time. Just my name, where it always was. Yeah, dude. All my life, I've learned that some people take longer to finally get it. After Vita's testimony, what kind of life can she expect here? Even I can see she'll always be looking over her shoulder. Especially if Estregan declares martial law, like my parents say he will. You think he'll actually take the witness stand later this week? That's why people are protesting in the streets. It'll get bad, man. If Vita needs somewhere to go, I'll take care of her. That's your role when you love. I don't know how anyone can just give up on a person. Seriously. When you see her, tell her I'm waiting at the finish line. Tell her, please, I'll ride the bus with her. She'll know what I mean. Come on, guy. Help a brother out, eh?

Vita Nova Transcript: 4 of 13.

(37:55.43—VN4.M4A)

Can you believe it? First people flood EDSA Boulevard, scared his absence was a prelude to martial law—and now a snap election? I know, right? Question is: Why? Just to stop the impeachment? Or prevent another People Power Revolution? Is Nando even gonna run? Or run away, I bet. Maybe his new neck brace means it's true he's deathly sick. Or sick and tired of fighting. Maybe the election's so that Vice President Hope doesn't become president—to pave the way for Farrah. What do you think?

(Inaudible)

Maybe. Could be. Nando's always been such a fanboy of Junior's family—merciless with everyone else but them. As in, daddy dictator and mommy diva flee with billions, to Hawaii; mommy widow returning years later, shamelessly; recently getting convicted of plunder, finally, after decades of investigations and countersuits—but Nando won't ever lock up that fat old Looney Tune, coz she's like ninety-plus and we're supposed to respect our elders, even when they've always disrespected us. Bet she's redecorating the Palace in her head already—tons of gold and damask and rococo borloloys, all baduy AF and a terrible example to honest strivers like me. As she famously said: "Nouveau riche is better than no riche"—though I think new money's less a state than a state of mind. So, who else you think is gonna run in the snap election?

(Inaudible)

Yeah, no, not really a fan of Hope, though I loved her grassroots response during the pandemic. Good woman, bad party—the Fuchsias ran the show for too long, if you ask me. Relying on the so-called *resilience* of the Filipino people to make up for the government's failures. You know who'd be amazeballs? Dr. Rita Rajah. But the good ones never stand a chance. I bet Filimon Lontok's gonna run, to wriggle out of any possible cases against him. And what about Rolex, and his renewed whistleblower fame?—the old fart who shook the nation. You saw his testimony last week—weeping and growling, more king-killer than king. Even breaking into song.

(Inaudible)

Heck yeah, I think Nur's running. And if he does, I'll support him. He's the guy you should interview, not the other liars. We were Whats-Apping this morning, actually—re: my support, since I helped him win his Senate seat, even though he dumped me right after, the jerk. But of all the Presidentiables, homie's the best, with integrity up the wazoo—ready, totally, though it's a striptease, this kind of thing. Remember how Fernando always played hard to get, to make it look all grassroots, peeps just *needing* him to run? Pinoys don't really trust eagerness—we like underdogs but *love* reluctant heroes, finally doing her duty. Me, what's sad is every presidential election gets like a hundred candidates registering—the kooks, cult leaders, has-beens, never-will-bes living their dream of telling their grandkids they were once a contender—yet it's so predictable who the COMELEC declares as viable: same old surnames and surly faces, the nth sequel to *Dumb and Dumber*. Just once I wish there was someone unexpected, who comes from nowhere with a fresh vision—someone actually in it for others rather than themselves. Just once, to prove it's possible. We're, like, Asia's oldest democracy, right? Shouldn't that mean anyone with good ideas, integrity, and community lovin' can rise even to the highest office in the land? I've met some amazing people in my travels: activists, neighborhood leaders, women running initiatives from their corner store, men going house to house learning what people need and helping them organize to get it—oh, and the ladies making everything happen at my foundations, for crying out loud! But all mostly stuck at that level, especially if they're decent. In our democracy you need guns, goons, and gold to win—even if you're just borrowing that from someone you'll owe. Ours is more a demo*crazy*—our dictatorship of dynasties, forever reelected. What's it—like, eighty percent of legislative positions controlled by a few dozen families? How's that representative of us hundred thirty million Pinoys? Seriously, let's be real here. So I campaigned for Nur— even before we fell in love—coz he's a disruptor. On fleek, especially compared to his competition. First Muslim Senate president, as you know. Now leader of the Opposition, as everyone knows.

(Inaudible)

No, when I was with Nando, their feud never bothered me, actually— coz the enemy of your friend can still be your friend—even if your friend's enemy is your ex who dumped you by text. As Nando says, politics is just weather—which to me's just like love: sometimes you're inside and cozy, other times you're out in the cold. Nando never asked me about Nur, surprising as that is. Not coz of boundaries or jealousy, he just wasn't interested in my past—which was hella refreshing, when the world's always judged you on it. That's why I'm kinda curious to hear your interviews with them manboys, and their justifications. What they believe about me.

(Inaudible)

I *do* believe in Nur, even if he hates cats. The irony of a campaign trail is you're straight up fronting to voters—your constant smiles and nodding concern—but you can't hide your true self from your team behind the scenes. As in, I'd spray fake hair on Nur's bald spot before rallies. So, yeah, I've seen him at his most vulnerable, kneeling at my feet. I just know he's in it to win it for everyone—not for ego, or clan, or the Muslim minority he represented on his way up (and still would if they'd let him). He'll be president yet, if I gots anything to do with it. Homie's complexicated, fersho—everyone has reasons to love him, and just as many to hate. Like I wouldn't talk to him for years. But having him there while I testified the other day, in that Senate chamber boys' club, I felt a little something something.

(Inaudible)

It wasn't that—I forgave his sorry ass years ago, coz his loss, totally. More like I appreciated his leadership in the impeachment, as I faced down those senators, all bulbous noses and bulging eyes, like dudes in a strip club without their hands in full view. Fernando's last few supporters scowling like scolded bullies as I read my statement, a testimony that felt almost unnecessary—after Kingsley's, after Rolex's, after everyone else's—and therefore, kinda petty. Making me a piñata again for the EES troll army, led by Baraka Vousfils—that nothing but a second-rate, trying-hard copycat. But in that hollowed chamber of horrorable senators, where once strode legislators of great substance—mostly men; just saying—this here country gal from Angeles City gave the performance of her life: authentic, impassioned, defiant. With Nur the magnet pointing me true north, once again. Like he did during my darkest days, after I quit drugs, and Red, and survived Bishop Baccante—my supposed spiritual advisor, leading the boycott against me—and after my mother's death, and my father reaching out, finally (by email—email!). In Fernando's eyes, Nur was always the barbarian at the gate. To the country, he was the convincing salesman you try not to trust. To his own people, the trailblazing traitor you can't reject. To my mother, the man who'd ruin my chance at eternal life—the Muslim from the far North, with two wives, in hijabs, who'd always be more important to him than I'd ever be. But to me, Nur was fascinating, with all his ambitions, contradictions, flirtations with our culture's Catholic guilt—his taboo jokes whispered in the bedroom, or kissing me after I ate bacon. To his Adam I was Eve.

(Lighter click. Exhalation)

People love misunderstanding him—you know?—mistaking his dignity for vanity, or superiority—like there's something wrong with preaching what you want to practice. Always the sharpest man in the room, predicting the future by influencing it. Me and him met at a rally, for peace and unity, after he gave a speech that had me captivated, after I sang a song that got him clapping like a maniac—both of us bonding over sweating bottles of Jaz Cola in the afterglow of the crowd's admiration. I admit, I found him hella sexy, with his legislative record and experience in governance—*Rouge* even naming him one of the country's Hundred Hottest Men, ranked strongly in the high fifties. Dark, brooding, salt-and-peppery, with his father's ratty briefcase and lunches he packs himself, his Nehru collars and pocket Koran against his heart, and his scholarly pout and prayer scar on his forehead like a raisin. He's the playing-coach of the Mythical Fighting Cocks (three-peat champs in the Congressional Basketball League), and runs a marathon like every six months, and talks with the authority of a game show host, and listens like a lawyer paid by the minute—seeming more like an exiled sultan than the rural tribesman he once was, or is, actually, though it's easy to forget. I admire that most: how his many worlds to him are just one—not just about autonomy for the Muslim North, but uniting our whole nation. Which some people doubt, coz it's easier—insisting he'll always be a militant, a terrorist, coz he once took the only option left and picked up arms. Authoritarianism needs a villain, right? His polygamy so weird to most Pinoys he could never win a national election—till I joined his campaign, reminding everyone, every day, that most politicians have mistresses or second families, while many of us commit premarital sex or even adultery, which we all accept as just human.

(Inaudible)

Excuse you—that's not whataboutism. It's what-about-the-truthism. See? Even you're struggling to unlearn your conventions. Nur's marriage is unhidden, honest, and within his faith. So who are the hypocrites? Islam allows up to four wives, as long as each consents and is treated justly. So I was open to seeing where it might go. And what I saw between him, Massarah, and Ayeesha wasn't about collection, it was about compassion. Massarah twelve years his senior, the widow of his brother, and Nur accepted his nephew Salaudin as his son. She tried so hard—like years—to give Nur their own child, and finally, after thirty-nine hours and a cesarean, they had Zafar (which means "victory"). Poor boy dying when he was only four, when he ran and hid from the soldiers who came looking for rebels and rolled a grenade into their house—Nur and Massarah restrained outside, screaming the truth nobody believed. So Ayeesha brought them hope, even if in the end she also never bore a kid—but that's a story I'm not at liberty to discuss. I respect her quiet majesty. Both women's, actually. Massarah always bringing a book—Nur's speeches: totally hers. And Ayeesha hungrily sharing stories—teaching me about her life and always super interested in mine. (Liking my IG posts till today, with clapping-hands emojis for every lowkey flex.) I cherish that afternoon I met them—my first trip up North, well into Nur's campaign for the Senate, drunk on barnstorming across the National Capital Region, a couple of months before elections—which I'm actually looking forward to again, those weeks electrified by purpose and possibility, waving from honking motorcades, belting at rallies, hanging with all sorts of people to hear their stories. Never knew how anyone can hate all that. Have you been to the North?

(Inaudible)

Me neither, till then—coz you're right, it's kinda scary. A blur of kidnappings, beheadings, massacres, bombings, violent mining companies, refugees, separatists—which we doomscroll past fast on our feeds; another tragedy in another place with another strange name. Coz death tolls are as abstract as the tribes we forget till Christmas-bazaar season, and their handicraft gifts for our foreign friends—like: Isn't this Badjao weave just wonderful? And this Maranao-inspired monokini just marvelous? Till election time, when every national candidate sucks up to Muslim warlords for the sort of landslides rarely seen in a democracy. As Bishop Baccante bemoans on YouTube how Muslims will martyr themselves while Catholics barely attend mass, and always come late. Meanwhile, Governor Rolex, born-again son of the Church of God, once again vows equal protection for Muslims in his province—honest this time, for sure, promise. As President Nando blames Islam for the Abu Sayyad—as if their faith in a different god explains their lack of faith in his government. Even Mama warned me, before I went North with Nur, "Don't tempt the jihads!" Looking for comfort in certainty, I get it, but as LeTrel once told me, there's violence even in our words. Which is why it was a turning point—back when I was with Furio—discovering Rita Rajah's poetry, about her faith and advocacies, then actually having her reply to my questions so thoughtfully in the comments section of her Facebook posts. And also going with Nur to his district, to meet his constituents and wives— that changed my life. Before that I couldn't understand how you can be both princess and peasant. But right when I stepped onto the sunny tarmac, a parasol was held over me as I bowed my head for flowers, some kids dancing a traditional welcome, a convoy whisking Nur and I away to the market he built for his town, where I got the corrugated-iron roof vibrating from the packed crowd singing—♪ *Heal the world, make it a better place* . . . ♪—then smiled for selfies till I saw stars when I closed my eyes and began to see this place more clearly. The fans were like fans everywhere: girls in headscarves all shy but daring, boys in basketball jerseys pretending they weren't staring. Nur beaming by my side, as ladies in the stalls giggled and wrapped me in batik, and an ancient man refused my money for the ankle bells I picked up for my next dance number on *Oh-Em-Gee!* But Nur's bodyguards were hella antsy, and rushed us out soon as they could, and were like double how many he had in Manila—I was surprised—our convoy blurring through town like an arrow, into his compound like a bull's-eye—the place prickling with guns and men hanging out of openings like chorus girls at the Moulin Rouge. Not what I expected for such a simple man, who'd learned his alphabet coloring signs for his father's protests, and endured Massarah breaking apart their first house to make coffins for the casualties of war, the two of them driving survivors miles and miles to the hospital—rebel or soldier alike—sleeping at their bedsides to protect them—whether Muslim or Christian, it didn't matter. With our convoy safely inside, his wives met us, telling me "peace" (which I've always loved), Ayeesha calling me "sister," Massarah pulling me into an embrace—their whole family welcoming me to a simple feast (uncles, aunts, cousins, kids—except Salaudin, because rehab). As an outsider I knew that I should be the one seeking understanding, and Ayeesha finally opened my eyes—about how Islam was meant to be a revision of previous faiths and their shortcomings, acknowledging human nature and guiding us against it. How Islam doesn't say that things are automatically sinful—like, alcohol or gambling, which the Koran admits have benefits along with harms, but because the harm outweighs the benefits they offend the god who blessed you with all you got, and why would you want to do that?

(Zipper. Rummaging)

I still carry this pocket Koran she gave me. Coz I loved that about discovering a new religion: being guided through thinking about what I believe in—rather than just being told I'll be condemned to hell coz someone like Bishop Baccante says so. Islam's laws were überprogressive, back in the day, and practical—halal's about hygiene and sustainability in the desert; head coverings remind us of the strength in humility. And unlike in our Philippines, till now under our Catholicism, Islam actually allows divorce—as in, a wife can ditch a bad husband, though a waiting period gives them three months to try working things out. Like I said: practical. Islam stopping people from worshipping idols to suit their own whatever, everybody gathered around a single purpose, kneeling together five times a day, to hold each other accountable in your individual quest to be better. Ayeesha was super open with me about their shared relationship, since she's younger and woke and therefore kinda defensive—which says more about us than it does them. "Instead of two people dividing into one couple," said she, "it's family multiplying through the blessings of a god shared by almost all religions." Besides, morals are like hemlines, shifting with time. King Solomon supposedly having like seven hundred wives and three hundred concubines—all the slaves of a king famed for his wisdom. And our own president has kids with four women—one big unhappy family—yet we voted him into power, twice. Honestly, philanderers like him are usually the most generous men around, so it kinda makes sense that polygamy's honest and unselfish—aren't we always taught to share?

(Inaudible)

Really? Subjugation? You've never loved something so much you kept it to yourself? Or felt fear so deep it's like love's twin? Till today, in many faiths, in lots of places, the definition of a dutiful man is one who ventures into the sinful world to provide for his family safe at home. I may totally not agree with it—as in, really, I don't—but if I'm demanding equality and freedom for everybody, then I gotta understand why some seem to me to surrender it. Walk a mile in someone else's shoes, right? Even Nur's supporters called him a hypocrite, coz here's a dude with multiple wives but a strong stance on empowering women. A Muslim who championed the Reproductive Rights Bill, and always says we waste fifty percent of our strength as a nation without equal opportunity for education, employment, and political participation. Even me, after talking to Massarah and Ayeesha, I judged him for never publicly acknowledging their roles in his thinking, but I also never bothered asking them if they wanted that acknowledgment. In the Westernized world we idolize, transparency and evidence are sanctified, but in Islam what's most sacred is kept hidden—while in Pinoy politics publicity is power. And as much as I love Boy—who'd make a visionary president, if only a badaf-badaf-forever could win—he once told me the reason Nur loved me was coz I offered what his wives couldn't: election victory. At the time, I actually liked that, coz the new belle on the block can't help but be competitive. But I know now that Boy didn't give us enough credit; he oversimplified us—Nur, especially, whose branding is that he's simple and decent, making his greatest vulnerability showing a hint of hypocrisy. Like Hairgate—remember? When his GLH—Great Looking Hair—melted during a rally, his opponents pounced. "If he'll fool you with fake hair," they declared, "what else will he lie about?" Exactly why I always advised against it, even while spraying it on him. Coz there's one cure for baldness: dignity—which is so denied to us baduy masses that we love catching our leaders acting undignified. They're just like us, we say, as Presidentiables take the stage to outdo each other with the Sexy-Sexy Dance—as if we're not laughing *at* them, but *with* them, just coz they're laughing, too. But sometimes you just gotta own it. The Baldies for Bansamoro Brigade was my brain wave. And those grannies invited onstage to spray GLH while he kneeled and winked at the crowd—"What man doesn't want to look handsome for the ladies?"—kisses on cheeks after. The crowds lapping up his show of humanity, though I cringed inside, and I'm sure he did, too—but a candidate's gotta do what a candidate's gotta do, which is why he dumped me after my concert fiasco. "We're only as useful as our reputations," said he. Coz Mr. Perfect can't afford to be imperfect—even if it hurts others, like imperfect me. So I super savor that memory of our one New Year's Eve together, at the Polo Club, the ball about to drop in Times Square, ten seconds to go, Nur in front of everyone insisting *his* watch still reads eight to midnight—his look of devastation as everyone cheers and hugs and celebrates ignoring him.

(Laughter)

I caught him later, adjusting his watch to the wall clock. A victory for time itself.

(Laughter)

Nur could be such an Orion. But his convictions also meant he never gave up on Salaudin—never blaming him for his addiction, the relapses, or pawning the TV, and selling the family van, or the wild-goose chases of several weeks looking for Sal—who I actually know from the scene.

(When me and Cat met, at the Metallica concert, Sal was with him.) And Nur's convictions are why he suspended his campaign to come help find my mother's body, and nurse me through my long guilt. Me and her had made up just seventeen months earlier, when I was coming down hard one morning from molly with Red and called her weeping over all those years we were estranged, apologizing—yet in the end I lied to her, because of Nur, while she was cat-sitting in my condo over Holy Week and caught that blind item in Kitschy Katigbak's The One-Eyed Woman column—something like: "Which sexy-sexy former weather girl was spied boarding a northbound plane to perhaps consummate a courtship with a certain steely legislator? She needs no golden Easter egg! Allah be praised that plural marriage can keep a darling in dancing shoes." Mama was so angry—she'd pray for me every day, but there I was, galivanting—exactly the word she used, in her very last text.

(Pause)

The irony was, out of all my friends, it was Massarah and Ayeesha who jumped on the first plane to arrange the . . . like, you know . . .

(Pause)

You know elephants are the only other animals to communally mourn their dead? I forget where I read that.

(Silence)

In the car, afterwards, I said some hella cruel things to Nur—coz I felt guilty for bringing him to her . . . you know—yet there he was, still gently supporting me when Boy got that email a week later, from my father, who'd heard, and was all like, "The past is passed and while we still live there's a future in the future"—and I was like, whatever.

(Lighter click. Exhalation)

It's funny: you spend your life imagining your first encounter—him approaching you at the red carpet at the Oscars, or emerging from the Amazon after searching for a cure for cancer, or rendezvousing in a café in Paris after the underground prisons of an ousted dictator are thrown open—anything but an email from suburban Utah, his automatic email signature an inspiring quote on motivation, in swishy blue font, by Vince Lombardi, former head coach of the Green Bay Packers (who I totally had to look up). So when Nur dumped me, by text message, after the massacre at my comeback concert, I was literally devastated. More than I've ever been, before or since. Doomed love's only sweet if you know in advance it's doomed. Guess I should've seen it coming, in retroflect. I think I know exactly the beginning of the end: in my condo, one weekend of moistened sheets, scattered childhood photo albums, tubs of ice cream melting by the bedside, when I asked him to tell me something from his supervast repertoire of taboo jokes—which I appreciated for their trust and intimacy, and how they unmasked our darkest of human frailties. Because these days sex and violence are boringly acceptable, but say something that offends someone somewhere and a mob storms some embassy and sets it on fire. Dance the Mr. Sexy-Sexy all you wish, but support the Reproductive Rights Bill and your career gets boycotted to oblivion—like that.

(Fingers snap)

So I wanted to see Nur as free as he was naked, and he puts on his professor voice, all like: "This is no joking matter," says he. "When Jesus was dying for your sins, on the cross at Golgotha, the place of skulls, he was watched over by his mother, Mary, as well as Mary Magdalene and another Mary who was the wife of Joseph's brother Cleopas, and of course the beloved disciple John, son of Zebedee. Jesus calling down: 'John. Where is John?' And John casting aside his fear of the centurions' spears to rush to the foot of the cross. 'Master, I am here. Tell me.' But Jesus was weak, his voice weaker and not heard. John ran from Golgotha to fetch a chair from his home, and returning he stood upon it, kissing breathlessly the knees of Jesus. 'Master, I am here.' Yet Jesus's voice was so weak John still could not hear and he ran home and returned with a ladder, limping because his ankle was sprained in his haste. The disciple climbing the rungs, in much pain, until he was level with his master's chest. Jesus spoke, but alas his words were still too faint. John climbed down and arranged the ladder on top of the chair, and the ladder woefully slipped, and the disciple fell and broke his leg and the ladder fell and broke his arm. And as Jesus breathed his last breaths, his disciple rearranged the chair and ladder in desperation, and asked the three Marys to hold it firm as he climbed, in agony, to press, finally, his ear to Jesus's lips. 'Master, I am here,' said John, 'tell me, Master, what it is.' And Jesus, hoarsely whispering, tells him: 'John, my faithful John, my beloved John, I can see your house from here.'"

(Laughter)

Jesus jokes are always funny. So I'm like, Tell me another. And Nur's like, "Why's Jesus rich?" and I'm like, Why? And he's like, "Because Jesus saves." And: "Why is Jesus never thirsty? Because he's the King of the Juice." And: "What's the difference between Jesus and a picture of Jesus? Only one nail's needed to hang a picture of Jesus." And I'm burying my face in his chest and telling him to be fair, and Nur's like, "Why can't Buddhists vacuum in the corners?" And I'm like, Why? And he's like, "Because they don't have any attachments!"

(Laughter)

And I'm like, What about the Jews? And he makes this face, like I-wouldn't-dare, but then he does: "Why did the bee wear a yarmulke to a bar mitzvah?" Why? "Because he didn't want anyone to think he was a WASP!" And: "Why don't Jewish mothers drink? Because alcohol interferes with their suffering." And: "What's the difference between a canoe and a Jew? Canoes tip!" And I laugh and ask about atheists. And Nur says: "Why'd the atheist turn to religion? Because he was sick of not having any holidays." And: "What do atheists moan when making love? 'Oh figment! Oh figment!'" And Hindus, I insist. "I only know one," says Nur. "What's a Hindu?" And I say, What? And he says, "Clucks and lays eggs!"

(Laughter)

Then I'm telling him again: Come on, be fair! Nur shaking his head, me twisting the skin on his arm till he nods and says: "Fine. Just one. About a tourist sightseeing in New York City, who in Central Park encounters a young boy being attacked by a pit bull, and so the man picks up a stick and beats the dog, but the dog won't let go and the man has to kill it. A reporter witnesses the incident and tells the tourist, 'Let me interview you! You're a hero! Your story deserves to be syndicated across the world. I can see the headline now: Brave New Yorker Saves Child from Vicious Dog.' And the tourist replies, 'But I'm not from New York!' So the reporter says, 'Okay, across the world the headline will read: American Hero Rescues Boy from Attacking Dog.' And the tourist replies, 'But I'm not American, I'm from Iran!' And the next day, the tourist wakes up to discover that across the world the headline reads: Islamic Extremist Kills American Dog in New York's Central Park." At that point, I'm up on my knees beating Nur with a pillow, telling him that's not fair, and he sighs and launches into another. "An atheist walks down the street and encounters a Catholic priest, and says to him: 'Three people in one God? A virgin birth? Body and blood of Christ? Such nonsense!' But the priest turns his other cheek. So the atheist keeps walking and encounters a Buddhist monk, and says to him: 'Meditation towards enlightenment? Reincarnation? Spiritual leaders found as infants in the middle of nowhere? What rubbish!' But the monk looks at him with detached compassion. So the atheist keeps walking and encounters a Jewish rabbi, and says to him: 'God's chosen people? You conquer Palestine because a book says so? You can't turn on machines on Shabbat but get goys to do it for you? Utter stupidity!' But the rabbi shakes his head. So the atheist continues walking and encounters a Muslim imam, and the atheist says to him: 'Good morning, sir. Lovely day, isn't it?'"

(Chair scrapes. Footsteps pacing)

By then I'm hella vexed, of course, me and Nur sitting up on either side of the bed, suddenly ashamed of our nudity—like an apple had been bitten. So I offer a few, in fairness. Like:

Nur pulling on his clothes by the end of that punchline, and I put my hand on his shoulder, and he turns like about to hit me but goes to the living room, slamming the door. We were okay the last weeks before elections, but never quite the same, come to think of it. That night, I'm not proud of—coz we should take each other's values seriously. Sometimes it's just hard to really understand what you believe.

(Chair scrapes. Seatback shifts)

Actually, maybe it started when I pushed him to show me the mosque he built, which isn't his province's biggest but supposedly its most beautiful—the main hall decorated with mosaics by local crafts-women, where now only men are allowed. Maybe then. Coz just as Nur's finally telling me, "Fine"—because anyway "it's not yet prayer time," and "the Great Mosque in Mecca isn't segregated"—that's when I insist that Massarah and Ayeesha join us, coz they'd never seen it. When they heard their names from the next room, and came in, Nur couldn't say no. That day, I'm proud of. Inside, a small dome soars like a miracle, like all domes do, sunlight streaming through windows at the top, the main hall clean and elegant with a sense of peace that made me proud of him. I'm striding alongside my two sisters, Nur some paces ahead, my bare feet cool on the tiles, and a voice sings from beyond like an angel—♫ *Allahu akbar* . . . ♫—taking me to ancient kingdoms and worlds I might never see—♫ *Ashadu an la ilaha illallah* . . . ♫ Nur looking at his watch like it betrayed him again, saying sharply that it's time to go, as men file in from all directions, first a few, then many, then more, rugs rolled like yoga mats under their arms, feet shushing across the ground. That moment, I'll never forget—the sound of the sea of their naked soles, an invisible singer and his faraway call, the charge of the forbidden suddenly accessed, with Ayeesha and Massarah on either side, and me at peace as one of them, while we take our time walking out, Nur now way ahead, the men glancing up as we pass, staring for the briefest second before looking away. They glimpsed, then looked away. Glimpsed. Looked away. And for a moment I felt we were the most powerful women in the world.

Senator Nuredin Bansamoro Transcript.

(32:04.13—bansamoro.M4A)

In the name of God, the most gracious, the most merciful, allow me, my friend, to first tell a true story of a life. You are a boy and the great North is your home—the Land of Promise, the place of broken vows. The town in which you were born will soon no longer exist. On the hill where your grandfather unrolled his prayer rug every day will stand a church of the Kingdom of Faith in Christ. You will know the mountains and valleys and rivers across hundreds of miles; your earliest memories will be of fleeing again and again with your family as the front lines shift. You will find, my friend, your life told by others who cannot understand, who speak only of separatists and schisms, bombed markets and broken peace deals, abductions and sieges of intractable cities that are left destroyed despite presidential promises. In history books, you will read of the ungovernable babel of tribes; of stolen lands, settlers, militia, and refugees; of logging and mining empires; of radicalized men, widowed women, raped girls, and teenage boys strung up, burned alive, hacked like meat in broad daylight. From a faraway city, leader after leader will have sent armies with guns and tanks to bring what they call peace. Even the most intrepid of travelers will not dare taste your people's hospitality, for there have been others whose stories did not end well.

(Pause)

Of everything you've seen stolen, hope is the most blatantly taken. Yet you watch your father refuse to follow the way of the bullet, for he has seen the bloody residue of previous generations. He beats his plowshare not into a sword but into a pen, fighting in the courts and newspapers with all that he has taught himself and learned from those around him. His pilgrimages to the capital, his protests in the streets, his pleas for reform, all yield pittances. The government offers only scholarships as panacea for our poverties. The congress of representatives of our nation's people commissions reports, only to conclude: "In their ignorance and in their trend toward religious fanaticism, the Muslims are sadly wanting in the advantages of normal health and social factors and functions"—our leaders' certain answer to the question of the chicken or the egg. Your life has enjoyed no such simplicity. Against the wishes of two families, your father married your mother, an educated Christian of quiet inner strength. They both practice their faiths with mutual respect, though you and your older brother are of course raised by your mother in the faith of your father, whose regular absence fills you with pride at his purpose while his rare presence fires you with the convictions of his cause. It is your mother who teaches you how to get through each day with an eye to the future, and you help her keep the secret of the money from her own mother, which she folds and hides away for your family's needs. You will never forget, for you won't want to, the morning your father returns and sits like a stranger in your chair at the kitchen table, closing his eyes as if he can hear the inevitable. Some nights you all stand with him in the front doorway to listen, approximating from how many valleys away the gunfire is coming. Your parents are the ones whom your neighbors follow when you pack to flee like animals before bushfires. If your parents are ever afraid, they hide it well, and throughout your life you will think of them when you need to find your way. Each time the fighting passes, your family returns repeatedly to what was your home, its doors stolen from their hinges, glass from the window frames, roof from the walls that have been bulldozed to erase all evidence of your existence. You struggle to make sense of such things. There are too many enemies in too many places—Christians, Communists, rival sovereignists, government loyalists, collaborators, soldiers, terrorists. You learn suspicion and hatred the way the young do, by hearing adults mourn over the evils of others. In time, you try such things out to see how they feel.

(Pause)

In one mountain village where you live the year you are eleven, there's a widow everyone calls Aunty Grandmother, who often frightens you with her list of human ailments before amazing you with nature's remedies for each. Sometimes she shows you the cavalry sword she captured as a young woman in a raid she led against the colonizers' garrison. In another age, she would be branded as a witch, for her potions and poultices made from the upside-down field of herbs and flowers drying from her ceiling. These days the whispers have tagged her as something else. One afternoon, after Asr, your group of friends is walking in the woods and you find Aunty Grandmother lugging a canister of kerosene. An older boy named Mohammed, who's nothing like his namesake, politely takes it from her. As she turns to smile and tell you something, Mohammed empties it over her head and pushes her to the ground. "Communist!" he shouts, and your friends join in kicking. "Communist!" you shout, though you don't know what that means. After one kick you find yourself running home and your father grabs and holds you in his arms, but you remain silent. The next day, when Aunty Grandmother's burned body is found, the villagers, of course, blame the Communists.

(Pause)

You will think of this at university, in the capital, as you witness the radicalization of your peers, each of you confused in different ways by the optimism of youth and the limits of society's offerings. Your shared independence brings both purpose and curiosity. With your roommates, Eddy and Farouk, you ride the jeepney downtown to the mosque, yet you three often venture instead to the Ideal Theater to watch the celluloid love stories of Elvis or Marilyn. You stroll the avenues as shop windows begin to light up on unaffordable goods and you all gaze at the Universal Genève wristwatches at the Estrella del Norte. Sometimes you linger with your friends in the red-light district, daring each other to enter a nightclub as a door swings open and you pretend you aren't peeking. Farouk, with his splendid enormous nose, can on most nights sniff out where the school parties are. Eddy, disapproving, nonetheless always joins, as interested in the light-skinned girls as they are in him and his white songkok, which he wears proudly as if it says more about his devotion to Islam than it does his rich father taking him on hajj. At the parties you try alcoholic drinks for the first time and you learn to dance the Watusi. For a while you even go around with your head bare.

Yet every morning you climb with your friends onto the roof of your boardinghouse—above the sounds of the radios and the scent of frying food—and you pray under the rising sun. It is in that city where you first experience the varieties of discrimination: the stares, intimidation, ignorant professors fortifying their petty views in classrooms. In your junior year, the constant stream of bad news from home, and criticisms from your imams and devout friends, take on profound weight when dozens of Muslim army recruits, hardly older than you, are machine-gunned by their comrades only miles from your campus and dumped into the bay—their sin: requesting discharge after refusing to be deployed against kindred back home. Had one man not played dead, and clung to driftwood for hours, the Dictator would have kept it covered up, and your life would have been different.

(Pause)

When Farouk returned home, to join his professor who founded the armed faction of the sovereignty movement, Eddy returned as well, to organize peaceful protests that went ignored and increasingly sabotaged by who knows what side. Yet you, my friend, stayed in the capital, heeding the wisdom Ibn Abbas relayed from the Messenger, in the *Sunan Ibn Majah*—that one knowledgeable man is more formidable against the shaitan than a thousand devoted worshippers. You studied and passed the bar examination, topping it at first place, after the last of your circle returned home to fight following another massacre, by the army's Fifty-First Infantry Battalion, of one thousand seven hundred and seventy-six worshippers in a mosque owned by a suspected rebel financier. You would have stayed your course toward national politics, despite exhortations and guilt, had your brother not been killed while protecting his wife from men who forced themselves upon her. That was in the refugee camp where your family finally settled years ago. Rolex Aguirre's Christian militia came over the provincial border before dawn, with picks, shovels, iron bars, and anything else they could find to kill women, children, and the elderly as they slept. They lit fires to hide their crimes. Massarah, your brother's widow, was found to be with child, and after the appropriate four months and ten days of mourning, but before her pregnancy came to term, you abandoned your plans in the capital and married her quietly on a hillside beneath ancient trees. She was unforgettable in her immaculate beaded raiment touched with the blue of the sky and the green of the forests. Your brother's son, Salaudin, you have raised as your own, for his is the great North, the Land of Promise, the place of broken vows.

(Pause)

For his sake, and that of his generation, I will not rest until their stories are entirely different from mine. This, my friend, is why I ran for the Senate, and why I'm running now as Hope Virdsinsia's vice president. For these problems are ever present, however far removed they may seem to some. The same unhappiness grows right outside your gated subdivision. North, South, Kibera, Shatila, Rocinha—it's the same. Smoky Mountain, Sultanbeyli, Orangi, Comuna Trece— it's the same. The unnamed streets, cinder-block walls, bricks on iron roofs, bare bulbs like blisters, obelisks of rebar, laundry hanged like flags of beggarly kingdoms—the same all over. The open sewers, burning trash, children on corners, walls everywhere plastered with politicians' faces and portraits of martyrs. Whatever language they're in, the graffiti and prayers say the same thing. What they express, the need, is simple, however complicated and contentious meeting it may be. I believe *that* path is neither the violence of separation nor the compromise of autonomy. I have always proposed a third path forward. For every war is rooted in inequality and injustice, and it was through division that our problems began, on scorched earth sowed with blood where great kingdoms once strove for peace. It took the Americans a decade to finally "pacify," as they put it, this ultimate of our nation's regions, quashing civilian support and breaking resistance through ancient Roman tactics like vastatio. This is what my grandfather suffered, his fields destroyed, the villages starved, the roots of famine taking hold, until he and his men traded their guns for pens and signed papers ceding the ground beneath their feet to overseers in the capital. Our traditional courts were abolished, our minority dismissed as barbaric, our communities excluded from development efforts. We were deliberately forgotten, skirted even by the Christian missionaries who promised other places progress and education in exchange for a willingness to hear about their faith. Law and order, and land distribution, brought settlers who did not even speak our language, to work our soil for the sake of the nation. They built churches, unfolded roads, shared among themselves crop loans and irrigation grants as their communities thrived. Our people grew poorer, outnumbered, even as new tracts of land were offered out. Our age-old suspicion of government, our lack of education, our ignorance of procedure, and our incapacity to pay fees saw many unable to legalize our claims to the homes our families had owned for generations. It was conquest by paperwork.

(Pause)

With the Second World War came more crisis for us and more opportunity for the ruthless—like Aguirre, the son of a Christian homesteader, barely in his teens when he fought the Japanese. His men were less guerrillas than bandits, yet they received arms and an official mandate that led to the power he still holds today. When that terrible war ended, we were the ones seen as squatters on the land for which we'd fought, while Christians such as him called in government troops to deal with people such as my grandfather, who would never accept token payment for what had always been ours.

(Inaudible)

Yes, my friend, yours is an astute question. You're right, poverty and radicalism are mutually propagating. But when you're underrepresented, when protests and peace deals go ignored, when change is not forthcoming, it can be courageous and noble to turn to violence. Its threat can be useful to democracy by ensuring fair treatment in unfair political circumstances. During our two decades under the Dictator's Martial Law, for example, violent conflict is what led to international support for our cause, from Islamic countries who threatened to withhold the government's supply of oil. Our violence was always deployed in good faith, and it was in fact a peace treaty that allowed the Dictator to hand power to his cronies among us, never intending to honor the agreement to let us craft our own laws, control our budget, and govern ourselves. Predictably, and reasonably, many of us returned to the gun, again and again, while every subsequent president held tightly to the leash despite vowing more slack. One offered autonomy but only if approved in a plebiscite held in regions that by then were a solid Christian majority. Another gave the responsibility of autonomy but retained all power of taxation and development authority. Slipping deeper into our frustrations, we on the same side fought bitterly with each other, splintering into armed factions, competing for control, prompting the next president to send even more troops, leading to more violence, more refugees, more poverty, more of the same cycle that began more than a century ago.

(Inaudible)

As congressman, I supported the reform movement, yet there's only so much one can do by representing your small district and writing national laws. As provincial governor, I later sought to help us deepen into what spaces were available, even with everything stacked against us, for the possible must never be limited by the impossible. I targeted bureaucratic bloating and red tape, and ensured salaries were paid on time, to deter incentives for graft and corruption. I expanded telecommunications infrastructure, to connect us with the world. My office sponsored IT literacy and blogging workshops in high schools, to cultivate stronger voices among young people. I made government finances transparent, to show how underfunded we are even when every peso is put to good use. Lastly, I invited national journalists to come lift the shroud off our region. Six years later, during President Estregan's first administration, when he washed his hands of the most promising peace deal yet, and passed it to Chief Justice Arriola Makapal Glorioso and the rest of the Supreme Court, who ruled it unconstitutional, what choice did we have but to take up arms once more? That, my friend, was when I decided to run for Senate. A national quest for peace requires a national platform.

(Pause)

More than thirty years had passed, the span of a generation, since the promises of the initial peace summit, but the yields were inadequate and the costs unacceptable. My father died a bitter man. My mother never recovered from the murder of my brother. Gentle Farouk was blown to pieces by mortar fire. Noble Eddy was shot at a rally. In total, at least one hundred fifty thousand people have lost their lives to conflict in our region. Two million people, more than half the population, have been displaced in their lifetime. None of the top brass have been held accountable for the military's human rights violations. Our region remains consistently at or near the bottom of national development indices. We are the poorest, most illiterate, shortest-lived of the Filipino people. Our natural resources are exploited by imperialists from the capital who refuse to invest in the communities from which they're extracted. Warlords like the Aguirres bring peace that is as brutal as Ivan the Terrible's, empowered not by local legitimacy but by the unwavering support of national leaders. Nowhere else could Estregan receive one hundred percent in the polls—a hundred percent! Estregan's nickname for Rolex is "Lazarus," for in Aguirre country even the dead vote. My old rival has a real talent for spinning gold from manure, and even from swine, as we heard in his over-acting testimony during our impeachment. Not only did Rolex give kickbacks from illegal gambling to the president, but billions were siphoned from the budgets of the United People for Progress party's congressmen, governors, senators, and ministers—directed to shell corporations that were ostensibly NGOs for agricultural development and post-typhoon reconstruction. Those involved in that scam, managed by Giannetta Napoli, each received their cuts of taxpayer money. Breeders only received pigs that were sick or infertile, and farmers got fertilizer so devoid of nutrients it was little more than dirt, yielding too many failed harvests before a scientist at the Ministry of Agriculture discovered the truth.

(Inaudible)

Rolex is likely behind the black propaganda now leveled at me, for I've never been afraid to bring attention to the illusions he conjures. Our rivalry in Congress extended beyond the bitterness on the hardwood between my Mythical Fighting Cocks and his Crusading Cagers, with me revealing him in front of the assembly at every turn. His Clean Air Policy bill would have uncapped limits on factory dumping in waterways. His People's Enhanced Remuneration Act sought to raise basic salaries by four percent while reinforcing the short-term contractualization that allows employers to terminate workers before they're due the benefits and protections of full-time contracts. Rolex did not block the Accessible Great Water Act because it was impracticable, as he claims, but because one of his sons owns the North's largest distillation facility while his other son manufactures plastic bottles. Rolex is the master of legislative acronyms and political sleight of hand, his tricks celebrated for their audacity and generosity. The old weaponry he and his men received to fight the Japanese were turned in during the cash-for-guns amnesty meant for disarmament, yet Aguirre invested his earnings, in partnership with current Attorney General Jehusepat Caldera, to establish the largest security-guard company in the nation, gaining unlimited firearm permits and an entirely legal private army. He raged against dynasties when he turned on his mentor, the Old Man Calvino, ending that clan's long reign by beginning that of the Aguirres. Through smuggling luncheon meat and cigarettes, he impaired his province's livestock and tobacco producers, whose businesses he bought for a song before very publicly clamping down on smuggling. He's enriched himself on everything from illegal logging to mountaintop removal mining, even as he proudly inaugurates his provincial marine and mountain nature reserves, lauding them as the largest in the nation. What was revealed at the impeachment, my friend, is a fight among thieves. Even in his sunset years, Rolex does not seek redemption so much as opportunity. It remains to be seen for which co-conspirator he's traded in his old mah-jongg buddy, Fernando. These next days and weeks will reveal who stands to gain the most through this snap election, which shanghaied our impeachment's efforts for accountability.

(Inaudible)

Estregan is clearly a coward and a fraud, as we saw after I accepted his debate challenge. Yet despite his recent conspicuous absence, and re-emergence wearing a neck brace, he is not down for the count. Where those like Rolex wield guns, those like Fernando wield favors. The presidency enjoys the personal appointment of more than six thousand key positions, with indirect influence on thirty thousand more. Estregan distributed juicy committee chairmanships to faithful legislators, ousted the Supreme Court chief justice and installed his own, and gave government vehicles to Catholic bishops in exchange for their support. He manufactured positions to establish a new layer of loyal bureaucrats, such as presidential advisors on dairy, social media, shopping malls, and water-buffalo development—even a presidential assistant to the presidential consultant on chiropractic education. As a man suddenly in power will suddenly have many friends, a man who maintains many friends will maintain much power. Controlling

Congress allowed Estregan to appoint loyal officers to key positions in the armed forces, which is why the military maintained their support even during the thousands of preventable deaths during the pandemic, until the impeachment laid bare the long list of his flagrant violations of the Constitution they're sworn to protect.

(Pause)

To my mind these are the most pernicious effects of the two Estregan administrations, which have made government less accountable and accessible to the people. By bulldozing limits to presidential authority, Estregan eroded the institutional checks and balances that hindered government's potential abuse. By pushing his Con-Ass, his assembly of sycophants sought to change our Constitution and cement his hold on power. Thank God we stopped them. I've long agreed with that notion that dissent is the highest form of patriotism, for a citizen must hold his leaders to account and a leader must be accountable to his citizens. Yet in quashing dissent, arresting Opposition politicians, attacking journalism, and swarming social media with trolls and disinformation, Estregan and his everlasting supporters have successfully conflated patriotism with partisanship and cultlike sycophancy.

(Inaudible)

I'm sorry—jokes? My friend, do I strike you as a flamboyant man? No, my apologies, however you may press, I like jokes as much as I do cats. Jokes are what helped Estregan gain the presidency. Joking is the excuse his supporters use to explain his misogyny and malapropisms. Accountability is not a laughing matter. What is a joke is their claim that the country is safer. Under Estregan, tens of thousands have been killed on the streets by police. General Rusty Batlog took his patron's mandate and executed it, if you'll excuse the tragic pun. Index crimes have decreased, yet murder and homicide have spiked two hundred percent. Some nine thousand Filipinos have been confirmed killed by police in drug operations, and an increasing number of suspected Communists slain by the military—which Kingsley Belli always claimed is acceptable, comparable to the Reyes administration. Yet at least thirty thousand more killings have been classified as DUIs—deaths under investigation. Where, my friend, are these investigations? Where are the convictions of rogue police officers? Estregan made his comeback by promising unparalleled violence, yet they claim he was always joking.

(Pause)

Meanwhile, they attempt to sweep this genocide under the rug. The family of Albeo Cruz, that seminarian killed at a temperature checkpoint during EWANQ—where could they go for justice? Despite the evidence of his innocence, the dead boy was condemned posthumously as guilty by even public prosecutors like Warden Cantuteh, whose loyalty to Estregan was his lone qualification to serve as his lead impeachment counsel. Albeo Cruz's family had no recourse but to approach us members of the Opposition.

(Inaudible)

No, my friend, I disagree. That's not politicizing a tragic incident. It's simply how our system works. Those in power will claim to be innocent of abuses, while those who seek power try to prove those abuses are evidence of the need to change leadership. Without that dynamic of opposing forces, without the threat of accountability, incumbent leaders will act with impunity. Our sole method for ensuring that our leaders act on our behalf is to make it worth their while, either through our support or the consequences of our withdrawing our support and giving it to another.

(Inaudible)

You're exactly right, it is self-preservation. Democracy, like capitalism, thrives on self-service. It is our ability to freely organize and advocate for our own interests that distinguishes us from absolute monarchies. Impeachment is one safeguard; elections are another. Yet what happens when impeachment is hijacked? What happens when elections are rigged through money, patronage, disinformation, and a willful lack of voter education? This, my friend, is the test now faced by our democracy. God willing, our next few chapters will reveal whether there's hope for our political system or if it's been perverted beyond repair.

(Inaudible)

To answer truthfully: I don't know. But I offer the two likeliest scenarios. The optimistic one is that voters entrust our Liberty Party with a resounding mandate so that President Hope Virdsinsia and I, as the first Muslim vice president, can chart a more peaceful and equitable path for our country. The pessimistic one is that this snap election is a ploy to circumvent the impeachment's likely result and rig the forthcoming polls so that Estregan, or his proxy, Farrah, will retain power.

(Inaudible)

I choose to be hopeful. We all deserve an opportunity for redemption.

(Inaudible)

Yes, as you say, exactly the case with my son. They accuse Salaudin of being an addict and a dealer, which under this regime can be a death sentence, executed by unknown assailants in masks. That his dependency on drugs still continues is interpreted as a moral defect as well as the impunity of a sitting senator's son. These are of a piece with the other slanderous talking points—that I'm imposing Sharia or establishing a caliphate in the North. They claim that my private nature is proof that I've much to conceal, yet that's fallacious. True patriotism's not waving flags but bearing responsibility with quiet resolve. The Sufi tenets teach us that faith must be intimate. Islam is a religion of community and the self; I'm personally devout, yet also a public servant who knows that separation of church and state assures equal protection to all communities by preventing the vested interests of one faith from dominating the interests of another. It's the same principle that makes freedom of speech a foundational right, one that allows us to fight for all other freedoms, especially of religion. Many disagree with me—common cause finally found between Muslims and Christians—yet the burden of proof is my challenge in blazing our third path forward.

(Inaudible)

No, my friend, I'm not avoiding your question. It's no secret that Salaudin has wrestled with addiction, while I fought to improve our government's policies regarding illegal drugs. I am not soft on the shabu issue, and Salaudin does not deserve to be plastered all over the news. He and I have had struggles, yet what father hasn't with his child? That so-called exposé in *The Bullet* said he sold our car to buy drugs, and that we tracked him to a beach resort and kidnapped him by helicopter to fly him to a rehabilitation center. I've never disputed that. Yet I didn't leave him to rot, as they claim. For months I visited him every week, even after he violently threw a checkerboard at me for not letting him win. I would never coddle him, through any relapse. The most recent, as you've read, was that morning when I found his car parked in the flowers, the door open, the radio on, while Salaudin lay unconscious in my study, his pants down and a racy magazine on his stomach. That's how we discovered him, I and the reporter who unfortunately was conducting a profile on me. What else could I tell my son when he joined us at breakfast? "Salaudin," I said, "wash your hands."

(Laughter. Sigh)

I struggle, I admit, with knowing what to do with him. At his age, I'd topped the bar and my practice was becoming successful. Salaudin, on the other hand, can be undisciplined. Like so many of us Filipinos. Yet he's my son. I'll always forgive him. As I said, we all deserve opportunities for redemption. Three months now he's been sober. I advocate for a drug policy centered on harm reduction because I've seen firsthand the effectivity of such methods. In so many countries, they are proven to succeed where Estregan's method of violence has failed and only driven the drug epidemic deeper underground. Harm reduction isn't capitulation, as he claims. It's simply a raft of pragmatic, evidence-based policies, programs, and practices intended to reduce the negative public health and social effects of drug use. It is both effective and compassionate. By meeting people where they are in their struggle, you increase their opportunities to succeed when they are finally able; without their readiness, there can be no real commitment to avoiding relapse. Shabu is indeed a dangerous and illegal drug, yet was I expected to have Salaudin arrested that morning? Would you turn in your own child if you found him with drugs and pornography? Or would you flush it all down the toilet, as his mother did, and get him help, as I did? The accusations of my enemies, many of them parents, are the only hypocrisy I see. I've nothing to hide.

(Pause)

That is why I'm proud to run with Hope, a kind woman and accomplished public defender whose isolation as vice president under Estregan only revealed the shaky legitimacy of his administration. From the very day of the results of last election, they've attacked her. In her first year they quarantined her, claiming she was the Liberty Party's Plan B to win the Palace, should Estregan and his UPP party ever falter—yet that is precisely the constitutional point of a political system in which the president and vice president are elected separately. This year, Estregan double-dared her to oversee his drug war, which she consistently criticized, only to fire her two weeks later once she began investigating the top drug lords, who, many believe, have a relationship with Estregan's sons, Judong and Mikki.

(Pause)

I believe in Hope's vision for the future. We will reform the social services, for the nourishment, education, and healthcare that families need for an honest life. We will address corruption at every level, starting with the reform of the judiciary and police, to give teeth to the laws we already have. We will abolish the pork barrel, to increase oversight of public funds, eliminate patronage and theft in Congress and the Senate, and prevent our laws from being manipulated in order to profit lawmakers. We will finally pass the legislation that our Constitution mandated and prohibit political dynasties, which clans like the Estregans and the rest always refused to pass. This is where we'll start, for how can you tell our lowly bureaucrat not to steal for his family when those in authority pilfer with impunity? As the old Arab proverb goes: "If the head of the family is drumming, don't blame the children for dancing." Long term, there's also electoral and tax reform, infrastructure development, national security, pandemic response, and modernization of our armed forces. Decriminalizing defamation, to finally protect the freedom of speech our citizenry needs to speak out when we leaders fail them. We'll repeal the foreign ownership laws, those good intentions which only deter investment by prohibiting noncitizens from owning more than forty percent of a business. Finally, and perhaps most urgently, we'll develop a workable long-term plan to address the climate change that increases the potency and frequency of our typhoons each year.

(Inaudible)

Yes, my friend, it was indeed the youthful and idealistic Vita who inspired me years ago to pursue a national agenda. Her connection with the people was profound at the rally where we met. The way she sang and walked among the crowds moved me with its power. Her Mr. Sexy-Sexy united the nation in laughter and joy, reaching the most remote of villages and the most unnostalgic members of our global diaspora. She and I saw in each other kindred spirits.

(Inaudible)

Ah, yes, I'm glad you mentioned. I've heard of the Vita for President Movement. A touching sentiment from her fans, but Vita's not ready. I told her this, even if she didn't like it. She's as sharp as broken glass and as engaging to watch as a lovers' quarrel in public, but she needs experience. This is neither a boxing match nor a beauty pageant. These are matters of life and death. Our failures are what lead others to violence. The day that desperate young man, Loy Bonifacio, tried to assassinate the president, I knew nothing could be the same. That was such a hot afternoon the air conditioner in my office failed and as soon as I heard thunder in the distance I went to open the window. The rain finally crackled like fragrant oil on a smoking pan. In its downpour, the boys who guard cars for a coin or two stripped off their clothes and slid naked on the smooth paving stones in front of the Senate building. I watched them frolicking and I pondered what the Holy Koran tells us, how the life of this world is but a sport and a pastime, an adornment, a source of boasting among ourselves, rivalry in multiplying riches and children. How easy it is to lose sight of the larger picture. Take those beautiful, naked boys cavorting, what choice will they have but to one day fight the old fights we lost? We cannot blame even those so desperate they take up arms, whether they be Loy Bonifacio or Communist insurgents. Or those driven to fight for rights by any means, like the Abu Sayyad, with whom I'm now negotiating directly for the release of the American and Australian yachtspersons they kidnapped. Estregan's strong-arm tactics have always failed and it's time we negotiate armed instead with understanding and compassion. My friend, ask yourself: What is your role in all of this? Where do you stand? For it is our responsibility to work together toward providing autonomy of life, opportunity, and faith, for whoever you may be, whatever you may believe, wherever you may live in our great nation. Only when we've made progress together will we finally have peace, God willing, in the North, the South, the West, the East. Only then will our blessed country rise as one. I hope I can count on you, your vote, your voice, your pen, in this, the most important election of our lives.

Vita Nova Transcript: 5 of 13.

(32:20.13—VN5.M4A)

How terrible. So terrible. And everyone's watching it—all over the internet, livestreamed, shared, retweeted. What kind of sickos want to see that? That poor American and his husband, beheaded by the Abu Sayyad—now just another weapon for the hot mess of the snap election, everyone blamestorming all over the place as if they care. Junior condemning Nur's negotiations. Estregan and his Everlasting Supporters equating impeachment with destabilization—and treason. The Fuchsias saying the strongman was weak all along, and now more innocents have paid with their lives. Were you tempted to look? Oh— please don't tell. I can't. I think I'd rather go first than be forced to witness . . .

(Inaudible)

Actually, I was texting with LeTrel; he said it's not the U.S. embassy's official line, but he believes it's a show of strength, against the government's vulnerability at this time. Coz that's terrorism, right? Daddy can't protect you. Meanwhile, elsewhere on social media, the trolls and incels are buzzing about Jane Virdsinsia's supposed CR nudies, which nobody knows if they even exist—supposedly hacked from her Huawei smartphone, supposedly by China, adding oil to the fire, like with those Hong Kong activists years ago: ruin their lives, ruin their power. So Hope may not run, after all—some saying she's protecting her daughter, others claiming she's just waiting out the storm. It's all so hard to navigate, even if we're all in the same boat heading for the rocks. If only empowerment was actually about who gets to steer, instead of who's by the lifeboats with all their friends and family— like our senators and presidential bodyguards, with their smuggled vaccines, months before the rest of us got anything. But faith's most important when the truth's hard to see—Bishop Baccante told me that, when he was trying to control me. This was after I'd made up with my mother, who asked me to seek spiritual advice, after my druggie days with Red, and I'd coincidentally gotten an email from Father Yoda—as Baccante's affectionately called, coz of how he looks and speaks and his green metal cane that he waves to make a point. Emailing that he wanted to chat about my soul, because of the Sexy-Sexy Dance, and my public support for the Reproductive Rights Bill. This was before all his moral crusading made him bishop. At first I was like: no need, I'm good—spinning like every weekend, at Kemistry and at Boy's latest rainbow haven, Geisha; getting mad respect, finally, as DJ ElectrxCute. (Plus my clubwear brand, Oomph!, was finally becoming a thing.) But as his students say, you can't resist the force of Father Yoda, with his Buddha smile and playful eyes and his old-man ears expanding like rings on a tree while the rest of him shrinks. That's how I first ended up in his office—to prove to Mama how sorry I was. Besides, I've always been a believer. I mean, I try.

(Lighter click. Exhalation)

So I'm there in the Arneo de Manille Université, like summoned to the principal's office, sitting on his pleather couch and reading his Footprints on the Sand poster. He's floating around on his office chair, redirecting the rattling air-con, chirping away like a disappointed Pikachu about the dangers of the Sexy-Sexy to the youth. "Other people's sins," said he, "are no enviable responsibility. Take it from me." And with a chuckle, he left it at that, knowing wisely that I'd never come back for lengthy lectures. We ended up just chatting about whatever—showbiz, my career, religion, relationships, my mother, even my father. It wasn't gossip, like with Furio, or shoptalk, like with Jojie or Boy. It felt deep and meaningful. He complimented my charity work, said the university could help, and that he'd put me in touch with the right people. Then he lent me a stack of books—I think C. S. Lewis, Henry David Thoreau, Gerard Manley Hopkins—and we planned our next appointment to discuss them. That's how we kept hanging out every week— even if he's one of those close talkers, and tends to spray it while he'll say it (and you pretend to scratch your face, then your pant leg)—his long digressions washing over me, a surprising antidote to the billion everyday things poisoning my attention span. I'd leave his office feeling surprisingly cleansed. Blessed, even. Actually thinking, for like a hot second, maybe he had a point: perhaps such dancing wasn't just harmless fun. I mean, partying had taught me a lot, but its peaks and come-downs and search for cosmic wisdom kinda left my soul empty—even if I knew it was just low serotonin. "In the sunshine is where you should walk," Father Yoda would say, about my late nights out—which I'd come to see as necessary, either a competition or investment, or both. He'd remind me that the Billboard Wars were just a showbiz media thing, not worth my energy, coz nobody actually cared about Jezhabelle Baratto's latest thirst trap stretching slightly wider than mine on EDSA Boulevard. (Except, of course, Jezhabelle Baratto.) Which should've been so obvious, especially after that supertyphoon toppled all of them onto commuters—but Jezh and I had history, ever since the final episodes of 3-Poll Threat. "The size of others," Father Yoda would advise, "should neither diminish nor define you." And he was right. I'd let it do both. Besides, have you ever tried that cocktail named after her at Club Coup d'État? Lychee liqueur's so 2004, for a reason.

(Laughter)

Sorry, not sorry; better savage than average. Anyways. So despite Father Yoda's gentlemanyak moves in the end, he did help me find my faith again. Before that, Cat and I'd go to Sunday mass, late, hungover from my gigs, towards the end of the homily or just before Communion, usually standing outside the back, smoking. When I was with Furio, the atheist, I'd hide my faith to avoid being debated into exhaustion. But I think I can almost say—coz hindsight's fifty-fifty—that my years without God were a chain of bad-trip choices and unhealthy situations, despite all my yoga. Cat never forgave me for his being rich, and I should've broken up with him earlier, instead of being stolen away by Furio, who treated me like clay to be molded soon as we met—at my solo gig in Forbes Park, the sweet sixteenth of some sour kid whose parents said was in love with me, though what he clearly loved was making sexist remarks about me to his friends while I played. All night long they faked appreciation with that over-acting gallantry of young Manila boys, sniggering as I did my best at singing, smiling, then politely sawing at the rubbery steak tornado while being ignored by my neighbors on the VIP table. And as I'm finding comfort impaling marshmallows by the chocolate fountain (coz "desserts" is "stressed" spelled backwards), this bald rando in a bad suit comes up to me. "Nolite te bastardes carborundorum," says he. "Don't let the bastards grind you down," he mansplains. "You're superior. They just don't know it yet." And I'm like, Yeah, sure, that's kind of you. And he's like, "Kind?" And to my polite smile he's like, "Really, I'm not. See the brat's mother, by that huge ice dildo that used to be a penguin? She's screwing her dance instructor. But good for her, because her fatso congressman husband—there by the pool, sucking down Blue Label with his cronies—he has a second family." Go on, I say. "Oh! You're that kind of girl? Good. That guy there, the celebrant's brother, dancing with that buxom blonde? He's a closet homosexual and everyone knows except him. And the grandma trying hard at the kid's table? Tonight's the first time in three years she's seen her grandchildren— her husband croaked and her kids sued and she countersued and the inheritance went to lawyers." How do you know all that? I ask. Friend of the family? "Some friend I'd be," says he, rubbing his head and flaking more dandruff onto his shoulders. "I'm Furio Almondo," he says, waiting, then wincing. "Sentenced to obscurity, clearly. Parties like this—my penance. Hard-hitting, prize-winning journalism, for the society pages." That's pretty fetch, I tell him, and he scoffs and shoves a protiferole into his mouth. I stick around coz there's nobody else, then chatting more coz he's actually interesting. After I sing happy birthday, the brat spit-spraying his candles out—so prepandemic!—Furio helps unplug my amp and roll up the cord, then asks if he can call me sometime. And that's how I found myself, almost every night, in the locked master CR—in case Cat came home early from working late—warming the marble floor by the phone to talk to Furio for hours, about newsrooms and underground poetry readings, society scandals and artists' love affairs, about hopes and dreams and his youth during the dictatorship, and how I had nothing to fear about getting my own place and living alone.

(Chair scrapes. Footsteps pace)

When Boy got me onto *3-Poll Threat*—ten young dreamers outsinging, outdancing, outacting each other as the country voted for our newest superstar ("The fight of your young life!" Jojie predicted)—it was Furio who helped me choose my dramatic monologue for the final acting showcase. Its theme: the Golden Age of the Silver Screen. His huge personal library—and the lists he made me—would change my life, and I trusted his advice almost as much as I loved rejecting it. But that monologue he nailed with one suggestion, from his favorite black-and-white film, after I'd spent days searching in vain—because do you know how few inspiring pieces over two minutes there are by female characters? Until today we get like only thirty percent of Hollywood speaking roles, and only like fifteen percent of movies have female protagonists. It's like we're expected to only be silent, or tragic, or defiant—the underdog by birth, undermined by art, underrepresented by history. Where are all the inspirational speeches by women? That roused the rabble, that claimed the streets? Once more unto the breach, girlfriends, we few, we unhappy few, this band of sisters—relegated to responses or repartee with silent-type men. Or rants declaring the obvious: that I exist, more than a bride, more than a daughter, I'm part of this . . . But who runs the world—girls? Me, I'd say so, or at least I'd hope so, because without us, boys wouldn't be, and men would not return from war, and no side would ever strive for peace. O, we women are not wee men—our roar is why we're feared, traded, impregnated, beaten, burned, or mutilated, murdered as newborns, or belittled for our militancy—yeah, baby, go crazy, burn your bra, grow out your pits, open your own doors, *serve* as secretary of state, be taken down the aisle towards loving, honoring, *obeying*—praying for the silent resolve of the queen of queens, Mama Mary. No wonder the unspoken question's been: You, too?—the answer already known, the violence already a given. Truth is, I need no man to live, no king to rule, no permission for pleasure, and no nod to speak. Our words have power, in both dialogue and monologue, and ground's been broken by our just declaring: This is *my* vagina! There's a whole world of vagina life out there! Vagina! Vagina! Vajayjay on Oprah! We can shout, walk topless in New York City, wear or tear off headscarves, break glass ceilings, run countries—but equality somewhere's not yet justice anywhere and there's no shame in demanding more. To be accepted, immodesty and all. To be respected, without compromise. To be loved, for who I am and not just what I could be. All the men I've known believed they had me figured out, falling for a mystery, writing me off as a certainty, asking constantly: "Vita, baby, what do you want in life?" My honest reply: I do not know! Because I don't. I have questions *because* I don't have answers. "Of course," they declare, laughing: "Just like a woman!" While I hold my tongue, thinking: Just like a man! Because uncertainty's not a female thing—it's a human thing. Even if every one of us—in *his* heart, or *her* soul, or through *their* lonesome experience—knows that things now are *not* how they should be, and we can start to fix things by saying so.

(Single clap)

How's that for a two-minute monologue?

(Chair scrapes. Seatback shifts)

I'm not dramatic—I just have flair. Anyways, turns out Jojie was right. The weeks leading up to the competition, the practices already had me crying in a CR stall—factions forming, secrecy reigning, one girl stealing another girl's act, and another spending more time healing her boob job than rehearsing. A couple of thots even throwing themselves at the producers, separately and jealously. Our candid interlude interviews carefully crafted for public opinion—like running for office, or curating your MySpace page: all generosity, quirkiness, and manicured humanity. The fight of my young life! From the starting swirling overture of boiling kettledrums and blasting brass; to the betuxed Illac Angelo Diaz introducing us in turn to the world; to the blur of false lashes, Lycra, media hype, and ten life-changing journeys towards that peak where there can only be one; to the torrent of text-voting for the face-off finale that bitterly divided our nation between two final finalists—Jezhabelle Baratto, the halfie London-born grad of the BRIT School of performing arts and official Pantene 2 In 1 Shampoo and Conditioner Queen, versus li'l ol' mongrel moi. In the most fantabulous spectacle the Philippines had ever seen (till *Cinderfella*, of course, the dragshow spin-off). All the streets empty, all the houses full, all the TVs locked onto Channel Seven, while our country was swept every Saturday night into an existential question: Which Triple Threat would embody our people's highest aspirations of womanhood?

(Finger drumroll on table)

The regal posh-accented princess, or the plucky underprivileged up-start? The barok hip-hop-dancing striver from Angeles, or the baroque piano-playing English major who wasn't caught always pronouncing pronunciation as pronounciation? After our duet duel, which I barely won, and our dance-off, which she barely won, it all came down to our dramatic monologues, to break the tie. And Furio, bless his heart, had helped me choose the perfect one, which was clear soon as Jezh was done and I took a breath and my turn in the spotlight. When my mother and I started speaking again, she said that was her proudest moment, as our neighborhood crowded around her TV, seeing how far I'd come from the Little Queencess pageant when I got stage fright and she danced in the front row for me to follow, my mother, the little tea-cup, short and stout. I think the reason I opened up to Bishop Baccante wasn't so much because he understood me, but more because he un-derstood who I wanted to be—like my mother in the beginning, and in the end. For more than a year Father Yoda was the only man in my life, and I'd see him like every week, just chatting—he'd buy me a bubble tea and we'd go for walks around campus, sitting under trees, talking about ancient and medieval history (what he used to teach)—the uni-verse opening up in ways I didn't think possible. When you're always looking forward, your perspective's only as deep as your vision— but looking backwards is when you realize the immensity of what was, and therefore what can be. But then it happened.

(Lighter click. Exhalation)

I was having such a sucky week—the reviews for *Heaven Only Knows* calling it poverty porn, with the critics highkey hating on my pros-thetic nose (never mind our Cannes nomination)—and I need to talk, like right now, so I follow to the army base where Father Yoda's blessing a shipment of assault rifles. The soldiers all overexcited to see me, so he brings me to the chapel and closes the door. We're sitting in the front pew, the light through the stained glass at our feet, like a cartoon magic carpet, and I'm crying to him, and he puts his arm around me.

And kissed me. I don't know why he thought . . . I didn't give any signals, not even mixed. No blurred lines. I didn't want it. But I'm crying, and he thinks it's okay, even if I'm pushing back, and he's really strong. I don't know.

(Silence)

You know, sometimes women accuse men of unwanted advances, and you guys think it's no big deal, it's just a kiss, understandable, forgivable, because it's so difficult for you to read . . . But he was strong, and I couldn't pull away, and yeah, at some point I sort of stopped pushing, hoping he'd let—

(Inaudible)

How can you even ask? I'm sure I didn't invite it. He let go coz I sort of played dead—only reason he stopped. That whole year, we were friends, I trusted, he gave off this paternal vibe, maybe that's why he thought . . .

(Silence)

My mother used to tell me how my father convinced her to run away. Her dad—who I never met—he was a laborer on a sugar plantation, my mom the frailest, blind in one eye, but the cleverest of her seven siblings, so she was the one they sent to school: their great hope, who loved math and trivia and had pen pals all over the world. When my father finally became more than just letters from Missouri, in person, his white short sleeves glowing, cheeks red as a devil—my grandma slamming the door in his face (coz she hated the temptations of other prophets)—of course Mama took his presence as his promises kept. She'd tell me stories of where they went—caves with mummies, hills like mounds of chocolate, an underground river, and waterfalls so high the water never reaches the ground—and, his promise, trusting him, to take her with him. "Home to Independence."

(Silence)

Who wouldn't believe in a place named like that? I asked once if she loved him. She said: "He was kind"—which I've always totally struggled with. How kind could he have been?

(Silence)

Afterwards, she tried to go home. Then turned to the Good Shepherd Sisters, living with them, learning skills to live without them: how to cook, and make the world's best jam; how to sew, which empowered her the most, coz clothing's a basic need as well as an opportunity for creative expression. The nuns helped choose my name: New Life.

(Silence)

When I was little she'd take me planespotting, outside the base. I loved the C-130 Hercules—giants! Imagining one would bring back my dad one day. Eventually, I imagined what it was like when he'd flown away. I'd ask: Wasn't it hard for him?

(Silence)

Coz it was for me. Like, boss-level hard. When we were about to meet, about four years ago, I was driving to the Peninsula Hotel, my mind turning on one question, like a dog who won't sit. From *See You in Our Dreams*, the movie I shaved my head for—my character, Natalia, looking for her dad before the cancer claims her. "Parents are supposed to have answers," she said, "but why are all my questions about my beginnings the same as the ones about my ending?"

(Silence)

Those are the sorts of things I'd talk about with Father Yoda.

(Silence)

When he did what he did, nobody believed. Coz I didn't have the answers. Why go see him again? Why bother returning his books? Why so many months before speaking out? You look at him and he's as harmless as your fave uncle. His weakness for fine brandies his only sin. But the guy puts the manyak in Armagnac. Charming without the *C*. Therapist, with a space missing. If he got his way. Totally. That afternoon in the chapel he told me to fix my clothes and leave. And somehow . . . somehow that felt like the worst part to me. When I mentioned that once, in an interview, they grabbed it and ran with it. So you wanted to stay? If not, why not scream? Why come out only now, when he's speaking out against the Mr. Sexy-Sexy Dance, and your ads for the RR Bill's Cover Up Campaign—only now that his boycott's killing your career? As if courage is always instant. As if there's no assault without bruises or scratches. As if we're wrong because we were wearing shorts—or doing shots, like when Senator Victorino "Toti" Otots III (aka the Turd), blamed that victim on national TV. And those people who stop struggling, to save their lives . . . or ask that at least the attacker wear a condom—I mean, you try seeing how safe you feel defending a sex-positive rape victim on Facebook. I dare you. Speaking out, it was . . .

(Silence)

But what if I didn't want to be defined by that? To be *that* girl? Why's that hard to understand?

(Lighter click. Exhalation)

So I stopped doing interviews—until these ones with you. Coz I wasn't gonna let anybody . . . Nobody gets to oversimplify your complications. No matter how difficult these things are, we should all bend our minds to it. To you, it may not matter—lucky you—but not everyone's so fortunate. When I started the Sanctuary, I learned so much. One in three is the famous statistic. Think of all the women you know and love and how every third one might be secretly carrying that weight. Did you know that three out of four rape victims know their attackers? More than half of all sexual assaults happen on dates or in relationships. I've met wives who told me: "I thought that's how all husbands act." My foundation tries to help, but barely five percent get reported.

(Chair scrapes. Footsteps pacing)

But that's news to nobody. Statistics, statistics, statistics. That's the thing. When I put a human face on it and my interview came out in *Extra!*, the Bishops Conference was oh-so-typical—one telling his congregation to buy all the copies and burn them. Deacons and little old nuns waiting at dawn for the delivery trucks, by the newsstands, like pigeons at breadcrumbs, tottering away under teetering stacks of *Extra!*—the bestselling issue in its hundred-eight-year history. That's when Dr. Rajah started commenting on my posts on Facebook, along with so many other RR Bill supporters, who became my online fam. I remember she wrote me: "You should not be punished for coming through in strength." So I filed a case, but Baccante was only charged with outraging my modesty; he filed a countersuit, and I was charged with alarm and scandal, libel, and unjust vexation. Our justice system, ladies and germs.

(Clapping)

In our culture—and the world—boys are taught that to be a man you gotta conquer others, especially women. I want to teach them otherwise. So I kept speaking out, appearing in another ad—the one about my body, my choice. Some saying I was brave, but others—enough of them—calling me a fame whore abortionist. At first, I was like: eye roll. Sticks and stones, right? But then my movies got picketed, and people started ditching my fan club—Baccante denying any involvement, naturellement—people vilifying my lawyers, bullying journalists who were honest about me, boycotting companies till they canceled my contracts. Democracy in action, the Bishops Conference called it. Fighting moral relativism. Protecting religious freedom. And because of all the gossip, and my past with Rolex—older guy, public figure, married man—even my mother, bless her soul, she had doubts. About me. Coz she could only blame herself so much. But all that brought the best lesson God ever taught me. My faith was finally free. "Walk with those seeking truth," says Dr. Chopra, but "run from those who think they've found it."

(Chair scrapes. Seatback shifts)

I'm seeking truth. Learning to be a feminist. A long road we should *all* travel, if you care about half of humanity. It's justice, actually— that's what Rita always tells me—and if you truly believe in an equal world then you gotta be willing to check your unearned advantages that made things unfair. That's why it's called privilege. That's why some complain it's revenge. That's why it's a problem to the bishops and Nandotards, the incels and racists—acting like victims, stealing the language of those who've fought so long for equity and using it against them—demanding tolerance for their intolerance. People like that don't want a better world, because a better world is a new world, and the old world's working just fine for them. It'll be interesting to hear what Baccante says, though I don't know why you bother. They'll always remember it differently, coz memory's a selfish witness.

(Inaudible)

Yeah, I still go. Usually when it's empty. Sometimes even attending mass. But I sit at the back, behind a pillar so I can't see the priest. It's comforting, kneeling when everyone kneels, standing when everyone stands, reciting prayers you've known your whole life, your voice lost among everyone else's. It's nice to be part of something. It's good, sometimes, to not be alone.

Bishop Verdolagas Baccante, OP, Transcript.

(48:38.16—Baccante.M4A)

Welcome! How glad I am to clear the air. I remember you still from my history class. Perpetually absent. Please, have that seat. But give it back after, ha?

(Chuckles)

How grateful I am for you coming on short notice. It was now or never. Snap elections approach, to switch the channel on the impeachment. You want coffee? Tang? Change your mind, you speak up, ha? I get thirsty thinking about your interrogation. Without a question.

(Chuckles)

I understand you want to talk about our dear Miss Vita Nova. Well, she's yesterday's news. Already we are mobilizing priests, seminarians, nuns—as is the habit—and the faithful laity, initially to protest on EDSA but now to watch for hanky-panky at the polls. Vigilant we must be. History shows the dangers of a power vacuum, into whose hurricane is sucked all the ambitious opportunists. I discussed that last week, in my YouTube show. Do you follow me yet? All that is not to say that Estregan is on his knees. While the other Presidentiables confidently make promises in Plaza Miranda, and dance the latest craze on-stage, in likelihood Fernando plots, most probably with Junior. Pay no mind to his neck brace. I tell you, beware an injured saltillo—or better, a parladé, with that white spot some have by their tear ducts that neophytes take for a defective eye. I've seen many a cocksure matador turn his back on a horny parladé. They get it in the end.

(Chuckles)

Fortunately, the past prepares us for the future. The wisdom from that perspective is a gift. That is why it's called the present—which we must unwrap, lest we repeat our follies through our blindness to their reblooming. The fault is ours if we do not nip what darling buds we may. All this does not remind you of Pope Formosus? That most famous of skeletons in the papal closet? Well, had you not cut my class constantly, you'd recall his fate. Back we must go, to the year 894, as Formosus gazes expectantly from a window of his palace—as Estregan is likely doing as we speak—the big papa's mind occupied by currents he accelerated beyond his control. A period of tumult and worry it is, as usupers and petty kings feud while the Church is courted and kidnapped for its imprimatur and protection. To the west swirls a vacuum that is rattling the cobblestones of Rome. Emperor Basil of Byzantium has died in a hunting accident and his heir, Leo VI—formerly confined by his father and almost blinded for conspiring—has exiled Photius, the patriarch in Constantinople, to a monastery in Armenia. Meanwhile, archbishops in Cologne and Hamburg squabble over the bishopric of Bremen while Count Odo of Paris and Charles the Simple fight in France. Pope Formosus, the once wily diplomat and bishop of Porto, now awaits a messenger with news from the battlefield at Bergamo. It is there that his alliance with Arnulf of Carinthia and Berengar of distant Friuli, king in name but not in power, faces the army of Guido of Spoleto; the pontiff's dangled prize: the Iron Crown of Lombardy. For the duchy of Spoleto sits too close to Rome for the pope's comfort, and Guido's coronation as king by the preceding papacy keeps our current Vicar of Christ quaking in his campagi. Too fresh in his mind are memories of his own banishment, defrocking, and clamber to power, followed by the ignominy of being forced to declare Guido and his adolescent son, Lambert, coemperors of the Holy Roman Empire. Exactly as with Estregran, Formosus did not endure exile, pardon, and abuse by his predecessors—in this case, John VIII, Marinus I, Hadrian III, then Stephen V—only to be ousted three years later by the schemes of his opponents. And so it is, quite literally, campaign season, as armies meet in Bergamo to determine the Holy Father's fate.

(Mouth smacks)

With news, a rider on a frothing horse now stumbles, kneeling breathlessly before Formosus. The duke of Spoleto has been sent running! And Guido's shrewd retreat proved for naught when he dies before rallying his forces, leaving on their own in Rome his wife Ageltrude and son Lambert, full emperor at fourteen. And so Berengar and Arnulf advance to complete the job, but on the banks of the river Po a fever savages their camp and drives them home. For his efforts, Formosus is imprisoned by Ageltrude in the Castel Sant'Angelo. Down for the countess, however, our pope is not, and he dispatches secretly to Regensburg emissaries inviting Arnulf to defeat Lambert, once and for all. Quick as an opportunistic presidentiable, Arnulf and his army cross the Alps, march through Italy, and arrive at the Eternal City to force its surrender. Yet Ageltrude is wilier than her late husband and she slips away to Spoleto, where her son awaits with their forces. Members of the Roman Senate, as fickle in their fidelity as our own Philippine legislators, welcome Arnulf at the Ponte Milvio and lead him to the steps of the Santi Apostoli, where our pontiff awaits with an emperor's crown for the Bavarian king. But while en route to Spoleto, to vanquish our pesky mamma e figlio, Arnulf is paralyzed by stroke—or poison, it is whispered. The ailing new emperor retreats home to his hearth by the Danube, leaving in charge, as subking of Italy, his illegitimate son Ratold—whose name my students never get wrong in a pop quiz. Alas, that same year, the days on Formosus's calendar are numbered, and the pope dies suddenly. Yet for him the worst is still ahead.

(Chuckles)

For the precocious Lambert has regained power by allying with his old foe, Berengar of Friuli, and together they send Ratold scurrying. As pontiff now steps in Boniface VI, for fifteen days, before succumbing possibly to gout, but more probably to Stephen VI, favored by Ageltrude and Lambert. And it is Pope Stephen, in 896, who gives a fateful order, and the rotting remains of Formosus are exhumed, garbed in papal garments, and placed on a throne to face allegations spanning fourteen years. To answer for the corpse, a deacon is appointed, and Stephen poses this question: "When you were the bishop of Porto, why did you usurp the universal Roman See with such a spirit of abandon?" Poor Formosus, of course, is speechless, though his history speaks for him, rewritten by the court to fit their schemes. In what we now call the Cadaver Synod, the finding is guilty, and all Formosus's proclamations are decreed null and void. Stripped from his remains are the vestments, and cut from his right hand the three fingers that performed consecrations. Again his corpse is buried, this time in a cemetery for foreigners, before again being ordered exhumed, tied with weights, and tossed into the slow churn of the river Tiber. Yet Formosus would have the last word, as Romans soon whisper that his corpse has been found on a riverbank, performing miracles. Crowds fill the summery city streets and Stephen is imprisoned and strangled in his cell—his spiteful papacy only fourteen months old. His successor, Romanus, is dispatched in lesser time. Then Theodore II seeks to be more decisive, despite his weak chin, reinterring Formosus in St. Peter's and decreeing that never again shall a cadaver face trial. Twenty days later Theodore is dead, succeeded by John IX, who strikes a wise alliance between Church and State by throwing in his camelaucum with Lambert, at least until the emperor's death soon after—from his horse fallen, it is said, or by assassination felled, it's more widely believed. Why anyone ever seeks power, never shall I understand.

(Teeth sucking)

I see your mind wandering, like always you were in my class. Fine, fine, let it—a mind is better open than shut, and history flows with words and moments, images and ideas, into which we are swept, even into daydreaming. For how else do we seek our place in this distracted world? Worry not, our story is nearly complete, as time sweeps inexorably on, and John IX's two years gave way to Benedict IV's long three, then Leo V's reign of hardly a month, until the odd tenure of Antipope Christopher, who ruled only three months—because apparently a coup can legitimize the most dubious of rulers but cannot, in the writing of history, make Christopher more than antipope. Finally, we arrive at the climax, or nadir, of this tantalizing tangle, with the suspicious crowning of the bald and the brutal Pope Sergius III—who'd been no friend to Formosus, who exiled him from Rome by naming him bishop of Caere. Nor friend to John IX, who'd defeated him in the papal election. Nor to Lambert, who'd exiled him again and destroyed his official records. But a very good friend Sergius was to Count Theophylact I of Tusculum, whose daughters and wife, Theodora, famously make a game of playing pontiffs, pretenders, and politicians against each other. Sound familiar?

(Chuckles)

Despite the trail of death leading to his ascendancy, history remembers Sergius most for life: in the form of his many children, including one sired with Theophylact's fifteen-year-old daughter, Marozia—a son who becomes, at the sage age of twenty, Pope John XI, the only known offspring of a pope to himself become pope. Some historians call the reign of Sergius III the Saeculum Obscurum, the dark ages of the papacy. Others call it a pornocracy, controlled by Theophylact's women who manipulate their husbands, lovers, and sons. Yet to we who can see the long spiral of time, it is but another loop of history's full circle, both resonance and reminder. For Sergius still has bones to pick with a skeleton he once condemned while cojudge in the Cadaver Synod. Our resting-in-pieces Formosus is exhumed, once again, and placed on trial, once again, the verdict, once again: guilty. This time, Formosus loses his head. And Sergius orders inscribed on the grave of Stephen VI laudatory words for beginning what he himself has now finished. What a troll, my students would say. Rewriting history itself. Until we, in hindsight, work tirelessly to discern the truth as it should be.

(Spoon tinkling in a glass)

Shall we similarly see now Estregan stripped of his insincere vestments? Must we storm the Palace to pillage his thousands of wristbands and run into the streets in his silk boxing robes? Or will his next act turn into a pornocracy, if we are not vigilant, with his Marozias extending their influence, Vita foremost among them? Come to pass that well may, if we fail to expose their naked ambition and parade their indecency shorn of its alluring curls. I tell you, that a strongman can be toppled by her manipulations proves how deeply Vita's polished claws have sunk into our society. What is our recourse? Can we only watch as Estregan hijacks his own synod? Are we still powerless to his bloody campaigns? Shall the battlefield be drawn, with us the conscripts at the front, led from the rear by either him or the Muslim senator? Each of those two bulls claims to be the matador, but whenever egotists meet it's always an I for an I.

(Chuckles)

Until we say enough is enough, as we did a generation ago when we linked arms and ended our Dictator's twenty-four-year reign. For without freedom there can be no true belief, as forced faith is no faith at all. Only a democracy can safeguard the free will God grants each of us, and we must utilize both decisively. Thou shalt not kill, every religion instructs. Was our Church expected to only issue admonishments and encyclicals as his supporters cheered Estregan and washed their hands of his rising death toll? No. We responded by opening our doors, offering sanctuary, establishing community-based rehab programs. Then testing and vaccination drives. And now, with the government's new vogue of red-tagging people as Communists, our parishes are safehavens for even the Godless lost lambs. Always the Church is on the front lines. We see firsthand the people's suffering. In my diocese is an orphanage, its occupancy now swollen, and how beautiful are the children, faces of joy when you visit; ask what they want to do when they grow up and some reply: "To kill police." Others say: "To kill soldiers." How early they learned to crave vengeance! Even I as a boy was not fueled by retribution after losing my family to the Japanese. To my generation the enemy was clear, but these children today are betrayed by those sworn to protect them; are we expected to sit idly as their hatred festers?

(Mouth smacks)

I speak to my congregation honestly. Never do I tell them how to think, only what they should know for themselves to decide. It was the same when I conversed with Miss Nova, about her role in society, beyond her dancing, parties, and romantic tribulations. Our actions, our words, lead to consequences for everyone. Even a comment on social media can cause great wretchedness. These years Hope Virdsinsia led the Liberty Party with utmost integrity, yet now she's fallen victim to cancel culture, blackmailed by the online mob into choosing between her candidacy and her daughter's privacy, the poor child assaulted for her youthful follies. So recklessly does our world move now that ignorance outpaces understanding, and so many of us judge without thinking.

(Slurp)

As Bansamoro and Estregan circle each other, we see Junior awaiting his chance, a cuddly shaggy-haired version of his father, preparing a second act for his family's legacy of despotic entitlement. This I fear most. Under them, how many thousands died or were summarily imprisoned? How many millions impoverished by their plunder and that of their cronies? Until enough of us said enough is enough and filled the streets, prepared to die. If again we must, we shall. The role of the Catholic Church has never been partisan; always it is moral. People, not politics. As the Supreme Court concerns itself with the laws of man, the Church is concerned with the laws of God. Decisions of policy are best left to our elected representatives; to the people we offer only wisdom in selecting who will best represent them. I tell you, our Church does not possess the tithing zealotry of Brother Martin's El Ohim, or the corruption of Padre Laverno Kidohboy and his Kingdom of Faith in Christ, or the political evangelism of Friar Edgardo Newton and his Jesus Is Savior Ministry, that seminal movement with an unfortunate acronym. My congregation practices safe sects. Safe sects. You understand? With *C* and *T*? My apologies, I didn't mean to be such an Orion, as my students are hashtagging these days. You didn't laugh, so I thought perhaps you . . . oh never mind.

(Inaudible)

Santa Banana! A one-track mind you have! Like a monorail. Regarding Vita, I simply offer my prayers; I've nothing to add about that Marozia. More concerning to me is her allegiance to Bansamoro and his prominence in the Liberty Party that I've always supported. Not only a Muslim, a polygamist he is, and a progressive. Proudly have I hailed our nation to be the stalwart defender of marriage as the last in the world without divorce. A country that celebrates our social tolerance toward the gays without ceding to their demands to deform an institution meant for one man and one woman. Thank the Lord for Rolex Aguirre, who alone had the courage to stand up to Estregan, not only during this impeachment, when it was expedient for many, but when certain parties were ramming the so-called Reproductive Rights Bill through Congress. Governor Aguirre brought the first Estregan administration to its ignominious end those years ago by admitting to its collusion in illegal gambling. Last month at the impeachment he did the same, helping topple Estregan's second reign by tearfully confessing to the continuation of their crimes. My gratitude and support Aguirre has.

(Inaudible)

No, child, I take umbrage at your implication; the Church is neither mercenary nor out of touch. What do you think this is, pre–Vatican II?

Corruption and violence shall always be condemned by our conference of bishops, although the reproductive demands bill was a Horus of a different color. We must choose the hills upon which we die, and that one was Calvary. Don't you agree that a government that forces people to sin against their faith is a government that must be challenged? Our Constitution guarantees religious freedom, yet are we the villains for standing by our beliefs, while abortionists and gay-marriage minorities feign victimhood, co-opting human rights to impose their agenda upon the majority? I tell you, I am shocked that you agree with Estregan on contraception and abortion. Granted, many Germans agreed with Hitler—until they lost. "Overpopulation is the problem," Fernando told me, "and contraception is the answer." Contraception is the problem, I replied, and good government is the answer. "Unlike your boss," he said, sadly, "I am not omnipotent." Can I then tell the world, I replied, that you are impotent?

(Laughter)

That one he enjoyed, his sharpness always proven by his sense of humor.

(Teeth sucking)

But what should one believe, as we are lectured by armies of pundits on both sides of any debate? Thus the importance of natural law, and morality that is not relativistic. In this era of alternative facts, truths remain truths, despite progressives' insistence that everyone is entitled to their own. They claim that a lower birth rate, more working-age adults, and less burden of children is the panacea for the degradation of our God-given world and the depletion of its bounties. The "economic dividend," they call it. Although a person with a soul can never be merely a number in an academic's equation. In truth, the poorest half of the population—predominantly the ones having children—produce only seven percent of the world's pollution, while the richest seven percent—the ones too busy to have offspring—produce half of the world's emissions. Obviously the problem is inequality, not a growing population. I tell you, better it is to think than to screech, ha? More people means a broader workforce, an economy of unbounded potential. If human capital is denigrated as a burden, we should not be surprised when our kindred who are unskilled, disaffected, or addicted are cast by our leaders as disposable, warm bodies to export or hindrances beyond rehabilitation. Nor should we be shocked when the frustrations of the forgotten, like Loy Bonifacio, mislead them to violence. A society's strength is not measured by its wealth or power but in how it treats its least wealthy and most powerless. Let us not take the easy path by devaluing human life via promiscuity, abortion, materialism, and selfishness. Let us make the hard decisions via self-mastery, responsibility, altruism, and community. Is it not reasonable to believe in the unparalleled resilience of the Filipino and help them be the best versions of themselves? Is it not unreasonable to demand that we surrender them to their weakness and sin? Cut us some slacks, my child.

(Chuckles)

History reveals that King Herod was dubbed "the Great" for bringing peace and prosperity, establishing vital institutions and regional unity, yet now we remember him most for slaughtering children to maintain his power to achieve such lofty goals. History shall judge as harshly those who permit the killing of babies in their mother's wombs, addicts on our avenues, and malcontents in the mountains. When working, as I must, with penitents such as Governor Aguirre, the sins of the present are far more important than the sins of the past. As reminds St. Jerome: "A friend is long sought, hardly found, and with difficulty kept." Above Estregan's head somebody had to wiggle the sword of Damocles. That friend was Rolex.

(Mouth smacks)

During the impeachment, many politicians feared they would be sacrificed by an Estregan acting like Caligula, or Moctezuma bloody-handed atop his pyramid. But the Roman Emperor was stabbed thirty times by concerned courtiers; the Aztec king either stoned by his people or assassinated by conquistadors when he could no longer bend his followers to his will. Rolex knew what was forthcoming, for the story of Estregan and his circle is as old as time. To put such in proper context is my responsibility. History and the priesthood share that mantle. Both weave together the personal with the universal. One life is connected to every life and it is in those connections that our purpose we find. Such was the counsel I offered Vita, who felt perpetually as if stumbling through darkness. I told her: Imagine yourself a traveler in a moonless night. The light of your torch illuminates only a few meters around you. What is it that keeps you walking into the darkness beyond, if not your faith? Who shall help you find your way, if not the people you meet? Of her relationships we would speak, of her mother and her father, of her faith and her anger. Anyone who had wronged her she was unable to forgive. She was troubled by how evil never seems to die while good succumbs repeatedly. I told her that constant may the Devil's work be, but that is only God offering us endless opportunities to do right. But in her mind, right and wrong remained relative. She thinks her sexuality is liberty, not realizing that liberty is a means to an end, not an end in itself. No matter how far one pushes the envelope, it shall always be stationery. No greater naivety exists than arrogance, and Vita is very arrogant. About me, she lied, played the victim, screamed that we were curtailing her freedom of speech when we only sought an apology for her slander. How heartbreaking it was, and is, to watch her being used. By Boy Balagtas, who enriches himself off her scandals that sell cinema tickets, musical albums, and Vitality slimming supplements. By Kingsley Belli, who had ideals until he dropped out of Communism school because of lousy Marx. And by Bansamoro, who changed his Christian-sounding surname to seem a Muslim patriot, and is using the poor girl to gain the presidency as he did the Senate. Vita's life is a cage so vast its bars she cannot see. I understood her strident idealism, although I counseled that what must shape her, and those she inspires, is quiet heroism—also known as humility. For on billboards, in bold scenes, over social media, she reveals everything, sharing too much of her life—although what she shares is selfish, like a fishmonger.

(Inaudible)

My child, don't be silly! I'd be happy to. But I do so without guile or expectation. Get comfortable now, for you've asked an old professor of history to share his story. You don't want Nescafé? Sure, ha?

(Liquid pouring. Spoon tinkling)

Imagine now the darkest of darkness, of a certain time and a particular night. Seeking the light, my journey began, after the defeat of the

Japanese. In my possession, only a flashlight, a family photo, a bottle with water, and rice cakes wrapped in leaves. Into the back I slipped of a U.S. Army truck that lurched and rattled from the seaside up the mountain then down over three days. In army blankets large objects were tied with twine and I unwrapped one to cover myself from the cold night. Inside, I discovered something I had never seen, raised as I was among war's deprivations: a landscape of such wonderment, a work of such beauty; a window to our divine world. Everything else I could, I unwrapped. Paintings, sculptures, a glossy piano, golden objects whose glitter seemed their sole purpose. When I was older I realized this was the booty the invaders had left on the roadside as their retreat grew more desperate. When the drivers stopped at night, I nestled in a nook between the treasures, in the comforting scent of old wool. With a squeal and a jolt we arrived at the capital and from a polished box I stole a glorious chalice, intending to find a priest and receive a reward. In the sun I squinted and dodged the legs of towering soldiers bustling everywhere. How terrible the desolation, in all directions, that no photographs ever could capture. Above the rubble rose the cathedral and through its huge doors I passed into the pitch-black narthex and through the next doors into dazzling light. How magnificent it was inside, the adamant walls holding aloft a ceiling of blue sky and white clouds. A squadron of fighter planes slowly made its way across. That was the first cathedral I encountered and the most beautiful ever have I seen. A lone priest was searching through debris of stones and fine wood splintered and shards of glass that looked like jewels. I held up to him the chalice, as if it was a bird I was going to release. The priest widened his blue eyes like Eddie Cantor, then smiled.

(Teeth sucking)

That is how I found my way to the Dominicans. I did their washing. I helped in the kitchen. I brought discreetly to Father Maximo his cruet of olive oil at the table, and he'd wink a blue eye at me. The oil was in rarest supply and in the kitchen I'd hold it to my nose, having never known anything so rich and clean. When the school opened in Quonset huts among the shells of the campus buildings, I studied. I excelled in English, Latin, Italian, reading aloud for the priests while they ate; they pretended it was for their entertainment. Herodotus and Plutarch and Thucydides I loved most; their tales of glory I devoured among Manila's ruins. That was the first travel I undertook without fear, through time. Books and conversation were how I discovered the world, until I was chosen to go to Spain for my doctoral. History was how I found my place in the cosmos, validated at key times through my own actions, the meanings of which opened in those quiet moments profound only to oneself.

(Slurp)

In the seminary, like all young men I yearned for excitement, and there is no greater adventure than idealism. There was a book we surreptitiously shared among us, which I loved so completely I did not pass it on. Its cover was lost and its title I never knew. It was about a priest in the 1920s riding into the sun with the Cristeros as they struggled against government persecution. That remained with me for years, and in Spain I would come to secretly read Juan Luis Segundo, Paulo Freire, and Camilo Torres Restrepo, who wrote, "If Jesus were alive today, he would be a guerrillero." I devoured the writing of Gustavo Gutiérrez, whispering Yes! Yes! as I leaped from my chair to pace over orthopraxis versus orthodoxy. How obvious, to practice what we preach, not preach for others to practice. How clear that the sins of humanity would manifest in the fabric of society. Is not poverty in this world of riches the greatest sin imaginable? Even after I returned here in the capital to tend to my parish, part of me longed to live like Father Balweg, Robin Hood of the Cordilleras, taking up arms against multinational loggers stealing land from tribal illiterates. I understand in this way the story of our friend Kingsley Belli, although my evolution was through strength, not weakness. Some of my old seminary-mates believed that the Church should serve local needs and not a centralized plan from the faraway Vatican. But such rationalizations are perilous in a country that has the world's longest Communist insurgency. Just as I did with Evel Knievel, I admired my colleagues, yet I foresaw their fate. By themselves they interpreted the tenets of our faith, yet are we not more lost on our own? Were not Henry VIII and Martin Luther selfish and impatient? A People's Church is not God's Church, and

God's Church is not oppressive. People are imperfect and elusive perfection is the truest oppression. Martyrs can be beatified, but a missionary need not be eaten by cannibals to give them a taste for religion.

(Burp)

Among my idealistic friends, only I remain positioned to do lasting
good.

(Inaudible)

Ah, yes, the so-called Mitsubishops; my colleagues whom I could not
defend for accepting Japanese SUVs from the president. "Even God is in
Estregan's pocket," people said. I had to be forthright in my testimony
to the Apostolic Visitator. People know my values through my weekly
column, Footprints in the Sand, which receives thousands of likes and
shares every Sunday. For example, my opposition to the quota system
of the Philippine Bishops Conference: two-strikes-you're-out for priests
who father or molest children. I maintain that one strike is more than
enough, however much I forgive their weakness.

(Inaudible)

My child, I must take umbrage! Of course I didn't want Vita to be my
girlfriend. I tell you, she betrayed me that day in the chapel. Never
should I have closed the doors; I sought to protect her from the soldiers
who would have clogged the entrance, elbowing to glimpse her. She
was crying about her father and my embrace was paternal. I trusted
her. The only thing worse than being a source of sin is enjoying it. Our
permissive society has brought that about. That is the danger of figures
like Rita Rajah and her Me Too movement, masquerading as equality;
how ripe it is for abuse by irresponsible women lashing out with the
vigor of their anger and regret. No longer without fear can I voice my
concerns about due process, thanks to the progressives and their outrage, which shall start right after I finish my sentence, in three, two, one.

(Silence)

There. You can hear them rioting in the distance, burning their own
homes in protest. That is why I caution you, if you want this book of
yours available in this country.

(Inaudible)

Yes, I agree, but free speech never comes free. Do you make jokes
about bombs when boarding the airplane? When you see onboard

your friend named Jack, you dare not shout "Hi, Jack!" Our Revised Penal Code, which has lasted since 1930, specifies imprisonment—imprisonment, ha?—for work that is obscene, that glorifies criminals, satisfies the market for violence and lust, offends race or religion, abets prohibited drugs, and expounds doctrines contrary to public morals. End quote. Does that sound like your book? All those characteristics are necessary for an honest book about our national politics, and the significance to it of our Miss Nova. I caution you. Only one accusation it takes to waylay a life. Vita's allegations are ludicrous to anyone who knows how I cherish the peace at the heart of celibacy. In my long service to the Church, the memories I return to most are of when I was allowed to be solitary, while pursuing history in a city whose present was both in flux and frozen in time. Its nights I savored, the shops shuttered and the darkened mesones in Plaza Mayor like caves in the cliffs of a slumbering volcano. Many evenings the streets were mine alone, save for occasional old Citroëns, burly and feline with hoods vast as coffins, speeding down shadowy avenidas to deliver some untouchable official. Still I hear the echoes of the serenos on their rounds and the message with which they began their shifts: "It is ten o'clock at night. Lower the volume of your wireless. You will be fulfilling your duty as a citizen, and you see that you can hear perfectly." Sometimes I would arrive home even later, finally alone, my head still noisy with the theological debates with friends, my cheeks still flushed from an excess of hot chocolates in San Ginés. At my locked portales I would clap twice and wait for the sereno's metal-tipped chuzo to reply, on distant cobblestones, like echolocation. Clap-clap. Tap-tap. Until he found me and grumbled and fished out his huge ring of keys. Five trudged flights above I would fall into bed, the chuzo fading on the street like a metronome guiding me into sleep. Never have I felt lonesome. For some, celibacy is success against temptation, an intimation of the divine. Others wear it as proof of obedience, readiness to do as they are called. Selfishly, I prefer the solitude. I welcome anything that brings me closer to Our Lord. Even death I shall embrace, for that is how God in His wisdom defines our earthly life. To pretend otherwise is hubris. Forget not the Caesars, in their salad days, parading victorious through Rome after conquests, and the slaves tasked to whisper, at intervals along the procession, these words in the ruler's ear: Memento mori. Remember death.

(Inaudible)

Yes! How astute—as with la corrida, for which everyone is surprised I have a passion. After Sunday mass, at San Isidro, I would rush like a perfumed philanderer to another kind of cathedral, Las Ventas, where in the cheap seats of the sol section I would wrestle with my conscience. Reminding myself that death remains life's greatest absurdity if we never see it. It was there where I witnessed the legendary El Cordobés wave away his banderilleros and turn his back toward the bull. At the last moment of the charge he put out his leg and death and life shared one possibility. That is what I learned from those dusty circles. In the Eucharist. In the baptism of a child. In the anointing of the sick. I witnessed that when I undertook my Rite of Ordination, prostrated before the altar, facedown on a carpet that smelled like a wool army blanket, in that cathedral whose roof had been rebuilt. With the bishop and the priests I prayed the Litany of the Saints and the verses lapped like the waves on the beach from my childhood. When the bishop laid his hands to recite the consecratory prayer, Father Max stood behind with the others and winked at me his rheumy blue eye. How sweetly the chrism smelled like olive oil. Vested I was with my stole and I waited in darkness through the absurd moment when the chasuble was being placed and my head couldn't find the light. I received the paten and holy chalice like a bird I had just caught. From every passing comes a beginning and I pray that Vita receives forgiveness for the hatred in her heart; that she will find in its end a fresh start. For her I have only compassion—not passion, ha? Do not misquote me in that book of yours.

(Inaudible)

Yes, of course, friend me on Facebook; I'll accept you, but you have to like my posts. I promise it's not all prayers and pastoral statements. I put humorous Bible stories also. As when a youth named Eutychus listened from a window to Paul's sermon, but so long did the disciple talk that poor Eutychus fell asleep and tumbled out! Haha! Acts is so good. I love that reminder. But Santa Banana, is that the time? I must bounce, as my students say. I shall pray for you. When you find yourself lost in your next chapters, unsure whom to believe and how to commit your trust, forget not the prayer of Reinhold Niebuhr, and ask God to grant you the courage to change what must be altered, the serenity to accept what cannot be helped, and the insight to know one from the other. Amen. And also: don't take yourself so seriously.

(Burp)

Vita Nova Transcript: 6 of 13.

(35:39.47—VN6.M4A)

I know, right? Sorry—just a sec. Messaging Nur. Nearly done. An offer I can't refuse. I'm still thinking about it. Almost—Argh! Autocorrect: my greatest enema. There. Send.

(Inaudible)

Crazy, right? Huge decision. Don't get me wrong, I want to help people—but imagine what I'll go through. Bad enough now. Like with that fame ho Red, which is so typical—never trust a ginger—talking shizzy, supposedly spilling the milk all over social media, for me to cry over. He's not even my ex—was hardly a fling. And that Paz Panot, at the *Metro Times*, trying to link me to Loy's attempt on the president; plus she's saying I should be tested for shabu. That karen's as egregious as her poetry, which deserves a visit from a death squad—let her come home from Strasbourg and see all the killing on the streets, maybe then she'll have something worth writing. Jojie says she brings shame to the trans community, coz Panot surfed that advocacy till she grabbed another wave: Estregan's drug war. And right beside her is DJ RedCentre—the pot calling the oregano green. Seriously. They know drug accusations are a death sentence these days. So I'll just own it: Sure, I experimented, before. Yeah, with everything, long ago. E, K, A, fashion, smileys, Vs, shrooms, nitrous, wari . . . but never needles. And stopped after trying shabu once. Okay, maybe twice—coz it scared me. What Red's saying about drugs is true, but to us back then drugs were spiritual, mind-expanding. Blue pill or red pill?—why not both pills?—how else you gonna know if the Matrix is a lie? Full disclosure: drugs transformed me. I used to be so uptight—like Paz Panot-level self-righteous—and totally uncomfy in my own skin. So I learned what they had to teach. As Red always said: altering your own consciousness is a human right. But I'm no addict—except maybe to Potato Corner. Besides—hello?—alcohol and nicotine: both drugs, both harmful, both legal, both taxed. And—yo!—coffee: millions of antisocial zombies would kill without their daily hit, seriously. And—like, dude—weed: don't even; did you know it was vilified by pharmaceutical companies scared of its organic medicinal uses? And by politicians afraid of the hippie counterculture's influence against the Vietnam War? Those EES are all Orions. I gots zilch to hide—I experimented, just like everyone.

(Inaudible)

Actually, Red was our dealer. The Atomic Shaman, he called himself—with his scenester swagger and golden dreads. And we were his Chemical Jedis, he said—an expedition to the center of the universe, searching for a peak to gaze from into the horizons of perception. All this was after Rolex, after I evacuated the condo he let me stay in until the eruption of Mount Abiola—his wife, who he never left, of course (thank frakking goodness, in retroflect). Rolex now the villain turned victim turned victor, once again: Yes, horrorable senators, huhu, I was forced by el presidente to govern with the gun, buhuhu, fund law and order with illegal gambling, buhuhuhu, because my province is poor, buhuhuhuhu, but my conscience will not allow me to allow these people to allow our country to be destroyed . . . blah blah blech! Phony as the sensational going-out-of-business sale of the rug shop that'll just move across the street. After him, no wonder I wanted to party.

(Inaudible)

Don't be ridiculous. Such lies—me and Red weren't ever together-together, though with all the eckie we were all dropping, maybe he felt we were. ♫ *Blame it on the boogie* ♫—of Manila's summer of love. You know, that high point every generation deserves, coz every opera needs its aria, every wedding reception its "New York, New York" played loud near the end, when the whole shack shimmies, zigazig ah! So high you just gotta wax poetic. About those rare moments, reminding you you're alive: like a secret rendezvous by the sea, or sitting in darkness beside your first crush with your hands brushing buttery in the popcorn. Moments that feel like they'll last forever, coz if they don't they're not all that. Thing is, every disco story's got a rise *and* fall—that's just disco, that's just life. Parties end, and the cool kids know when to head. I guess you were there, since you don't seem to remember.

(Inaudible)

Really? Oh, homie, you missed out. You got your American degree while Manila got its moment, for just over a year, when every kid could be cool—every Friday, every Saturday, sometimes even Wednesdays, Thursdays, at ABG's, at Insomnia, at anonymous warehouses, on beaches, in homes, passing out gum, passing out zines, passing out bumps, dancing alone, dancing with everyone, all without shame. Just kids, of the night—like anybody searching for something bright to guide your way—exclusively inclusive, embracing all who offered an open soul: the freaks and geeks, ravers and rockers, divas and fag hags, yuppies who rushed over from working late and left their ties hanging on their rearview mirrors. Introducing our old selves to our new selves and ditching our masks—the clans, cliques, classes—everyone knowing your name, and everyone who knew your name could be your friend. Your only entrance fee was giving as much as you took. And you'd feel the party before you'd hear it: the bass, blocks away, through your steering wheel or under your feet, the chaos cozy, spilling into the parking lot, you throwing your bad self in like one more branch in the bonfire. All platform shoes—so fab—and sweat and pleather pasted on skin—so hot—and glowsticks cracked and shaken—so trippy, in endless arcs and loops—with a candy crush of dyed hair on the dance floor till the music swirls and we all peak as one, our souls in urdhva hastasana to heaven. And onstage, on many a night, on the decks like a maestro with a passionate youth orchestra, there was Steve Robert— as in: Superstar DJ RedCentre. As in: fricka-fricka-fresh. As in: so cool you'll catch a cold. As in: icy hot, making big noise, ♫ *kicking his banner all over the place.* ♫ So don't blame me—trust me, I already blame myself.

(Lighter click. Exhalation)

Red first caught my eye in Boy's *Brief Encounters* coffee-table book, frolicking in the surf in tighty-whities, smiling like sunshine and splashing two other male models. He also DJed for some *3-Poll Threat* wrap-parties, and we'd see each other out—you know Manila—always hey-

hey, kiss-kiss both cheeks, big melting hug if either of us was peaking. Always a bit too crunchy granola for me, with his flip-flops and Thai fisherman pants and Bintang Beer wifebeater and peeking-out armpit hair—though his accent was charmant, how he called even girls "mate," like an offer. This was during those nanoseconds when Maori tattoos were actually fetch for non-Maoris. His rough sailor's hands all sexy, and he wasn't like other guys who told you sweet things they don't mean—he told me mean things to be sweet. I'd toss him a five-peso coin and be like, Hey, Steve Robert, buy yourself a last name; him handing it back, saying: "Hey, mate, for last night; keep the change." Come on, don't look at me like that; there are times in life when that's fun—guys being brash for your benefit, like a peacock fanning, or Stanley Kowalski shouting up at your window. And those eyes—oh, em, gosh, like Brandon Walsh's, flashing like a wild animal in the woods. Did you know that cats' eyes flash green because of the tapetum lucidum? The bit that reflects and magnifies luminosity before it enters the retina and appears in the brain as an image. I love that: seizing light from the darkness, reflecting it off each other. Like Red arriving at a party, with his glowsticks and sunglasses and knack for the perfect moment—like we couldn't reach the next level without him—crowing: "It ain't a party till we cross the point of no return!" I still don't know what that means, but it sounded so true. Like I said, I'd just dumped Rolex and was single and ready to mingle, cash and ciggies tucked into my bra like a laundrywoman rolling up her sleeves. So one second I'm dancing with Red in the middle of hundreds at 78Orange, the next second we're making out as if the whole world's fallen away and the music's just for us. I pull back and accuse him of having a girlfriend—this grimy girl named Sugar, with the long hair and short shorts white guys love. (He thinks his yellow fever makes him culturally progressive.) "We broke up," Red said. And I'm like, When? And he goes, "Right this second," and slides his tongue back into my mouth. And that's how we started hooking up. ♫ *Bad boys, bad boys, whatcha gonna do?* ♫ . . . when they come for me, I swear, they're kryptonite—or used to be. These days I'm feeling more the gentlemanly writerly type.

(Pause)

Look at you, blushing.

(Laughter)

So anyways, Stevie wasn't all bad—give me some credit. You'll see when you talk to him. There's decency deep down, somewhere. Like, he was friends with everyone—the society kids as well as their body-guards. And he patiently taught me how to DJ. And called his dance parties "therapy," wanting to bring that vibe to the people—at malls and political rallies as much as clubs and raves. Red lived in Boy's pool house rent-free a few months and never cared about Boy and his co-terie watching with binoculars when he swam or tanned—unlike other male models who'd move out in a huff. He was a total fagnet but deflected their come-ons with kind firmness—no pun intended—gracious about their admiration, and they respected him for it. So we pulled a French exit and headed to his place, for a magical night I don't remember, and a terrible morning that I do—waking up in a black hole, his windows taped over with aluminum foil, his blacklight buzzing like a headache, his Nokia shrill in my ear—one of those recorded person-alized ringtones assigned to specific callers: "Hey baby! Wazzaaaap!" Sugar's voice. "Hey baby! Wazzaaaap!" Red reaching over to reject it with an "effing B"—but like really saying the words, which was why I get up and look for my clothes, drawing the line at such disrespect. His place is gross, sand coating the soles of my feet, though we're like hours from a beach. His filthy toilet not flushing. I on the fluorescents in the kitchen and roaches run like picnickers in a lightning storm. Plus the whole condo smells like his dreadlocks. Sometimes I wonder if the reason Western civilization used to be so advanced was coz they don't waste time on personal hygiene—like China now. So anyways, like I said, me and Red never dated-dated: just bumped into each other at parties and left together—always one last time, I'd tell myself. I mean, yeah, no, there were some real moments, TBH. Driving home from a party high as kites, Chicane on the stereo lifting us higher, both of us all like *Wheee!* as we soar up and down overpasses—hella dangerous, which was kinda the point. Stumbling arm in arm into his building, mumbling promises for matching tats, both of us covering an eye to see straight coz we're screwy-kablooie on Special K. And lying together under the covers as the speed drains away, feeling like kids who found the best hide-and-seek spot ever, your body so still it senses the world in motion—the roosters outside, carts squeaking, kids chatting their way to the pump. It was sweet, I admit, passing out in Red's spicy arms, my Vicks inhaler still stuffed up a nostril, closing my eyes and opening them one breath later to find a whole day had passed. Some afternoons we'd wake and bake, mining through his hash from tribespeople in the mountain rice-terraces to the south—and he'd play his music low— Delerium, Sigur Rós, Fischerspooner, Enzo Lim—and I'd watch him at his turntables, so gaunt his ribs stretched his tattoos—Japanese carps, the stars of the Southern Cross, his ta moko of whale teeth, and a swirl of birds and a setting sun—wearing only a sarong, his head tilted into one headphone like someone was whispering the secret of life to him. Reminding me of an angel of death, actually: bony, androgynous, fatal. But I couldn't. Honestly, too many things irritated me. I never invited him to my place coz I kinda worried he'd steal from me. And he's as cocky as a line chef on cooking shows, but I faked all my orgasms so he wouldn't pout all night and keep me up trying. And I hated how he'd play up being different, but really wanting to belong—a social climber acting hella street. We all know the type.

(Inaudible)

Hardee har—good one, you're so funny. I'm match more complexicated, son of a whore, I shall spill the milk and box your perflexed face there, worst comes to shove. But seriously, I hated how Red could be so condescending, pitying my sitcom references—coz he's too good to watch TV—and playing music nazi—making barfing noises while he flipped through my CDs in my car, all like, "Céline Dion's what they play in the elevators in hell," or, "Enrique Iglesias is the Danielle Steel of pop music."

(Inaudible)

Why? Because our after-parties held such sweet surprises. Me and Stevie smoking ourselves into marshmallows, holding in bed like we're one person, whispering about his past faintly in my ear, like we're telepathically connected and riding the black light into the spaces between the neon planets in the velvet poster on his ceiling. He's an interesting guy, actually. I once took him to a poetry night—where I first met Dr. Rajah in person, to my great thrill—and Red closed his eyes and listened so sweetly when I read, then he got up there and recited from memory that "Invictus" poem he said was by Nelson Mandela. Homie can herd sheep, drive a tractor, sail yachts, and dive in open water. He can cook well, sew, and navigate by the stars. Red hitch-hiking from his small town to the coast, where he worked on boats of the rich and not-famous, ending up here after crewing for this lonely hedge-fund guy named Clayton, who was trying to sail over the edge of the earth. I was addicted to Red's tales of places that don't seem real—like drugs I wanted more of. Like the volcanic Tikopia—a ring of sand around a freshwater lagoon, divided by four tribes who bury their dead inside their houses. Or Rapa Iti—where only five hundred people speak a language that somehow appeared in the dreams of this six-year-old kid in France, who grew up and met a sailor's Rapan ex-wife in Rennes, speaking the language in his dreams, and they moved to Rapa Iti, which to the guy felt like coming home. Trippy, right? A marvelous world I'd never see, and so I kept seeing Red, despite myself. My fave was his story about crossing the Indian Ocean to Madagascar, three hundred miles to go when their boat starts leaking and they find a dot on the map called Tromelin Island—once named Île des Sables, isle of sand (I love that)—not even half a kilometer in size, where no trees can grow because of cyclones. And it's either luck or a curse—coz they know its history: Three hundred years ago a French East Indies ship called the *Utile*—the *Useful*—got wrecked in a storm and half the Madagascar slaves drowned under hatches nailed shut, the other eighty left on the island by the French sailors who built a boat from the wreckage and were never seen again. The castaways—the perfect word—making shelters out of coral and sand, surviving on shellfish, turtles, and birds, keeping one fire going for fifteen years—imagine? Only fourteen people alive by the time a lone Frenchman struggled out of the sea and helped them build a raft, setting out with six of the men to get help, the women and children left to wait. Until one day a war-ship appears on the horizon, *La Dauphine*—the dolphin!—to rescue them all, including a grandmother, her daughter, and the daughter's baby daughter. The island getting its name from the captain, the Chevalier de Tromelin. A place I'm doomed to never see but will never forget—so small Red and Clayton only spot it when the bang of their flare sends up a spiral of birds against the setting sun, a cloud rising from what he first thinks is a whale—Red actually shouting: "Land ho!"

(Inaudible)

Come to think, I don't know—you should ask if they reached Madagascar. Red called his stories yarns, and they'd go on like a ball unrolling till the final thread led into sleep. How could I not let myself get tangled? To be honest, I'm shocked by his bitterness now. That was all years ago. And the moment we shared was a huge part of me finding myself, after *3-Poll Threat.*

(Inaudible)

Yeah, check out the monologue duel on YouTube. The Golden Age of the Silver Screen. Decide for yourself. Jezhabelle entering stage right, hair pulled back, face in cold cream, wire hanger in her hand as she growls: "No wire hangers! What are wire hangers doing in this closet? . . . You live in the most beautiful house in Brentwood and you don't care if your clothes are stretched out from wire hangers, and your room looks like a two-dollar-a-week furnished room in some two-bit backstreet town in Oklahoma!" And she's on her knees, whipping an invisible child, capturing the frustrations of a mommie dearest wanting more for her kids than she had. Absolutely captivating; incredibly stupid— leaving the stage forever the typecast snob, as I stride on as a sexy Charlie Chaplin dressed as Hitler, the crowd gasping as I stand in the lonely spotlight, proving that a true artiste should leap to the challenge of inhabiting their most distant opposite. I become the Great Dictator.

(Chair scrapes. Heels click)

My body shaking but my voice strong.

(Footsteps pacing)

"I'm sorry, but I don't want to be an emperor . . . I don't want to rule or conquer . . ." By the time I get to, "In this world there is room for everyone. And the good earth is rich and can provide for everyone," the clapping's like a rising tide. And when I reach that part about how "the way of life can be free and beautiful, but we have lost the way. Greed has poisoned men's souls, has barricaded the world with hate," I gotta pause, the applause so deafening. And when the bell rings to signal my last ten seconds, I know I'm going to win. "The hate of men will pass," I declare, "and dictators die, and the power they took from the people will return to the people. And so long as men—and women!—die . . . liberty! Will! Never! Perish!"

(Silence)

The house lights sudden. Everyone on their feet. Their ovation the most gorgeous deafening.

(Chair scrapes. Seatback shifts)

Then, after the long commercial break—all the votes electronically tallied—me and Jezh and the eight others onstage, arms woven around shoulders, emotions pushing behind our eyes, our slo-mo journeys projected above (all the practices without makeup, the bloopers and cross-eyed faces, tightly shot breakdowns, sisterly hugs, shared laughter . . .)—that's when Illac Angelo Diaz strides out in his velvet tux, waving the envelope. "The country has voted!" says he, and rips open the result, pausing forever to look at Jezh, then me. Then Jezh. Then me.

(Finger drumroll on table)

He reads my name. I break down crying. Of course. Runner-up? WTF, right? Jezhabelle Baratto: the country's newest star. And Furio, afterwards, not even there for me—using the backstage pass I got him, rushing to be the first to interview Jezh the Triple Threat. Imagine? So don't you dare make that same mistake, you hear?

(Laughter)

Just kidding. Not really. Don't talk to Jezh.

(Laughter)

And that's how I arrived at the Kilikili Klub—with my judy, Jojie—brimming with sadness, purpose, and Alizé. And how I met LeTrel—tall, Black, and handsome—and I'm like, Enchanté!, coz I'd never been with an African American before. Plus he was a fan. "You rocked your monologue tonight," says he, that slightest sweetness going straight to my head—as we dance, and walk to the casino, and flirt as he teaches me roulette, his hand on the small of my back feeling exactly like a thrill. Furio knew he deserved my scorn, judging from his energy in defending me the weeks after, as the media focused more on my supposed crash than Jezhabelle's meteoric rise—like they always do with us women. (Britney, can I get an amen?) So I melted down while hosting a perfume launch—whatevs. And got drunk at Venezia and fixed some chick's face with my drink—she deserved it! One headline read:

"Triple Mess!" Another said: "Schizo-Threat!"—Changco rags always making a fortune hating on me.

(Lighter click. Exhalation)

Poor Furio. I thought I cheated coz he betrayed me, but maybe I just needed to get up on my own after my defeat. I've learned, from my limited experience, that infidelity starts with excitement but continues by filling the gaps in your life. Furio, I'm pretty sure, blamed his karma— stealing me from Cat, me being stolen by LeTrel. But I wasn't stolen. Those were my decisions. Sometimes I make good ones, sometimes bad ones, sometimes the bad ones turn out to be good ones. Like I had mad props for Jezh—so talented, so gorgeous (if her cheekbones were higher they'd be horns)—but as winner she overcurated her career. While I, as runner-up—aka: top loser—took what I could get, working to make every opportunity pop, modeling, hosting, singing at corporate parties, doing cameos on TV. Jezh turning down a cheesy movie lead that I—an aficionado of baduy—seized: the feisty dancer in *Sexy Nights: Shadow of the Forbidden*, following her dreams to the big city, where she fails again and again before inventing the Mr. Sexy-Sexy, the dance society tries to repress (though when people come together to be free they can accomplish anything). The theme song was fire—heard everywhere: infants humming it in their sleep; the oms of monks beginning to resemble its beat. ♫ *Ooo, my sexy, sexy. My Mr. Sexy-Sexy. I dance this dance for you . . .* ♫ Our country's biggest ever viral dance sensation. Everybody, as in every body, doing it: matrons at the smoky Starlight Room; urchins on the smoggy starless streets; grade-school kids on variety shows at noon—hands on knees, butts bumping up and down in V formation. Even this paralyzed patient at Philippine General supposedly moving and moaning to my music video on TV. Miraculous!—the whole thing: leading to my first solo EP, *Waiting for I Do*; contracts left and right; mobs everywhere; mothers literally tossing me their babies for pictures with them. Jezhabelle was our nation's Triple Threat but I became our It Girl—coz in a culture that loves underdogs, sometimes the best way to win is to lose. Even though losing was what the media seemed to want more of, especially after my bold scene in *Delirium Tremens*, coz people love confusing sexuality with permission. Reporters trying to catch me drunk at parties, paparazzi angling for upskirt photos when I slid out of cars. I was even snapped in downward dog at Bikram yoga from the fire escape across the street. Then came the unfounded rumors, which stuck like spilled glitter: I was pregnant with a Black man's baby; I got my boobs did in Rio; I was skinny thanks to shabs; and having an affair with my *Ready! Set! Go!* cohost. Yadda, yadda.

(Laughter)

At first I was, like, whatever you say so, I'll box you there in the face— but after a while it made my bangs hurt; as annoying as a hot girl hamming for Insta at the next table. And then came the infamous camel-toe incident, while shooting an ad for Wildcat Deodorant. Which honestly made me seriously consider what LeTrel had to offer—that fine Black man waving a green card and a new start in the U.S. of A. But in my line of work, you gotta accept a codependent relationship with the media. From the moment you go public, you kinda have to live out loud, and silence can feel like giving up. Either clap back or straight flex—a puffer-fish charade that I first learned during Furio, mastered with LeTrel, used to cope with Rolex, until the charade wasn't a charade by the time I hooked up with Red. You asked earlier if I loved him. Honestly, I loved Red's capacity to surprise me with his depth, his way with words, his freedom. He offered me what I needed, at that point in my life. If it feels like love why figure out a magician's tricks? But honestly I wasn't ever really comfortable with him and his crew—though as Dr. Chopra reminds: "People are doing the best that they can from their own levels of consciousness." That's why I tried, at their after-parties at his beshie Nolimon Lontok's place—his wing of his skeezeball dad's mansion in Dasmariñas Vill—until ecstasy and ego was no longer their combo of choice and they got into the shabs.

(Inaudible)

Just twice, as I mentioned. Okay, maybe thrice. But crystal meth's scary as; centering and multiplying everything you are, like a Voltes V robot volting in—as in, I thought up, wrote down, and finalized the entire concept plan for my women's shelter, the Sanctuary, all in one sitting. Lots of people get into shabu to be productive, to like work extra shifts to feed their families. Problem is, too much brings out the ugh in ugly people. Like Red, who'd talk nonstop about people he looked down on—who didn't party, or were religious. Or like Noli, who'd boast for hours about his dirty work for his dad's SuperMegaOceanic Corp.—all the kickbacks from developers, the Chinese land-reclaiming company, highway contractors, material suppliers. So when I heard Fernando and his crones on my recordings talk about SuperMegaOceanic, and how fires were used to clear squatters from the land, that's when it clicked: Noli's shabs talk was all true, ongoing for years, with everyone in on it. Filimon and Nando's feud just like the one with Rolex over illegal gambling. Because allies are made by giving them what they want, and enemies made by taking it away. There's always a red line.

(Inaudible)

Mine with Stevie and co. was when Noli's little sister, Ultima, brought in her new beagle puppy—this adorbs little thing, all big paws and floppy ears, and Noli reaches between its legs and plays with its birdie then throws the ball for it to fetch, poor puppy running and shuddering and whimpering—Ulti crying after him, all the boys cacking themselves. Yeah. Good times. May their tribe decrease. Out of all the Nandotards, I'll never forgive the ones I used to party with—supporting the drug war now, just coz they outgrew getting high, or are rich and protected whenever they still do. Like this former friend now living in Paris—Snow White, let's call her—all over Facebook attacking even friends like me who've actually gone into poor communities to witness the fallout of Nando's violence. Yet last time me and her hung out, peeps were crushing and mixing Vs with fashion, and there was Snow White, hoovering the fattest lines of all. I was like, Really? Guess there's no higher high than hypocrisy. Coz it's been years since I touched anything—even before Nando clamped down to get reelected. And I'm not just saying that because Nur wants me to run as his veep—vice prez! Imagine? So let Red and the Changco brothers media spew their whatever—I'm so not afraid. Someone even sending this bullet after Spaz Panot's recent so-called exposé—my jeweler turned it into a pimpin' pendant. See? Coz haters gotta hate; that's what haters do. Defending the undefendable, with blood on their hands. Even if I could forgive, I could never forget.

(Inaudible)

You're right, absolutely—some *do* say that about me with Nando: How could I love a killer? But nobody knows what I'd tell him behind closed doors. I sincerely believed I'd do more convincing him in private than calling him out in public. At the time. I've been making up for it, haven't I? So let Red try to ruin me. He's just bitter, all these years later, as if *he* wasn't the one who wanted an open relationship. Our last party was one Halloween, me dressed as him and him dressed as me—coz nothing turns on Anglo-Saxon men more than wearing drag. Yet there he was, in the club, in the CR, in my clothes, in Sugar. Imagine? Me catching them coming out, him claiming they were just doing fashion, but when I get my daisy dukes back that night I find her smelly crust all over the fly. Gross! Red trying to win me back by saying he'll quit drugs and choose me over her, in a note with really careful bad hand-writing that accompanied an expensive purse—a Dior that I did not j'adore, and ended up giving away, to Ultima Lontok. And I hated every song on the mixtape CD he made me. Neither of us talking for like over a month—yet when Noli and him run over those morning commuters, while screwy-kablooie on K, *I'm* the one Red calls? Suddenly *I'm* the only person he trusts to lend him bail money? Seriously, germs, some advice: when wooing back a lady, the three words she wants to hear aren't "I'm in jail."

(Clap. Laughter)

Of course, they both went free, like a day later. For punishment Noli got sent to New York City—as if partying at Twilo's any penance. And Red didn't cross my mind for years, till he started attacking me these last weeks. Some people I'll never forgive but will forget, just like they deserve. I don't know why he's so angry with me. Can you find out? All I know is thanks Goddess we didn't do our matching tats—Latin, in Old English font: Omnia mutantur, nihil interit (or something like that). Everything changes, nothing is lost. I forget where he got that, but it's kinda perfect. Coz that first night the undercover cops appeared in ABG's, you knew who they were because they refused to dance. Then our names appeared on narco lists. And places got shut down. Then house parties became more exclusive. And fear came back, and minds closed; then that was that. But I learned so much, so very much, that year we felt that we were all the same, and that love could change the world.

Steve "DJ RedCentre" Robert Transcript.

(42:04.20—Red.M4A)

Nah. Record away. Got heaps of goss. Vitatas. Boy. V's ex, Cat. That Vegemite-driller Bansamoro, who ruined his son's life. You want it, I got it. I sound like a yob on a street corner, hey?—flogging swag in his jacket. Hope it's cool I'm sitting here in the back. Epic balls, mate; I like to spread. You can hear me from there, right? Ripper. Left here, please, then second right. Would you look at it come down! Fuck, I hope my flight's not canceled. Ta for the ride, mate. You don't mind if I vape, hey? Good thing you caught me before I split. Flying south, to Woop Woop. Election season's always bonza. Spinning Junior's thank-yous bash for his supporters. Technically not a campaign event, since candidates haven't announced yet. Want some coffee? Choco-almond biscotto? Bit of a dingo's brekky I brought, but I'll go halves with you. Did you have a big one last night?

(Muffled)

What? Mate! Should've caught my set at Coup d'État. I came, I saw, I crushed it. It was massive. At the light, turn left. So, like V, huh? For her book, huh? I'm writing a book, too. *All I Really Need to Know I Learned from Shrooms.* That's the title. What's she calling hers? No worries. Be secretive. I'll gladly tell you *her* story. Not much to it. She's the town push bike. That's it. That's her story.

(Muffled)

Oh. Alright. Got me first gander at the fashion show of the Warp guys, Brando and Ronald—you know them, hey? Brilliant muchachos. Post-apocalyptic theme, bondage-inspired clubwear. All spikes and shit. Vitatas the finale—vampire briiide! Freaky makeup and fangs and blood dripping down her chin. I was like: Ooft—check that long-legged, brown-crested, mongrel warbler. She's a fair bit of alright. Gown was, like, bondage straps and zippers covering her bits with this big, like, uh, ruffle, I guess, from, like, across her tatas and around her hips. Walking like figjam in mega high heels. I was like: Aw, yeah! Gotta stick me long foot in there like a door-knocking Jehovah's Witness. Cuz everyone knows she's a Betsy Popwood. If you get my meaning. Such a silly sko she thinks foreplay's joining three others for a rootfest. Not smart enough to know she's dim, but at least she knows she's a fucking beaut. You know how some birds are, hey? Nah, yeah, I totes wanted to bonk that hornbag. Bloody inevitable, too, I reckoned. We had this profound connection. And in this town RedCentre's kinda legend, to be honest. Like, the most loved DJ, humility aside—always bringing the vibe.

(Muffled)

Well, what rock you been under, mate? Even the povos know Red-Centre. Cuz I get that everyone's gotta get legless once in while. That's my genius. So, like, me and Vitatas first hooked up at a rager. Ferry Corsten at 78Orange. I opened and after my set me and her start pashing in the middle of the dance floor. Of course, I'm loving it—she's the meat magnet every bloke's cracking wood for that night. We start to hot up and she pulls me to the loo and locks the door. I'm like, Go on, we're not here to fuck spiders. Dude, the root-rat couldn't unbuckle me daks fast enough. Starts in with a two-handed sloppy gobbie, all twisty and shit, pinkies pointing all dainty like she's sipping a cuppa with the bloody Queen Mum. Fucking legend, mate. 'Ken oath. All like, "Fuck my face!" and I'm like, Strewth, if you insist. Next I know, we're legging it down the footpath to a taxi queue, stumbling in each other's arms we're so fucking high. The cabbie going hell for leather to my place cuz I slipped him a fifty. Me and Vitatas snogging in the back like lives depend on it. I'm knuckle-dunking to warm her up.

(Muffled)

Mate, chillax. Like oh my god, why so serious, bruz? Look, you want the truth or not? Nothing new from what I posted on Facey. And, like, good on her for owning her sexuality, hey? I mean that. Aw fucking hell, would you look at that traffic. Typical. Let's get comfy, I reckon. May I go on? Cuz we can end the interview if you're gonna be a wowser.

Okay, so anyways, we're at my place, J. K. Rowling on the molly. V's jaw's grinding, eyes fluttering. But I'm worried my chubbie won't rise to the occasion, I'm that smacked. I pull my lips away and go to the deck to chuck on some sounds. Oakenfold, *Tranceport*. Classic. V stands on the bed and starts gyrating, like being tickled slo-mo. Starts sliding off her clothes. Mate, word of advice, since obvs you fancy her: shout a schmancy dinner, with like fancy plonk and shit—she'll give you a go. Toeyer than a Roman sandal, that one. Thing is, I'm spewing inside, thinking, The galaxy of drugs you got, bruh, no Viags? But then she, like, bends over and pulls down her superhero-tight cargos. Mate, wait till you get a gander at that badonkadonk. Turns out no need for a dick pill, mate. My snag was raging like a mob of wogs at a race riot. Oy, what's with your sour mug? Like, you don't want to hear her story? About her famous funbags? Fucking A—or double-D, actually. Like weighing two bags of gold. Them tatas dinky-di, let me tell you—or pretty fucking convincing, and I'm something of an expert. So I get nudie lickety split and she grabs me knob, like opening a door, and leads yours truly by the willy to the bed . . .

(Muffled)

Pushes me down and feeds me her pink taco, my manaconda up her throat, and I'm finally impressed. Cuz I generally dislike sixty-nining chicks I don't love, cuz you know how tang can reek like old tae kwon do pads—but hers, mate: worth a sticky beak. Right tasty. I feasted on them umami twatflaps, then—

(Muffled)

Just a tick, mate—I'm getting to my point. Then she moves up to mount me reverse cowgirl. Like, coy smile. She didn't come down in the last shower, let me tell you—

(Muffled)

. . . hold on. So the wily cock-socket slags on her hand and slips me up her Hershey highway. Bareback, to boot—

(Muffled)

. . . should've insisted on a franger, considering all the randos that sluzza's shagged. But Asian girls are clean, and hooboy was it tight. Like, ethnic tight—

(Muffled)

. . . circumcise-me tight, mate. Cuz tight brown holes make white junk look just massive—that's objective fact. Six times the little snagbag came, and my jammy hadn't even touched her punanny—

(Muffled)

. . . just let me finish, if you want this interview. Then I laid pipe in every orifice for an hour before marinating her mug in me baby gravy. Red-tagged!

(Muffled)

Probs felt my phantom dick for like a week . . .

(Muffled)

Okay! Jeez. Calm down! Don't be so sooky, bru. She'll be apples. She made her reputation, she's got to lie in it. Okay. My bad. No details. No worries. Just saying. My point is we became fuck budd . . . friends with benefits. Is that okay to say? Politically correct enough for you?

(Silence)

To be honest, I wasn't all that into her. She wasn't half bad, but you know how it goes—I got ninety-nine problems but a bitch ain't one. And V's a bi . . . bird who'll bring you nine hundred ninety-nine problems. Exhibit A, the president, mate. Most powerful man in the country, toppled by a honey-glazed ham wallet.

(Muffled)

Oh, soz. Come on, mate. Don't get shitty. We're just chewing the fat. I'm just saying onya, V—using all she got to get all she wants. Honestly, you think I'm dissing but I got big mobs of respect. She's a sex-positive feminist—like, in this country? The chicks here love to fuck—but, like, shock horror if they ever admit it. But don't hate the player, mate, hate the game. Society makes repressed liars of all of us, I reckon—well, not me, clearly. Haters just jelz cuz she gets it. Totes. Vita's a down-ass bitch. That okay, bruv? Can I call her a down-ass *bitch* if it means a good sort who's up for adventure and novel experiences? Hang a right next crosswalk and we'll hit the highw—bloody hell, they caught another. See that taxi? Happens in this spot all the time. Coppers get some bloke to stand on the corner and hail a ride soon as the light goes green. Cabbie stops, blueboys get him for obstructing traffic. Doesn't stop, he's refusing to convey a passenger. Same bribe either way. My mate Nolimon Lontok clued me in. He's the mayor's son; scams fascinate the fuck out of him. This one's called "stars-that-sparkle," cuz not all stars sparkle. Problem with having a nice cab. As I was saying, me and V had genuine affection. She's a modern woman. Never came by without cold stubbies. Never pressured for commitment. Made your schoolboy fantasies come true. You gotta respect such a forthright sheila. Who loves to smoke and root and blast the Jimi. Who swigs Cazadores while riding cowgirl. She took what she wanted. Let them feminist grizzlers spit the dummy. It's a new millenium, bruv. She gave up heaps to get hers. I remember when those nonce priests were boycotting her movies. Them puritan poofs just won't admit everything's better with a whiff of sex. The Bible's chockers with it. The best parts. All the begatting. Like, what's really wrong with Vitatas digging wang sandwiches cuz how powerful she feels having your schlong in her mouth? Or just enjoying giving pleasure? If a jackaroo says this, he's a male chauvinist. If a jillaroo says that, she's an unwitting product of a chauvinistic society. Behind every great man stands a woman, fondling his nuts. Behind every great woman stands a man, schtupping her K-9. That's equality, I reckon. Fuck them feminazis! I sat through Vita's *Vagina Monologues*. I know what I'm on about. "Vagina! Vagina! . . . If your vagina got dressed, what would it wear? Like a Ralph Lauren skirt or lots of glitter? Or probably a red boa? Or something from the forties?" Bloody hell! Vita was *so* empowered at the play's after-party, sucking up praise from thick-waisted lezzos with spiky hair and fawning pooftas in scarves.

(Muffled)

You for real? Don't cancel me, boyyo. Not a bloody thing wrong with being a lezzo or poof, mate, but if you're a lezzo or poof I'll call you a lezzo or poof. Just cuz I'm not some snowflake bleeding-ass pinko tosspot, sending anyone who disagrees to the showers for a whiff of Zyklon B. Political correctness is our last taboo, and taboo's where the rot ferments and spreads. Look, mate, you see this all the time. Wowsers be whingeing like, Oooh, Vitatas is partying, what a screamer. Oooh, check them socialites, fiddling whilst Rome burns. Get your hand off it, mate. Sometimes your shit just gotta go fallow, hey? As if silvertails don't got their own worries, frustrations, and dreams. Mo'

money, mo' problems. Without money, you got just one problem—
getting some. Most these kids were born with what they got—you
reckon they should just chuck it all to the Commies just cuz everyone
else is povo? Give up what their ancestors worked for? What their own
ankle biters gonna need? Like the world's not cruel even to the big-
note man—especially with cucks like that Loy Bonifacio, going troppo,
ready to assassinate yous for perceived humiliations. Not saying there
aren't heaps of spoiled eggs. But get to know some of them, they aren't
half bad. How about sympathy and compassion for all, hey? Like those
kids of generals caught smuggling cash into the U.S.—I've partied with
a couple. Top blokes—decent, generous, born into a tough position.
What you gonna do when daddy tells you to whack a shoebox of dosh
in your Rimowa, to hide in your family's house in Malibu so enemies
can't flog it? Bit of a sticky wicket, hey? So you follow orders. Wrap the
box in a Foot Locker plastic bag. Chuck it between your underdaks and
toiletries. And hope for the best. Only thing at stake is your freedom
and soul. Just cuz their daddy rorted the system doesn't mean I won't
snort lines with them. Nuh, I don't mind admitting. People should
totes get high once in a while. But some are weak. Scared of the truth.
Not everyone's cut out to be a bolt of lightning. Or a new prophet with
his first revelation. Or a two-toed sloth, the pole-dancing rainforest
pimp daddy watching the world below speed toward oblivion. Like,
look ma, check what I can do—with only two toes! Less you talk about
drugs, the longer they'll remain in the shadows. Get in that lane, mate.
Buses stop here higgledy-piggledy. We'll be stuck for hours. I once saw
one hit a cyclist then back over him. Funerals cost less than hospitals.

(Muffled)

Abso-bloody-lutely I know they're illegal. But who says drugs are
wrong? Yeah, fine, alright, the shonky government says—the government that can't even feed its people. And the religitards, who know
shit-all about life cuz they've never had orgasms or seen the insides
of their minds. It's about liberty, mate, not partying. The Man doesn't
want yous to think. The Man wants yous addicted to the stupid-
making drugs, shit that controls yous—corn syrup, cable TV, God.
Why do dealers get jailed and not doctors writing scripts for the self-
medicating rich? Why's sentencing for crack cocaine like ten times

higher than for powder cocaine? Inequality, mate. Meanwhile, pikers in customs, border patrol, coppers, judges, diggers, pollies—they split the shmoney. I'm not saying society needs drugs. I'm saying society needs a proper convo about drugs. You can't even discuss it without being dismissed as a druggo, then shot. The country that can talk sanely about drugs, mate? That's the same country that can talk sanely about racism, sexuality, and difference.

(Muffled)

Fair dinkum I care about those things! Just cuz I'm not virtue signaling like Vitatas all over Facey doesn't mean I don't. Doesn't it scare the bejeezus out of you, living in a country where just chinwagging can land you in the boob? Like, 'ken oath, mate. Fat cats need villains. Long live Tommy Chong! All hail Shulgin! Truth is . . . Oh, shit, mate, take that exit there. Mary fucking Joseph. You can hardly see in this deluge. Like, where's Noah? You know where to go from here, hey?

(Muffled)

Yeah, so, like, my dad, after his stroke, his sciatica was always killing him. I was like, Just try some kindbud; he just wouldn't. Not a puff. The world convinced him it was wrong. Meanwhile, every morning he hacks his lungs out, cuz forty years the world's been selling him Peter Jackson Menthol Milds. Does that make a lick of sense to you? Yeah, nah, politics in the Philippines is equally fucked, mate. All just Skeletors, hey? But I reckon *that* makes sense. A country like this, choosing not to rort's like starving at a buffet and not eating. Everyone knows it's an open slather. That Bansamoro bender's always banging on about every Joe Blogs deserving a fair suck at the sauce bottle. Tell him he's dreaming, mate. No wonder them Taswegian woolie woofter and his Seppo hubbie got beheaded. I reckon Estregan's got the right idea. Yous guys need a firm hand. Some people just can't handle their shit. Virtue of selfishness, mate. You never read Ayn Rand? Only reason Bansamoro's cool with drugs is his son's a druggo. Sal's true blue and all, but I'm not gonna lie. I reckon the second strangest thing about your country is your pollies, mate. Their song and dance actually includes singing and dancing. You'd never catch, like, Obama dancing the Sexy-Sexy for a crowd. Or Angela Merkel singing "I Will Survive" on a noontime variety show. You might see ScoMo taking it up the bum from the miners and smiling, but I reckon that's nobody's idea of entertainment. Except Tony Abbott's, probs. I do love playing for the crowds at campaigns, I have to say. One weekend, I'm all posh, spinning tech house at the Coup d'État, next weekend I'm in a rice field so dry the ground's like cracked into little stop signs, spinning the Macarena so that Junior and his family can act the fools for voters. I reckon he's not a bad bloke, far as Decepticons go. Never done wrong by me. And his rallies are killer, mate. I love them povo kids, dancing with zero self-consciousness. Then come the grannies, cacking themselves till everyone joins in. I especially love them security blokes. They'll lay some trippy yarns on you. I got this pic on my phone . . . hold up, they're all like tough sneers and aviator shades and paunches, and I'm, like, holding a Tavor assault rifle. Israeli-made, mate. Check it.

(Silence)

Pretty fucking rad, hey? TAR-21. They let me shoot it, bruh. Like, chk, chk, boom! And here's me and Mayor Filimon Lontok, when he was still commissioner of the po-po. Like I said, his son's my wingman. My flat got broken into one time and my decks got jacked. Noli had me talk to his old man, who's got like a line of people waiting to see him, like bloody Don fucking Corleone. Two days later, couple a coppers are pounding my door at like nine in the fucking morning. I'm freaking, you can imagine. Was about to flush my stash but had a feeling. Chucked on a pair of sunnies and swing open the door, all nonchalant and shit. Copper's like, "Good morning, sir. We've apprehended your stolen property." Two days! Reckon Mayor Lontok has to be a toe-cutter to keep his citizens safe.

(Muffled)

That's right—me, Noli, Cat, Sal. Not besties, but we partied together for a hot minute. Not much to it. Till I started bonking Vitatas and Cat got cross as a frog in a sock. And Salaudin got chucked into rehab. Yeah, we're in Bora, tripping balls on the white sand, and this helicopter descends like from heaven and his three woggie parents pop out with two orderlies and carry him away. Saw him recently, in the mall, getting an ice cream with his dickhead dad, like a retard smiling and licking on his Very Berry Strawberry. Good as lobotomized, mate. Shabu, mate. That shit just about scared me straight. Vitatas, though, she loved it. Total coke whore meth mouth. She'd earbash all night till I stuck my bob in her gob. Oh, soz. Take it easy there, captain. I forgot what you're like. Nah, yeah, Cat and I, we hung out before. This whole society's incestuous. He'd hook shit up—like, shout massages at Tagaytay Highlands, postparty. Good times, speeding along in his van—the Mystery Machine—siren blazing, getting giggly on his infamous tank of nitrous. Me and him always had a rivalry, which he reckoned was an excuse to cockblock. Sometimes he'd even win, though the sedentary fatwad reeks like rotten avo. He may not be a stud, but his wallet makes a thud. Till he got sick and lost his sense of humor—happier staying home wanking his little doodle to internet porn. Loser! Mate, there was this time, I'm sticking it to Vitatas and Cat rings my mobile . . . Bear with me, for sure you wanna hear this story. V, the randy beaut, she's like, "It's Cat? Answer it." I'm like, Alright, darl, whatever floats your tinny. I'm trying to have a chat to Cat and Vitatas swallowing me balls deep . . . Hold on, bruv, this is relevant. Just inhaling me, my whole ten-incher—and I got a curve . . . Just a tick, mate, this is character development for your book. So, like, Cat knew something was going down. Lol. I leaned over to give her the shocker and she starts squealing, totally wanting to be heard—

(Muffled)

Mate! Mate, I'm just having you on. Just mucking about. Come off it. I'm starting to think you fancy the scallywhop. What happened to journalistic objectivity, mate? You want to get in there, hey? Just like, uhh-uhhhh—split that rumpled-slitskin. Dontcha?

(Muffled)

Okay! Alright! Calm down. Gee, you're bloody sensitive. And like, what do you mean, "hate her"? Like I said, mate, I'm appreciating her. Why, if she rang right now, I'd wash my pits and shave my balls and cane it to her place lickety-split. I was always chuffed being with her. Hundred percent. It was like . . . like this—one of my besties told me this once, whilst sailing. Remember Kathy Ireland? *Sports Illustrated*? Nineteen eighty-nine? Hella stacked? Feline eyes? Fully sick in a stars-and-stripes bikini? Yeah, that Kathy Ireland. So this bloke's shipwrecked with just her. Remote desert isle. Nothing but heaps of fresh fruit and coconut water. Rescue probs won't come before death and surely not before boredom. Best thing to do is root. So they root every morning. Root through the day. Root in the surf. Root beneath the Milky Way. A bloody dream come true for him. But one arvo, this, like, homing pigeon lands on the beach and the bloke grabs it. He knows he's got just one go to send a message to the world. Bloke scribbles something on their last piece of paper. Attaches it to the pigeon. Releases it into the sky. Bird flies over terrifying oceans. Dodges hawks and eagles. Grazes hunters' buckshot. Hides in caves during storms. Finally reaches his home coop, in like this naval station thousands of miles away. The ancient admiral's glad to see his pigeon. He greets it by name. Calls it old friend. He'd reckoned it was lost for sure. He's even more surprised to see a message attached to its leg. The admiral grabs it. Unrolls it. Takes out a honking-big magnifying glass. Reads the message carefully. It says: "Dude! I'm fucking Kathy Ireland!"

(Guffaw)

That's what it's like being with V. You know that feeling. Bloody fantastic. A real catch. Part of me wishes I could've stuffed and mounted her. Rather than just mounted and stuffed—okay, okay, okay. I'm just yanking your chain. You a bum bandit or something? Don't be so up yourself, darl. Let's change the subject. What you want to talk about? Seen any good movies lately? Read something stimulating in *The New Yorker*? Go for your life. Ask away.

(Muffled)

My folks? Not much to it. Bunch of dole bludgers, if I'm honest. My family tree was a cactus: everyone on it was a prick. Never could do anything right by them, so I was like see yous when I'm looking at yous. My old man, he was your typical unhappy battler—hard yakka, pub sanger, footy on the telly and Darwin stubby in his favorite risqué koozie. We dubbed him King Bazza, cuz he was always shouting from his throne in the dunny for me and my brother Wayne to listen to our mum. Couldn't even form a proper crap, that's how useless he was. Only thing he ever wanted for Father's Day was a good shit and a golden drinking ticket. My ol' cheese, on the other hand, was a rancid nellie in a wheelchair. She figured the world owed her for her legs. Princess Di, we called her, cuz she was doomed to unhappiness. I was like nine when I vowed to get far and never come back. This was during the only family holiday we ever took—Fantasy Glades. King Bazza up and disappeared while Princess Di made me and Wazza push her through the queues of kids. She wanted a go at every ride and whacked everyone aside with her cane. I never understood why people in wheelchairs get to go to the front of the queue. They're fucking sitting down. They don't have to stand around, shifting weight from hip to hip. My older brother Wazza's the only one I miss. Me and him were a pair of hairy-bum farm boys. He's a couple of sandwiches short of a picnic, but never said no to anyone who asked for a hand. Lazy fuckwit liked nothing better than hooning around in his fourth-hand Holden. I used to work in the drive-through at Hungry Crack's and every Saturday night he and his chick Schapelle rocked up to lean on his red Commodore like they were the ant's pants. An aggro gronk and chilled-out ranga, chain-smoking the Winnie Blues that Schazza pinched from the servo, cuz her boss was a tosspot. Match made in heaven, bless their fucking cottons. I'd look over like seeing my future, counting how many times he checked himself out in his tint, loving himself sick. I was that bored, and he did have a bonza mullet. An education in contrasts. Screamed: Yes, sir, sergeant! Go get stuffed! I couldn't wait to rack off. When I was ten I got on the local news, for driving our tractor twenty clicks till I ran out of petrol. Trying to get to South Africa, which shows what a minda I was, thinking South Africa was an improvement. Highlight of my childhood was when the cane toads came down. Eating through our fragile ecosystems. The council issued a reward for every toad killed. Me and Wazza had ourselves an Olympics. The salt heap. Dettol douse. Fire triple-jump. Cricket bat. Toad golf. Javelin roast on the barbie. Firecrackers up the butt. Suffocating them in bin liners. Bike squish. Tandem toss, which is tying two together by the legs and chucking them over the powerline—makes a hell of a stink when they rot. Invasive species aren't welcome in the Lucky Country. Like you Orientals, apparently—thanks to the likes of that cunt, Pauline Hanson and her Yellow Peril. Sounds like a fucking indie band, hey?

(Guffaw)

I left and never looked back. Not much to it. Ditched the paddocks and hitched a ride on a road train. Woke up in a hotel in Kings Cross covered in bedbugs. Pulled back the sheet and saw a gash in the bed filled with the buggers, like the devil's snatch. Fucking disgusting, but, like, the disgust felt real. Reckon there's no luxury like waking up disgusted and just racking off to somewhere new. I worked this boat owned by a pommy bastard, a real diamond geezer—that's what he called people most like him. Mate, I fucking loved the sea. And them alien lands. Not a bloody word familiar. Couldn't decipher a sign no matter how long you stared at it. No clue if you were eating beef, goat, or dog. Locals still uncomfortable wearing shoes. Fucking loved how everyone looked at me funny. So much better than at home, where everyone's expected to be the same height poppy. Can't you tell I'm one of a kind? They don't represent me. I washed up on these shores cuz yous speak English, and I stayed cuz your chaos agrees with me. Only thing that drives me bonkers: your fucking religion. Bloody gallahs, the lot of you. Vita gets molested by that bishop, rubbished by the Church, and still she believes? What a joke, mate. Look, if I said aliens come every night and chat to me, I'd be chucked into the loony bin. If I said I converse every night with fairies and dwarves, I'd be stark raving mad. But if I say I speak every night to this invisible being who grants my wishes and sent his only son to be butchered on a wooden cross for our salvation, then I'm pious? It's obedience forced out of blood sacrifice, titted up over the centuries. And you can't say anything about it else you get crucified. Lol. Ironic, hey? Mate, I know what I'm on about. I was Catholic, born and raised. My parents true-blue. Prayed the rosary whenever they needed something, which was all the fucking time. Sacrificed me to an all-boys Christian school, which just about ruined me. This one time, Year Four, we had a spirit rally for our footy squad, with this raffle for a stereo. Every student's name got chucked into a lucky-dip box. Mr. Fallon, the principal, would draw the winner. I really wanted that stereo. Princess Di was always hogging the one in the front room, just cuz she couldn't walk. So, like, I start praying. Please God, let me win the stereo. I'll be good to ol' mum and dad. Never miss confession. I'll fucking quit swearing. I told God: If you let me win, I'll always believe in you. Mr. Fallon stuck his hand in. Pulled out a slip of paper. I was like, Please, Mama Mary, order your son to give it to me! I begged Jesus. I even begged the Holy Spirit, who I never paid mind to before.

Mr. Fallon read the name out. Crikey, mate, it was mine—a bloody fucking miracle! I'd spoken to God and He replied. Fucked me up for years, I was such a believer. Till I wondered why He never answered my prayers about me mum's legs. Or my dad's stroke. I blamed myself, cuz you can't blame God. I sat by ol' Bazza's bedside, listening to the machines breathe for him. My strong dad reduced to a lump of wired flesh. I prayed and still got a vegetable for a father, so it must've been my fault. What kind of prick god gives you a bloody stereo instead of what really matters? After a while, I was like, Fuck God. Fuck that cunt Mary. Fuck the little baby Jesus up his motherfucking fairy ass. Spent years in that trap, mate. Hating God's still holier than not believing in Him. Vita called me an unbeliever, but that's not true. You have to believe in something to hate it. Now I know enough to believe in something real. We're our own gods, you know? You're the only one who can control your life, brother. You want a god who's both mortal and immortal? Have a gander in the mirror. We invented God in our own image.

(Muffled)

What do you mean, do I believe V? Shit yeah. I say believe all victims, even if she don't look like one. Fuck that Bishop Baccante. Seen it before, too. Firsthand. Bestie in Year Eight was this bloke named Hector. Broken family. Half-Abo. Acting the dill in class for attention. We got on right off. We had this teacher, Paulo. Good Catholic wog who set the town's girls buzzing when he arrived. Everyone loved him. A real nutter. He'd sneak up on kids and hoist them over his shoulder like a sack of potatoes, make like sticking you in the recycling bin. Even when he'd catch us smoking behind the big gum, he'd just stand and have a chat to yous about whatever, never dobbing anyone in. I always stood in his line at mass cuz it was nice having him smile at you and place the host on your tongue. Paulo gave a whole lot more to kids like Hector. He gave sanctuary. They did homework at his place after school. Parents even left their kids with him when they went to the pub. I used to rock up on my BMX cuz something was always happening— a cricket match, shooting tins with his flash new BB gun, taking turns at Sonic on the Sega. I always had to leave early for tea and hated seeing Hector on the lounge beside Paulo, neither of them looking up from the telly to say see you tomorrow. So when Hector told Mr. Fallon that Paulo put his fingers down his underdaks—not once, but thrice—yeah, mate, like, the whole town believed old pious Paulo. Hector was making shit up. Poor sod. Years later, turns out Paulo groomed heaps of kids. Slowly, from like horseplay to, like, hugs and caresses, over months. Why you think this shit comes out so long after? Nobody believes the kids. They're always mistaking harmless affection. But, like, real talk: Hector told me about it before anyone and I kept it to myself. It's fucked-up, but I didn't want him taking all the attention again. So yeah, I believe V about that bishop and his fake fatherlyness. Hundred percent. She didn't deserve that. There's a sweet part to her, I'll give her that. Those quiet moments when we got to talking, honest like. She'd read me poetry from that Rita Rajah chick. Or yabber on about her own dreams. Said she was afraid to meet her dad, but only cuz she was scared she'd be disappointed by him. Said that would break her heart. If that's even possible.

(Silence)

So, like, what did she say about yours truly?

(Muffled)

Yeah, nah, seriously, go on then. Give us a try. I can take it.

(Muffled)

You're fucking joking. She said that? What fucking arse-piss! Don't believe it for a second. Besides, what matters is I didn't fake mine. Reckon if you can make a sexy slurry lie about orgasms, you're golden. Any wanker can pay a slag for sex. How many can get a prozzie to lie for free about loving it? What a fucking smegma gobbler. I wouldn't fuck her with your di—

(Muffled)

Aw, come on, mate. Mate! Don't be such a cuck. You've got to be joking. It's fucking pouring out there.

(Muffled)

Yeah? Well, bugger off then. Both of yous. Loose cunt'll give you herpes just like she—Hold on, that's off the record, mate. I . . . Aw, fuck it.

(Microphone friction)

. . . Fuck you and your fake news; I got more followers than you. Fuck your small-dick energy, disrespecting me like this. I just ripped one in your sad-ass car . . .

(Door slam)

(Silence)

(Knocking)

(Window hums)

Hey—hey, mate . . . Mate, take it easy . . . I'm not trying to get back in your stinking Daewoo—

(Door handle clacking)

Would you just . . . Hey, hold on . . . fucking stop the car just a tick—

(Knocking)

Would you just—

(Banging)

Hey, just fucking . . . Mate, just fucking pop the fuckin—

(Hollow pounding)

Hey, pop the fucking boot . . . I need to—Mate! My bags, mate—

(Hard pounding)

Why you gotta be such a dick?

(Window hums shut)

Vita Nova Transcript: 7 of 13.

(43:32.03—VN7.M4A)

Well, well, well—look do we have here. So Nando's not running after all—imagine? Because colon cancer. But can you believe he's snubbed Farrah—his own daughter—and endorsed Junior?

(Inaudible)

I know, right? That son-of-a-dictator's gonna struggle to make daddy deadest proud, up against Rolex, and Glorioso, Lontok, and Nur, and especially Dr. Rita Rajah, who'll steal the Muslim vote—and maybe my support, coz I'm still not sure I want to be Nur's veep on the Liberty Party ticket. I won't be used again. Besides, would I even be a contender? Look at those ninety-eight other strivers, destined to be disqualified by the COMELEC as nuisance presidential candidates—though bless them for dancing into their moment in the circle, in our disco democrazy. Coz every citizen deserves to stand at the podium and challenge the powerful, right? Even the rocker who goes by Archangel Luciferus—ordered by his "master," quote unquote, to be the whistleblower on all our country's sins. Or that engineering student envisioning a plexiglass dome over Mega Manila, for air-con and increased productivity. Or the self-proclaimed future prince of Caress Reyes, that stalkery guy who campaigned for her brother, and watched every episode of her talk show at least twice. Or even Padre Laverno Kidohboy, the so-called "anointed Son of God," whose Kingdom of Faith in Christ rose to fame on copyright confusion over its initials and branding in food courts everywhere—I saw him on TV last night, pushing his old claim that his invocation stopped that earthquake in the North seconds after it started, saving hundreds more lives (though he couldn't stop his own detainment in Hawaii with that plane-load of cash—remember that?). But *my* fave's that grandfather who was pulled from the podium, weeping for our country, saying only a poor guy like him from a community like his knows what a nation like ours really needs; so moving, and very true. But some Orions out there say these so-called nuisance candidates are proof we need a higher threshold—like our politics should be even less inclusive. But what about those sure losers with winning ideas worth talking about? That civil servant and his blueprint to reform the Social Security System. Or the law prof with that plan to abolish dynasties.

(Plastic crinkling)

It's up to the COMELEC now to deliberate then disqualify those who can't mount a realistic national campaign, or are mockers of the democratic process, or are paid voter-confusers with convenient names— the Roxel Aguirres, Fanfilo Lintiks, and Gloria Makupal Arraykos of this world. I say bless them all for refusing to live in the margins of our shared story. Hey, maybe you should run, too. Make your father proud! Be my vice prez. Joke! Can you imagine me as president? This week's gonna be hella interesting, before the deadline to file candidacies. All the commotion at the starting gate. Only Lontok's declared his running mate already: Lucy, naturellement. So we got six days till the rest announce their veeps. Thirteen till campaigning starts. Twenty before parties finalize any substitutions for their candidates. Exciting!

(Inaudible)

No, not just coz Dr. Rajah's a woman; I support her because she's an activist, a human rights lawyer, and the public prosecutor who wasn't scared to investigate Nando's kids. She beat cancer, and has totally made up for running with Junior last election, and she lives like she's got nothing to lose. Yas, queen! Besides, you can't hide your true self when you write like she does. Her poetry saved me, actually, when I was with Rolex. And she's been such a mentor these past years—going from my Facebook pen pal to sitting on the boards of two of my foundations. Did you know I was the one who got her to do the ice-bucket challenge? Actually, if there's anyone you should interview, it's her—she'd be responsible with my story. So, no: gender doesn't matter—character does. We need a leader, finally, who's not from the so-called elite. I'm super grateful to Nur for his offer, but I think leadership should be by example—like sometimes knowing when to follow those who can do better.

(Lighter click. Exhalation)

He'll be hella disappointed—my not running, with my army of fans. But when I dumped Rolex I made myself two promises, knowing I'd never find happiness till I kept them.

(Inaudible)

His chances? Rolex just runs so he can sell his percentage of the vote to the highest bidder, as per yoozh. Question is: This time, who can promise big enough? "I'm a man of appetites," he told me, in the beginning, and we all know his appetite's for everything. Mayor, congressman, senator, longtime governor—what kingmaker's not finally tempted to be king? After all those years so close—mah-jongg buddy to Nando, who got a taste for blood through boxing, just like him. Nando always royalty, he could really stick and move—and did, to the top—while Rolex was the dodgy brawler, in rural beer gardens, against bullies picking fights with the former governor's son. A huge chip on his shoulder, from the very beginning. To escape his father's shadow, and the burden of his widowed mother, Rolex bought a one-way ticket on a steamer to Honolulu, to become a paniolo, a Hawaiian cowboy. But just as he's leaving, in town for one last rodeo, a bull escapes and runs down main street, right into a mirror factory, Rolex running after and roping it in one go. And when it turns to charge him, Rolex stares at all the rampaging bulls, bets which one is real, and throws a single punch, knocking it out cold—proving his credentials to govern, and getting elected mayor. Because of course. His campaign slogan till this day: "No bull."

(Inaudible)

Yup, this was the hotel he owned—back when his wife was warming his governor seat and him and his son, Abex, were in Congress and needed digs here in the capital. You really don't want anything? Green-tea frappuccino? So, yeah, upstairs, in the penthouse suite, that's where we first met in private, though it's not what you think, I honestly had no clue—to me it was just dinner. We'd met on the set of the biopic he was producing—*Rolex: The Man for Our Time.* I was playing his wife, Abiola, filming in the central market of Abiolaville—that scene of the second assassination attempt during his first run for governor, when Rolex shoved his bodyguard to safety and jumped into the crossfire to save the little orphan girl who ran out to save a mommy cat who ran out to save her kittens. The director had just called cut, and everyone was congratulating me and Birdie Patilya, who was playing Rolex, and the stunt crew was reversing the army jeep from the fish stalls, and PAs were chasing kittens, and there were fish bits on everyone and fake blood in my hair and clothes. Suddenly, the real Rolex strides onto set, clapping like a flamenco dancer, coming to shake my hand. And me, starstruck speechless. Here was the man with *the* best hero-origin story: leading a resistance brigade against the Japanese when he was only thirteen; taking five bullets in his back while saving that orphan with Down syndrome; grabbing the governorship, once and for all, from the clan who'd fought his family for three generations; and relocating the provincial capital to a city he built from scratch. Rolex slaps Birdie on the back—all like, "The resemblance is uncanny—though I was naturally athletic"—then smooches my hand loudly for all to see. "You look exactly like young Abiola," says he, "only ten times more beautiful!" I know, right? Must've been mad eye rolls from the crew, though I was too dazzled by his bright smile—realizing only later his gold tooth was glinting in the sun. (Even that: kinda pimpin'.) Afterwards, I'm in my trailer, combing fish scales from my hair, when there's a knock on my door. First thing I see is sunshine and an umbrella, held up by a driver in uniform, and out from its shade steps Rolex, extending a gallant written request for the honor of my company at dinner when we return to Manila. "I'm sure you'll go on to win a Golden Durian," says he, "but only if you truly understand your character. I can help." And that's how I find myself fetched by his driver, a week later, blurring through this lobby and taking deep breaths before inserting the keycard and pushing *P* on the elevator— its doors closing on all the chattering Koreans in matching sun visors, my reflection coming together to look at me like one last warning, as I rise and rise with my stomach trailing till it catches up and I shrink an inch, my reflection splitting to reveal the Emperor's Suite: Rolex waiting at a table with white padded cloth and bubbles of glass and a chorus line of silver cutlery, two waiters at attention like Mr. Carson and Barrow in *Downton Abbey.*

(Inaudible)

Yeah, hella surprised Abiola wasn't there. But Rolex, to his credit, was a perfect gent—his thin hair neatly striped across his head, his barong immaculately tailored around his roundness. He got up—awkwardly—and pulled my chair. Complimented my blouse—his word. And we stood small-talking for a good while before I decided to sit down. I was relieved it was more like a private dining room, with the door closed to the bedroom and the bed a forgotten fear, and these huge windows and the cityscape jangling across—making me feel somehow hidden and on full display, which was surprisingly not uncomfortable. I'd never seen Manila from that height. Or been treated like a real lady. And the food—wow, the food. Before that I thought the term molecular gastronomy had something to do with intestinal cancer. His personal chef was a Spaniard with a cocaine and ego problem that got him fired from the world's finest kitchens. All so exciting. This first dinner happened around the time I was losing faith in showbiz. Like, the fans still loved me but the media was relentless—about the wardrobe malfunction while shooting for Wildcat Deodorant, and going out with an African American, and my post–*3-Poll Threat* success that they implied wasn't deserved. I was having a legit quarter-life crisis and was looking for ways to diversify—like starting a sunglasses and perfume line, or running for office. So I listened, like I do, and Rolex talked, like he loves to. He thinks his entire life's a teachable moment. I gotta say, his stories were inspiring: giving up his father's cattle farm, entering public service his own way, building his security guard company into the country's biggest, and getting into construction and real estate, all for his sons. Took me months to realize the cowboy'd wrangled himself political power, a private army, and a cash cow for kickbacks from his new provincial capital, built far from his enemies. But, like, don't most big politicians legitimize their, um, entrepreneurial instincts? Look at Lontok and the Villas and SuperMegaOceanic Co.; and Nando with the Changco brothers' media empire; and Reyes and the sugar barons; and Junior's fam with the taipans who laundered the billions that family hid in Switzerland. In the car, after dinner, the driver bringing me home, it hit me that Rolex never asked me about myself, not once—but he did mention several times that I was an excellent conversationalist. Thing is, for some reason, I wanted him to know me. So a second dinner followed, then a third, and a fourth—him calling each time with a new enticement: a sushi chef flying in with a shipment from Tsukiji market ("When I think of fish," Rolex said, "I think of you!"); or a bottle of Moskovskaya from the Russian ambassador and a tin of caviar ("Sterlet," he said, "like you!"); or a case of Cristal champagne ("I've heard you love Negro culture!"). I know, right? What was I thinking? So young, so naive, so willing to be wowed by his attentions. Sigh. Did you know that Cristal was created for King William of Prussia—for his Three Emperors Dinner with Prince Otto von Bismark and Tsar Alexander II and his son, in Paris—in clear bottles, so that no bombs could be hidden? Guess transparency's actually important, huh?

(Inaudible)

Of course I did—all those other stories: his gambling empire; his amulet against bombs, bullets, and blades; the wrist casts he made his son Xelor wear to cure him of being gay. Or having a northern white rhino lured outside a nature reserve for his seventieth birthday hunt. Or shooting Aguinaldo the Eagle, who used to nest by the eleventh hole at Manila Golf—swapping his rifle for a two-iron and telling his caddy to stick the bird in a cooler to be taxidermied later. And of course, how he treated Abiola—all his shameless cheating, and that time he caught her beating a sulky maid with a stingray tail, in an exorcism he said was sinful, and he whipped them both with it so badly the incident earned a Kitschy Katigbak blind item. Rolex has no problem with betrayal—expects it, even—but don't you dare embarrass him. Remember when Changco's papers photographed him with three girls at Cupid's Hydro Massage, and Abiola got back at him, all smoochy-smoochy with her dance instructor in a private booth in Where Else? Remember what he told the media when asked to comment on their hospitalizations? "Be glad I didn't kill them." Me, if I were her, I would've left him; but I totally get it—Rolex's intoxicating cocktail of tenderness and danger. And he treated me so well; plus it's exciting, not getting caught. Abiola was the one who scared me, actually. Like any fierce, philandered matrona, she relishes using her strength, usually deliciously dramatically—extinguishing many a starlet, grounding many a stewardess, ruining many an application to elite kindergartens. Long before becoming one of the most powerful congresswomen ever, she was the most faithful of the Dictator's wife's Pink Ladies—the haughty courtier who stayed to face the mobs and protect the Palace artwork the night the First Family fled. Till today, Abiola can set a party amurmur with her breezy arrival—people more comfortable fearing her husband than fearing her. I always wondered how she got so tough.

(Lighter click. Exhalation)

For Roly I felt . . . I guess, pure sympathy—which can feel like forgiving someone who's so obviously unhappy. On our fifth dinner in his penthouse suite, after discussing the next day's pivotal scene—when he strode from Congress to the Palace through a lightning storm, to tear up a bill restricting settlers and dump it on the Dictator's desk—Rolex takes my hand over the crêpes suzette and asks to continue seeing me. I say something like, Of course, Absolutely, We're friends—his expression getting super earnest. He's like: "Vita, dear girl, you must know how much I admire you. I have a secret not even my wife knows. Will you safeguard it?" And I'm like, Absolutely, Of course, Tell me. "The Lord blessed us through our uncanny collision," says he, "because I have only three months to live. My last wish is to taste, one final time, that feeling of love with an amazing woman." And silly me, I said yes. To a man thrice my age, who hollers into his cell phone like it's a can attached to a string. Who speaks such fancy nosebleed English, even though his accent gets him subtitled on TV. The outsider never welcomed in the capital's glittering social circles—just like me. Three months came and went for us, and death didn't come for Rolex. "God's miracle!" said he. A miracle named Vita. "Finally I have something to live for, and the credit is wholly yours." He'd pay me back, somehow, he said. And I fell for it, like an Olympic diver. Loving the flood of flowers in my trailers and dressing rooms—with their poetic notes, always in different handwriting. And the lavish Wednesday penthouse dinners—with their sweet endings, me popping Teuscher champagne truffles one by one, as two by two he popped pills for gout, GERD, and hypertension. And how we'd sit together on the bed to sing videoke—

Roly serenading with his signature "Bésame Mucho." At first, I refused his extravagant gifts: the mink teddy bear inside a pink balloon; a rose-gold Pearlmaster for my Golden Durie nomination; the sterling box of Turkish delight flown from Istanbul after I mentioned I'd betray siblings for some. Till Boy said people were judging me, "coz a mistress sans swag is just a homewrecker into saggy seniors." That's when I realized that's what I was: a mistress. Not just a lover, as I called him. Or partner in crime, as he called me. I was his mistress—the other woman.

(Inaudible)

It wasn't easy, I won't lie. Not so much because I cared; more coz others did. What my mother thought still mattered, even though we hadn't talked for years. Whatever little integrity I've got, I learned from her— single mom, working by day in the air base canteen, by night our community's seamstress, all the neighbors treating us with such respect (they had to: she knew their measurements). Admired most, by one and all, for her self-reliance. Mama could fix any item, mend any situation, and even had a side business to her side business, buying from the PX store the Stateside snacks that weren't available here—Butterfinger, Cheetos, Jelly Belly—to resell on our street. Even running a lending library from our house, with the books and magazines abandoned by soldiers who shipped out—*Time* and *National Geographic*, my first portals to the world. Plus she had the greenest thumb, the veggies from her hanging gardens making me strong. And she was so much fun, always game to play with me. (Only when I filled out her death certificate did I realize she was so young.) Scrabble was her fave, which is why I'm so darned good at it—the strategy is many little words hugging what's already on the board, and never giving your opponents openings, and planning your next move at the expense of this one—I could never beat that jiujitsu master. Most of all, Mama loved music—when she sewed, I'd cut patterns, and we'd duet—especially country western, with its tragedy and defiance. The way she sang "Jolene" broke your heart. ♬ *Your voice is soft like summer rain, and I cannot compete with you, Jolene . . .* ♬ So beautiful, my mother. Sometimes I'd tease her about finding a man—or partner, I realize; back then my mind was still shut in its heteronormativity. Mama would just harumph: "Why bother?"

she'd say, "I have you." I loved that—just her and me and the universe that orbited us: Joe, who owned the corner store, and taught me guitar; RJ, the neighborhood ngongo, who we all saved up for one year to get his harelip fixed, sorta; and all the parlor's ladies and gentlegays, who were our family; and Tita Henny, of course, who'd come over after closing to tell us the latest, though Mama just listened, laughing politely but never cruelly, never adding or commenting, coz deep down she didn't believe in gossip, though she never judged Tita Henny for it. Even when Loy came into the picture, and I started to change, Mama treated him like a son. Teaching by example. We never spoke about it, when we were finally speaking again, about the simmering scandal of me and Rolex that drew a bright red *A* on my chest—after Abiola got suspicious (when he started trimming his ear hair), and caught us in his suite months later ("Well, well, well," said she), then spilled the milk to the media (who lapped it up). I knew Mama hated even thinking about it, but not because he was untrue to his wife. "If you can't be true to yourself," she always told me growing up, "who can you be true to?" So when me and Loy left for the big city, I thought she'd understand that I was being true to my dreams—though that's what hurt her most, I think: knowing she wasn't included in them. At least for a while. Then my shame kept me away so much longer.

(Lighter click. Exhalation)

After we made friends again we spent eleven days together—as in straight—bingeing, from start to finish, on every season we missed from each other's lives. It was hard, and we tried until it became easy. She'd become an antidrug Zumba instructor and we'd dance in my living room till the neighbors banged on my floor. We talked about everything, except my time with Rolex. She never asked and so I always knew. You know how it is: there comes a time when the ones who love you most understand you least, because they know who you were, not who you're becoming—still seeing who they hoped you'd be, not who you've become. So you hide things, for your sake, and theirs. Like when you first keep secrets from your parents—not those lies to save you from trouble, but those things you leave out to not trouble them. You remember that moment, right? That end, of something . . . childhood? The start of what you think is adulthood, until she's gone. When Mama found out about me and Nur, from that Kitschy Katigbak blind item, I couldn't reach her, she wouldn't pick up—next thing I know, I'm walking in a warehouse among rows of bloated bodies, searching for the Versace blouse I bought her, which she'd wear whenever she was by the sea. Blue and white, with knots and anchors and life preservers all over. That's how I found her. My mother. Her name was Serena. We had hardly a year back together. I'd waited too long. But I had to. I just did.

(Silence)

Truth is, all relationships are transactional. I hate to admit. Some give you joy and guilt, some give headaches and fulfillment. You see a mom or dad giving their kids everything and you can't help but wonder who they're really doing it for. Rolex thought he deserved a world's-best-dad trophy for sending Xelor to that expensive clinic for "reparative therapy," quote unquote, to "cure him," quote unquote. And he taught Abex and Patek how to be efficiently corrupt, just like papa. Same gift he offered me, helping start New Life Distributing—providing uniforms and supplementary educational materials to public schools. That's Rolex's style of largeness: giving what he thinks you need, not what you ask for. Like government gigs to his reliable madams and the mistresses he could no longer see—gifted opportunities in a chauvinistic world. Alongside his code of honor for his philandering: never haggle with a prostitute, or safely use the same pet name for each girl. (Unlike Nando's Estreganettes, all called "my queen.") Rolex was so proud of his loyalty to Abiola—never abandoning her, claiming that other women made him appreciate her more, and that the extra he got elsewhere helped him accept her shortcomings. I really hope, somehow, that he knows by now that his deepest selfishness was the absence of his presence, which she deserved. And that his greatest failure isn't so much to his wife as it is to the man he thought he'd be. Deep, no?

(Laughter)

Maybe that's what you need to do as a provider—convince yourself you're the best, coz the best is what your loved ones deserve. Like that mother with a crying baby in the plane snarking back at your sleepless glare: "You'll understand when you get here." Like Junior's loony mother gushing about being the grandmother of our nation. And Fernando grumpily embracing his supporters calling him Papa Nando.

When you take upon yourself such burdens, any criticism, any opposition, becomes painfully personal. And that's how a leader becomes a ruler becomes a dictator: fooling yourself about the value of your selfless intentions. After all Mama's sacrifices for me, she deserved to believe exactly that: that she'd done everything right. And so I accepted all the blame for leaving with Loy, for leaving her alone. And when I did finally meet my father, no way could I forgive him, coz if me and Mama weren't free, he didn't deserve to be, either. Freedom—that's what Rolex said I deserved, and tried to give me. Like his empty condo he asked me to maintain by staying in till the rental market picked up. Like financing my acting-directing debut, *Demonia*, to help him diversify into film producing. Like setting up my New Life Distributing with contacts, consulting, and government contracts—Rolex getting fifty-five-all (that's fifty-five percent), while the rest of the SOPs (standard operating procedures) were kicked back to everyone else: the companies who made uniforms and flashcards, maps and posters; the clerks at the Ministry of Education; even my competitors, who got a little something something for not undercutting my bid when it wasn't their turn. The pricing strategy Rolex taught me I dubbed the Hemline Equation: raise it so high you can't lose. My own take-home, just twenty-all, was more than I'd make shooting a movie. When I testified about this, at the impeachment, it was like a great weight fell away. But I don't think Rolex feels betrayed by me. He always advised: "If your conscience bothers you in private, do your penance in public." Like read to school kids, or establish charities, but never sacrifice my interests, coz that only benefits my competitors. "Money's dirty like a mop is dirty, but you need a mop to clean up a filthy world." Which was classic Rolex: justifying the lines he crosses, especially by drawing the ones he won't. "Don't get involved with textbooks, or desks, et cetera," he'd say. "Necessities are sacrosanct. Be a good Christian." And I believed him—at first coz I wanted his final three months to be happy, then because I'd come to care. Aren't love and pity strangely related? Like, don't you think he wanted to be a good man to Abiola? That once upon a time they were madly in love? Coz it always starts so wonderfully, till one fight she retaliates, unsheathing her tongue, saying that all these years she only forced herself, that she pried open her legs out of necessity. "Forced herself; pried open her legs"—words Roly told me he couldn't forget. Words that made me love him more. Coz there's nothing more tragic than dead love, especially in a society where divorce is forbidden. "Fidelity's a terminal sentence," he said to me, when he didn't die.

(Inaudible)

How'd I know you'd ask that? Feeling close, huh? No, actually, never. Not even once. Just look at him: in a TV ad he's not so much the silvery Viagra guy on a salsa-dancing date; he's the granddad out hiking with those weird ski poles, confident and comfortable in improved diapers. Honestly, Roly would just talk, I'd just listen. I would ask, he'd advise. His moonshot meals, his verbal flights of fancy, his circling digressions that seem pointless till you think about it after—*that's* sex to him, which you'll see when you interview him, since you insist. At least you'll be well-fed. The few times we tore off each other's clothes and rushed achingly to the bed were so I could rub efficascent oil over his arthritic joints, which was more intimate, in a way. I even wrote a poem, about untying knots, tracing rivery veins, the scars like borders, and ghosts of bullet holes like bombed-out cities across his body's yellowing map of who he was. Me and Roly recognized that courtship's the most erotic part of romance—without even touching: the formality of dressing up, zhuzhing hair, spritzing scent, finding each other in the dimness of the bar. Who doesn't love sitting across your date, seeing yourself reflected in their face? Sharing silence as the sommelier uncorks the wine? Synchronizing spoonfuls of foie gras, eyes closed to hum a duet of mmms? Is there anything wrong with accepting what the person you love offers?

(Pause)

Seriously. I'm asking—is there? I loved him and I took what he gave, and he did exactly the same. I was happy with my independence and our semisettled stability; I couldn't be bothered with anyone else . . . Well, sometimes LeTrel—coz who can quit a mystery you can't crack?

(Laughter)

Old-school shenanigans nobody can get away with today, with our smartphones and social media. But don't you think it's at all romantic, spiraling into forbidden love? Sharing a secret? Expanding each other's experiences, beyond your life that was so complete until they walked in? Isn't that more meaningful than, like, hooking up with someone single and sick of having to mingle? Honestly, I admired Rolex's loyalty to Abiola, but I won't lie: sometimes I just wanted his promises to me to be more important than his promises to her. People usually think mistresshood is the ultimate tragedy—the word *mistress*, in our culture, a bygone conclusion. What's its opposite? *Master.* Mistresses are mastered. Our only tools: affections and tantrums, threats and truth. You're the ultimate luxury, but luxury's always extra—extraordinary or extraneous. Birthdays, holidays, sometimes it felt like independence was the terminal sentence. I remember one Valentine's Day, all my messages on his beeper going from sweet to angry, and suddenly I'm parked outside his house, getting cold feet when the guard walks over, ending up in the mall hoping all the consumerism would convince me of that day's meaninglessness. And it was there, beneath all the hearts decorating National Book Store, where I stumbled upon *Etiquette for Mistresses*, by Jullie Yap Daza—which the whole town was talking about. Unethical, they said, undermining family values. But to me it was clouds parting for heavenly light and angel song. I read half in the aisle then half in the car. What a relief, knowing I wasn't the first to chart this course through this folly, with all its compromises and fever dreams that few dare to understand. Thanks Goddess I wasn't the only one stumbling under hope and all its expectations. Like, following his schedule coz maybe one day he'll follow yours. Like, committing to the sometimes coz maybe one day he'll commit to the always. Convinced that being better is the best way to be equal. Thing is, did I actually want any of that? Just coz a little bit's amazing doesn't mean more will be amazeballs. Love should never be that confusing.

(Silence)

But no regrets—except how sad the way we ended. That day I was at a public school, reading to kids, and I ask to see the desks from New Life Distributing, but the students are like Siamese triplets behind the old ones, and the principal takes me aside, sucks his teeth, and explains. That evening Rolex brings Abiola to my premiere, of *Demonia*—remember that rotten tomato? "*Demonia*, a tale of lust and deception. *Demonia*, the story of a good girl gone bad. When society comes between her and true love, she becomes a . . . demonia!"—the two of them front-row center, and I'm introducing the film from the podium, Abiola staring like she's just realized but isn't sure. That night, I couldn't sleep, thinking about what was coming for him—alone again with his pain, surrounded by suck-ups waiting for handouts, his sons as demanding as they're ungrateful, a wife who despises him, and their hatred that was also a sort of empathy—driving them apart, pulling them together. I was always—*always*—the only one free to walk away. Next day, Rolex is of course refusing. His pleas fill the penthouse, about all that I owe him, and cutting off the contracts for my business, and taking back my condo that very night. Coz when you tame something, you want to be the hero who sets it free. And to a man of appetites, with all the riches in the world, your final hunger is for heroism. People say I'm a lot of nasty things, but one thing I know I'm not is an ingrate—so I gave him that much: thanking him, taking his hand, telling him, Go home to your family, before you really die, go make it up to Abiola—his wife's voice behind me suddenly ringing clear and loud. "Well, well, well," says she, "look do we have here—demonia!" I turn to face Abiola, looking me up and down, and we both know what's next. I'm in the elevator by the time they started screaming old blame at each other—Rolex shouting, "She seduced me!"—the doors closing, my reflection becoming whole again, and I felt myself grow taller as I fell into a memory from my favorite book, *The Alchemist*: "The Soul of the World is nourished by people's happiness. And also by unhappiness, envy, and jealousy. To realize one's destiny is a person's only real obligation." The doors opening and the day bright. And that's why I never regretted those years. And why I was true to myself, even with Red, and Father Yoda, and onwards.

(Inaudible)

My two promises to myself? Let's just say the first I intend to keep— you're watching me live it; it's well on its way. The second: to never again be a mistress. I know, right? And I oop.

Governor Rolex Aguirre Transcript.

(170:52.69—Aguirre.M4A)

Respeto! Bring the rouge for our guest! God maketh "wine that gladdens the heart of man," though Rolex alone madeth our country's wine industry. This is our signature Chateau René-Pogel, a plushy Syrah from terraces hewn into limestone foothills above my ranch. Enjoy, please. As I explain this slapstick sarswela. Everything is under control, we just don't know whose. Please, let us be relaxed. My back brings me grief. Have you ever fired a harpoon at a whale? We have connections in the Chukotka Autonomous Okrug. Spine-rattling, but you feel like an Ahab vindicated. Now that America is drowning itself, we must dance with Russia. Respeto! You forgot the amuse-bouche! We must spell things out for this twinkletoes. But I am tolerant. At least he will never betray me for a woman. The poor boy's pathology is Satan's plan to eradicate humanity; nobody can get pregnant in that hole. I hired him when Reyes became president. Respeto! Inform Chef Toogy we are ready! Good food, the fulfillment of public service, the Lord's providence: nourishments in our ninth decade. When I was younger, Vita would pester: "Take care of yourself!" That now is my modus operandi, with my tai chi, jigsaw puzzles, avoiding stress, every year making pilgrimage to Villa Medica, in Edenkoben, Südliche Weinstraße. Fresh-cell therapy, injections from the organs of lamb feti. Abiola warns I will grow sheeplike. "Baaa!" I reply. Life is too short to not live boldly. Vita used to rub my potbelly, as if it's not a boast of vitality. Do you dare pick a fight with a DOM with love handles and a clutch bag containing a Glock? Of course you don't. Six-packs are for homosexuals. Self-respect is what I strive to reclaim for our people. Independence, defiance in the face of China, that is our pride, after centuries being colonized. Estregan making vassals of our people was the camel's last straw. Filipinos excel too much in service, forgetting that respectability comes from will alone. Fernandito became popular through his joke book about his own ineptitude; as calculating as young Vita. Though if you stoop, how do you pull others up? Despite all I did to empower her—opportunities, books, linguistic tutelage, etceteras—she maintains her youthful tricks: her weaponized I-love-yous, her dramatic departures wielded like a baseball bat. She is still as stunning as an Akhal-Teke, with her laugh as lively as a dinner party, though her smile now is sharp with time's cruelty. After the darkness of a discotheque you might lay with her, though in the light of the morning wonder how beautiful she used to be. Past her prime, the time passed for a decent husband, or shaking her bottom on the television. Though now independent and finally better than I envisioned: a worthy adversary. And legally old enough to aspire to the Palace. There is only one way for people like she and I to escape the powerlessness of poverty. Following the Laws of God—capital *L*, capital *G*. Assiduus usus uni rei deditus et ingenium et artem saepe vincit. Always that way. I learned this when the Virgin Mary informed me of my destiny. Respeto! Please kindly obtain my coffee-table book about Abiolaville! You can gaze upon all we built, despite the laws of men, and what they regard as hubris. Ozymandias, they called me, those same people who made assumptions, because Vita is no fortress. But alas, even then, at my age, the only intercourse you crave is spirited debate. A stroke can betray the bravest heart; the Lord our God had already blessed me with three score and eight years of pleasure before that. Only a fool does not change with seasons. How liberating to shed the leaves of desire, of distraction. When you fear your body will betray you, adoration becomes better than sex. As sloppy sometimes but much less wet. I turned instead to a different erection, a city built from a swamp, as you will see— Respeto! You illiterate flitterer! This one is *Rolex: Tropical Caesar*! Fetch *Abiolaville: City of Dreams*! Almost as retarded as his namesake—Aha! So cometh our first course: mint and pea mousse, I see, cooked tableside in liquid nitrogen. Careful, Respeto! We pair this with the Domaine Barmès-Buecher's 2019 Gewürztraminer Herrenweg—because we are men enough for a spicy Gewürz.

(Pouring)

Mabuhay!

(Glasses clink)

As I was saying: Vita was only a companionable masseuse; much more palatable than the cows at the golf club spa, with their acid reflux and heels like cheese rinds. Her succulent body a blessed lever, consoling me, her faint grunts only a fond reminder of my passionate yesteryears. Through her supple hands the Lord revealed immense wisdom: that life's greatest pleasure is the cessation of pain. Better even than vengeance, for my critics are not even worth killing. Baaa! A lion does not concern himself with the opinions of sheep, as Vita used to advise. I was a rebel, a populist, self-taught, like our Christ, guided by God's Law of Morality—capital *L*, capital *M*. It designs our destiny's true path, beyond the pompous legislations of mankind. As Reverend Kidohboy teaches: "We sinners cannot blame God for testing our weakness." Divine law is clear: Accept Jesus as Lord and Savior and He will forgive you—but first you must deserve it. Estregan prostrated himself to the Catholic bishops only to make pawns of them, before betraying them and the country with his so-called Reproductive Rights Bill. Just as the Communist writer Furio Almondo hides behind man's laws of free speech, defaming us holy vessels, brainwashing Vita, and encouraging her to take up with that Islamist terrorist, Nuredin, who uses her as his beard; really he is only her fashion accessory—like a hat, or a handbag, or a homosexual friend who cracks audacious jokes. Vita's fame shall prove toothless, as the Law of Necessity—capital *L*, capital *N*—reveals the necessities of the people as the supreme dictatum. Leadership has been as absent as Fernandito. By sacrificing ourselves as turncoats, Kingsley and I proved that democracy is too important to be a popularity contest. All Filipinos are my family. When they are sickly, suffering, I am sick, I suffer. My wife, my two living sons, we are only stewards. In my heart I am not Ozymandias but a Cincinnatus, called to save his homeland—task completed, he relinquishes his dictatorial powers and returns to his farm. Respeto! Second course! Respeto! My wife says I should tinkle that bell to summon him, but that's undignified even for a tinkerb—Oho! Here comes our medley of three caviars, brought from my trip—ossetra, sevruga, beluga, with steamed La

Ratte potato and crème fraîche, from the blessings of our garden and ranch. Try, try . . . The salty creaminess is exciting against the potato's nuttiness. Chef Toogy suggests Perrier-Jouët, though I prefer my own Grand Curvy, in its shapely, clear bottle—a shrine to our country's very first méthode-champenoise. Mabuhay!

(Inaudible)

You are correct—the RR Bill was not wholly bad; I supported its educational provisions, to teach the dangers of sex, because if you do not know your gun you might shoot even those who do not deserve it. The Lord forgives only if you take responsibility for your sins. I am against irresponsible sexuality; girls must be taught how to control their bodies, and Western propagandists be held at bay, and abortionists face the fire of the electric chair. Sanctity begins with knowledge. I have many studies—some decades old already—proving co-relations between the idiot box, objectification of our girls, and adolescent sexual deviancy. Even science shows the miracle, blooming in the microscope, the instant a sperm fertilizes an egg: twenty-three chromosomes from the man, twenty-three from a woman, creating a child with forty-six chromosomes. In all of God's universe, only we humans have forty-six chromosomes, a sacred number: the six days our Lord created our world plus the forty days His son spent in the desert redeeming it. Forty-six—sum total of the divine grace spanning creation to salvation. Those women—like that nonmedical fake doctor, Rita Rajah, who influenced Vita to rally in the streets—they are but pawns of Western corporations seeking a market for condoms and pills. Our population of one hundred thirty million is big money—those women's urges blind them to that bigger picture. Even Saint Paul says, in the first book of Timothy, chapter two, verse twelve: "Do not permit a woman to teach or to assume authority over a man; she must be quiet." That is why the best chefs and surgeons are men, because the biology of women's hormones is not conducive to accuracy. So let us empower our girls to raise children, the most important job of all. I admit I am old-fashioned, but that is our country. Why should our values be defined by Westerners? Their invisible genocide would rob us of our greatest resource: people. Godless Westerners malign our family values and cast as corrupt our ingenuity for survival. Nepotism, they shout, when you provide for your family—as if they would not appoint their brother as their second in a duel, as if Saint Paul himself does not tell us, also in the first book of Timothy: "If anyone does not provide for his relatives, and especially for his immediate family, he has denied the faith and is worse than an infidel." Only two of the twelve apostles were not related to our Lord Jesus Christ. One was doubting Thomas. You can guess the other one. Corruption, the Westerners accuse—as if it is something tangible to be measured, to define the success or failure of our values. Do you know what is corruption? The inequalities they imposed on us colonized nations, controlled until today by their niggardly organizations. Values? Their elders allow their offsprings to address them by their first name, then they eject them from the nest before they can fly. Jiminy Christmas! Their virtue of independence is evil! What is evil is their selfishness. The Lord taught me this painful lesson. Abiola's choice, to use birth control pills those years before becoming pregnant again, with our second son—he was born premature, defective, my gentle, thoughtful, creative boy now no longer with us—Aha! Our third course! A selection of tasting sashimi: fugu, wild-caught bluefin tuna, and uni, the foie gras of the sea. Respeto! The wine pairing! Ah, here it is, the Louis Roederer, Cristal Brut. 2000. The bottle made for an emperor; transparent against Trojan horses.

(Pop. Pouring)

Mabuhay!

(Glasses clink)

Vita loved this champagne, due to her fascination with Negro culture—from that CIA thug she persisted on seeing, as if I was not aware she was being unfaithful to me. "Champagne for my real friends," she would say, "real pain for my sham friends." Indeed.

(Inaudible)

Yes, I do not deny your allegation. Ninety years old, and who among us can cast a first stone? I am equally as imperfect as all God's children. The Lord had one Son on earth without sin, Saint Augustine reminds us, but never one without suffering. I discovered my place upon returning after the war, marching from the jungle to find my father on his deathbed. The next day I galloped fifteen miles, back from city hall to his wake, to confront his brother, who was losing generously at the mah-jongg table and pretended he was not the one who filed my death certificate years earlier. If we were not outside a church I would have shot my own uncle. When he inherited our cattle farm, and threw my mother onto the street, and forced us to journey by cart to seek land in the wild North, that was when I learned how toothless society's laws are against suffering. Only God's judgment is the law. On the night we departed, the Lord took my uncle in his sleep, peacefully. Someone slit his throat. Like Moses we journeyed, leading my old companions in the Resistance, who like me had returned to only our antebellum indenturements. We went with certainty, for he who walks honestly, says the Book of Proverbs, walks securely. It was then, as on the road to Damascus, I discovered the Divine Laws, capital *D*, capital *L*. The Blessed Virgin visited upon me as I scouted ahead alone. On December 21, at 9:21 p.m., or 21:21 on the twenty-four-hour clock, atop a cliff in the Sierra Padres, the full moon became the face of the Virgin, her voice the most beautiful sound I've heard. She instructed me to guide my flock to righteousness. Ever since, I follow God by leading.

(Inaudible)

Yes, as you say, my critics call me a warlord, yes, because I am a leader in a war-torn place in a time of war, a humble mayor called to serve. Truthfully, my Civilian Armed Militia Organization brought peace necessary for prosperity, to rescue the ranks of impoverished who would have become godless Communists or extremist Islamists.

(Inaudible)

What do you mean, child soldiers? They are hardly—Aha! Our fourth course! Chef Toogy is a triumph of the Filipino race! White Alba truffle gnocchi with lobster, chanterelles, and fresh peas, with Domaine Jean-Marc Morey's Meursault Burgundy, 2009. Imagine? A white burgundy—as rare as an albino Negress but equally delicious. Mabuhay!

(Glasses clink)

As I was saying, in the real world, childhood is a luxury. I was a man already at twelve. Children can be the most cruel creatures, their consciences undeveloped, so I have offered orphans moral leadership. What right do you have to tell someone he is too small, too young, to protect his family? If someone takes your home, will you not protest? If your neighbor would reap what you've sown, will you not pitch a wall of plumbum? God's Law of Common Sense, according to Reverend Kidohboy. A strong ruler will never draw his sword if his voice is enough. Nor slay when he can maim. Sometimes the fist is necessary. I mentored Fernandito in that. For too long he kept his wrapped in padded gloves. This old vaquero taught him fear is a hand's shadow, gentler than the hand itself, and usually more effective. During the war, without radios to coordinate our attacks, we used the drums of our ancestors—boomboooboomboombom!—shaking the bones of the Japs, turning them in their tracks, saving the lives of our own. Let me show you something. Respeto! Respeto! Kindly please obtain my sword from my bedside. The blessed meek may inherit the earth, but do they know what to do with it? The rich will only swindle and evict them. Yes, my sins are legion, yes, but—Oho! Our fifth course! Roasted ortolan bunting, à la François Mitterrand. As prepared by Alain Ducasse. Try . . . eat them whole. You want a towel, to cover your head? Reyes! Reyes! A towel for our guest! To savor the fragrance, they say, or so God cannot see you devouring his songbirds. Paired with Nail Brewing's Antarctic Nail Ale, from Australia, made from ice from Antarctica—making this, of all beers, the oldest and purest. Much like myself. Mabuhay!

(Inaudible)

Not at all . . . at my age I can do without the presidency. I seek only to serve. Let the rest hide their intentions under patriotism and promises. Junior, to please his mother, wishes to resurrect his father's legacy. Lontok is running for his life, to dodge the ubiquitous allegations of wrongdoing. Glorioso, the unbreakable mustang mare, she is maneuvering for Speaker of the House. Rita Rajah is the big surprise, the secular Muslim candidate who can temper Bansamoro's extremist policies; now she is unexpectedly the front-runner even he cannot match, praise God. For a woman, she has spine, but can still be convinced to see reason. Perhaps she will be the one to unite our divided country. She alone finally brokered peace between me and Nuredin. But if *that* bading becomes president, I will launch a crusade against his theocratic caliphate of secret pederasts. His religion promises war, not salvation. I wrote this in my latest newsletter, to mark next week's anniversary of that massacre of fifty-eight by men from the Armpiturangutan clan, that Muslim governor and his sons who acted with all the impunity of those who can be punished by neither man nor Christ. Thirty-four journalists, several lawyers and aides, half a dozen unfortunate nearby motorists, and the wife, three sisters, an auntie, and a cousin from their rival's clan were all shot, then buried with a backhoe emblazoned with the name and face of Governor Dandy Armpiturangutan. These victims' sin? To be part of a convoy en route to simply file certificates of candidacy to challenge, at the next election, the incumbent's decades of rule. Those animals raped several women, and most of the female deceased were shot in their vaginas, by members of a family that traces their lineage to Shariff Aguak, a preacher who helped bring Islam here centuries ago. This is the violent tradition Nuredin comes from. We Christians would never commit such excess— Aha! Our sixth course! Langoustines, gazpacho espuma, and tomato jelly, as prepared by Ferran Adrià. Before he closed, I offered to buy El Bulli, but you know Spaniards, how lazy. Paired with Ridge Vineyards' Lytton Springs, 2017—seventy-one percent Zinfandel, twenty-two Petite Syrah, and seven Carignane. Mabuhay.

(Mouth swishing)

If I kept it maybe one more year the blackberry notes would be mellower. Aha! Respeto finally manages my sword, my signature at rallies. You should have seen the size of the sawfish it belonged to. Just when my guerrillas were nearly crazed with hunger, in the last days of the war, the Lord brought me this monster and I leaped into the river, ready to die. That is what sacrifice is: you prostrate thyself to forces larger than you. My campaign slogan has always been: "My Vice is SerVice." And also: "No bull." In my province my name is everywhere, on every streetlight, every fence, so that one and all know whom to call for any injustice, illness, inefficiency. I will fight, unnoticed, with a sword, while Nuredin wields a broom on national television, in undershirt and shorts, barefoot and bathed in nostalgic colors, to sweep dirt from his childhood home before turning to the camera to mouth anticorruption lip service. That hut is only how he maintains residency requirements in his district. My critics complain about my banners, that I am campaigning early, but I do not need to waste my children's hard-earned inheritance on—Oho! Our seventh course. Seafood treasures in a curry-coconut foam, as prepared by Guy Savoy. With a 2017

Sancerre blanc—Henri Bourgeois La Côte des Monts Damnés, that is how wickedly delicious. Mabuhay.

(Inaudible)

Yes, of course, yes, I take responsibility, but Jesus Himself showed us sacrifice can redeem sin. In our towns, numbers gambling ties communities together, and offers hope to entrepreneurs and participants alike. What, really, is corruption? Being kept ignorant by colonizers while the local elite grow rich, that is corruption. Fighting invaders and being eaten by the jungle while our leaders surrender and collaborators prosper, that is corruption. It is a voice on the radio, ordering you to run the most dangerous mission of the war, your men falling one by one as we cross a field, so that our liberators can land safely. It is sacrificing your place as mayor to win a seat in Congress, the landed gentry then claiming electoral fraud, sending you home with nothing because you lack firepower to defend your rights. So you return to find your wife, your sons, already strangers to you, your bed a promise of nightmares. Good men turning to evil to wrest from chaos some semblance of peace. And more wars, against countrymen who want only the same necessities as you. Corruption is your being ignored by the powerful in Imperial Manila, until they need your dirty work. How can corruption be survival? Or desperation? Or resilience? Or duty to those who depend on you? Tell me, young man, what is corruption? Respeto! The calamansi-vodka sorbet! Our palates need refreshing. Emperor Nero was the first to enjoy a version of honeyed wine with snow, passed hand to hand by his minions from the mountains to his palazzo. Imagine all he could have accomplished with a conscience.

(Muffled)

Tipsy? Good! I am also. In vino veritas. For your interview. Tacitus wrote that the Teutons drank during councils, because drunks make bad liars. Though I testify that is false. Estregan fooled me, over cases of his Johnnie Walker Blue Label, his livestock procurement scheme like quicksand to any who followed him in. I listed the process, under oath during the impeachment. Number one, if you did not participate, the Ministry of Agriculture would cease future allocations of livestock to your constituents. The Fernando V. Estregan Pig Program was also our party's flagship, under which the MoA would allocate five thousand pigs to farmers in each province over five years. Except, second of all, the FVEPP was immediately hijacked by fake deliveries, by shell corporations Babs Agri-Breeding and Goldstock Resources, incorporated only days before implementation of the FVEPP by the MoA—as revealed by a Securities and Exchange Commission report, sent to the Ministry of Justice, that found BAB and GR's scheme operating in sixteen of the nation's seventeen regions—not just my own. Yet, tertiarily, the MoJ handed the report from the SEC to the government's Barter and Agricultural Credit Assurance Convention, who convened a six-person Presidential Pig Program Special Task Force to conduct ocular inspections independent of the MoA, and even the MoJ, to search beyond BAB and GR, via the SEC, probing suspected connections to entities owned by mah-jongg buddies of FVE. Letter D: as determined by the PPPSTF, only five hundred breeders received sick or malnourished livestocks from the FVEPP, while four thousand five hundred farmers were made to sign receipts-of-claim, receiving no pigs and only four hundred pesos each—totaling a mere one-point-eight million out of the allocated sixty million in unaccounted taxpayer funds. Number six, while the Commission on Audit investigated, operatives from our party, the United People for Progress, lobbied for disbursement of additional pork barrel funds to allies among the two hundred eighty-six Members of Congress, to convince the House of Representatives to expand the FVEPP with a more generous, more lucrative, Fernando V. Estregan Pig Program Expansion Bill. Finally, the Office of the President, whitewashing all the evidences, released proactively on its website a watered-down three-hundred-twenty-page investigation, titled *Cultivating Transparency: The Office of Fernando V. Estregan*. That is the document the red writer Furio Almondo dubbed the *CulT: Of FVE* in his allegations based on Vita's recordings, revealing what Filipinos now know as the Swine Swindle—which ran from BAB to GR, through the MoA, via BACACON's PPPSTF, ignoring the SEC, sidestepping the MoJ, who brushed aside the CoA, due to incentivized MoCs in the HoR, bribed by the UPP, upon orders from the OP to pass the FVEPPEB to protect President FVE. And that is the A to Z, a pattern across many scandals that—Aha! Our meat course! Our duo of Kobe and Matsusaka beef medallions over charcoal, with 2010 Screaming Eagle Cabernet Sauvignon—scored perfect by Robert Parker. Mabuhay.

(Muffled)

Yes, as you say, I am complicit. My sin was my lack of courage in not speaking out sooner. Maxima mea culpa, ad infinitum, etceteras, until I am forgiven. Even if I was only one among many. A lowly bill folded into a thick stack is not responsible for funding a corrupt act. I have knelt publicly, humble and contrite, confessing all the facts. A more interesting fact is that a pig, when it comes, produces two pints of sperm; while a congressional budget, when it comes, produces two hundred eighty-six thieves—Aha! Our accompanying final course: triple-cream blue pepato cheese delicately gratinated over roasted beetroot, with toasted pili nuts, on a roquette salad—*Eruca sativa*—to rouse us men. Quoth Virgil: "Et veneris revocans eruca morantuem." Because we must be awakened now to what must be done. It is clear the government in the capital is rotten through and through. Whistleblowers like me are lauded, used, cast aside. What will change is nothing and everything, irregardless of who is president. Bansamoro is misguided in his faith in a national solution—top-down has never worked. If he stepped out of his closet he would see the real work is in local governance. As I did in Abiolaville, we must drain the swamp, then build from the ground up. The people first and foremost must fill their bellies, and the solutions are obvious to those who do not hide within walled compounds. There is no reason anybody should starve. Every year we waste half the Lord's bounty—two hundred fifty pounds per person, discarded uneaten in rich countries, while in poor countries that amount is lost to spoilage and vermins. Urban politicians like Uranus Jupiter Kayatanimo-Uy and Ambassador K. Sisboy Pansen woo Western supermarket chains, because it is easier to monitor, control, and tax entities like Woolworths and Walmart—while our farmers and local government are not prioritized. I built storage silos across the province, farm-to-stall infrastructure, refrigeration facilities, all leading to Abiolaville Market. Five hundred tons of produce pass there every day, serving farmers, fisherfolk, distributors, fixers, resellers, logistics companies, vendors, clerks, buyers, restaurateurs, janitors, consumers, mothers across the Northern Philippines. Respeto! My guest surrenders! No need to finish—what matters is you enjoyed. Reyes! Dessert! Mr. Twinkletoes will bring my favorite: a popped black sesame ball filled with chocolate, green-tea dust, caramel-hazelnut Pop Rocks, and lollipop. Paired with the Director's Special Reserve Vintage Port, by Taylor Fladgate. Mabuhay.

(Grunt. Belt buckle tinkling)

You look stuffed to the eyeballs. You see? Dessert is just like wealth: unhealthy only if not shared. I have one last wisdom to offer before we end our blessed repast. You asked about corruption, but do the poor complain when Robin Hood steals from the rich? Of course not. As the saying goes: Money makes the world go 'round. Whatever its color, however you call it—cash, quid, bucks, bread, dough, moolah—our need unites us. It can be a peso, a rupiah, a ruble, a rupee, a ringgit, a kwacha, a baht, a somoni—all money, all the same, not dirty, not clean, not a god, but given by His munificence: a slice of rock, a leaf of paper, an electric pulse sent with faith between secure servers—individually almost useless, but together, that's a different story. Take, for example, this lowly crumpled bill, emblazoned with a dead hero's face. Here, hold it. It's like a feather. How did it find me this morning, after I bought an anniversary gift for my dear wife, Abiola? How, when it was likely recently fished from the jean-jacket pocket of a salty Overseas Filipino Worker, back on dry land to buy his retirement home? Fished and dropped between snotty fingers of a glassy-eyed boy on the street, who shuttles the moist crumple to his mother beneath the underpass, who stuffs it into her bra with a grunt. Until night brings the syndicate man to collect his percentage, bending our note into the roll he owes the police who let him work that neighborhood. In the precinct past midnight, those officers converge with the share for their sergeant, who on his way home passes a councillor's house to leave a bundle with a domestic helper who prepares it for the secretary who fetches it every Wednesday for her employer. After dinner, the mayor—a former student radical, now golf handicap of nine—sits in yellowing Jockeys on his bed, slapping his palm with what's no longer livelihood, charity, or savings, but grease, SOP, small thanks, coffee money, or sweetener, rubber-banded and stashed in his safe with a comforting clunk. Until his wife purrs at breakfast for an advance on her allowance. "Have fun with this," the mayor will say, handing her a stack that includes our intrepid note, which isn't spent with the others at Starbucks that morning, or at Prada that afternoon, but is folded into the hands of her driver, far more than usual for his dinner, as he waits outside the church, when really she's in a condotel overlooking the neon steeple, between the biceps of her pilates instructor. This chauffeur, however, is as frugal as he's faithful, and he hums over his stomach to the Bee Gees on an FM station, arriving in the a.m. finally home, gone again at dawn with pockets emptied for his wife's business—doctoring labels on expired medications. Onward goes our little bill, licked by a male nurse into a bulging envelope and delivered to the House of Representatives, to a secretary named Vangie, who whispering-counts the amount beneath her desk before placing it coincidentally on Matthew 21:13 in the Bible in the drawer of her jefe. Hours later the congressman sits in a circle of lamplight in his empty office, adding the bundle to the stack in a pastry box before rushing to the Palace for Thursday's mah-jongg. As he arranges his tiles, the sweets are lifted from his side by a presidential aide named Jhun, who is dim and odorous but very reliable with deliveries to a Veritable Bank branch in the CBD, to the checking account of one "Pidal Velarde," who does not exist but nonetheless wires a very real sum an hour later to a numbered account in downtown Zurich. Barely a weekend will have passed before a hairy-knuckled Schweizerdeutsch fund manager transfers it back to an escrow belonging to the First Lady, who may or may not even know of its existence. Another trusted underling, also named Jhun, leaves a different Veritable branch after lunch, and separates in his windowless office bricks of five hundred thousand, packed in small boxes and wrapped in Christmas paper, even though it's November, to distribute after dessert but before Nescafé, to the eighteen congressmen, senators, and legal luminaries on the Constitutional Assembly supercommittee, who burp either porterhouse or salmon while shaking their presents and joking about having always wanted iPods. Among them is a former police general, on his first Senate term, his head hairless and his shoulders trustworthy, who sends his present that includes our stalwart bill to an Indian money changer, to transform it with others into notes bearing a bemused man named Benjamin. These, as I'm sure you've heard, are placed in socks in the suitcase of the general's son and carried, westward ho!, to California, to pay for a condominium overlooking the Golden Gate Bridge. As reward, this balding boy earns fifty Mr. Franklins and flies home for his birthday, and asks the family Indian to convert five notes into what they once were, before buying from a friend of a friend four sachets of shabu—

(Belch)

. . . And so our saga continues, from dealer to supplier our intrepid note goes. To the muscled lieutenant of the city's triad king. To the Fil-Am people-smuggler working for a Chinese POGO. To the offertory basket at Sunday mass. To the archbishop's coffers. To disaster relief for a supertyphoon. To an unscrupulous aid worker. To his boss. To her boss. To his boss. To the assistant minister of the Interior, then to her clever but ugly daughter, then to the city inspector who's savored delaying the opening of the girl's shop, which will sell phone accessories and is called, without irony, Cell Mate. From there, the quick-witted, slow-footed inspector lopes back to city hall, chancing on the vice-mayor who holds out his hand in his doorway for her monthly dues, meant for the proposed light-rail development, which, I'm sure you've heard, will bring investment to a ramshackle part of the city, though only after a certain magistrate rules against the pesky residents of a shanty-town. That respected judge is a God-fearing family man, who wires his daughter in Iowa her semestral tuition, for the creative writing program where she crafts indecent poems and earnest short stories, some of which her father admires for their indignation over the corruption in our Third World nation. And thus, through her full-fare international-student payment, to the construction of a new science lab named after another Jew, to a MAGA-loving contractor doing plasterwork, to a drive-through ATM in Reno, Nevada, beneath a blue desert sky, we bid adieu to our lowly, intrepid bill, who has definitively become—with the vigor of the colonial mentality—a foreigner, a greenback, an eagle clutching arrows, a pyramid and all-seeing eye, a Washington crossing the palm, to be stuffed into the panty of a graying macho dancer, to be thrown across stained satin sheets, to be handed to a panhandler holding a sign declaring "War Veteran in Disparate Times," to be spent on antidepressants from happy Big Pharma, to be swallowed by lobbyists on K Street, to be dumped into super PACs of representatives on the Hill, to be positively used on negative campaign ads, to be trickled down to small businesses, to be taken into middle-class taxation, to be dispensed on defense budgets stockpiling surgical masks, to be sent as foreign aid to dictators investigating a threatening opponent, to be lost in the gyre that is the world economy, that makes our planet spin, that brings us all together, only to find its way into my change at the Crocs store this morning. And now between your fingers.

(Burp)

Keep it. Some call it necessary, or a religion. Some call it venal, or the fruit of hard toil. I know only to never to call it yours. Money becomes filthy in the hand that won't let it go. But where would the world be without it?

(Pause)

See? You have no answer either. Maybe now you understand what motivates even noble Vita. Respeto! My Colchicine! It prevents the uric crystals from forming in my toe. And commend Chef Toogy! And bring our postprandials! Do you prefer Dong Hao Pao, an oolong for honored guests? Or Kopi Luwak, from beans processed through the digestive system of the palm civet? Reyes! Bring both! Come, sit beside me—this photo was taken from my helicopter. Abiolaville, the nation's largest city, in terms of square miles. Also the safest, in terms of nonfatal crimes. Jiminy Christmas, how this brings me back. These pages hold all my good memories. No photograph exists of me before my wedding day. This mountain, I used to climb with my friends; with clear skies you could see the sea, and view the view. These were our colonial-era granary, train station, stationmaster's house. Streamline Moderne, by the fellow who built the Capitol Records building in Los Angeles, the one in America.

(Inaudible)

No, they're gone, for the road to our market. Law of Necessity. Here is my childhood home, at the end of that row. I'll never forget it. My father built it. No, wait, it's this one. I'll never forget it. I would await the squeak of cart wheels in the darkness to hear if it was my lucky day—I'd ride to school with a farmer going to town. The potholes were

so gaping a small child like me could fall in and never be found. I remember the heavens would slowly change, from black to indigo, and
in the single breath of God the shoulders of the mountains emerged,
like monsters chasing away the stars. This was the village pump, now
Abiolaville city plaza, modeled after Brasilia's Praça dos Três Poderes.
Here's my Fountain of the Martyrs, to commemorate all who died in
the wars: Christians, Muslims, animists alike. I shall install a plaque
for that revolutionary, Loy Bonifacio, if Estregan makes good on his
promise for the death penalty. Bah!—ignore that statue of me; a birthday gift from my wife, on behalf of the people. Big, no? Look how he
offers up his sawfish sword to the Lord. It is so embarrassing. The tall-
est in the countr—wait, don't turn the page yet. The resemblance is
well-done, no? It makes me blush. All these city blocks here remain
empty, a free-trade zone—people joke the bodies are buried there. In
the meantime, a bird sanctuary—providing more than a dozen jobs to
capturers of cats. They release them over the border, into Nuredin's district. Ah! This is my market. Inspired by Brasilia's Supreme Court, because commerce is real justice. How modern, with tiled stalls, each with
drains. Electric fans, and screens to keep away insects. Respeto! The
assortment of single malts! Choose what you like—Scottish, Japanese,
even Indian, would you believe? It doesn't even smell bad. Abiolaville
has the country's lowest crime rate. Per capita. If Rita Rajah is to be our
country's next savior, she should come see what good governance looks
like, instead of making spurious claims. In my city, even the sexiest
women can walk safely at night. The karaoke curfew is 10:00 p.m., so
one and all can sleep and wake refreshed, ready to contribute. Simple
governance innovations that empower the people. All that, Fernandito
tried to plagiarize, as if he was Senator Toti Otots ototcopying again.

(Laughter)

I like you. You can appreciate humor, despite how you look. Give Respeto your email later, for my newsletter. Oh, look, here is my Coconut Museum. My Agricultural Museum. My hippodrome. This is our
Governor's Mansion, a replica of Rome's Pantheon, but entirely out of
coconut shell and timber. On either flank: our army barracks, CAMO
training HQ, and police academy—a reminder that force is subordi-
nate to democratic office. This is our main thoroughfare, named for my

parents: Roland and Alexandria Aguirre Promenade continues across mountain ranges, vast planes, endless bridges, all the way to Manila, so that my people will never live as a distant notion to the imperial capital. Every year Abiolaville is voted cleanest in the nation. One and all wants to move here. We regularly clear squatters from these agri-parks, ecoparks, industriparks. Eventually everything will hum with prosperity, if our next president doesn't destroy us all. Come, be my guest. My people will drive you all over. You cannot walk, Abiolaville is too grand. Launch your book there! I'm so glad I thought of that. Hospitality is our lifeblood. In fact, you may never leave, until I am satisfied you understand. Abiolaville will be the capital of our country, if God smiles down on his most humble of servants. Reyes!—este, Respeto! Where are the Teuscher champagne truffles?

Vita Nova Transcript: 8 of 13.

Who'd do such a thing—right? I can't believe it. Disgruntled Islamists? Drug lords? I can't believe it. Furio thinks Rolex is involved, because gambling—and her son owing money. Hope says Communists have infiltrated government. I think it's Estregan, who of course pins it on Nur; the EES love their vigilante conspiracy theories. It was like a bad dream, when I found out this morning. Still is. I cried and cried. Still am, inside. What's this gonna mean for all of us?

(Silence)

These years under this president, anyone with a grudge can get away with murder. Sprinkle drugs or rumors of radical socialism: guilty as not-even charged. Like a thousand bucks, U.S., to hire a hitman, even less. Which is what they're now saying about Loy's attempt on Nando, hired by the Liberty Party, supposedly—his trial not even started, they're already preparing the lethal injection. I was WhatsApping with LeTrel this morning, but even the Americans have no clue who did it. He just said be super careful. Even offering to guard me, and we haven't seen each other in years. Can I just say, he was the best guy I ever fell for: gentle, confident, mature—but hella lost. And the one I took least seriously, I don't know why. Probably coz he's a spy. The CIA knows everything—One-Mig always said—coz they're behind everything. But what would the Americans get out of killing her? Maybe the Chinese—to pave the way for Junior? The trolls claiming she was recruiting Communists from universities. Sorry, I'm rambling. She was, like, super sweet, sending her bodyguard home early on his daughter's birthday. Just half an hour till the next one's shift started. He found her. Imagine? Execution style. Living room. Apparently refusing to kneel, from the position of her body. A copy of Chairman Mao's *Little Red Book* in her pocket, supposedly. I can't even. Dr. Rita Rajah is gone.

(Silence)

And so's our best chance for change.

(Silence)

Imagine if Junior wins. Or Rolex—right? Makes me want to run, almost.

(Lighter click. Exhalation)

I'm actually serious. I could at least save Loy.

(Silence)

So, you recovered yet from your Rolex food coma? Did he serve his infamous Chateau René-Pogel? The country's first wine producer—two-dollar wines for soccer moms at Trader Joe's. Bet he didn't mention the farms he sequestered, and how he now has to import rice from abroad for Abiolaville Market. Can't believe nobody's realized what René-Pogel is spelled backwards. Super class.

(Inaudible)

He said that? See? This is why interviewing them's a waste of saliva. Of course they'll spin things. I'm totally getting editorial veto on my book. But yeah, okay—sorry, not sorry: I did see LeTrel while I was with Rolex, sometimes—didn't I mention? Not my fault you didn't ask—you're the super keen journalist. If Rolex had Abiola, why couldn't I see LT? But he was never a booty call. That's unfair. My feelings were real, despite myself. During my Lost Years—with Rolex, Red . . . Father Yoda snapping me violently out of it—LeTrel was actually the one reliable thing in my life. Which is ironic, since his style was sweet-talking me with promises of freedom—such an American obsession. Freedom from what, right?

(Sigh)

That was LT, the Lion Tamer. And I the lioness, purring at the mention of his name. Tall, dark, handsome. Strong silent type. The kind who never, ever, talks about his feelings. A cliché and a half. With a voice like a sheriff. After we first hooked up I'd snuggle on his chest, feeling the rumble of his stories—puzzle pieces that kinda fit, but not in a way that showed you the whole picture. Growing up in Cali, moving to Atlanta for his mom's job, trouble in school, finding himself through the navy, as a radar operator in an E-2 Hawkeye. (I knew those planes from growing up; they look like lamps.) Watching like God, as he put it. That's how LT ended up here, with a ho-hum desk job at the embassy—so he claims. I won't lie, he started as my curiosity, coz who doesn't want to explore clichés at one point in your life? To be part of what's said. But he was like literally the nicest man ever. The sort who doesn't need to master others coz he's mastered himself. Nothing bad to say about nobody. With these long lashes that curled like a little girl's (my Waterloo, apparently). And *so* fit, scooping me up like a kitten in his arms to make like throwing me over the balcony. Jojie was the one who hooked it up—such a judy—at that Halloween party at the Kili-kili, after Furio ditched me post–monologue showdown. Jojie was Posh Spice, I was Scary, but my real costume was pretending to have a good time—fooling everyone, myself included. You know the loudest person at parties? That's what faking looks like. These people were going around with bamboo cages filled with butterflies, and when they got to me, they were all dead—the butterflies, not the people—littering the cage like paint chips. I started crying for some reason—it was all too much—so Jojie pointed out LeTrel and his white B-boy friend across the crowded dance floor. Daring me. I made excuses: Furio, fatigue, and LT being, well . . . you know how racist we Pinoys can be. So Jojie waved them over, like giving the go signal at a drag race—that B (coz what are beshies for?).

(Inaudible)

Like I said: I was curious. Cat used to show me interracial porno, which was somehow so taboo, and I grew up on rap videos on MTV, super crushing on LL Cool J and crying for like literally a week when they shot Tupac. I think we Pinoys, especially Fil-Ams, we identify with African American culture because of our shared experience—you know: conquered, stuck in cages, made to serve. So I acted all cool when LT shook my hand, but inside I was bursting with fruit flavors. I mean, his pants fit proper. He smells nice. Has a slender nose. Articulate. Good grammar. I was pleasantly surprised. We made our way to the bar for the drink he offered and he didn't gentlemanyak me around by my waist, or grind up when we danced. He was fun. Jojie, the four-time ballroom champ, was leading his friend Dwight all over the dance floor, and she'd spin herself over to give me an encouraging eye. I didn't

know what to do. Part of me wanted to pull the plug—coz of last time
she got into trouble, when she didn't tell the guy, his hand jerking up
so fast she didn't see the fist coming. The wingwoman's dilemma: keep
your beshie safe or keep your beshie happy? Besh you can do is respect
her judgment and hold her hair or get ice for her black eye. Does she really gotta give a disclaimer on who she is? Like it's some trap? You
really gonna punch someone whenever they defy your expectations?
But when LeTrel flashed me his glowing smile, and suggested somewhere more quiet, I was like, Lead on, McBuff. Part of me wanting Furio
to catch me on LT's arm, seeing where it would lead, my heels snapping
friskily down the street like the dot-dot-dot at the end of a suspenseful
sentence. Coz at that point in my life I needed a sense of possibility.
Dot, dot, dot. Because Filipina girls are always forced into this fantasy of virtue and purity—priests sermonizing that if Eve listened to
Adam we'd all still be in paradise. Cat making me his project—what
to wear, which fork to use—and Furio trying to save me (save me!)—
mansplaining maturity and promising he'd be proven right. So when
LeTrel looked at me the way he did, I thought to myself: Go on, bawse,
live a little—don't let your inner goddess shrivel up and die. So we're
in the casino, by the roulette table, and he's dropping some bills for
some blue chips, his whispers curling into my ear. "What are your favorite numbers?" (So charming.) Small stacks go on eight and seventeen. "And your birthday? You don't have to tell me the year." (What
a gent.) Blue covers twenty-five and twelve. "What about your statistics?" (His warm breath making me shiver.) The rest goes on thirty-
four, twenty-three, thirty-five—his smile caressing up and down my
sides, in confirmation. I know that if we win tonight I'll surrender
myself to this romance-novel love. The croupier spins the ball into the
blurring red and black while the ring and clang of the casino fade and
I can't breathe till it click-clacks then lands . . .

(Pause)

Back at mine: money's scattered all over my bed, LT kissing like he
wants to taste my every inch, my body limp in his strong arms he's
almost carrying me, the zipper of my dress like ice down my spine
before he crouches at my feet like a rescued Madagascar slave I want
to set free, removing my shoes and putting my toes into his mouth,

and I'm like, Um, maybe don't, wow, okay, yas. Kissing behind one knee, kissing higher behind the other, me holding on to his head like it's the only thing keeping me from waking, his hair like the soft half of Velcro getting stuck on my prickly soul. His eyes flashing in the dim light, his smile finding my trembling yoni, and I want to sing an aria. Tumbling backwards towards the bed, I pull him up to my face, tearing open his shirt—buttons clattering on the floor like pearls in a mugging. His chest like the trunk of an ebony tree sculpted into a warrior's, wished into life by magic and need, animated by a spirit either benevolent or cruel—or both, depending on what you deserve. I can't hold back when he kisses my heaving bosoms; I'm like, Goodbye, good girl—tugging at his belt, unzipping his jeans, sliding them down slowly like Galileo Galilei at a telescope discovering a new galaxy inch by inch. Sliding lower and lower without reaching the end, as exciting and frightening as infinity—my breath like I'm fighting the corset of history, of society, of my past existence. No, I say, in disbelief, or warning. No. His manhood swinging up like a hand that knows the answer: Yes—the head nodding yes, glowing like a ripe plum. Yes. I open my mouth as wide as I can. I become his hungry Desdemona.

(Lighter click. Exhalation)

It was so good the neighbors had to smoke a cigarette after. Like I said: a cliché and a half. Perfectly too big, like a button in a buttonhole. Like making love to a centaur chieftain on the eve before a doomed battle. In relationships, size really doesn't matter, because love makes everything bigger. But when it's just sex, logic beats illusion. I admit, I first liked LT for his body, later for his mind and heart. Didn't seem to bother him. Not like he was first interested in my personality. Just saying. So I othered him, so what? Let's be real here. We're all influenced by our endless scroll of media. We all fall for someone's beauty or profession, sense of humor or style, or even just freckles and green eyes—so you really gonna give me grief for liking the contrast of my hands on his skin? To me, LT came from another world, dripping preconceptions like it was bling. And sometimes our first travel's through something as far as an accent or exotic face. To a bikini-clad belle in Boracay, even the gaze of men can be a geography lesson: Aussies come right up to talk, Italians stare as if it's appreciation, Frenchies try to make you laugh, Chinese peep as if uninterested, and Arabs peer like it's their right, while Pinoys will ogle like schoolboys till you catch them, jolting their gaze into the sky dreamily above your head. LeTrel, my African American lover, proved and disproved my presumptions. Isn't that a good thing?

(Inaudible)

How long? Eleven, maybe thirteen, or more like eighteen, actually—yeah, eighteen months, on and off. I measure relationships on the CR Scale, as I call it—brushing teeth side by side comes after the first great night; bathing together's on the first romantic getaway; farting, a serious milestone, six months to a year, if you're careful; peeing in front of each other's when you're really committed—one year to two, max. Pooping in each other's presence, while chatting about an interesting article, that's at least two to three years—and the start of the spiral when romance gets flushed. Me and LT never reached farting. From even the beginning, I knew. Like I hated the way he talked about Jojie—as if the joke was on his friend Dwight—and he refused to call her "her." I'd try to enlighten him but he just couldn't. Don't get me wrong, it wasn't a Black person thing; it was a LeTrel thing. Which was sad, because they had so much in common. Jojie's into mountaineering and breeds dogs, and LT backpacks across the country and was always missing his chocolate lab back home. But love's about timing, right? He was one of those perfect partners still working through a major flaw neither of you can get over. As Dr. Chopra says: "The secret of attraction is to love yourself. Attractive people judge neither themselves nor others. They are open to gestures of love." I tried to be exactly that. Go on, said Jojie and Boy—both of them, who rarely agree—go take him up on his offer. You'll love the States, they said. It may be your last chance to escape. I was hella tempted, at that point, coz me and stardoom have always had a love-hate thing. According to the Myers-Briggs test online, I'm an introvert—

(Inaudible)

That's a misconception, actually—we do like people; we just can't stand shallow connections, which is unfortunately a huge part of my profession. There's no business ♬ *like show business* ♬—I know, but it can highkey mess with your head: you're scared nobody really sees you, and if they do you're scared they see you the way you see your-self. Fans are forgetful and fickle. Show them too much, they resent your shortcomings for reminding them of their own; stay too dis-tant, you're ungrateful and feeling superior. Like what happened during those infamous Billboard Wars—a career peak that came lit-erally crashing down. Back when my techno-hop EP, *Curricula Vita*, was selling like scented candles before Christmas, and at every rave I was performing its hit single—"P, L, You, Are"—singing about peace, love, unity, respect. While snagging ad campaigns left and right—coz partying makes you skinny—and I got my first billboard, the coun-try's largest ever: me, thirty feet tall over South Super Highway, in a Triumph Amourette 300 bra and a Daisy Desire hipster shorty. And because our country loves nothing more than a trend, every landlord was soon renting out their rooftops, every fashion label assembling record-breaking signages, every agency making giants of their top talent for the commuting gazillions. All of us: me, Jezhabelle Baratto, Heart Aquino, Criscris Rebolvar, Peachy-Pie Pilar, Georgia Thompson, even Tootsi Pahotsy, flaunting proudly her brand-new bolt-ons in a Billabong bikini. (When in doubt, get 'em out, right?) And, of course, my nemesis, Baraka Vousfils, who was obviously the so-and-so back-biting my new Levi's billboard at such-and-such a party, according to a Kitschy Katigbak blind item—saying I was jelly over her Silver Swan Vinegar spot because it was like four feet taller than mine. When the tabloids asked for comment, I made the mistake of saying raw denim was classier than stinky condiments, along with some objective obser-vation about her jeggings and generally sour attitude—and everything went craytown. The shade so creative it was like the golden age of trash talk. Retaliations following reactions. And you couldn't hit the clubs without your crew ready to throw down. The billboards getting bigger and bolder, magazines keeping score, newspapers offering infograph-ics, and models cutting their fees. Till that morning the season's first supertyphoon blew all the billboards down, one of mine just missing a school bus while Baraka's famous ad for Red Pagoda Ultra Filtered—mouth parted suggestively, puffing real smoke—fell and flattened like a dozen commuters at a crosswalk, leaving one survivor stand-ing trembling between Baraka's lips—like many a cock . . . amamie innuendo—without a scratch and suddenly a celebrity: bagging an endorsement deal with Lucky Me instant noodles, strutting her stuff on the noontime variety shows, then the religious programs, then the makeover vlogs, before returning to obscurity, hooked on showbiz, and so depressed she took her own life.

(Chair scrapes. Footsteps pace)

I could totally relate. Coz for me came the camel-toe incident—in that black pleather catsuit for Wildcat Deodorant—all over websites like manyak.com and cameltoeoasis.org, instantly more famous than I ever wanted to be. Just before LeTrel was heading back to the States, to put his stepdad in a nursing home, and suggested I come. I kept telling myself the infamy wasn't personal—that anybody's wardrobe malfunction would receive the same reaction. Except it wasn't anyone else's—it was me who'd be defined by that image; me who opened my trailer door to find the entire crew, led by my champion, Boy, who'd been holding his ear to a glass as I sobbed to LeTrel in what I thought was my privacy. All so dehumanizing it was worse than being naked. You know gossip: it's not about the truth, it's about creating doubt about the subject. Like those latest political memes about Nur's supposed secret Korean cosmetic surgery: implying self-hate and homosexuality, coz we're almost ready to finally elect a Muslim, but apparently not a badaf. Memes meant to undermine his dignity, coz these days what passes for bravery is shamelessness—the opposite of owning your shame for your shortcomings, which is actually courageous. Like, I'm not perfect (I contour), but I'll never hide—not behind filters, façades, or fake news. Not anymore, at least. Especially not from all the hate-following trolls out to cancel me. So when LeTrel suggested I escape to New York, I'm ashamed to admit I almost did, telling Rolex I was going shopping, packing two Rimowas, ready to never return. Like most Pinoys, I always dreamed of moving to America, and it felt almost right when the setting sun filled my plane with orange as we circled JFK—the famous skyline beneath my feet like a movie: the Chrysler's chrome spear, and Kong and Fay's rendezvous spot, and Carly Simon singing in my head ♫ *let all the dreamers wake the nation.* ♫ Knowing that seeing LT would be like a romance novel sequel: either better or worse than the first—and I'd find out which soon as he lifted my feet off the ground. We know those books are fiction, but you can't help but believe that whatever can be imagined could always come true—coz reality needs fantasy like a damsel needs the hero (or the hero needs the damsel?). So I pop a mint, and zhuzh my hair, and dotdotdot into the surprisingly crappy terminal, automatic doors revealing LT, fresh off fifteen hours on a Greyhound—if that can be called fresh—leaning against a pillar, arms folded, smile cocked, his duffel bag slouching on the ground like a faithful hunting dog. We literally had the best week ever—all those New York City promises: wading through Central Park, leaves as bright and loud as fire; crashing a reception in the Plaza Hotel; dancing till dawn on a Tuesday in the basement of a Chinatown restaurant; watching the sun rise over the river from under the Fifty-Ninth Street Bridge, LeTrel leaning me against a lamppost to kiss away my disappointment that Annie Hall's bench wasn't actually there.

(Chair scrapes. Seatback shifts)

The big galoot making it all sound so easy. "Let's buy a cheap convertible," said he, "and drive cross country till it breaks down or we make it back. Jazz in New Orleans. New games to learn in Vegas. Winter in Big Sur. Let's get a copy of *Roadfood* and hit every clam shack, hot-dog stand, and custard joint on the way to everywhere. When days get hot we'll jump into motel pools, and bounce before they realize we're not guests. Let's get Elvis to marry us," said he, "it's cool if it's just for a green card. I get how it is and I'm down." He said I'd charm the Southerners, and would love imagining which house overlooking Charleston Harbor we'd fix up. His friends would introduce me to Hollywood agents. I could finally qualify for *Jeopardy!* LT so darned tempting it broke my heart. Coz I knew how he felt about me, even if he never said it—that word so hard to say, like Worcestorshire: *L-O-V-E*—and all its promises. Offering me himself. Offering me America. But the problem with such dreams: What happens when you wake up? America, and its promises to us Pinoys, where'd they get us, a century later? What happened to the equality, democracy, freedom, security? When Fernando speechified against their massacres of the Philippine-American War, a hundred plus years ago, he was right, in a way. How many more hundreds of thousands of us Pinoys had to die, fifty years later, before General MacArthur kept his promise?—"I shall return," after abandoning us. Artemio Ricarte, now *there* was a hero who kept promises: a Pinoy patriot fighting to oust the Spanish, repel the Americans, organizing while exiled to Yokohama four decades, returning with the Japanese forces to free us from our Western colonizers. Ricarte the liberator, a traitor, gone too long. LeTrel actually thought I could be happy leaving our country, with all its issues—but it's mine, and yours; it's ours. You know, Nando ditching America for China and Russia was just logic: no strings attached to their promises—arms to fight the Communists (which is ironic), loans for infrastructure and defense (also ironic)—with none of America's demands for human rights and democracy. He betrayed our old ally because their promises ask too much from us. Coz democracy's imperfect, especially ours— that's what makes it a forever process. Which is why so many no longer believe in it.

(Sigh)

Naive as he was, I always had mad respect for LT. He hated his embassy job—like, every weekend escaping from it across our archipelago—but his sense of duty kept him committed. Thing is, that night on the ferry to the Statue of Liberty, when he told me about his sick stepfather, and asked me to stay, it sounded like promises he could never keep. How could he, if he didn't believe in them himself? Next day, I took some time away, catching some old Manila friends who'd kept canceling till my flight home was tomorrow already—our whole coffee spent talking new babies, past parties, and Brooklyn real estate. On the subway back to LT, I got off a few stops early so I could walk and think. You know, with Deepak, I tried harder than I should've because I always wondered about life with LeTrel—what could've been if I only understood what he was running from. When LT kissed me at the door of our hotel room, I kissed back like everything would be okay. Because he seemed to have found in me what I couldn't find in him. But as he held me, I thought to myself, What about *my* promises—the people I told: I shall return?

(Inaudible)

Well, for one, my new talk-show segment, "People's Patrol," had just started on *Oh-Em-Gee!* and I knew what it could do for our shallow noontime variety shows. My first guest before I left was Helen, mother of twin sons—one killed, the other jailed by Rolex's CAMO militia, for poaching endangered wood in the Abiola Conservation Reserve. I'd met her outside Rolex's office one afternoon—she'd been waiting for him eight hours. Our segment helping her son walk free; Helen shaming Rolex into action. Did you know that the first newspaperwoman in America, Anne Newport Royall, got her start by changing the mind of President John Quincy Adams? He refused her request for an interview, because she only had a vagina, but she'd heard he liked swimming nekkid in the Potomac, and she sat on his clothes on the river bank till he agreed to talk. The president so impressed he even helped her find justice in a case involving her late husband's pension—and with those funds she started *The Huntress*, a newspaper that became an icon for asking hard questions. I'd like to think that's what I'm doing with this book—sitting on people's clothes while they shiver naked. Like a huntress lioness. So anyways: LT. In the end I had to choose my promises. That's why I broke the one I made to him. And why I've now decided: challenge accepted—thank you, Rita. (Rest in power.) I shall accept Nur's invitation to run. Vice presidency, here we come.

NOV 24, 9:48 P.M.

PO2 LeTrel Dyson Transcript.

(56:78.00—Dyson.M4A)

Listen. My bet's on Vee. No doubt. She'll do good. She's a do-gooder. She got the stuff. She got the story. Sometimes story's all you need, if it's the right one. Right time. Right place. Know what I'm saying?

(Inaudible)

Yeah, man—the Philippines is home now. The years I used to live here, it's not like I didn't care. But I'm all in now.

(Inaudible)

These days? Freelancing, mostly. Research. Reports on the region. The outfit's called the Global Initiative Against Transnational Organized Crime. No slim pickings here, for us do-gooders. Status nominal: all fucked-up. More protests in the streets. The American embassy's under siege. My old colleagues are texting me, scared of another Benghazi. It's not like the United States killed Dr. Rajah. The CIA's always a great scapegoat. Right now it's just leftist groups with slogans, university kids with picket signs—all's needed is some nutjob to toss a firebomb, some lone wolf like that Loy Bonifacio, and the whole world changes, just like that. Somebody's trying to incite riots. To break the ceasefire with the Communists. Restrict election campaigning. Vee better watch her back. Given all the chatter I'm getting from certain channels. Chaos offers everyone opportunity, large or small. The other day, I was getting my driver's license. As I said: all in. So I sweat an hour in line at the Land Transport Ministry. Get told I need an updated residence permit. Sit an hour in traffic. Freeze an hour at city hall. Get told I need a utility bill. Four hours later I'm back with my paperwork from PLDT. Wait another hour. Get told I need an LR22 stamp. Wait forty-five minutes upstairs. Another thirty back downstairs. Same guy tells me: "Sorry, sir, this is an OR22. You need LR22." I fill out a new application, because the stamp invalidated my old one. Chaos. All the while, random opportunists keep sidling up. "Facilitation fee? Fifteen minutes. One hundred only." I don't bite, cuz I'm the dumb foreigner with principles. Next day, I'm back at oh-nine-hundred. Wait an hour in line. Submit my documents. Get given a slip of paper. I'm like, Ma'am, where's my license? Lady says: "Sir, temporary license." When's my real license card coming? "Sir, five to eight months." I look at the paper. This one expires in three. I ask. She tells me, come back in two, to apply for an extension. "Unless you want an ETL." An ETL? "Sir, Extended Temporary License." I vibe what she's saying. "Sir, five hundred pesos." I hand over the cash. She takes back my slip of paper and passes back another. "Sir, keep that safe." I can't help joke: What if I lose it? "Sir, obtain an affidavit of loss from the police precinct and return back here to apply again." On my way home, in the crowded MRT train, my pocket gets picked. For real.

(Inaudible)

Exactly. A maze that leads back to the start. Know what I mean? So props to Vee for busting through its walls like a wrecking ball. She's bloomed into something real special. We gotta amp what she's saying. Before they shut her down.

(Inaudible)

Not really—she was always a surprise. From the second I walked into the Kilikili Klub, where we met. Place was popping, dirty hip-hop pounding, ladies whale-tailing in low-rise denim. But Vee stood out, in this elegant leopard print and curls. Different. In the middle of the chaos, still as a statue. Unreal. Surrounded by darkness, face lit by her cell phone. Special. And she was crying. I had to find my opportunity. And shake my wingman, Dwight. At the embassy folks called him D-White. Dwighter Than White—he tried so damn hard. Always "dawg," or "homes," always either cockblocking you or honing in with Cuervo shots for the disregarded ladies, cuz he lacks courage. So he and I are scoping from the bar when I spot Vee again, dancing with her friend on the stage. So fine she gave me nerves. I was thinking my way in was to make eye contact with her friend, but when I looked it was like one of them 3D posters you stare at blurred before it slides into perspective. Remember those? Maybe the arms, or bony brows, but all a sudden I knew. I'm not proud of how I felt about things then, but that's the way the night went down. He . . . or she, actually . . . or they—right? That's what we're supposed to say now?—they catches me staring. Man, that grammar kills me, but sure. They looks at me, they looks at Vita. I look at Dwight, then look back and flash a smile. Tooth for a tooth, guy for a guy. That's a joke, man. Just what I thought at the time. So anyway, next day at work, Dwight catches me by the watercooler. He's all: "Wassup, Cochise! You raid it?" I hold up my hand to show Vee's digits. He shrugs like it's nothing. "Yup yup," he goes, all baller. "My shy little filly kept pushing my hands away. But I got tongue action. And a date mañana." So I bet him a hundred, in real money, USD, that he couldn't get head. Another hundred he couldn't snap a picture, as proof. He smirked, straight flexing. Gave me a dap and took the bet; I almost wet myself. Told him: But what if we win?—that's the punchline to one of his favorite jokes. Like I said, I'm not proud. I'm telling you this story cuz when I told Vee after, about the wager, you could tell she didn't know how to react. When she sort of giggled I figured no harm done. Not like anyone got hurt. Know what I mean? But she never forgave me for making her do that. And she wouldn't react that way now, for sure. Back then she was figuring her shit out. Fake it till you make it. I can't hate on that. She's not faking things no more. Problem is, that might to cost her more than she expects.

(Inaudible)

I don't know, man. That's a tough question. I'll be straight with you: I did care. But love's a big word. Maybe I did. Yeah, I guess I did. Fuck it: I did.

(Inaudible)

Listen, no resentment from me. It wasn't like I knew what I wanted, either. I used to tell her: Careful what you ask for, debts always come due. At the time what she wanted was to get famous. Like it was the answer—but what was the question? Know what I'm saying? We make our own currency and that's all we got to spend. Mine was being what she wanted me to be. Hers was being what she thought men want women to be. I was in no place to convince her otherwise. Then the governor came in heavy. Toothbrushes. That's as far as we got. A blue Oral-B in her bathroom. A pink one in mine. Vee always played it cooler than the other side of the pillow. So I did, too. Pretended. Acted all player. Bounced before she woke up. But the truth is, I was happiest when she was unhappy and needed me. I'm man enough to admit that now. She'd play the guitar, or sing at the piano, and it was like you finally saw her. Singing "Hallelujah" like she's the girl it's written for. "But all I ever learned from love was how to shoot somebody who outdrew you"—coming from her, that shit felt true. Then her guard would go up and there was nothing you could do. She gave a lot of heartache, but I'd do it all over. She was addictive. Blooming. Getting famous. Catching her on the tube—the Weather Fairy on the morning news, in her little outfits, or tiny yellow raincoat, or this furry bikini and Russian hat—there was no bad forecast with Vee in the world. I just gave more than I should've. From day one. Changed a month's salary in chips at the casino. All for her look of pure hope. She puts my very last money on seventeen, just as the ball starts rattling for a place. The croupier's pushing a stack to us across the baize, and Vee's hugging me, smelling so good, screaming: "Always bet on black!"

(Inaudible)

Man, what do you think? I hated that shit. Just cuz she heard Will Smith say that in a movie doesn't give her permission. She was always "fer shizzle my nizzle." Know what I'm saying? Made me feel like a game being played. Introduced me to her friends as her Magic Johnson. So I called her my Fortune Cookie—playing at a fair trade. She loved the scandal. Said if folks were going to make shit up about her, why not own it with something true? But there was her truth and there was my truth. Like with   . She'd throw that word round like it was harmless. I should've told her there are things in this world she can't ever own. That words are tools but anything that scars is a weapon. And weapons must be used responsibly. Yeah, that's it—she treated me irresponsibly. I let her. Like you do the ringleader of the cool kids—that kid cussing up a storm in the bus, shooting spitballs at your old best friend you outgrew. That kid who sucks up to your folks all mocking-like. That kid you follow like a shadow. Because hope's a fucked-up thing. You want them to know you, but you just can't make them listen. Vee always reminded me: "This ain't no relationship." When I knocked up at her pad she'd sing out behind the door: "Booty call!" But I didn't clap back once. I just bet on my constancy. Through her *3-Poll Threat* disappointment. Through that dumb camel-toe scandal. I liked being needed. Took my pops getting sick for me to see. I got fired from my job for an excuse to go. I asked her to come, but you know. Vee gets that life's a transaction. You got to do what you got to do to get it. Everybody says relationships are give and take. She gets that better than you or me. But if I blame her, I'll hate her, and I ain't that weak. Already enough hate in this world.

(Inaudible)

No. Back then I couldn't see all that. When I split, I split angry. Charles, my father, he'd fallen again. Yeah, technically my stepdad, but only technically. Social services found him. On the kitchen floor, a day later, bruised and dehydrated. Hardheaded son of a bitch never took help from nobody. The nurse they sent—this Fil-Am named Charmane— she'd worked with my mother and was the only one who'd put up with his obstinance. But even her patience was running thin. They said he started calling her a "gook." Told her to dance and threw coins at her. Hard as all that was to believe, I had to come. This was the gentleman who always said manners distinguish humans from apes. Who never let anybody call him Charlie. Who checked every payphone for change. Who spoke like an English teacher and refused to code switch, always telling me and my brother: "Don't sound like an immigrant in your own country." That was the Charles I knew. My moms said he got back from Nam gentler. That's how strong he was.

(Inaudible)

My mother? She passed away years before that. About a decade. Vee always asked why I didn't talk about my folks. I just never wanted to talk to her about regret.

(Inaudible)

Yeah, sure, Vee and I had that in common. Myles, my brother, he remembered our biological dad. His memories of him are all the ones I got. My mom took us when I was three and Myles was six, soon as she graduated. It was better that way, except we didn't see her as much. She was always working. Even most Sundays. That's why I don't really do religion, except under fire. Know what I'm saying? I wasn't about to share with Vee secondhand memories. I got my own memories of what I called home. Like after my moms met Charles, at the VA hospital, and they decided to marry: city hall in the morning, ICU shift in the afternoon. Nice lunch in between. Changed from her dress to her uniform in the bathroom. We dropped her off at the hospital and drove home with Charles. Myles and I had tied cans to the bumper, like in the cartoons. I remember that.

(Inaudible)

No. Charles worked at home. I'd help round the garage. He restored cars for rich people. "Passion augmenting pension"—that's what he'd say. Both my folks worked hard. In such a damn hurry. They had this thing about time. My moms had no intention to retire just to nurse his bony old ass. They had real plans. Charles was fixing up a 1960 Cadillac, Series 62, in Persian Sand. To visit forty-eight states. Write a book on old diners and track down lost relatives. They were a perfect match. He loved erasing time. She loved defying it. He resurrected life. She delayed death. It's why genealogy was their hobby. Hers, really. Charles'd drive hours, on our family trips, to graveyards and archives, for my moms. She'd been the first in our family to get past high school and she wanted to study history. My granddad said there was no future in the past. He got cancer and died just before she got her nursing license. I wonder if he realized just how wrong he was. He still exists only because I remember him. Know what I'm saying?

(Inaudible)

On his side, my mother's, his father, my great-grandfather was one of the first Black men to cast a ballot in Alabama. A freed slave. Lined up the morning the Fifteenth Amendment came into effect, to register to vote. Five years after Abolition. About a century before the Civil Rights Movement. He ended up voting just once in his life. "Knowing your own story," Charles always said, "is your first line of defense." Charles's pops, he got home from the Second World War and tried wearing his uniform to get served at diners. Was told one time, with a sympathy he felt worth mentioning to his son: "I'm sorry, sir, we just can't serve   ." My mom would nod at these stories. "The world's always going to try," she'd say, "to tell you who you are." On her maternal side, my mom's great-grandfather was Chinese. Probably where I get my head for numbers. He drove ties on the transcontinental railroad. The only women those workers could marry were Black. That was as far back we got in our history and it frustrated my mother. "The deeper the roots," she liked to say, "the wider the branches." Then she'd grab me and Myles in this huge embrace and lift our feet off the ground. Larger than life. That's pretty much how I remember her. Boys aren't raised interested in the inner lives of women. Mothers, sisters, teachers—mysteries. Hidden in plain sight. At her wake, hundreds of folks visited. I didn't know so many folks loved her.

(Inaudible)

No. I'd rather not, please. Hope that's cool. Won't discuss my military service, either. I know my story and neither of those endings need to be part of it. I'm here now. Like I was saying, I split angry, a few weeks after Vee's camel-toe scandal. That shit got heavy. Remember, she was just coming up. Shooting this commercial for Wildcat Deodorant. Thirty-six hours of freshness and confidence, they said. A world record, with armpit whitening. Everybody's waiting on her big entrance. Hyped. Buzzing about her skin-tight latex cat suit, by some up-and-coming designer. This was when *The Matrix* was big. Some thirty people in the lot. Crew, stunt and safety, extras, media. Paparazzi in position. Vee would be racing up a fire escape, running rooftops like a wild cat, absconding in a helicopter with a stolen diamond beauty-queen tiara. Never breaking a sweat. Her trailer door opens. Vee steps out. Big smile. Hands on hips. Feet planted like she's about to take off into the sky. This whisper ripples through the crowd. Years later, it feels like that whispering's never ended for her. Know what I'm saying? That's why she's unbreakable now. Vee's dead game. My manok, as you Flips like to say—she the chicken my money's on. All instinct and conditioning.

(Inaudible)

You for real? Never been to a cockfight? It's your culture.

(Inaudible)

Man, that's a misconception. They're given a charmed life. A chance for more than just adobo. Without us, they'll fight to the death anyway. Gaffs keep it civilized. I seen a naked-heel fight take eight hours. It's nature that's brutal. Know what I'm saying? So yeah, Vee's my manok.

Hell, she'd even make a great president, if they don't paint her as a Communist and pop her. The irony is she's the best candidate to stand up to President Xi Jin-Pooh; China don't got a single yuan on her. If you all don't do something, you all will be their next province, bought with development loans, compliments of your Papa Nando. All you all speaking ching chong. Just saying. Colonialism doesn't end on independence day. In my humble opinion, you folks should fear the superpower that's so slick it can enslave two million Muslims. A system so calcified their dictator killed seventy million, during peacetime, and still gets a huge-ass portrait, guarded by soldiers with fire extinguishers, in pride of place in their most famous square. I'm not even saying that as an American—there's no love lost between me and my homeland. But at least America forces lip service to democratic opportunity. Every two years we confront who we are.

(Inaudible)

Man, I'm not about to argue with you. Listen, I'm very clear eyed about the U.S. of fucking A. Can't you tell I'm woke?—woke up rudely from the Dream. Let's be honest: the United States of America wasn't never great. Conquest. Genocide. Slavery. Colonialism. Racism. You Filipinos know what I'm saying. All men are created equal?—brother, the only truth held as self-evident is it's every man for his self. But that's not why I left. Call it unrequited love. Greatness is generous. Generosity is shared. What made America great was its unity in diversity. That shit's even on our money. Out of many, one. The founding fathers couldn't free themselves from hypocrisy, so they gave us mechanisms to fix what they couldn't. The Constitution's a living thing. How else we get twenty-seven amendments? America's a process.

(Inaudible)

I guess I'm just sick and tired of that process. Sick of shouting that for all lives to matter my life must matter, too. Tired of searching for shared humanity in morons who can't stomach that our history's a legacy of oppression. You know what? This last time I went home, I was fully fixing to quit the Philippines, to go home for good. I'm sure Vee told you. My father had a finite number of lucid moments left and I wanted to savor each word of every story. But I had to support us and job prospects were fucked. I was mowing neighbors' lawns, man.

One evening—one of his good evenings—we were out on the porch and I was telling him my grand plans. He looks at me like I'm a damn fool. Starts laying down some knowledge. Ever hear of David Fagen? Corporal in the Twenty-Fourth Infantry Regiment of the U.S. Army— occupying America's new colony, the Philippines. He got real famous back home Stateside once he quit taking up the White Man's Burden. Deserter tired of being just a   . Found more in common with the gugus McKinley shipped him in to kill. Fagen turned heroic guerrilla captain. Fagen turned seditious rebel traitor. Charles asked: "Which are you going to be?" I said, Aren't they the same? He said: "Depends on which history you believe." One story saw a bounty paid in dollars for Fagen's decomposing head. The other saw Fagen marrying a Filipina and hiding happily ever after in the boondocks.

(Inaudible)

I'll tell you which. I believe life's not as simple as a sad ending or a happy one. Know what I'm saying? All the paths in the maze lead to right back to the start. My brother Myles got militant and left. I got enlisted and left. Where'd that get either of us? People used to come up to me in airports, to shake my hand like I was famous. Thank you for your service, they'd say. An improvement from Charles's dad. But soon as I took off my uniform I was just some Black dude in a hoodie. Served, sure, but too often with suspicion. Never mind I enlisted right after 9/11. For what they called a just war. It's just a war, man. No polish could shine up that turd. "Never forget"—that's what folks always said. That old promise. You won't be forgotten. Growing up, everybody knocked at our door, saying the same thing. Baptists. Jehovah's Witnesses. Brothers from the Nation of Islam. Republicans. Democrats. Girl Scouts. Everybody soliciting your support in exchange for some cookies. Know what I'm saying? But if you can't afford the cookies, it's your own damn fault.

(Inaudible)

Shit, man, at least in the Philippines you all are honest. Come with your dollars, you all tell us. Marry our women. Start a business and a family. Have half-breed kids who become models or sports stars. Some folks come because they start with an advantage. I've come because I got sick of being told I'm not whatever enough. Know what I'm saying?

But what Vee never understood is that just because it's home doesn't mean it won't betray you. I seen it, man. Growing up. One lost hockey final. One injustice caught on tape. One brick through a window. Thousands rush into the streets, looting stores, flipping cop cars, torching property. That's what's normal. You know what's abnormal? Suburbia. Stock markets. Civil discourse. Supermarket franken-chickens. Plastic in the seas. And thirty-six-hour deodorant. At first I thought the whispers were because Vee was damn fine in that catsuit. So tight it looked painted on. Then her cocksucker agent gives his famous laugh. "What a cute little camel-toe!" Motherfucker even points. And all civility up and leaves. Flashes flash. Shutters click. Vee looks down. Looks up. Looks stunned. Locks herself in her trailer and they're gone, buzzards off to email the story and pics. That night, the outline of her vagina broke the internet. Someone even made an animated gif that went viral—Vita Nova looking down, looking up, looking stunned, for eternity. What kind of civilization inflicts shame like that? Just like that, her life was different. She was afraid to leave her pad. Ate her feelings. When I got the call about Charles's condition, I tried to paint a pretty picture for her—a great escape, priceless privacy, freedom. We'll throw some camping gear in the back of the old paddywagon—the '79 Country Squire that used to be Charles's taxi—and point its monster V8 toward the coast, to secret coves I knew. Stop at Mrs. Wilkes's Dining Room for lunch. Sweet potato soufflés. Okra gumbo. Best fried chicken you'll ever taste. Get to know my pops before he kicks it. I very much wanted her to meet him. Let's go, I said. Grab your passport and split. Just like that. She said she was worried what her sugar daddy would do to me. But I knew. Rolex was powerful, but I was free.

(Inaudible)

Hell, no, I wasn't scared. Other than Vee, I had no reason to stay after getting pink-slipped. That was some bullshit, too. My superior at the embassy was this well-meaning white boy with a stupid-ass pony tail. Dale. The woke chipmunk. Cited HR 4238. Said President Obama banned the use of the word *oriental*. Said government employees must be circumspect on social media. Said I had to take down my tweet about Manilans calling their city "The Pearl of the Orient." And my Facebook posts about the handicrafts at the annual Negros Trade Fair.

And my Insta pics of love potions from Siquijor, in the province of Negros Oriental—especially that double whammy. Along with my picture, at your National Museum, by the flag of those revolutionaries who
ousted the Spaniards, cuz of their initials: the KKK. Because apparently
how we Americans interpret words matters more than anyone else in
the world. Know what I'm saying? I used to play this game, after Myles
left. After my mom moved us from L.A. to Atlanta. Walking home alone
from my new school. When I came up on any dudes on the sidewalk, I
wouldn't share it. Just walked right at them. Fuck the social contract.
I wanted to learn what it felt like not giving a shit. Eight times out of
ten, I won. Guys'd step off into the grass. Or wait till last second to angle sideways. But sometimes some dude would refuse. Boom. Just like
that, our shoulders hit. Chests puffed. Time to make a choice. Who's
gonna apologize? I always did. I didn't need to fight. Just wanted to understand the limits. Of peace. Of violence. Of the choices in between.
With Dale up in my face, I couldn't deal. Not in my padded cubicle
at the embassy. Not with all that was going on at home. I made my
choice. Told him to go fuck himself. "No, sir," motherfucker squeaked,
"you just fucked yourself." White boy had me escorted out by military
police. Like I would hit him. Or steal stationery with official letterhead.
Snowflake even watched me packing. Arms crossed. Constipated expression. More drama than when Vee and I said goodbye.

(Silence)

Vee, you see, she didn't treat it like goodbye. She said she'd meet me
in New York City. I said I wasn't going to be in New York City. She said
she always dreamed of seeing New York City. "Concrete jungle where
dreams are made of. There's nothing you can't do." She sang that to
me. Kissed me. Said I was so lucky to be going home. Then she shut
her door. When I got to Atlanta, I wasn't feeling very lucky. It was hot
but didn't feel like summer. Summers are joyful. Like I said, I took to
mowing lawns, like I did as a kid. Wouldn't have got even that, because of Mexican illegals. But neighbors are neighbors. I found a lead
out in North Carolina at a new factory that was going to make armored
Humvees for our troops in the Middle East. Far from Charles, but bills
needed paying. The owner was a vet too and we hit it off. But AM General, the competition out in Indiana, they had connections in D.C. and

held up the bidding process. Allegedly. So no job, no protection for our troops, let them fry and die a bit more in tin-pan vehicles for pennies on the dollar. As if we taxpayers didn't pay a couple hundred mill per day for those wars. My salary back during my deployment was two thousand eight hundred seventy dollars and sixty cents. Per month. Blackwater security guards made fifteen grand. Per month. No fucking wonder we lose twenty vets to suicide, every single fucking day. Know what I'm saying? And Vee said I was lucky to be going home.

(Inaudible)

Charles? My bad—let me backtrack. Day I got home, I was trying to be positive. I'd written up plans on the plane. Charles and I'd take a trip up the coast, like I wanted to do with Vee. Drive all the way to Fenway, to sing "Sweet Caroline" at the bottom of the eighth, like he always dreamed. Just like he did in front of the TV, and Myles and I would make fun of him. The Sox were his team ever since his godfather—his dad's boss at Wells Fargo—ever since he brought him a cap when he was seven. Never mind they were the last major-league franchise to integrate. Truth is, I wasn't sure if Charles would even speak to me. Last time, after I was discharged, after Afghanistan, I cut his driver's license in half. For his own safety. And others. There'd been an incident. That was brutal. Telling your father he can't drive the cars he assembled piece by piece. Suffice to say we had some reconciling to do. He was on the porch when I drove up. Rocking. He acted like he saw me just yesterday. A sign of his illness, I figured. I unlatched the front gate. "How's life?" he said, like always. Pretty good. "Why you back?" he said. Just am. "You should know better." I don't. "Find yourself a good woman yet?" Not sure yet. "Beer in the fridge," he said, gesturing with his head. "I'd like one, too." Why not three, four? His favorite pun when I was a kid, when I'd ask for a cookie like my brother. Charles finally smiled. "Visit your mother yet?" Charles, Mom passed years ago. His smile disappeared and he weighed his eyes on me. "What kind of senile fool you take me for, son? She died in my arms, on that very sidewalk. What I meant was have you visited her grave?" Drove straight here from the airport. "That your new vehicle?" A rental. "Good. Never approved of those Asian jobs." I asked if he heard from Myles. "You think after all these years?" Just asking. "Was hoping he got in touch with you, son." Nope. I did hear you fell again. I waited for Charles to say something. Stared. He was always lighter-skinned but now it was like he was fixing to disappear. House is looking good, I told him. Don't you get lonely? "I do not." I worry about you. "That's your affair, isn't it?" Sorry I took your license away. Charles shrugged. "State would've anyway. You just saved me from socking a stranger." Want to go for a ride? "In that Korean tin can?" In one of your whips. "Check the garage." You sold even the Caddy? Charles closed his eyes. I asked if I could stay a while. "If you cook meals." I did.

(Inaudible)

Yeah, I was hoping she'd come meet him. But you know Vee by now, don't you? So Charles and I eat spaghetti on the porch and I don't mention her, as much as I want to. They'd set up his bed downstairs but he won't let me fuss. "Go on," he says. "There's always tomorrow." The second step from the top still creaks. Charles calls up: "Welcome home, son." My old bedroom smells like something almost remembered. I push back the curtains. Streetlight and dust filling the room. Everything just as I left it. You'd think it would've felt like home but it was just the opposite. The old tennis posters. Swim trophies. Model cars. In my bedside drawer, my *Playboy* magazines, stolen from my brother who knew. They were the first things I packed before we left L.A., sandwiched inside *National Geographics*. Hidden at the bottom of my suitcase like treasure. I open one to the centerfold and remember everything. That year after the riots, when Charles got denied a gun license the same day my moms saw the job listing. Sitting round the kitchen table, discussing. That week, when Myles threatened to split. I'd lay in bed listening to them shout. That morning of our flight, his bags and boxes gone, just like that. His note on the kitchen counter. He was college-age, but still. That broke my mother's heart. I leaf through the magazines, remembering those women. How they used to be so much older than me. Always from an alternate dimension. Know what I'm saying? Kymberly Herrin: White skin golden. Tan lines like an ivory bikini. Knee-high boots the color of her sable coat. Aviators. Kidskin driving-gloves draped on the hood of the red sports car she's leaning up on. I forgot that I'd never forget her. Or Debra Jo Fondren: bending over naked to comb her golden hair, like Rapunzel's past her knees. Or

Alana Soares: Sun-kissed on the river. Braids and kayak. Juicy and cute in that eighties way.

(Laughter)

There you go, you remember her—Miss March, '83. All them Playmates always from exotic places. Albuquerque. Concord. Honolulu. Anchorage. Their questionnaires saying they spoke second and third languages. Were of Irish-Scottish–Native American descent. Chinese-Jamaican-Swedish-Italian. Portuguese-Welsh. Each woman so whole to me, like they had it all figured out. While I was lying on the bathroom floor, back against the door with the broken lock. Knees shaking. Searching. I'm pretty sure lust's based on pure envy. I always envied Vee's ability to forget, until I was sitting again on my childhood bed, trying to re-member. Almost hearing my moms getting home downstairs. Charles singing something sugary to her. Sounds of the kitchen promising din-ner. TV blasting on. The theme of *Benny Hill*. The theme of *M*A*S*H*. The theme of *Roots*, then British voices. Outside, a car stopping. A door opening. A rush of Grandmaster Flash. Myles saying something and a slam. Me rushing to put his magazines back under his bed. Till this day I can see him out our window. Strutting up those front steps forever. Vintage dashiki. Black-power medallions. Hair like a halo. I always en-vied his certainty. Know what I mean? When the riots came he took it one way, I took it another. One minute, you hear the crack of wood on rubber outside. Neighborhood kids at stickball. Good kids we played with. Worked part-time after school. Next minute, Charles says game's canceled, we're not watching the Clippers beat the Jazz for my birth-day. My mom forbids me and Myles from leaving the house. Out the window, smoke towers in the distance. Just like that, the same good kids are running up the street, sticks in hand. One makes to smash a side-view mirror but pulls back. They all laugh. I looked at my brother beside me. I couldn't figure out why he was smiling. That was the day the white truck driver got beaten. And that Chicano guy. We thought it would end there. Next day, a Thursday, our whole family's ready to watch *The Cosby Show*. Final episode of the whole series. Popcorn and sodas all set. Room goes dark all a sudden. Television crackles and glows a few seconds. A portal closing. Just like that. Myles and I run to the upstairs window. Sky lit like pictures of Desert Storm. Serious shit.

Enough to cancel Michael Bolton at the Hollywood Bowl. Charles had tickets for their anniversary that Sunday. My mother loved Michael Bolton. Said he had a voice like a fine Black man, and a baron's face from the cover of a romance novel. The riots canceled even his concert. My moms took a shift at the hospital. Charles drove her.

(Inaudible)

No. I was too young to understand. We heard about Reverend Bennie Newton saving that Latino from being beat to death with a car stereo. Mrs. Landsdown, our neighbor, leaned over the fence between our houses and told Charles. In her usual tone, like she'd predicted the event. The reverend got between rioters and the man they were beating on. "Kill him," he said, "and you have to kill me, too." I couldn't believe I actually knew a hero. He used to come round to talk to Myles. My brother had his share of trouble. Frustrated genius. Built a robot and won the Grade Eleven science fair. Charles turns to my brother, raising his eyebrows like they'd slide off if he wasn't careful. "Next time that man visits you," he says, "you best listen to what he has to say." Myles never listened. People talk about riots as spontaneous, like the ones right now outside the American embassy. Eruptions of anger at avoidable injustice. But the hottest flames burn so low and long the eye can no longer see them. Know what I'm saying? Everybody talking for months about what would go down if the four cops got acquitted. When you're a kid you pick up on adults' conversation like you're a ham radio catching signals from another galaxy. Incomprehensible and too distant. So for me to know what was going on meant I was finally part of it.

(Inaudible)

No. I wasn't angry about Rodney King. Too busy wanting a Game Boy. What got my attention was Latasha Harlins. Shot dead, back of the head, a few months earlier. By this Korean grocery woman. Myles went to Westchester High, same as Latasha. In our old neighborhood. By the airport. They were in different grades but he had friends who said they knew her. I was in Grade Six, at Raymond Elementary. Five minutes from our house on Brighton Ave. Do you know L.A. at all? That was near the store where she was shot. That's how I knew it. First thing my moms ever let me do on my own was bike to my swim lesson at the rec center on Hoover, if I bought her milk at the store. I remember setting out, cycling standing the whole way. Got me a pack of Big League Chew and went to the counter. I remember the stink of chlorine off the towel round my neck. How good that smelled. Soon Ja Du—that was the Korean woman's name. I remember now. Must've been the lady behind the cash register. She was nice. Smiled as I counted out my coins. Called me *sir*. "Thank you, sir." I was thrilled. I remember. Few weeks after, fifteen-year-old Latasha's shot in the back of the head. Just like that. Mistaken for stealing a bottle of orange juice. A buck seventy-nine. Coins. Growing up, I thought about that a lot. Violent crime wasn't novel in our community, but this was different. Myles and I would bike by that very store. By Westchester High, to Dockweiler Beach, to squeeze through the fence and watch jumbos fly low right over us. The Korean lady said it was an accident. Her son was threatened recently by thugs. She got sixteen for voluntary manslaughter. Reduced to five years probation, community service, and a five-hundred-dollar fine. Coins. The white judge went on to be mayor of Manhattan Beach. During the riots, Damian Williams shattered a white truck driver's skull with a cinder block. He beat the attempted-murder charge. Got four misdemeanors. Myles said Rodney and Latasha were vindicated. Two wrongs made right. So I thought so, too. I was eleven. Like I said: rage burns low and long. Probably still would, if not for the navy and my years in Manila. Ironic—you know what I mean. Can't we all just get along? Fucking Rodney King. The barrier between civilization and chaos is a plate-glass window. You never see the brick coming. A girl gets popped. Four white cops caught on film. One court's decision. Just like that, gunships overhead. Barricades by the corner store. Soldiers on the way to school. Your brother leaves. You move away. I fold up the centerfold and shut the magazine.

(Silence)

Next morning, I go downstairs to start the coffee. Charles is at the kitchen table. His back to me. I tell him I need his advice about this girl I met. I tell him I'll get us some breakfast. Chik-fil-A biscuits. His favorite. No reply. I tell him again. Nothing. I come round and see. Charles, it's me. He nods. Don't you recognize me? Nod. Who am I? Nod. You feeling sick? Nod. Like a foreign tourist pretending to understand directions. I play his favorite CDs. Bring out photo albums. The four of us in Disneyland, by the Carousel of Progress. Myles and I helping strip the '66 Mustang. The house on Brighton Ave. My moms cutting my hair in the backyard, Myles spinning a basketball. Stuff even I'd forgotten. Charles nods politely. There's a knock and Charmane the nurse comes in, smiling. I remember her from when she worked with my mom. She moves Charles. Feeds him. Bathes him. Like it's normal. I tell her about last night. She nods and hugs me. Asks why I didn't find a nice Manila girl to make me a home.

(Inaudible)

Yeah—sickness like that's tough. Especially when they're lucid enough to remember their anger at you, but not lucid enough to remember they're sick. That illness, there's no closure. The disease runs its course in four to six years. That's what I was told. Every case is different. Some live twenty years. I mowed a lot of lawns that summer. Finally brought myself to put Charles in a home. Cleaned out my room and all the rest. Had a yard sale and sold the house. Vee never replied to my messages. When I'd pick Charles up they had him set in front of the TV, like a baby someone forgot. Tucker Carlson on Fucks News. Charles used to call him a waste of air. Like maybe the world would be better without him. What's wrong with just asking questions? Know what I'm saying? On bad days like those, I'd take Charles on his favorite drives. Up the Meriwether-Pike byway, to Warm Springs. For the healing waters. At Roosevelt's Little White House. On nice days, we'd go up Northside, to the Chattahoochee River. He liked the site of Pace's Ferry, where Union and Confederate troops fought for the crossing. On good days we'd go to Fox Bros, or Community Q, for ribs. Chicken and waffles at Gladys Knight's. He'd be nodding off in the car but didn't want to head back. "No!" he'd shout. "No!"

(Silence)

I would drive round the block till he fell asleep. Like I keep saying: the maze leads to the start. After dropping him off, I'd wait out rush hour in this rest area off the highway. Thinking where to go. The nights were cool and I'd lay down on the warm hood of the car, the engine ticking like a clock slowing to a stop. Thinking if Charles can't remember, then what's here? Beyond the trees, vehicles left red lines of light, going home. Thinking maybe if I'd stayed, or hadn't cut up Charles's license . . . Know what I mean? Fixing cars keeps your brain working. He'd go sit in his Caddy, just sit in the garage, too scared to take it out and get it impounded. Just start it and sit alone.

(Silence)

That fall, Charles had some good moments. Finite days. But I went and met Vee in New York City anyway.

(Silence)

I guess I couldn't bear the burden. When I told her that, she looked at me like she didn't recognize me. Be careful what you wish for, she said. Then she split. Just like that. On the Greyhound back, I got a call. It was about Charles. Charles fell again. Charles was gone. Just like that. I watched the road. Twenty hours. Thinking about that corporal, David Fagen.

(Silence)

My buddy from the embassy, Dwight—he has this favorite joke. President Estregan convened a joint session of Philippine Congress. To discuss his brilliant idea. "My fellow Filipinos," he declared. "Look at the enemies America vanquished. Germany is now a global leader. Japan, an economic powerhouse. Italy, a cultural luminary. I propose that we, too, wage war on the United States. So that we, too, will become a wealthy developed nation." All the great and good statesmen, all the honorable and wise representatives, all of them nod and buzz with excitement. They move to pass the motion. Just as they're about to bang the gavel, to declare war on the world's foremost superpower, someone pipes up at the back. "But," she says, "what if we win?"

Vita Nova Transcript: 9 of 13.

(43:32.43—VN9.M4A)

Namaste! That crowd, right? Amazeballs. The campaign's going super good. Top of the polls! Me and Nur, only two weeks from victory day. Don't I look fetch in fuchsia? Thanks for coming all this way. Let me close this door . . . There. ♫ *Just the two of us.* ♫ Feels like ages. Have you been working out? Your aura's so gangster. While I've been busier than an orthodontist in Britain. Rallies, motorcades, door-to-doors, town hall discussions—which nobody does like we do. Thank Nur's grassroots organizing skills. We're even launching an app. Haven't been this exhausted, ever, and that's saying a lot. The Comeback Kid— hardest-working gal in showbiz! It's hard being your own role model. You know what I'm super loving? Seeing everyone share their stories. Coz most politicians just go around selling themselves—like gracious gods explaining why you should worship them; yadda-yadding like used-car salespersons making promises: farm-to-market roads, water infrastructure, Wi-Fi—handing out calendars with their ugly smiling faces on them, or shirts with their smiling ugly faces on them, or book-marks slash health insurance vouchers slash ugly face smiling (printed together on one card; as valuable as cash and totally illegal—but *you* try objecting to healthcare access for the needy). Yadda, yadda. Except I'm no politician. I just listen: who voters are, what voters want— coz voters know best what voters need most. Me, I'm just here to help them help their communities. We in this together, homie. Have you seen my social media lately?

(Inaudible)

Hella fetch, right? All thanks to my army of woke college kids—so cute, such inspiring. And guess who's leading them. Jojie!—former Boy

Scout and current photography buff, curating everyone's stories and their selfies with me. On everything from Facebook to TikTok, which I've yet to embrace. Furio calls us citizen journalists, but we're just amping others—why's that so revolutionary, right? Used to be that my pics on, like, a yacht chillaxing, or at the club flossing, those got the most likes—followed by gym booty, action beach volleyball, or arrogant yoga, then pregame mirror duckface, hot friend shoutouts, outfit of the days, sun-kissed legs and sandy feet shots, awkward Throwback Thursdays, business-class humble brags, behind-the-scenes antics with the production crew, food porn, nail art against single-malt bottles, lowkey-flex hiking panos, cat gifs, inspirational quotes, feeling-profound infinity perspectives, hashtag-blessed book recs, then, at dead last, my events at my charities (too real, I guess). But it's finally different and I don't think it's the algorithm. Peeps be liking what matters. Furio told me the other day, looking out on the crowds: "I don't know what you're doing, kiddo, but keep doing it." He disengaged from social years ago, after his plagiarism scandal, but he lurks—one of those weirdos at like 3:00 a.m. liking a dozen of your pics from last year, and another dozen from like four years ago (and never commenting). You know the type.

(Plastic crinkling)

I love that *he* sees me as the mystery, when it used to be the other way around. Furio, my first *man*—so much so he started as Mr. Almondo to me. First guy with baggage from a life that was full rather than still empty. Cat, One-Mig, Loy: just boys. Fu had the musk of experience, loss, and Drakkar Noir—as bald as he was fond of his body hair. Old-guy corny cute and absolutely in love with love—such passion; what melancholy. I was still just in my twenties, he was just still in his forties—prehistoric, though I've always appreciated the life lessons of others.

(Whack. Whack. Whack)

His wife had just left him—sent him out for cranberry sauce before Christmas dinner and he got back to find her gone, with their daughters. That's why he was the way he was with me: like an old rescue pit bull, forever scowling about the bandana around his neck but ready to rip out the throats of your attackers. Hard-fought—that's how he described his life. I mentioned we met at a posh birthday party, right?—me their streaming-on-demand, he their mirror-mirror-on-the-wall—his *Magnum, P.I.* pornstache tickling into my ear as he murmured bull's-eye cruelties towards the socialites treating me like trash. Fu's legit. ♫ *Too legit to quit* ♫ . . . don't let his filterless cigs and flask of Fundador fool you. Without him, there'd be no Sexy-Sexygate. Thanks to him I didn't end up a packing-tape mummy with shabs in my pocket after Fernando found my little thingamajig recording.

(Lighter click. Exhalation)

Me and Furio talk every day now—full circle from how we began: phone marathon all night, drifting me away from Cat, coz nothing says romance and revolution like whispering till dawn. First time we went out, I said just as friends, but I tried on so many outfits getting ready, and his nervousness was clear from the uppercut of aftershave when I stepped into his beatboxing Super Beetle—washed shiny blue for our whatever-it-was outing, though the upholstery smelled like a laundry hamper, and corners sent books and bottles on the back seat rushing to and fro. He took me to Megamall for a movie: *Dying Young*—starring Julia Roberts, theme song by Kenny G—and I left the cinema in tears, rushing to Odyssey to buy the soundtrack. When Furio called it sentimental claptrap, I was hella insulted—but wanted to know why he thought so (and what "claptrap" meant). Cat was always at work late, prepping for the bar, so I'd escape with Furio to karaoke joints, where he invoked the bonding technique of many a Japanese sarariman. Back then videoke wasn't like now, with private rooms and complexicated cordless mics. Ours was old-school dingy: one TV for the entire bar, everyone snaking the long microphone wire over tables piled with Red Horse and sizzling pig face till it finally reached you—and you stood up to that delicious dread and took a deep breath. There's always a kind of sex in performing in public, and Fu'd gaze at me as he crooned about a moon and a big pizza pie, or one for his baby and another for the road, or how she's always a woman to him even if she's kind of a B. While I belted the big numbers—Shirley Bassey, Eartha Kitt, Édith Piaf—about the heartbreaking grandeurs of life.

(Laughter)

I so wanted to impress him, even with my drinking prowess, and one night I was drunk enough to suggest a nightcap at his—which felt so empowered—and he's freshening up in the CR while I'm snooping in his living room at the picture frames. There was Furio as a boy licking an ice-cream cone dripping on his brother on a tricycle. Furio in college, long-hair-don't-care and slim as a sword sheathed in polyester, slouching so confidently it's like he's standing straight while the world's slanted. And Furio in a turquoise tux, half-bald and clean-shaven, his bride beautiful in white with eighties hair that's hipster again these days. I think I fell for him then, looking at those photos of who he used to be—endeared by how he clings stubbornly to it, even up to now: still almost wiry in baduy flared jeans and bezippered boots, his Indian shirts unbuttoned to flaunt his chest hairs like an old-school ascot—*hairs*, coz you can almost count them; he probably gives them names. His beard, a sparse failure but full effort. And his nipples' whiskers—don't even get me started. (Cockroach antennas—just saying.) Not to mention his BO, which he just about cultivates: museum-quality, as gross as it's fascinating—you can hardly resist sampling it, but resist you must. That first night we didn't even kiss—which hella surprised me—he just showed off his library, which changed my life. Honestly, it took us a whole month to get jiggy, when he was surviving a man flu and my mothering instinct sent me over with chicken soup for his soul. Fu's on the sofa, burning up, sneezing back at K. Sisboy Pansen on the TV news. I'm scooping Vicks VapoRub onto his feet—a secret remedy for coughing, believe it or don't—when I notice these red polka-dot scars shining on his soles. "Fire-walking," says he, as I replace his socks. "In the circus." His body trembling as I explore the rest of him with a cool sponge. Don't be a baby, I say—which is what you tell a man when treating him like a child. And he's looking at me with these eyes as sharp as the tent in his boxers. Suddenly I'm on top of him, his embrace like a furnace, our first kiss the hottest ever in all of history. Furio tearing off my clothes like they're on fire, me enveloping him like the sea—his fevered phallus like the rising sun, our breaths moving like the tides from here to eternity, rolling like we're in the surf, and he's staring down at me in wonder, his body a thrumming E-string between our touching foreheads and his white tube socks. The bedroom, I whisper, but he keeps going till he shudders and rolls off, thud-thud-thudding to the CR and slamming the door. It was cold and I went and waited in his bed. His voice was sweet, calling out for me in the living room, but when he found me, his face crumpled like a beer can on a jock's forehead. "Get out of there," he growled. "Actually, just go. Please leave." Something in his eyes making me move quickly. I grabbed a taxi and cried all the way home.

(Inaudible)

I had no idea. When I saw him a few days later, he apologized and kissed me, as if that explained everything. After that, we made love a few other times, usually when we were drunk, but always on the sofa—both of us ignoring the beer sloshing around our tummies, the way you do queefs, or the sounds your chests make when they suck against each other. Guess I had unfair expectations of him taking charge—me being half his age, and him always trying to teach me about everything, which I'm super grateful for even if it's what ruined us. You know, I actually thought I liked overbearing, because I never had a father—until I met my dad, after my mother died, and he tried to be someone he never was, instead of just appreciating who I actually am. At least Furio listened to who I wanted to be, and pushed me to be the best version of that self. I got my first condo alone and he helped me move my suitcases, waiting politely in his blue punch-buggy while Cat and I fought bitterly as if it wasn't our last time. I couldn't afford much furniture—just a mattress on the floor and a lamp on a box—so I was always at Furio's, lying on his shag rug and playing his old records. Or sitting with him on his couch surrounded by towers of books. He even took me to my first public poetry reading, where I was pushed and pulled inside myself. And brought me to my first real library, in Arneo de Manille Université, losing each other in the maze of endless books, till I halted on the unexpected rows on feminism, and he found me there a short eternity later and pulled out all the ones he said I should read, starting with the First Wave. I know, right? But honestly, before that, I always thought a library was a place of polite words and much shushing—not actually a superhero's secret armory, stacked floor to ceiling with the loudest, most dangerous stuff. And there's no place more intimate than a reader's personal collection—revealing ambitions, memories, escapes, and dreams. Me and Fu talking for hours about what his different books meant, to history and to himself—

dipping in to read me passages that made me feel small and huge at the same time. He collects banned books and I devoured them, loving the forbidden and challenging my own beliefs. It seems kinda quaint these days to think a novel can get banned—because interwebz. But just look how they try to censor me. Or Ramona, who got her period and doubted her parents' religion. And Scout, questioning justice and the wisdom of our elders. Henry losing himself in his sexuality only to find himself through his words. And the politics of those verses blamed on Satan, which actually prove that the real evil comes from trying to silence voices and keep books shut.

(Clap)

So credit where credit is due: Professor Almondo introduced me to "serious literature," as he called it, giving me reading lists like an explorer with deteriorating knees dumping *all* his maps into your arms. At first, I found many of his recommendations hard, but he guided me with the patience of an eager snob. Telling me once: "If you want to understand the man I am, read Dostoevsky." I did. Didn't help. Probably his point, in retroflect. But when I discovered *Tess of the D'Urbervilles*—on my own, in the bookstore—that's when I first realized literature's not just a window, it's a mirror. That story could've been Cat and me—and all those years suddenly made sense; they weren't wasted after all. Sometimes you go into the world searching for something that's been there all along. Till today, Furio pooh-poohs books I adore—like *The Alchemist*, which he's never even read—but I now enjoy clapping back at him. Because whenever I'd ask for recommendations of female writers, he'd give me one or two, then three or four of the men who'd influenced them—which I think he meant to be encouraging, in a totally effed way: to get me writing poetry again; coz I abandoned it after Loy, when poetic words felt so useless. I'm a dropout, remember? Reading was always an escape to somewhere far away. I never had classes where you analyze writing or discuss current events—least not till it was almost too late. I'll always love my bodice-rippers and self-help, but Fu showed me even the romantic usefulness of newspapers— "Dispatches from the world," he called them, "to help us find our place in it." And the importance of mythology—all the human truth in those mortally flawed heroes, like King Sisyphus, which I misheard and mispronounced and earned my nickname: Sissypuss. And Fu showed me how poetry finds its greatest freedom through discipline. He fanboyed over Alfred, Lord Tennyson; I was more E. E. Cummings—with his derring-do intimacy and pornostar's name. I would read Furio my own drafts, and he'd read me his, like a sulky singer elbowing his way to the mic. I loved that I inspired him to write again. My fave's "The Days the Birds Died"—

(Inaudible)

That's the one about the young cadre in China: their leaders saying the sparrows are devouring the harvest, and his entire village sets out to catch them, him and his friends stringing carcasses around their necks, as the women bang pots and pans so the birds can't land and rain from the sky, dead from exhaustion. But next harvest a cloud of insects descends like night, without the birds to eat them, and people begin to starve—including the young cadre's family (yet he still believes). How that story got Furio red-tagged as a Communist, I'll never understand. Then there's *Desert Shadows*, his long-listed novel that got him banned from Saudi—I still choke up thinking about Job, leaving home to work, hiding his homosexuality, and everything else he is, to support his family back home. Oh, and of course Furio's classic poem about Metro Manila: "built deep / like the bay's confusion / black and blue / going and coming / with a loud / silent roar." Exactly like our relationship, pretty much: deeply confusing, born from black and blue, making me scream inside with frustration. Fu showing me that men are just boys: insecure, in denial, infuriated that they can't fool us anymore about any of it. As in, Professor Almondo can rock many a classroom or hold court in any dive bar, but bring him to a nightclub and he's a slug in salt—still calling them discotheques, and was always so jelly whenever guys asked me to dance. Not like he ever took me out for a twirl, except this one time he hammed it up like *Saturday Night Fever*, which proved just tragic. And so by the bar he'd lean and drink, chatting with my friends while I fidgeted in frustration.

(Inaudible)

They loved him, actually. They still rub his bald head and call him Buddha—hanging out just them, even, for like bubble tea, joking and opinionating, and gossiping about me, I bet. Boy and Furio going way

way back—way before Boy opened his iconic club, Mandible (or as the drag queens call it: the Jaw)—back when he still dressed mannequins at Rustan's, and was getting famous for their Christmas windows. And Fu and Jojie clicked so fast I hated it. Like, I had to learn from him about Jojie's mom, imprisoned during the dictatorship: seven months preggers, twelve hours' labor alone in her cell, Jojie plopping onto the filthy floor, too premature to cry—whisked away for adoption by a general and his wife, till Jojie's mom gets freed in an amnesty and finds a job as a maid in their house, one day locking the nanny in the pantry and fleeing with Jojie wailing in a pillowcase. And how her mother joined the Kingdom of Faith in Christ and noticed that her child's not the typical Boy Scout, Jojie finally leaving about the same age I did, after she was told: "I stole the wrong baby." All this Jojie revealed to Furio, for his article on her butch beer garden, Brew-Ha-Ha?—that place a super big deal; so much so it got shut down. We Pinoys are conservative but pretty tolerant of feminine manifestations of homosexuality—coz we accept beauty as a valid way out of hardship—but lesbians, especially masculine ones, they're too threatening to Pinoy machismo. And fear can be so unreasonable, which is why I understood Jojie never telling me about her past; pity's a scary thing to receive from your beshie. So big ups to Furio for being unafraid of LGBTQIA identities—despite his toxic masculinity towards a dance floor. I'd have to lean with him by his Fundador while he tried to make conversation: "WHAT DO YOU CALL THIS GENRE?" (Shouting in my ear.) "I DIG IT!" (Nodding and sipping.) "GOTTA GET ME TUNES LIKE THIS FOR MY POWER WALK-ING!" (Gazing at the decor.) "GROOVY PLACE!" (Turning in wonder.) "WHAT'S THIS AESTHETIC? RETROFUTURIST?" (Sipping and nod-ding.) "LET'S DECORATE MY HOUSE LIKE THIS!" (Expecting me to laugh.)

(Laughter)

A fuddy-duddy—that's what he was. Affectionate like that tita who says you got fat whenever she sees you. When my toilet wouldn't flush again, he'd tease me while fixing it—celebrating my poo as "doe-like and dainty." (And so, my other pet name: Bambi.) Proudly thinking his jokes were so bad they're good. When I'd off the light to sleep, he'd whisper this sweet nothing: "If you want to make love tonight—pull my penis once. If you don't want to—pull it two hundred times." Quelle romantic, right?

(Laughter)

He really did crack me up. But he'd cross the line making fun of my praying. "Hail Mary, who gave up her cherry to some Pharisee with sexy curls," he'd say, "then told Joseph it was God who knocked her up." Always so disrespectful. Even suspended twice in university—once for switching the organist's sheet music with "Stairway to Heaven" and again for vandalizing a CR stall, writing "God sees all. Wipe well." When Baccante and the bishops attacked me over the RR Bill, Furio'd call him a Damaso, and the rest "dumb mass-holes"—which made me feel supported, till I remembered that's how he saw *my* faith, too. He was so dogmatic—ironically. Talking about his values till you're about exhausted into surrendering yours. And I've never known anyone with so many enemies—and that's saying a lot. So many he'll surprise them by saying hi in public, then lean over to me and groan: "I forgot. I hate that guy." Like I said, a pit bull—can't let go of a bone. That's why we had no future, and why we lasted so long. I just couldn't bring myself to leave, as he braved the showbiz beat he resented, every penny for child support, rent, cigs, booze, and dinners with me. Scraping by on freelance gigs he felt were beneath him: copyediting corporate annual reports, teaching undergrads, ghostwriting autobiographies—as if that's not one of the hardest jobs out there, right?

(Pause. Laughter)

But the guy never let me pay, not once, for anything. It wasn't generous, or sexist, or paternal—just plain old pride. Which was the root of our problem: Furio refusing to let me outgrow him even if all he wanted was to help me grow. Like, he hated hearing about my past, but would ask anyway. "I only wish I'd been there," said he, "to love you right." One time I mentioned Cat and me used to watch porno together and Furio broke the pencil he was holding. "That explains everything," he exclaimed, explaining nothing. Honestly, I don't think you can call a relationship healthy if you have to hide things, and there's nothing more telling about a person than how they judge you—Cat, actually, teaching me that. First time I caught him watching porno—me waking up to pee, him lying down on the living room floor, his pajama pants a pillow and his leg stretched to pause and fast-forward the VHS with his big toe—that first time, I judged him, and judged myself. Wasn't I enough? Cat responding, surprisingly patiently, helping me understand, at my pace. Making it about *my* sexuality, *our* intimacy—the "pornoisseur" (as he called himself) introducing me to the best stuff of whatever I was ready to handle. But Furio had long decided such things are oppressive to everyone involved, whether they know it or not. So we never talked about it again and I hid my solo playtime. As Steven Covey says: "Most people do not listen with the intent to understand; they listen with the intent to reply." Sounds to me kinda like masturbation.

(Silence)

I get it—I do: Furio finds comfort in certainty; but I was young and wanted to explore even my uncertainty—not be warned off it by someone else's old wisdom. Furio could be such an Orion that all the endearing aspects of our relationship started feeling like a bad-trip haircut before a big event—embarrassing, frustrating, petty. Like resenting his shirts tucked into his boxers. And him calling contemporary music derivative. And how he'd send texts without vowels, like the nineties themselves were messaging. It sucked, being told how to be when I couldn't even suggest he pluck his nipples—my tweezers left politely on the CR counter, though he never took the hint. Anyways. Did you know that in yogic philosophy, age is measured not in years but in the fitness of your spine? The merudanda—the axis of your universe. I'd like to think I'm an old soul with a supple center, able to do the hard, necessary thing, eventually. I remember in Grade Six, changing out of my school uniform, my mother looking at me like reading my future. "Vita, always think with your head," said she. "Never think with your heart." But with me and Fu, my heart just couldn't bear ending it. Till one day, LeTrel uses my CR before leaving in the morning, and Furio comes over for lunch and goes to jingle, returning to the kitchen, all like, "Bambi, was another man here?" And I'm like, Whatever do you mean? "Because there's a mammoth turd in your toilet." So I go and look at it, realizing I have two choices. But how could I lie to him and destroy my doe-like femininity that he so loved? I reach across and take his hand and nod sadly. Furio staring into the toilet, his head going crimson. You could tell he was trying to make our ending more poetic than it was turning out to be. We waited what seemed like a lifetime. Then he flushed.

(Sigh)

Anyways. I can reveal all this coz the past is passed and it's all future for him now: the country's most famous journalist; named Stud of the Year by *The View* magazine. Everyone loves a redemption story, right? Besides, that silly old baldie knows I adore him. We weren't friends again while I was with LT, of course, but he was the first reporter to stand up for me when that camel-toe thing dropped—writing a piece for *The Graphic*, on what the scandal said about showbiz, public life, body image, gender, and how I was being scrutinized and ignored simultaneously (his essay poking at consciences and finally turning the conversation). After that olive branch, I saw him more regularly, every month or so, chatting over mango cheesecake and Nestea, about my life, my jobs, even the guys I was seeing. He hated me with Rolex, and worried about me with Red, and helped me find my voice during the whole Reproductive Rights saga—coz he wanted to stick it to the mass-hole bishops, but still. "Fight emotions," he advised, "with facts." So that's what I do. Did you know that fifty percent of pregnancies in the Philippines are unintended? That one in three Filipinas between fifteen and forty-four have had an abortion? And every year more than half a million abortions are performed in seedy back rooms—scraped away with wire hangers or broomsticks, or massaged out like a black-head being popped. And nearly twenty percent of those women—almost a hundred thousand, a small city—get rushed to hospitals for complications. About a tenth of those—more than a thousand!—die in terror: blood pooling in the sheets, cramps tearing them in half as they face the hell they're told they're destined for. You probably know all this, but it bears repeating till it's fixed. So how could I not support the Reproductive Rights Bill? It'll always be a man's world—unless women vote. Plus I'm a Christian—aren't we supposed to help each other face the consequences of our sins? I started New Life for women suffering such complications. And the Sanctuary, for trafficked or abused women and girls. And the Mustard Seed Foundation, which offers microfinanc-ing (and a venue for assassinating an evil president, apparently). Coz some people still believe Coca-Cola's a spermicide, and that you can force a miscarriage by jumping off your roof, and that there's nowhere to go with your problems if you're a girl like me who's sinned. Like Furio said: fight emotions with facts.

(Chair scrapes. Footsteps pace)

Fact: it was only in 1967 that a woman ran alongside men in an official marathon—though registered as K. V. Switzer, instead of Kathrine Switzer—people believing a woman's uterus would fall out if she ran more than eight hundred meters (male race officials even trying to shove her off the road there in Boston). Fact: science shows the HPV vaccine drastically reduces the chances of cervical cancer—yet the bishops got it banned and they attacked my ads supporting it. Fact: Furio's always been my biggest defender, through all my public adversities until today. Bless. That's why he was my red-carpet arm-candy for my best-supporting nomination, for *Heaven Only Knows*, at the Golden Duries. And read lines with me before my theater debut—as Big Sister in *Chinese Belches*, Met Rep's controversially satirical and short-lived musical. And when I left Channel Eight's *Ready! Set! Go!* for Channel Nine's *Oh-Em-Gee!*—my haters calling me ever-unfaithful—Furio was there, reminding me to do what you have to do to move up in this world. All while his own life continued its downward slide: first his terrible luck with dating sites, then the terrible cliché of dating one of his undergrads—this skater-girl from the University of Santo Tomas who looked like a Muslim princess and had a blog about books, booze, student governance, and emo music (so perfect for him it could only end badly). That was when I was abroad with Deepak, and wasn't the best emailer—Jojie keeping me updated, saying I should've been worried. Though honestly I was proud that Furio'd learned something from me: the point of reckless love, reminding us of life's possibilities. But in attempting to impress his Muslim princess, he ototcopied clever Facebook status updates, and instead of apologizing for his totally relatable status-update anxiety, the old Foolio doubled down. "I was just sampling," he claimed. "Paying homage!" Everyone expecting more from such a respected writer, who played his elder statesman slash gatekeeper card, rage-blocking his critics. Everyone taking sides, of course— this was during the Reyes presidency, when we could afford to fight

over unimportant things. When his Muslim princess dumped him—
poetically, on social media; epically, for another girl—all us friends
worried about his decision to quit writing for good. A man of so many
words with no more words left? So I called and called soon as I returned after Deepak.

(Chair scrapes. Seatback shifts)

A couple weeks later he finally met me in the park outside the National
Museum, where he used to school me on art history. We sit and share
scars in the shadow of the statue of the great writer and revolutionary.
Furio is unshaven, patchy monk's crown on his head, smelling like he's
given up his toothbrush for Lent—going on about how he longs to see
his daughters, how he misses reading me poetry, how he rewatched
all my movies while I was abroad. "They're better the second time
around," says he. "Especially *Booba 2: Here They Come Again*. So funny!"
Bending to tie his shoelaces and squinting up at me. "Some sequels are
just better," says he, "don't you think?" Oh Fu, I tell him. Not usually. I
tell him our friendship is priceless. He asks if I'm seeing anyone. And
just as I'm about to mention meeting Kingsley, he interrupts, knowing
it's not going where he hoped. "I must leave," says he. Oh, come on, I
say, Don't be like that. I couldn't let him go—not back to that empty
home and all its echoes. He pulls his arm like my hand burns him.
After a few steps he turns around. "I'm sorry," says he. "Especially that
time we . . . you know . . . in the beginning, when I shouted at you for
lying in my bed. It still smelled of my wife." Ancient history, I say,
Mythology even. He closes his eyes and nods. Then gives me that *Magnum, P.I.* smile. "Goodbye, Sissypuss," he says. "Keep on rolling." And I
did, and so did he—with each punch and every kick. Bad grass don't
die and here we are: Sexy-Sexygate, impeachment, poor Loy's televised trial starting next week, and the election nearly upon us. It's on.

(Knuckles crack)

Furio got the chance he'd given up hoping for, and it's like everything
now is in some way because of him. Nando making desperate moves by
red-tagging all his enemies. Nur still leading the polls, despite trending
allegations about his homosexuality and son's addiction. Even Hope's
courageously returned, to fill Rita's former spot in the Unity Party,
though it's probably too late. And tonight: the final announcement of

the tickets—me backing Nur; Lucy Lontok backing her father; Birdie Patilya supposedly joining macho forces with Rolex. Glorioso fingering as her veep either the ratchet fame-whore K. Sisboy Pansen or the human rights lawyer turned spokespologist Hari Pukeh—though his pandemic pics wriggling among dolphins at Oceanland torpedoed his cred with anyone who was locked down (i.e., everyone). And rumor has it Junior may offer his VP rose to the bachelorette Caress Reyes—which would be cray, since his dad imprisoned her dad back in the day. But you know the Philippines: everything comes full circle. Me and Fu attending society parties again, now as prized guests—but still standing by the chocolate fountain to skewer marshmallows and anyone who deserves it. I love that I'm still that person to him. I love that he finally treats me like an equal. I love that I could help him be the person he always hoped he'd be: bylines to the left of him, bylines to the right of him, cover stories that volley and thunder—out of the valley of death rode Furio Almondo, beat reporter who toppled a president, word by word by hard-fought word. But will that fight be enough to make a difference? Tune in next time, True Believers, as we race towards the climax of our unwritten destiny, and decide who will lead us into it.

Furio Almondo, MFA, PhD, Transcript.

(42:11.76—Almondo.M4A)

Vita. Light of my pipe, fire of my dream. Our sin, our star. Vee-tah: a smile of the lips, then a tap of the tongue, before a tsk-tsk and a shake of the head at what I had but lost. Vita: amor, felicitas, dolor. Galatea of the silver screen, boob tube, and showbiz blind item—for whom my treacherous heart once beat humbert-humbert, humbert-humbert. Now, as a panoply of politikos pander to da Pilipino peoples, who'd have thunk it would be Vita revolutionizing the present by promising the future? Not I. Not long ago I was too busy to care—massaging my aching head with a bottle of Bulag Gin. At the door went a knockity-knock. In sauntered a sultry ghost from my past: a sight for sore eyes, a sore spot in my soul—like angina. Vita! I hid my bottle but it clinked and she knew. Her smile told me she was unsure I'd be up to the job. Her eyes said I was all she had left. Thanks to her bravery, the rest of us are now blessed with choices, such as they are: the new Junior-Farrah tag team, the Lontoks' squadgoals, wily Glorioso with wormtongue Pansen, and our abandoned great Hope with her necessary bedfellow Rolex, all versus Bansamoro at the top, basking in the glow of our phosphorescent super Ms. Nova. Yet which winningest pair will be anointed by brothers Changco and their fellow tax-evading, campaign-donating oligarchs? The answer's simple: whoever's likeliest to win on December 12. But every tangled catch-twenty-two has roots, and this particular one began that desperate, sweltering Saturday night, in my tawdry living room—Vita placing on my crumby coffee table her little recording thingamajig and telling her story in a quiet, assured voice, which wavered here, and quavered there, but never stopped. She, the lone witness to a ten-thirty-one on the corner of Governance and Greed.

The Estregan Gang had struck again! Well. I took the case, of course—she had me at knockity. My only plans, anyway, were an appointment I kept postponing with my mortician. I sent Vita to a safe place. I positioned my laptop before me. I poured one last drink.

(Glasses clink. Liquid pouring)

As the crystal kissed my lips, memories slugged me like yet another jealous husband. Vita! All our late-night calls. Her eyes in the diner like a Hopper painting. Her face like a sunflower tilted to storm clouds. How she had taken control, even then. How she peeled away my clothes and defenses. Removed my shame and my Jockey shorts yellowing, my undershirt with armpits matching. Her breasts were like motherhood, then incest. Followed by the best four minutes of my life. Ending with Vita embracing my unclenching soul, whispering: "Promise you'll never give up on me. Promise we'll always have each other. Somehow." I always keep my vows. Eventually. God damn those goddamn memories. I poured myself one more one last drink. I wrote. I logged on. I clicked and I posted our first story: The Fart That Shook the Nation. Sunday morning's front pages follow, spiraling and blurring. Extra! Extra! We read all about it—the effluence of allegations of corruption, collusion, extrajudicial killing, the Swine Swindle, the Fertilizer Farce, the "Hello, Roly" electoral fraud, the HealthPhils pandemic plunder, the vaccine smuggling blunder, the payola from blood sport and numbers rackets, the embezzlement of the Presidential Intel Fund, the drug-smearing and red-tagging of dissenters and opposition voices, and all the racist, misogynistic, and, frankly, unsurprising idiocies recorded by Vita from the loose lips that would sink Estregan's ship. But in our moment of history, the truth is no longer enough to get rats scurrying for the life rafts. A few things first needed to transpire to make them perspire.

(Coughing)

As Vita posted online, and I wrote on record, Commander-in-Chief Estregan's outrage, at what he dubbed a blatant political smear, was worthy of another Golden Durian. "I will step down," he emoted, "if there is a whiff of corruption." His commender-in-chief, Kingsley Belli, announced an investigation of the investigation. "The ones who smelled it," he vented, "dealt it." The Changco brothers and their minions frothed with tabloid sanctimony about the elites they wished to replace, while my own paper was too long-chilled into self-censorship. So, I, like a belligerent Woodstein, armed with Vita's recordings, connected, day by day, week by week, one by one all the dots that comprised the cover-up: from committee, ministry, commission, task force, Congress, the Court most supreme, to the UPP and the highest office in the land—till my pointillism became a portrait the country couldn't condone. The evidence had always been hiding in plain sight, like a ledger lost in a library.

(Match flares. Exhalation)

For we da peoples had always seen what we always knew. Albeo Cruz, the seminarian martyred in the wrong country and wrong presidency, a statistic now among tens of thousands. The bishops' sermons bought with luxury SUVs. The cake-boxes of cash brought to mah-jongg nights at the Palace. The wiretap recordings on electoral fraud, as candidate Estregan greeted kingmaker Aguirre: "Hello, Roly? Will I win one hundred percent in your province?" All the multi-millions of unli-allocations siphoned to Panama. All of that, we knew. All the Veritable Bank accounts of the fictional Pidal J. Velarde—we knew. We heard of the paper trail to his mistress Tootsi's twelve-bidet Trevi Mansion; and the rumors of billions from Senator Bingo Bobot's warship acqui-sition; and the charges of kickbacks from the familia Glorioso's mili-tary helicopter deal; and the Changco brothers' in-law's cut from the Ministry of Tourism's ad budget—acquittals notwithstanding. Just as we've known exactly why our cons in Congress still refuse to legislate the Constitution's antidynasty provision. And why our sinner senators passed the No Spoilers Act and have wielded with glee their Cyber Libel Law against critics—even college kids merely exercising their dismay on social media. And we knew, most of all, about the nobly named shell companies siphoning dozens of legislators' pork barrels earmarked for disaster reconstruction, infrastructure development, and public education. To me what was scandalous wasn't the vast-ness of the lie but the callousness of the theft. And the death by a thousand papercuts of our ability to do anything about it. All those journalists and media organizations silenced; all those Opposition fig-ures jailed, killed, or hamstrung; all those civil liberties paused then purged during the pandemic; all those efforts by the desperate Lontoks and opportunistic Bansamoro to push impeachment proceedings—yet it only took one domino tipped in the right direction to topple the rest into a wave.

(Liquid pouring)

When Vita's drip, drip, drip of recordings revealed that conversation between the president, Rolex, Kingsley, and Rusty Batlog—then still police chief, not yet senator—implicating Aguirre fils, Patek, in distributing drugs via the family's network of community numbers gambling . . . well, that's when the wily wizened warlord secretly went witness for the wicked opposition. Drugs kill, these days more than usual, and that good provider's larcenies have always been for the well-being of the Aguirre clan. So Rolex's sudden conscience publicly emerged, after Kingsley's testimony left him no choice. And in earnest surged the impeachment, with its hijinks and low drama, its pageant of witnesses hosted in the airport-lounge shabbiness of our most-sacrosanct Senate chamber—as the president's petulant dance instructor, waddling Warden Cantuteh, dueled with Senator Nuredin Bansamoro to tell the better story and sway the outrage of da Pilipino peoples. But Cantuteh's slut-shaming shenanigans were meant as nothing more than ruination for the homewrecking, bishop-tainted, drug-using, butt-twerking, scorned-woman Vita. "Who is to be believed," he sniveled, "the betrayer or the betrayed?" A dickish deflection by the tall-tale-telling ambulance chaser, complacent in believing neither facts nor audio evidence could sway our political capi to throw their capo di tutti under the bus. When the truth has so long been dictated by Dear Leader, and legitimized by polls of uninformed opinions, and validated by dubious ballot every six years, even the real, factual, true truth can no longer threaten power. What it took this time, was, well . . . time—and its scourges, as the slugger had grown sluggish, as his guard drooped lazily, as the only betrayal that could finally undermine him came from his own body.

(Coughing)

Following the Commander-in-Chief's five-day absence amidst the impeachment and the aftermath of the coincidentally named Supertyphoon Nanding—while the media questioned, and netizens hashtagged whereisthepresident—his new chief commender, Senator Bingo Bobot, released that infamous selfie, with Estregan at home in a T-shirt emblazoned with his own face, the day's newspaper conspicuous beside his breakfast of unadorned congee. Yet even Sweet Mr. Suavé's signature dukes-up pose couldn't conceal the infirmity in his face. The next day, the king of the ring returned truculently, resurrected to address reporters outside the Palace, denouncing what he called "that court of kangaroos," while sporting a neck brace to convey the debilitating injustice of the impeachment trial. But that, to use one of his favoritest phrases, was a wrong mistake. The pantomime of medical frailty only succeeds if most of da peoples know it's not true. Threats of a Revolutionary Government only work if you've the military's support, which had eroded after he used the same gun to fight the pandemic as he did his drug war. Seeing an animal cornered, and fearing a desperate declaration of martial law, crowds sweated onto the streets, intoxicated by familiar chants and comforted by communal purpose—amassing, once again, for a mass and prayer rally on EDSA Boulevard, at the feet of Our Lady of the Many Revolutions. These typhoon winds of change had cracked Estregan's closet open for his conga line of dancing skeletons—a gathering tail of fleet-footed turncoats, one by one.

(Match flares. Exhalation)

Rolex had been the first to follow Kingsley's beat. True to form, the other wavering dominoes tipped: Money Villa, T. T. Gordion, Uranus Jupiter Kayatanimo-Uy, Hari Pukeh, and all the rest so deft at playing musical chairs in those seconds between power ballads in our country's long cotillion. But it was Vita—the quadruple threat: star, martyr, whistleblower, heroine—who performed the coup de grâce, testifying like a feisty Cio-Cio-San unfolding her colors. But Fernando V. Estregan had learned from the past. In volume one of his tragicomedy, an uprising led by his spiritual advisor, Brother Martin, had resulted in his ouster by book's end. In this sequel, our old antagonist has refused a similar narrative arc. Twisting the denouement, he refused to testify and instead called for snap elections—because a boxer knows that, at times, the best way to take a punch is to step into it. Nando was always a helluva inside fighter. Clearly, the People's Champ is no chimp, for it was he who revolutionized the vogue for Everyman Ruthlessness—battering his opponent pulpy, then smiling like a simpleton and tanking da Lord Jesus Cries, and his madder and his espouse, and itch of da every all Pilipino peoples, who are of course the sole purpose he fights for such lucrative purses. He will not go down easily, this twice-elected president who perfected democratic dictatorship. Hail his new world order, comrades! Totalitarianism's only for the loony or lily-livered leader—how passé, how outré! Any on-trend authoritarian knows that nobody overthrows a government that provides us with just enough. As Joplin sang: "Freedom's just another word for nothing left to lose." So give me security or give me death! And give me death only if it's not mine or that of anyone I like. Estregan gave us the circuses and he gave us the bread. Free healthcare and education—both substandard. The Citizens Dividend—fractions from our natural resources sold to China. And the Charter of Communal Rights—swapping universal human rights for whatever the State dictates we all need. Give the hungry enough crumbs, satiate enough undersecretaries with slivers, feed your minions enough slices, and the whole cake's yours to have, and eat it, too. Nando knows this. His allies know this. Every all knows this, except da Pilipino peoples, who swallowed his swollen story, every inch—down to his hirsute sack. Ensuring all the gobbling was his Goebbels, Kingsley, the churnalist so power-hungry he twisted our country into one of the most lethal for journalists. The slightest infractions earn you the most colorful troll-mob death threats—like when my blog exposed Estregan's shirtless, ropeless, cliff-scaling selfie as just him crawling on rocky ground with the crew's camera angled strategically sideways and skyward. The photographer who gave me those raw files met a predictable death by duct tape and antidrug signage.

(Coughing)

Well. This December 12 snap election is not at all Sweet Mr. Suavé up against the turnbuckle. It's simply the ol' rope-a-dope strategy. The beheadings, the assassination of dear Rita, the protests outside the U.S. embassy that turned violent, and the coming trial of that disillusioned Nandotard, Loy Bonifacio—all just a soapy opera to lather up Junior and Farrah. All just loosey-goosey huff-and-puff. Just willy-nilly, hither-thither helter-skelter. For the namby-pamby nitwits hollering and howling for the cozy yoke of oppression. No shit, Sherlock? Dig deeper, Watson. The bitterroot of disillusion's down there somewhere. Take presidential propagandist Belli—please! Alas, poor Kingsley, I knew him well. The Trollmaster General forgave neither the rich nor poor for his middle-class upbringing. His sudden testicular fortitude— what he called his "patriotic imperative of conscience," as he performed at the impeachment, like Hendrix blazing at Monterey—nothing more than sugar-coated self-service. Like eating with his mother's maids— the college rebel discomfiting both household help and his madre, the poor Tita Baby, with her principled aspirations toward decent society. While she lived, her son was a long-haired hippie Communist. While she spins in her grave, he's a money-grubbing capitalist opportunist.

(Inaudible)

Oh, the King mentioned that, did he? Yes, he brought me to my first protest. We shouted and sang solemnly in Plaza Miranda—aflame with purpose, not blessed with your generation's cynicism, which will keep your failures from festering into trauma. Arms linked like newly-weds down the aisle, Kingsley and I marched, amidst the comman-deered church bells clamoring juicily down University Ave, the two of us raising fists in unison—evidence of the people's clutched emp-tiness. He and I faced phalanxes of lacquered shields, batons like pol-ished femurs, as my heart moved backwards while comrades behind pushed me forwards—only my greater fear of cowardice shoving me toward courage. We two were so kindred people thought us brothers. So aligned in what we had to say, our voices rhymed. Yet decades later, I stayed the course, accepting the lessons of my mistakes, rejecting the ignorance of always being right. While nothing feels quite as right as might for the likes of Kingsley, who served as Estregan's toilet brush, thrilled at being useful. Former editor of *The Bullet*—or *The Bully*, or *The Bullshet*, as his tabloid is often called—he gained entry to the inner circle through the success of his ingenious Make Your Own Meme app, designed to recruit and empower rabid FFS supporters in his over-arching grassroots disinformation campaign, which proved as organic as Astroturf. Now Kingsley's a hero, lauded for his brave treachery.

(Liquid pouring)

But who is to be believed, the betrayed or the betrayer? He considers me a dinosaur, I know, naively gazing into the sky at the pretty Chicxulub asteroid growing more magnificent and imminently impactful, lighting up my demise. I do remain dazzled by the power of story, but I never lost faith in fact and its need for our searching vigilance. Kingsley sees it as a product. I know it to be a process. While his certainty led him trekking into the misty Marxist mountains, my uncertainty led me into the coffee-and-cigs cacophony of the newsroom. I arrived bright and early, brash and earnest, my pencils sharpened—the fastest Gregg shorthand writer in my graduating class: two-sixty-five, buster. And I never left. Journalism's purpose jibed with my ideals, with my woeful compassion for the worst and my awful skepticism of the best that humanity has to offer. There's superhero power in exposing what's hidden. A cop carries gun and badge and uses force as persuasion; a newshound carries pen and pad and through words forces persuasion. Oh, how I worshipped that monastic code!—ask why, explore every angle, never settle for easy answers. As you know, balance and objectivity have nothing to do with harmony. A journo's job is to be contrarian. The Nandotards paint me as a Fuchsia because I don't share their groupthink and I challenge their faith. Never mind that I held Respeto Reyes and his ilk to the same standard as all our presidents—on whom I've reported for forty years. Never mind that I briefly supported the second candidacy of Estregan, as the best choice among the worst, until I went into the poorest communities in the first weeks of his drug war to see for myself—encountering too many crime scenes that looked more like executions by police than criminals fighting back. Never mind those inconvenient facts, from us, the fake news. Oh the falsehood of reporting what Estregan does or doesn't do as part of his job! Oh the bias of quoting him verbatim! Oh the insolence of asking questions! Oh the duplicity of doubting the doublespeak that excuses his gaslighting jokes and sarcasm! Oh the callousness of asking after his cancer and whether it's now Senator Bingo Bobot pulling his strings! And so we newspersons are discredited whole cloth—as destabilizing, tool-of-the-oligarchs hypocrites—thanks to our harried process and its not-infallible standards, with our updates, developments, corrections, retractions, as stories rapidly evolve toward a truth revealed through gradual, collective effort. Our uncomfortable quest for certainty crucified by those comfortable with their certainties.

(Coughing)

Was it intolerant or invasive of me to reveal how Estregan first met Cantuteh—years ago at an auction of Nazi artifacts, Fernando's Schutzstaffel banquet-set displayed beside Warden's watercolors by the future Führer? I believed then, and I believe now, that their shared hobby is relevant to the public interest. And yet I was slapped with a libel suit, tailored by the nakedly guilty, in a country where libel's a criminal offense: the "public and malicious imputation of a crime, or of a vice or defect, real"—*real!*—"or imaginary, or any act, omission, condition, status or circumstance tending to cause the dishonor, discredit, or contempt of a natural or juridical person, or to blacken the memory of one who is dead." As a law, that's somewhat self-serving, wouldn't you say?—if you even dare say it, lest you dishonor the lawmakers who benefit from our silencing: those who are protected no matter how real their crimes, vices, and defects may be. Those who—like the well-connected businessman Waldorf King—will press for the jailing of journalists whose only sin was reporting on allegations and investigations into a purported crime.

(Match flares. Exhalation)

But what can anyone do? Look at Senator Toti Otots the Turd—if you've the stomach to—and what he did after the Cyber Libel restrictions became law, which he himself championed in the legislature. As the new Senate president, he demanded the removal of old online news articles about the alleged gang rape of the starlet Pepsi Paloma—and how he purportedly used his influence to save his brother and friends. Then he demanded, on top of that, the removal of online reporting about even his denials of said reports. What a whitewash! And now Junior's family's following suit, using trolls and lackeys, I suspect even in the Ministry of Education, to burnish the Dictator's past, and prepare his offsprings' future—funded with the billions they stole from us, da Pilipino peoples, whose next generation will be fed fairy tales and YouTube videos about that family's victimization and largesse.

(Liquid pouring)

What can you do, we of the lumpy proletariat? How do we demand accountability from those who can rewrite the rules, and even history itself? How do we safeguard history, so that it can be studied to prevent old tricks from being repeated? Is my only option to be fitted for another libel suit? My wardrobe's already full of them. They're never out of style to thin-skinned politikos—like their weekday man-purses and weekend penny loafers. By filing a case that costs them little, the most dishonorable, discredited, and contemptible natural or juridical persons can guard against dishonor, discredit, and contempt—however deserved. They force underpaid journalists to travel to the jurisdiction the politiko controls, to face judges the politiko appointed, to risk as many as six years in the politiko's jails—nowadays up to twelve for online transgressions, for as little as an overly candid comment or two-hundred-eighty-character rant against a politiko and their myriad malversations. What can we do? Except forge our swords of truth to proffer to the gods as they battle on Mount Olympus, while we watch and pray that the more benevolent will prevail.

(Coughing)

Not too long ago, art remained our final refuge—our novels, stories, songs, and films protected and enshrined as free expression, where we mere mortals could immortalize the sins of the sinful. Then the onion-skinned Estregan signed the No Spoilers Act—protecting netizens from social media posts that spoil the plot twists and cliff-hangers of our favorite TV series. But the death of parody, satire, and artistic creativity hid inside that Trojan horse—criminalizing "public, reckless, or deliberate expressions, misrepresentations, or misinterpretations, on digital or traditional media, that inhibit the reasonable privacy, agency, dignity, or satisfaction, of a natural or juridical person." So, for example, even creative and fanciful words, which no one in their right mind would either believe or imagine to be real, are now potentially criminal. As an illustrative example—offered purely in the spirit of free academic discourse—I would never dare write about an S&M orgy involving Toti Otots, Waldorf King, Mother Teresa, an adamantium alien robot octopus from Betelgeuse, and Cicciolina, with a naked Estregan in fuchsia nipple tassels sipping cold butterbeer from the tiny skull of Orion while he imagines the totally fictional bukkake finale onto the ahegao face of Senator Low-Hanging-Fruit.

(Laughter)

I chortle because it's so obviously untrue. Yet we cannot write that even as obvious hyperbole. We can't even say it out aloud as long as there's somebody to hear it. We can, however, for now, still enjoy the constitutional freedom to privately think it—though why would anyone conceive of such preposterous absurdity? When they take our words, our thoughts are next. And what tools now, what weapons then, will we have left? How can we pull down curtains from glass houses and unlock doors of power? How can we, the media, empower the public with knowledge to guide them at the ballot boxes? How do we, the public, push those public servants who only act when faced with consequences, whether praise or punishment at the polls? If we're powerless now to punish, are we only to praise?—like offering sugar or screen time to terrible twos in midtantrum.

(Match flares. Exhalation)

I will not go gently into that night! When Vita asked for my help, to tell the world all she witnessed, I was prepared to die for that story. I barred my door and subsisted on instant noodles those weeks I wrote, sheltering in place once again from an invisible enemy outside. While my blog posts went viral, Vita superspread her testimonies, from an undisclosed location, with the unmatched spite of a woman scorned. Safely apart, we stood together. Because if we citizens can no longer punish insensitive rulers even when they do wrong, our oversensitive rulers can punish us citizens even when we have done no wrong. To quote my hero, my colleague Maria Ressa, we must "hold the line." Kingsley and I learned that, in our first protests. A voice starts alone. Then is joined by another. Then three. Then thirty-three voices, holding the line. Then three hundred. Three thousand. Until three hundred thousand make heard our shared demands. In the public squares. At the doors of parliaments. At the walls that hold back our bodies but not our voices. Walls behind which cower those with power, their fingers in their ears.

(Inaudible)

Well. That's a fair question—you're right: if the media is to wield its power, its power must be wielded responsibly. As the saying goes: "Can we defend it at Plaza Miranda?"

(Liquid pouring)

I'm the first to admit what we do isn't perfect. My stumble from grace makes that clear. I've no illusions about the system's sins and short-comings. As a cub reporter all I had was disillusionment, discovering the venality up and down the mastheads. My first wrong mistake was believing I could remain beyond it. My second was thinking I'd achieved enough status to safely expose it—all the transactional relationships, retail and wholesale buying, AC/DC schemes, and the rest. Like a wiseguy Icarus forewarned by the wiser, my fall was swift, from firebrand city editor into the sea of ecru menus and bold-typed guests at the birthdays, nuptials, and diamond jubilees that became my beat. My vanquishers had hissed about the hypocrisy of my past compromises—accepting at Christmas cinnamon-scented candles, or bottles of Johnnie Red, or Ray-Bans from a congressman's import-export business, all so I could cultivate key connections, without promising bias, or even coverage. We say no to cash but accept ILTs—"In Lieu Thereof"—which are less transactional than strategic, to bond with former colleagues gone to work PR for politicians or corporations. At times we must compromise the ethical for the promise of the moral, our means justified by the end truth we seek.

(Coughing)

I learned that when I landed my first byline above the fold, thanks to my first ILT—a group of us on a congressman's junket to both Bumbay and Lahore, the era's most famous male entertainment palaces, across each other on Quezon Ave. When their ribald rivalry later led the mayor, public prosecutor, and police chief to raid Bumbay, instigated by Lahore, it was the aforementioned junket that had armed me with the contacts for my story—about the lined-up working girls in handcuffs calling out the pet names and preferred services of those crusading city officials. Life must be lived if we are to discover the truths in it. But I swear on both my daughters that I never succumbed

to envelopmental journalism's cash-stuffed stationery—or ATM journalism, as it's known in our era of direct deposits. Not even when one
of my old mentors, who'd left to work for a certain political family, took
me to lunch to celebrate my making city editor, and offered to put me
on retainer—thinking he was only sharing, helping me provide for his
goddaughter. That's known as subsidized reporting, when you serve
as eyes and ears and helpful hand with a press release—or "praise release," as we call them. To some that's hardly a sin on your soul.

(Liquid pouring)

What leaves a blemish is retail buying: when you create, curve, or kill
stories for cash—your soul sold but left with you to face at night. And
then there's wholesale buying, when your whole news organization's
damned, and you with it—bent over by new ownership, huge ad buys,
company-wide payouts, lucrative land deals, or postelection appoint-
ments into government for the loudest of loyalists. Such was the worry
for the once-venerable *Philippine Daily Inquirer* and the fate of the now-
venereal *Manila Times*, when their owners were strong-armed out. To
rulers like Estregan, oligarchs are only enemies when they aren't allies.

(Coughing)

Meanwhile, broadcasters routinely offer election-season packages, with
campaign ads, candidate interviews, and special reports by respected
hosts. And movie stars move to star in politics, blurring the line between A-section and entertainment pages—hard-news ethics dodged
through lifestyle puff-pieces. And eventually some ugly ducklings among
the Palace press corps swan into courtiers, pawning objectivity for access. Even the journos once united in reporting on police abuses in
Estregan's drug war now squabble for diminishing international attention and dwindling foreign grants.

(Match flares. Exhalation)

What can we do?—with our low pay, long hours, institutional vulnerability, and proximity to power and its temptations. Journalists like
Marlene Esperat get murdered while orgs like ABS-CBN get shut down.
Well. Myself, foolishly, I shat where I ate, exposing a pair of prominent
editorial writers, one at *The Sun*, the other at *The Bullshet*, who colluded
in an AC/DC scheme—Attack-Collect, Defend-Collect—one funded
by a challenger to savage the incumbent, the other retaliating for the

incumbent against the challenger. "Dirty Deeds Done Dirt Cheap"—
that was the great hed given to my sexy masked exposé, in *The Graphic*,
an article which my managing ed at *The Sun* recognized by its alliter-
ative eloquence. Despite pressure, she couldn't fire me for reporting
the truth; instead, I was promoted horizontally, to the land of cubi-
cles adorned with dusty teddy bears, celebrity cutouts, and loved ones
smiling in heart-shaped frames. My own heart broke—I'd wanted to
reach the world since I was four, sitting on my mother's knee as she
tuned her ham radio in the attic, both of us entranced by the sudden
clarity of Sputnik, its beep, beep, beep constant to anyone who cared
to hear. I'm too right-brained to be an astronaut, so I chose the next
best thing. Clear and constant. It breaks my heart, what it's become.
The jibber-jabber chitchat of social media mobs. Blogging influencers
bought for their burning sycophancy and fart-warm punditry. Viral
articles—which sounds like underwear you shouldn't touch without
gloves and an N95 mask. And churnalism—mass-produced clickbait
about hero dogs, or internet outrage, or how some guy did something
vaguely inspiring that'll make you laugh or cry and like and share. All
of it, with every eyeball, exhausting us into apathy. Well. We must
hold the line. Besides, the paycheck kept me in pencils. And Bulag Gin.
But then in danced Vita Nova, and her Sexy-Sexygate, refreshing my
faith in the truth. And its urgency. At stake in its conflict, climax, and
resolution is nothing less than da Pilipino peoples' soul. Our job as
writers is to unpack the past, confront the present, and imagine the
future. If you dismiss storytelling as irrelevant to the realities of the
streets, then your story will be for others to tell in those streets and
beyond. And in it, you'll be absent. Or worse.

(Coughing)

Have you noticed that each presidentiable has handpicked a veep
who can tell their tale for them? We've the purple-prose profanity of
K. Sisboy Pansen. The dutiful daughterly dignifying from the one good
Lontok. The beguiling butchy brash belligerence of the president's only
competent kid. The bloviating bigliness of Rolex. And, of course, the net-
savvy siren-song of our Sexy-Sexygate Circe Nova, who, unfortunately
for Bansamoro, has a much better story than he does. I respect Nuredin, though he once made me jog alongside him for an interview—he

in his track suit, me in my only nice brogues and tie. But in this race, he can't keep up. They've hamstrung him. The patriotic name change. The GLH hair-in-a-can. The High Guy–brand elevator shoes— discovered by a *Gazette* reporter while Nur was in the mosque. Last week's Nosegate—allegations that he had cosmetic surgery in Korea to look more Western. Now there are photos of habitual butt-slapping, after every point, during the Congressional Basketball Championship between his Mythical Fighting Cocks and the Triumphant Tarsiers. I know stepping aside would be a lot to ask of him. More so to ask Vita to step up—she who had big dreams of being much less than our savior, risking her life for the rest of us. But the baby is now a lady. Well. Seems like only yesteryear that I was gloating like Henry Higgins as she bloomed, holding her own among my literary friends, their eyes needling her for an opinion on the latest anthology or agitprop. "Well," Vita would reliably say, "consider James Joyce!"—which always yielded resigned nods, conceding sighs, or lustful looks of startled admiration. She didn't need to know how an elevator worked to take it to the penthouse. She never planned to be a mistress, or a messiah, either—but we rarely get to choose our love, or the good we can do.

(Inaudible)

Vita, with her ear to the people and a voice so clear, presents a singular vision in a country constantly divided into false dichotomies. Such as killing suspects versus being killed by criminals. Such as a protective strongman versus opportunistic oligarchs. Such as kowtowing to China versus waging a war we will lose. Such as enemies of da peoples versus patriots for da madderland—as if cloaking yourself in a flag isn't just hiding. Such as the enduring false dichotomy of the old dictatorship of Junior's family versus Respeto's recent admin—as if the thirty years between didn't drag us through plentiful presidents of different dynasties and manipulative motivations. Oh how insulting!—them thinking we can only wrap our heads around two ideas. Oh how obvious!— their straw men set up again and again for them to knock down in crowing glory. Oh how convenient!—the way they have us obsessing about political celebrities, and not the plutocrat vultures I once listed left to right, like a police lineup of socialites, whose land-grabbing, insider-trading, money-laundering racketeering is what funds all the campaigns, influences all the policies, sets all the national agenda. The chilling effect of Estreganism isn't merely the rejection of nuance and facts, it's the embrace of blindness and conspiracy. Nothing feels more real than emotion, and no emotion feels more real than anger. If our anger is real, then the stories of what we hate must be true. If the stories are true, then our hatred is justified. If we are justified, then what we hate must be stopped—at all cost.

(Coughing)

What sort of anger, what sort of hatred, felt so real to that Loy Bonifacio? So true that he came home with his savings from years abroad laboring, bought a gun, took a long taxi ride on a hot day, and waited in a community center filled with women to try to assassinate the president he once loved? Bonifacio's trial begins this coming week, and his diseased and desperate president shall invoke law and order to push for the death penalty. Because Estregan fears the universal disillusionments that underpin his alleged assassin's motives.

(Inaudible)

True! You're right!—it is now up to all of us. Bonifacio's spirit must make our manifesto. To each whose voice isn't heard, to us empowered with useless votes, to they at protests silenced or ignored, to those who work for less each day, to we who are crushed by debt or toil, to all who suffer selfish leaders far too long: Raise your voices, make them loud! Charge your smartphones, modern pamphleteers! Take to your keyboards and touchscreens. Retweet in unison. Unfurl your memes. A hashtag's a chant, so start one now. Let metaphor plagiarize the facts. Let caricature revolutionize the blind item. Let sarcasm describe the crimes of those whose claims of innocence may now acquit but never exonerate. The future will never forget, for we won't let it: not our lawless lawmen, courts without bite, slavish Senate, Congress of the corrupt, omnipotent oligarchs, and clerics indulging in their own salvation. We must satirize such fools, parody the perverse, point our fingers, raise a stink. To those who claim politics smears even the innocent: we are watching. To the crooks who roam unpunished: we will wait. To you who move to silence us: we will create, to immortalize your infamy, defame your legacy, and tell your children and their children's children the truth of all you did and failed to do. We will harass you in heaven and taunt you in hell, to punish you through perpetuity. Our words will bear witness and our stories remind and our justice will sound like laughter. We whose weapons are nothing more than pen and paper, vigilance and memory, and truth spoken freely for all to hear.

(Coughing)

Well. At least that's *my* manifesto. I'm working on living up to it. But how this book ends is up to us. We're its protagonists, facing a tough decision. Which side will you choose?

(Liquid pouring)

The truth is, a desperate broad sauntered into the washed-up gum-shoe's office and rescued me with her certainty. Even now, I'm still terrified she'll meet the same fate as my dear friend Rita. But I asked Vita that night if she was ready, because the only fights worth fighting are those you're unwilling to lose. She nodded without hesitation. Because it's never wrong to make the right mistake. We went to work—she facing the world, I facing an expanse. My cursor nagged, constant and clear, as I raised what I feared would be one of my life's last salutes—mabuhay!

(Glasses clink)

—and I swallowed it in a gulp, thinking about a colleague who worked as a correspondent for the Associated Press. One day, while dodging the chaos of crossfire between soldiers and insurgents, she turns a corner and finds herself alone. Surrounded by peace. Standing among craters. Seized suddenly by the realization that she's wandered into a minefield. At first, she edges forward. Foot by foot. Step by step. Then she decides it's best to run.

Vita Nova Transcript: 10 of 13.

(51:14.32—VN10.M4A)

We're all in trouble. Want some? Seriously, nine days from elections and all this goes down. Don't shy, have a fry. Leave it to Rolex to charge Nur with sodomy after our Abiolaville rally. You sure? It's Potato Corner. And of course the Communists break the ceasefire again, coz Hope's surging ahead. I'm starvin', Marvin; hangry all day. You didn't hear on the way? Couple hours ago, cadres bombed an army base. No thanks; I don't ketchup. They burned the Reyes sugar plantation, where strikers were massacred before. And in unrelated related news, the Abu Sayyad strikes again—kidnapping a missionary family, Americans: father, mother, tween triplets. Meanwhile, different factions are stirring up shizzy at rival campaigns. We're like heading for civil war. Security's doubled for our town hall event later—Nur says I'm quite the target now. Bomb-sniffing dogs and everything. I've discovered that nothing makes you feel less safe than having bodyguards. Everything's literally a hot mess. Markets in chaos—this snap election shaking confidence. People upset at the inflation—and drug dealers back in the communities, allegedly. As a strongman, Fernando was crooked, but at least that crooked man was strong—so say Junior and Farrah, of course; those two wrongs will never make a right. Fear's a great motivator, totally, but the discipline they claim we need isn't really discipline if it doesn't come from ourselves, right? We'd all follow the rules if we're sure others won't take advantage of us by breaking them.

(Paper bag crumpling)

Exactly why me and Nur are running. If we leave fixing the system to someone else, of course they'll fix it for themselves. So I gotta learn how, to teach others. Those years I was with Nando, I thought we needed a leader who'd do anything to do what's right—even if it took doing wrong. But, like, Loy—isn't that what he tried to do? He listened when the president told everyone to get a gun and kill those who'd lead our country to perdition.

(Inaudible)

I can't—I'd rather be talking to you. How can they televise that spectacle? I can't watch Loy just sitting there, not saying a word in his own defense, everybody grandstanding around him. I tried, but first love never dies. I still can't imagine why he'd want to kill Estregan—nobody does. We were both such Nandotards, growing up. Maybe Loy saw how orderly things were in the Middle East but here at home so hopeless. Broken promises drive people cray. It won't be like that under me and Nur, I'll have you know. (I'll have everyone know.) Have you tried our T&A app?—for nekkid Transparency and Accountability—launched over the weekend. You can read about each candidate and their platforms, so that voters actually know who they're supporting and can hold them to their promises. Imagine that for not just December 12, but also the local elections next year. And I'm highkey stoked about the Rate Your Reps feature—like Yelp or TripAdvisor, but for politicians. Just a tap to email your concerns straight to their office, or post your feedback and pictures of their projects, or judge their performance via one of five emojis: halo-face, smile, flat-mouth, frown, devil-face. Coz scrutiny's a public service most public servants avoid if they can—since it's human nature to hold on to what you got. ♬ *Doesn't make a difference if you make it or not.* ♬

(Lighter click. Exhalation)

But we got each other, and that's a lot. Coz fear's a helluva motivator, for the poor but especially the powerful. Look what happened with Cat's dad—and look at Cat: wealthy and weak, connected and soft, paralyzed into inaction by his uncertainty. I bet you know what I mean; on some level everyone does. Coz the walls meant to keep people out also keep you in, and the tint on your car window makes the world a dark and distant place. That's why some people are so blind they believe they deserve everything—till they get what they actually deserve. Like Narciso Odyseo Jang-Salvador IV, aka El Cuatro, or Cat to his friends—though I used to call him Snake. I still haven't forgiven him, even if I've given up trying to figure out why he did what he did. Coz I should've known—that entitled jerk, from day one, walking right up after the Metallica concert, despite One-Mig beside me the whole time, nodding to the music like someone trying not to disagree. Cat had caught me staring—as he headbanged by the stage, bathed in red light, his hair swirling like blood in water. His boots so James Hetfield, and he reminded me of the cute twin from Nelson. When the boys in black covered "Tuesday's Gone with the Wind," for their encore, it was Cat who started the flame salute—a lighter in each hand, tears down his cheeks as tongues of fire rippled across the stadium. After they opened the houselights, that's when he stumbled up, sucking both thumbs, all like, "Hey . . . Aren't you kinda famous? Vita Nova, right?" Then: "Your little bro here needs to make his curfew, and you and I gotta go backstage to say hi." One-Mig tightening like some karen about to call the manager, grabbing my belt to steer me into the crowd—which was exactly why I called back to Cat, What's your name? Him curling his hair behind his ears with a gruff reply: "Call me Snake." I know, right? So deliciously baduy, especially when my phone rings the next day and it's him. And I'm like, How'd you find me? His voice like five o'clock shadow: "Destiny." Turns out he'd contacted Boy, saying I wrote my digits on his hand, but they got all smudged—a bold lie I appreciated enough for me to be upfront: I got a boyfriend. To which he's like, "Is he so insecure you can't have friends?" And I'm about to hang up when he goes: "Come on, live a little. Let's get some gindara at Polo Club and I'll introduce you to my horse." Live a little—a challenge like catnip to this kitten, half smitten upon arriving at the veranda as he bounced off the high board, twisting through blue sky into a white splash. And more than half interested as he pulled himself out of the pool, arms and legs furred like a Basque lumberjack's, the rockin' tats and hairy whorls on his back hypnotizing me—completely opposite to One-Mig, who was like a Chinese emperor just past puberty, about to be murdered by his dowager grandmother before his first night with a concubine. Cat drying himself off, deadma-smiling, bumping his eyebrows up my way, then he lit a cigarette. Back then I couldn't tell arrogance from confidence, and he was so magnetic my cheap jewelry pulled me over—to his golden mane, green eyes, swagger like a thug in a seventies leather jacket, his thick hands made for fighting, bass guitar, and chainsmoking—with pen strokes along the sides for every cig he couldn't quit on (his jeans bulging with lighters he accidentally snags throughout the day). More brutish than feline; less cat than catfish. Did you know they can live nearly a century and grow more than ten feet long? (Catfish; not cats. Obviously.)

(Inaudible)

I know, poor One-Mig—especially what him and his family were going through, with Glendys, his twin sister. And the guy did try, with schmancy dinners and purposeful passion. But how could I not savor my first time being fought over? My first time deciding for myself what I needed. And ♬ *he's gotta be strong and he's gotta be fast and he's gotta be fresh from the fight.* ♬ A hero, that's what I thought Cat would be, as we flirted in a dark corner of Insomnia Café—One-Mig finding us somehow after the fight I picked with him for taking my CDs out of the changer in the car. The poor guy carrying me, kicking and squirming—him pleading; me hissing, It's over, It's dead—wriggling away to get back to Cat, who whisked me on his Katana to his mansion in Forbes and sat me on the diving board beneath the stars as bats swooped down for a drink. Me and him plunging into a kiss, which I liked so much we ended up living together two and a half years—my longest—in the guest house across that pool from his parents. He was twenty-one, studying law, his father wanting him to be a Supreme Court justice—Cat wanting to be just a supreme partier, like his folks before him. Obeying, nonetheless, so hungry for their admiration it was like he didn't hate them. Such a Scorp. Anyways, the dad was nice to me, so nice he was skeezy—quick with a compliment, ready with a joke, but always like he'd never forgive my not rewarding him with a smile. The mom hating on me, of course—we were too alike. I'd grown up watching her movies, singing her songs, and it was a tragedy seeing her beauty queen's smile tucked and nipped into a grimace—as if she'd never forget her airhead answer at that heartbreaking Miss Universe final in Athens, despite her arrival to a film career and our country's top bachelor on the tarmac in his ivory gullwing Mercedes and a Ring Pop of a diamond at ready. Such sparkling sadness in her society-page photos; so bad trip to peak at nineteen. Cat claiming she was just pious and didn't like he and I living together out of wedlock—you should've seen her face when I'd touch up my lipstick in public (plus she thinks tampons are sinful)—but the truth was, she lived for Cat, and the jerk knew it, threatening to move out every so often just to keep her nice to me. Imagine the dynamic: Cat's mom doting over him, me sucking up to her, his dad making cute to me, Cat trying to win his admiration, the dad needing the mom, the mom ignoring the dad, and me and Cat fighting every day over the stupidest things. Sundays were the absolute worst, piling into the Rolls for mass, nothing bringing a family together better than confined spaces, divine judgment, then public scrutiny at brunch at the Turf Room—his parents and me in our Sunday best, Cat in like skinny jeans and a cut-off Zappa T, hair around his shoulders, so defiant but so demanding. Till this day I freeze when I feel a foot under the table, half expecting it to rub obscenely, or step on my sentence, or kick me towards the right fork. That family was so obsessed with manners it was rude, though I did learn a lot—how cutlery service goes outside in (like parentheses), how to fold my napkin (pardon, *serviette*) for either lunch or dinner, how to draw the soupspoon away from you. And not to burp after a meal— like One-Mig's grandmother (which is healthy, actually).

(Burp. Laughter)

I adored Cat, recklessly, even if I'd never live up to his expectations. He always said he thought he'd end up with a girl "of a good family," quote unquote, and I never forgave him. Wasn't my family *good*—even if I left them behind? But as they say, all unhappy families are unhappy in their own way, and his parents were happy spoiling him till they blamed him for it. That big kid, with his love of cars, chicks, animals, and rock and roll—in his black Trans Am T-top with a silver firebird on the hood, me rolling a joint in the passenger seat, around my shoulders his African python named Mandingo, us rushing late to our gigs. For a while we were so good for each other, introducing me to partying, encouraging him to study—coz he's smarter than he thinks, even if the only nonschool books I ever saw him read were about horses (he can tell you how Affirmed nosed out Alydar at Belmont as if he was there, or the Argentinian polo team's chances this year). Both of us growing side by side. And because the universe was against us, we clung to each other, hard. What good girl doesn't love a bad boy showing her off?—him acting the fool in public so that everyone sees him making you laugh. What could be happier at that age? We'd hit San Mig Pub, where the rich kids went, then Dredd, where the rockers hung. We were even raising a puppy we named Psst-Hoy, till they needed him to guard Cat's farm. It was an innocence I'd never known, before or since. Cat so free from everything I worried about, whispering into my ear during mass—"Let's go home, smoke a bowl, and listen to Neil Diamond" (his fave, and the reason I took up guitar)—and we'd excuse, excuse, excuse ourselves down the pew, me holding my tummy and mouth like I'm ill, Cat not giving a frak what people thought. That first time I heard "Girl, You'll Be a Woman Soon" was like a whole night fading across the walls—♫ *I'd die for you girl and all they can say is, "He's not your kind"* ♫—the crackling silence after like the sound of a new dawn, and me in it with clear eyes. I was always so obsessed with that—the future, and how everyone saw me—but Cat showed me the glory of making out in the corner of a crowded bar, letting people sneer with disguised envy; or smoking a joint in the CR of the movie house before *Night of the Living Dead*; or spending all day listening to records, gazing up at album covers, grabbing the guitar to pick through the melodies. The two of us trying on rebellion and modeling it for each other. He'd skip school and we'd watch his VHS tape of Woodstock so often it became fuzzy. "The brown acid that is circulating around us is not specifically too good." That was one of the lines that specifically cracked us up, for some reason. Or, "Hey, if you think really hard, maybe we can stop this rain!" Me and Cat really thinking, really hard, that we'd last forever. But you know how sometimes you love someone so intensely you feel it's impossible for them to love you back as much? Like they must be crazy, or lying, to not hurt you? Love so bright it blinds you both; so deep it's like quicksand—and nothing could be more wonderful? That was us. ♫ *We had the right love at the wrong time . . .* ♫ Or the wrong love at the right time—our fights the most epic in human history, about anything and everything: like my stubbornness about my posture and pronunciations; like his wandering eyes, picking fights with randos, or trying to rob the C-word of its violence by saying it all the time—which is like shooting victims to maintain the peace. As

Eric Hoffer said: "Rudeness is the weak man's imitation of strength." Exactly Cat. And us, actually—me and him fighting to feel powerful. Coz at that age you're fascinated with your ability to hurt someone so bad yet still be loved enough to be forgiven again and again—all that so spectacular it makes peace feel kinda boring. In private, we were our own audience for our fights, relishing our lines and props of sloppily packed suitcases. While in public we tested each other, jumping out of the car in traffic, the other following with resentful apologies, people pointing and laughing then honking—though what could those fools know of love? Just like Cat's mom and dad—how could they know, either? As RuPaul says: "If you can't love yourself, how in the hell you gon' love someone else?" That's why Cat loved a girl he knew they'd hate, coz they'd taught him that love's a weapon.

(Inaudible)

No, je ne regrette rien. Not really. I guess maybe never speaking up when they mistreated their "servants," as they called them—till I convinced Cat that wasn't PC, and they became "domestic helpers" (even though they're more like do-ers, of all the domestic work, while you masturbate your life away). Cat claiming they were like family, his supporting theirs for generations: sisters, brothers, spouses, in-laws, cousins from the same village. "But don't get close," he'd say, when I'd hang with them. "You'll confuse them. Next thing they're borrowing money from you and creating a tough situation for themselves." But he did try, I'll give him that. He was just shy—his word—surrounded by strangers twenty-four seven: bodyguards, drivers, cooks, maids, laundrywomen, houseboys. Mangling his way through Tagalog—which he only knew in present-tense and the imperative, when Taglish wasn't enough— asking about their families, totally sincere but limited by his luck and lofty education. And always so hard on himself after shouting, like his father did, when they'd get confused by his instructions. So I'd try to make up for him—swapping stories in the kitchen with the sisters Mercy and Susan, or with Inday and Lek Lek as they shelled pistachios for Cat's dad, or in the garage with Edgar, Mercy's husband, harmonizing with him to power ballads on the radio while he shined rows of shoes. I'd even cut patterns for Honorata, who came once a week to make his mom's dresses on a squeaking foot-powered Singer. And

I'd gossip about showbiz with Noel, who used to be a security guard at Channel Three before becoming a cop and getting assigned to Cat's dad. Yeah, that's my regret: not having the courage when Cat and his parents laughed over dinner about IQs, or dented Porsches, or discouraged love lives—afraid the smart ones would find work at Shoe Mart, or the talented ones get pirated by relatives and start a family feud. When most of them were fired, I was heartbroken—after Cat's mom left to live with her sister in Cali, after his dad . . . you know. Just me and Cat—and Mercy, Edgar, and Susan—in that empty old mansion, as he studied for the bar, and I tried to get my music career going. Our fights becoming about money—why I wasn't earning, even though he'd always said that if this country had royalty his family would be part of it. Even though I'd made the household hum so efficiently he was deaf to it. Cat always needing someone to blame.

(Lighter click. Exhalation)

When he hit me, the first time, he apologized by making it seem like it wasn't his fault. That night, I watched him while he slept— I remember—trying to recognize him again. This was after we moved into the main house, with its faded seventies interiors, into the master suite, with its clouded mirrors on the ceiling. Staring at our reflections and wondering how we got there. Sometimes I'd pick fights just to drive away, parking by the airport and watching planes unstick and roar over me. Coming home to find Cat in bed, stoned, exhausted with worry that I'd abandon him, like with One-Mig, and I'd undress and slip beside him without a word, letting him hold me till sleep became the apology we settled for. I still have nightmares—running to the Trans Am like wading through water, Cat getting smaller in the rearview mirror, screaming something I can't hear but can feel. We loved so much we even loved the pain—mistaking anger for its twin, passion, both of them so delicious. The make-up, the break-up, the one-last-time sex—which somehow fixed everything, for a while. I'm not ashamed to say that Cat was important to my sexual blossoming— even if I resented him for it.

(Inaudible)

Coz I wanted to save it. I was so traumatized by Loy leaving me after taking my virginity, and—you know. Then me and One-Mig were more chaste than a convent of fugly nuns. But with Cat I moved in after like a week and I guess I wanted us to prove our priorities. "It'll be worth the wait," he'd agree, kissing my neck, his hand snaking up my thigh till I pushed him away, again and again. A month later, I found out he cheated on me, so I gave in. Yup—gave in. Super terrible. Flipping me through positions like modeling for those instructional workout posters in the gym. When he was behind me I cried, hiding it in a pillow, and he didn't understand and kept spanking me.

(Laughter)

I know, right? But it got better, eventually. Coz we were young and in love and forgave each other more easily than ourselves. After I learned what he liked, he learned what I liked. If you're lucky, sex when you're a teenager's the best—you're not just discovering another person, you're discovering yourself. Spending all day together with the blinds down, a gazillion miles from everyone, deserving that safe place—two lost souls guiltily titillated by everything, including the word *titillation*, giddy as twelve-year-olds in geography class discovering Lake Titicaca. Cat may have been one confused cad—hating his father's philandering, though addicted to porno and macking on chicks—but there was no confusion about how he worshipped me. Standing me in bed to unpeel my clothes, never releasing his eyes till we were both finished. "Making love to you," said he, "is like driving a Countach." Even today, if I hear Whitesnake, or Nine Inch Nails, or Ted Nugent's "Stranglehold," I think of Cat—not necessarily the sex, but everything around it. Of making out in his car with the top open, beneath the stars after a gig. Of holding tight on his Triumph when we raced the rain home from the beach, no helmets, me in my bikini, us singing "Take Me Home, Country Roads." And of hitting his six-foot bong and having silverback sex till he tumbled breathlessly by my side, curling like John with Yoko, our bodies still ringing, washed in the crashing waves of an electric guitar. No wonder we lasted. "Love isn't need," he said once. "It's choice. That's what makes it freedom." And that felt true—as bad trip as it got, I chose to stay, and I felt free. But that night I first caught him watching porno, nothing was the same after, to be honest. Some ways it was better, because I grew, but in many ways it was worse, coz we didn't grow together—at least towards the end, when he started pressuring to make our own. Like for his birthday, or our anniv, setting me up with a candlelit dinner, sparkly gift, lingerie, dancing me to the bedroom, blushed with wine, to the bed, with a tripod and a camcorder pointed at it. I'd tell him no. I'd tell him, I'm all yours now, but if we end, you can't have me this way anymore. So years after we ended, when I went to an internet café to see that infamous clip with my own eyes, its fifteen seconds ruined every moment of our two and a half years. Remembering that bedroom, and that very night—how we were so in love. It's funny how it's okay to do love scenes in my movies when it's appropriate to the narrative—art and artifice projected on screens thirty feet high. But a grainy bootleg of real intimacy was so wrong—both because of the betrayal and what society did with it. I think a lot about consent, in this world that forces itself upon you, where you almost need permission to be who you are.

(Inaudible)

Actually, no—at first it was exciting, Cat sharing his porno collection, like discovering a secret passage at the back of a wardrobe. With his library organized by era and region, the proud pornoisseur made watching together feel like unboxing a fresh perspective on beauty, pleasure, emancipation—some bodies misguided into fantastical fakeness, but others imperfect and unashamed. On the big screen in the entertainment room, Cat introduced me to Anna, Anita, Asia, Belladonna, Racquel, Rebecca, Nikki, Zara—confessing that he cared for them, grateful for their sharing intimate moments in careers that I guess could seem like awakenings: from solo to lez, soft to hard, extreme to retirement. He knew their ethnicities, origin stories, and personalities in such detail it seemed kinda respectful. And really confusing to me. Coz it's an addiction people don't really talk about, I think because it can't be blamed on a substance, so it gets blamed on the addicted person. And sexuality's always suspect, right? But I won't lie, I did see artistry in a lot of it—stuff from Vivid, Andrew Blake, Michael Ninn, Private Video—and Cat was pretty convincing about how it was ruined by instances of exploitation, and misunderstood on purpose by puritans afraid of themselves. Starting me on couples pornos—cinematic, narrative—progressing to gonzo, with its fantasy of authenticity: girls prescene talking about escaping their own limits and sharing their journey with their fans—us fellow misunderstood rebels, who made it all possible by supporting their work. Intriguing, I admit. But I always felt . . . I don't know—not sad, more like . . . complicit. Coz everything's connected in this universe: buying a diamond funds dictators and armies of child soldiers; filling your gas tank drills holes in the seabed and pumps poison into the air. Cat wasn't just paying for the laser disc, he was paying the store to pay the distributor to pay the producer to pay the director to instruct the casting agency and photographer to tell a hella unsure young woman to take off her clothes, put the penis of a stranger inside her, and try to enjoy it—since anyway the choice is hers and she's making bank. But no girl dreams of that when they're six, or twelve, or even eighteen—you dream of ballerina, teacher, movie star, president.

(Inaudible)

Actually, no—I don't buy those comfy clichés that all sex workers were abused as kids. Or that because it's sex the industry's automatically more exploitative than others. But I bet you anything that most of those women at one point took a deep breath and thought: "This'll get easier." And to me *that's* not really okay—coz it does, little by little, get easier; coz consequences pass, bit by bit; all the sacrifices just another price we pay in a world where everything has a cost. At least it's kinda fun?—doesn't hurt anyone?—could be worse? I don't know. I mean, I don't disagree that Sasha Grey is a sex-positive feminist—coz none of us sinners has the right to dis her way of getting the most from life— and I admire Stoya, Jenna Haze, Monique Alexander; I think my life lets me empathize with their choices. So I won't lie: I understood Cat's fascination. But I couldn't ever stop thinking of any dreamer at six, or eighteen, or twenty-eight, living to never see their dreams come true—the domestic helpers or insurance sellers, the telemarketers or bikini-waxers, the vice presidents or pornostars. It wasn't so much the sex that seemed obscene. To me, it was deeper. And Cat's addiction was kind of a metaphor for that. I'd find bits of toilet paper pasted to his penis and I knew our lovemaking would disappoint, while he'd joke about his exhausting trip to Wangcock, Myhand, for his date with Palmela Handerson—preferring his locked cabinet filled with fake loves to one real love he could lose. And making me feel prudish, and insufficient, for saying so. Look at him now. Did you know that according to pyschodynamic psychology, depression is rage turned inwards? Oh, when you interview him, if the white leather sofa's still in the entertainment room, don't touch it—just saying. Anyways. Want to hear his favorite joke? How do you titillate an ocelot?

(Inaudible)

Oscillate its tits a lot.

(Laughter)

So we hadn't spoken for years when he called out of the blue—a couple of days after that tragedy on my "Someday" comeback tour. Because Cat knew—from all our going to each other's gigs, all the setups before and the Carlsbergs after, all the CR sex and those times we tried to jam together onstage—he knew, of all people, what my music meant to me, and he always had impeccable timing. Nur had just dumped me and I was well into my pity-party, huhu, in the darkness of my hotel room, my fave break-up mixtape CD on loop—which Cat had burned for me, actually, one of those nth times he begged me to stay. Do you ever catch up with your exes?—like bump into them somewhere and smile wistfully over small talk? It was like that: reminiscing with a familiar stranger about the war you each thought you won but both lost. TBH, I always wondered if he followed my life. Like, turned up my songs on the radio, or nodded to the sermons and op-eds calling me a harlot and a liar. If he felt angry, or guilty, or at peace. If he thought of me at all. Coz I did—think of him.

(Silence)

The way he used to watch me sing—like he always knew. Told him so, too, when he called. That he would've loved the ride. Coz I'd prepared my whole life for *La Dolce Vita*, which went platinum thanks to Boy finally giving me my shot, working with the industry's best: vocal coaches, songwriters, sound engineers, video directors, choreographers, production crew, stylists, PR experts, and, especially, the dynamic duo of CAOS—those mysterious producers who wear Power Rangers masks even in studio. Remember the Hell o' Kitties' smash hit, "Sabotage Love"? ♫ *This is my tragedy, I am who I wanna be. Sabotage love! Sabotage love! This is my reality, I'm not who I wanna be. Sabotage love! Sabotage love!* ♫ That was them—coz hit music's teamwork, that's what makes the dream work, these days often very strategized: potential hits identified and offered to the highest bidder, who stamps it with her star quality and certifies it with success. So in the deep-space silence of the studio, CAOS unveiled their alien beats, riffs, chord progressions, as well as the lyrics drafted the day before by a topline writer—as they're called—who developed the stories, melodies, and hooks that got everyone bobbing and smiling through the soundproof glass. Until I arrive, finally, fitting my headphones, moving my pop filter, taking a deep breath to bring it all together—each song bedazzled with as many hooks as possible for our ADD age. "Mr. Sexy-Sexy," for example, has like seven—in the intro, first verse, prechorus, first chorus, second verse, second chorus, bridge, rapped verse, and outro. We laid that out, and all the rest, in a single studio weekend, getting all the techs dancing, needing just four takes for the "The Banana Song"—♫ *Pick it, peel it, push it, bite it. You say day-oh if you like it. Banana, nanana. Na-na, na, na!* ♫—along with just one go for "Bounzy Baby," which only proved to be the club hit of the decade.

(Three finger snaps)

La Dolce Vita—my first full album, not some four-song EP like I used to do. We're talking fourteen cherry tracks, from dance anthems to radio pop tunes, though it was the three unplugged ballads that were closest to my heart: intimate offerings of my craft over many years, for my real fans. "Unli You." "Maybe Isn't a Safe Word." And "Someday," of course—which is dedicated to Cat, in the liner notes, coz he was there, in the dawn-light of our relationship, on the beach beside me while I strummed it out the first time, never dreaming it'd top the charts. So when my tour was canceled the way it was canceled, of course he guessed what it did to me. After I'd skyrocketed from young actress in the recording studio to pop star just four hits and seven months later, planning an eleven-city national tour, kicking off sensationally—sensationalistically even—in the Big Dome, the Araneta Coliseum, where Ali fought Frazier in the Thrilla in Manila. Boy slow-dripping more hit singles to the public while I choreographed and drilled with dancers, brainstormed costumes, and prepped for my big chance—coz your early performances are vital to any performing artist's career, entire reputations made on a couple of ten-minute extravaganzas. Think

MJ at Motown's twenty-fifth anniv, in '83, introducing the moon-walk and sending the crowd into a rapture. Or the MTV awards in '95—"Dangerous," with suits and fedoras, and that little kid. Think of Madge at the '84 MTV Music Awards—a bride singing "Like a Virgin" on a giant wedding cake—or in '89—the running man, light-up stairs, crotch grab, and Gaultier ice-cream-cone bustier. Did you know that in American Sign Language, you say "Madonna" by making cone gestures from your chest with both hands? Icon!—and the one who taught me that a woman can be feminine and brassy, provocative and classy. My "Someday" concert tour was going to be an homage, but better—all hope and glamour, two sides of the coin that's defined my career. Every-one talking about how even Nur was investing in the production—his proof that he didn't just tolerate my work. Jojie and I developing a my-thology theme, and Boy's Boujie Boys dancers in costumes repurposed from his Victor's Secrets fashion shows—dwendes, satyrs, genies, tamed tikbalangs, and a gang of fallen angels. With set pieces that de-fined fab—Aphrodite stepping out of a clam; Cleopatra entering Rome; Cher partying at Studio 54; Helen of Troy singing "Someday" from her window as the armies of the underworld battled below in interpretive dance. Totally better than it sounds.

(Laughter)

And the finale should've been literally the best thing ever. Me as Che Guevara in revolutionary chic: low-cut camo, raspberry beret, a mic like a huge cigar, getting everyone up with "Bounzy Baby"—♪ *Big, juicy, round. Baby what's that sound? Bump, jiggle, pound. Can you feel the ground? Oh, my bounzy baby. Oh, you drive me crazy* ♪—climaxing in to-tal darkness, pyrotechnics from a gigantic magic lamp, a sixteen-piece band, a children's choir, B-boys, aerialists, the entire crowd on their feet chanting my name while dozens of extras from the army rush down the aisles in uniform with golden AKs and red-sequined turbans, as I'd tear off my army fatigues to reveal a red-sequined catsuit—camel-toe tight, biatch!—segueing seamlessly into our showstopper: me and those sexy Sikhs in formation—hands on knees, butts bouncing, the entire stadium—and the world, via simulcast—dancing everyone's fave: ♪ *Ooo, my sexy, sexy. My Mr. Sexy-Sexy . . .* ♪ If only!

(Silence)

If only the bodyguards of the VIP politicians in the front rows didn't think the soldiers were Nur's Muslim coup, and open fire, the music stumbling like a machine falling apart, the crowd stampeding to the door.

(Lighter click)

Dozens died. Along with my entire career—but never mind, people perished; and all any of us could offer was thoughts and prayers.

(Lighter click. Exhalation)

"Bloody Someday"—that's what one Changco paper dubbed it. Eighty-nine shot or crushed. Me and my investors losing a fortune in settlements. My contracts withdrawn. Bishop Baccante calling it divine retribution. Tensions between Christians and Muslims spiked and Nur broke up with me, by text message, from his secretary, who spelled my name wrong, twice, two different ways, as if it's not just four letters long. All the online threats of rape and death sending me into hiding. None of my friends daring to go to my condo to feed my cats. My career kaput: the rise and fall of Vita Nova.

(Clapping)

Cat was pretty much the only one who called me after. "Oh, Silver Girl," said he, "is that Ozzy playing in the background?" I said yeah. "Don't tell me you're having a crying-fest." My voice broke when I said no. "Oh baby. The weather's looking fine, and I think the sun will shine again. Do you want me to beat them up?" I tried to laugh. Yeah, I said, All of them. "You've survived worse," said he. I'm like, Yup—you included; you especially. He's like, "Was I that bad?" And that old anger boiled in me again. So I asked, Why you calling anyway? He's all like, "I just . . . I just miss you. I miss . . ." But I hate you, remember? "Yeah," he says. "I'm so sorry I wasn't the man you believed I'd be. I think about that a lot—that belief. It's kept me going." His voice very small, like when he read the eulogy at his father's funeral—fishing for pity. Then he goes, "Vita, you should know, I'm sick." I'm like, I've been saying that for years. And I wanted to hang up, but I needed to know. How could you do that to me? I said. It nearly ruined my life. And did you really have to wink at the hidden camera? Cat was quiet for a bit. Then he spoke and I could finally bury it all: everything I regretted, cherished, and still wondered about all those years—our passions and fights; our shameful secrets and proud nights out; the sexual awakenings and pillow-talk dreams; his father's death and wishful stories about his own son; his punk band Supektibul and its demise when he joined De Borja Anting Valdes and Partners; my career taking off and the compromises I made for him; and that last fight when he told me the other junior lawyers weren't bringing dates to his boss's garden party, but I saw all the WAGs in the society columns the next day—then me watching him get smaller in the cracked side mirror of Furio's blue Beetle, and the years wondering how he could've done what he did if he ever truly loved me.

(Pause)

"Oh, yeah," he said. "*That.* I'd forgotten." Yeah. That.

(Silence)

Sometimes it's like we all live in alternate realities, ignoring what matters to everyone else. Alternative facts, people now call it. Like, nobody bothering to ask Loy at his trial *why* he wanted to assassinate the president. And the cops not even really investigating who shot Rita—though I'm meeting with someone later who claims they have information. And everyone's buying into that sodomy charge against Nur, irregardless of what he says—all thanks to that gif someone made of him supposedly caressing Bazooka Reyes's leg in the huddle at the Senate-Congress Basketball Friendly; plus his hacked Huawei smartphone with all his shirtless selfies (so many!); and that viral vid someone put on YouTube of him on the campaign trail, with cross-dressing hairdressers, cancan kicking to "It's Raining Men." Hallelujah, his opponents now cheer. A lot of supporters and pollsters saying maybe he should consider possibly perhaps stepping aside—for me to take his place atop the Fuchsia ticket. Poor Nur. I really don't want that. Though, yeah, no, of course—if I have to, fine: I'll never duck my duty to serve. But for the record, he's got my support—a gazillion percent. Coz this election's just, like, only for the very soul of our nation. Right? Just saying.

DEC 4, 4:20 P.M.

Narciso Odyseo "Cat" Jang-Salvador IV Transcript.

(101:01.69—Jang-Salvador.M4A)

Joder, macho—Vita's going for it, no? Qué barbaridad, bud. Our savior! Glad I won't see how that changes her. Thanks for coming, meng. I don't get out much. How's your mom? Give her my regards. Let me just . . . clip this—

(Muffled)

. . . mic. Rock and roll. Yah, meng, this was *the* house. Once upon a time. Solid, no? Party central in the eighties. Imagine? Built, I think, 1936. By the National Artist who did Polo Club and White Cross Sanitarium. Fitting, no? Maybe '37? My mom would know. She's one of those militant matronas saving our nation's inheritance from nouveaux ignorance. Look, by that window—bullet holes. Liberated from the Nips in '45. The wifey wants to sell and move to Menlo Park. Bad juju, she says. Especially after my dad. Fucking just sage the joint out! I was born here, let me kick it here. Then she can join the exodus, clutching their pearls before Junior and Farrah conquer. Come, let's do the grand tour thing. So. My great-grandfather bought this property. My grandfather built the house. My father and mother landscaped. I try to keep it from falling apart. The Salvadors, my dad's side, were the stingy sort of rich. Sugar, soft drinks, guar beans, real estate. They knew. My dad's earliest memory: from that window, waving to his dad, who drove an old army jeep to work because all the money was in land. By grade school, my pops was dropped off in a third-hand Studebaker Champion. At his high school grad, my grandfather had him drive them home in their new '61 Mercedes 190D. My mother's side was the opposite: their beauty and breeding were the only assets left that couldn't be gambled away. Here's her garden. My dad's pool—complete with grotto.

(Inaudible)

Classic, no? After inheriting, in '81, he wanted like Hugh Hefner's, but my ma was in charge of renovations. So his grotto's less Playboy Mansion, more Lourdes miracle. Sums up my 'rents. The guy never even swam because her fortune-teller said he'd die drowning. Almost right, I guess. There's the garage. Every New Year's Eve that wall would be covered with sandbags. Ever fire a Tommy gun? Dude—the fucking best. The neighbors had their fireworks, my pops had his firearms. Imagine? You're thirteen, drunk and horny as fuck, Uzi in each hand—bratatat!, like Chuck fucking Norris. Solid. Chased that feeling ever since. Supposedly there's a cache under the pool, from Martial Law. According to my ma. Over there's the guest house Vita and I lived in, but it's rented now. Here's what's left of my dad's collection.

(Inaudible)

Yah, jake, that's a '75 Silver Shadow—bought the day I was born. Connolly leather, walnut, lambswool, and a face-fucking two-hundred-horse V8. For sale. The electric gearshift's a gremlin; I'll make you an offer you can't refuse. That scent, no? Old-car smell—someone should package and sell it. You should've seen his Willys MB, named Eugene—the garage-queen—an exact replica of my grandfather's. My pops would only drive it down the street to Manila Golf. Sold last week. He loved taking things apart and rebuilding them. Had even a Ferrari—a Mondial, but still—which the king, with all his horses, and all the king's men, couldn't put back together again. My ma taught me stick on that old TD diesel conversion Defender, which we keep for rainy season. But most of all we had Porsches—real ones, not those I-don't-know-what mom-mobiles. As a kid I'd sneak in, to tip-toe and see how fast you have to go to bust the speedometers. My fave was the first she sold, afterwards: the 356 Cabrio, in James Dean silver. The one that got away. Used to steal it when my folks were at the hacienda. Vita would put her seat back and let her hair fly and watch the stars and intreccio of branches blurring by on Pasay Ave. The best things in life are free.

(Breathing)

God, I loved Vita. As in, holy shit. From the second I spotted her and went to say nanu-nanu. Nineteen, dancing queen, like a steel-town girl on a Saturday night. So beautiful. Like a young Racquel Darrian: sweet, rangy, dusky, shaggy fringe cut—perfect. A thoroughbred. A Maserati. And just as bad an idea. You get it, dude, don't lie. If you've driven, ridden, and fucked thoroughbreds, you get it. Come, before it rains, let's go to the house. So humid out. Step into my Tardis. Tada! My mother's life's work. This fine grand foyer, señoras y señores, represents the epitome of what scholars term the School of Neoclassical Socialite style. Solid, no? Not too often these days are you greeted by a pair of life-sized naked negresses. My wife, Franny, she hates those statues. But they bring me back to my puberty. Those perfect Nubian de-des. Don't worry, the wee-men are out. She took our daughter Shiloh to a playdate—that term's so weird. To KidZania—another weird term, like pedo pornland.

(Inaudible)

Yah, my mother moved back after my tita passed. After I was diagnosed. She's been bearable, surprisingly. Having grandkids changes everything. Except in college, when I knocked up my girlfriend and my ma said cut and run.

(Inaudible)

Yah, this floor, I used to play chess, one stuffed animal per tile. Lots of memories here. Good. Bad. Arrivals. Departures. Dignitaries and delinquents advancing across the board, sniffing at hors d'oeuvres. My ma shouting "That's Murano!" when my G.I. Joes' parachutes snagged in that chandelier. Cops handed plates and beers, to not shut down the party. Or my pops—dropping his hand-carry, and the packs of peanuts he'd get for me from business-class, when I'd run down those stairs and launch into his arms. Remember that feeling? Knowing you'll be caught?

(Breathing)

Fuck, meng. I hate what's happening. I'm scared I'll drop Shiloh when she jumps. Come, the bar beckons, bud. Let me introduce you two. Watch your step. This is the living room, evidently. You're not epileptic, are you?—they liked their mirrors. For the filthy few, the Dictator's era was our country's most narcissistic. Lots of handy surfaces, too, for my dad's happy habit—and I'm not talking See's Toffee-ettes. That peeling wallpaper bugs the shit out of Frances, but if she starts she'll renovate us into the poorhouse. Why can't she just wait? When my dad kicked it, my ma totally renovated—her entire life. Stayed with her sister in California, got into riding again, started her memoir, which she self-published, eventually. *All That Glitters*. That's the title.

(Inaudible)

No. But I have copies, if you want. I can't, bok. Too close. My Tito Crispin praised it on the back cover, even if he and my dad weren't friends in the end, so I guess the book's good. I'm happy for her. Everyone deserves a new start. Me and Vita, the day after my ma left, we moved into the master bedroom. Playing house was . . . I don't know. Yah, sure, we threw some parties, but nothing like the bacchanals of my parents. Honestly, bud, I had enough growing up. I just wanted to, you know . . . Life with Vita felt . . . I guess, normal, finally? Like, I'd get back from work and she'd run down the stairs and into my arms.

(Inaudible)

Yah. Exactly. We even got a puppy, who I'm convinced got eaten by the workers renovating the neighbors' house. But you know how it is, jake: crave the crazy ones, stay with the sane ones, till you figure out which one you are—crazy or sane. But by then it's too late. You've lost all your chances. You live with your choices. You can't handle crazy ones like Vita too long. As much as you want to. Can't bring her home to mother. Which at the time is the fucking point. But you learn. You cherish. You grow. In that corner was the white baby grand, though none of us played. Over there was the dance floor, which lit up in rainbow colors. Parties spilled onto that terrace and out by the pool. That big-ass portrait, jake—we sat for a week, my ma and I. What a fatty—with my chronic asthma, so we thought. My dad got painted in from a photo. Check us out—royalty. Fucking pornographic. The princeling and the princess and their little pea.

(Breathing)

In public, they'd work a room; a match made in heaven—meeting on the other side to gaze lovingly, laughing loudly, admired by everyone. But in truth, their relationship stank. Like when you're in public, somewhere crowded, and your chick lets out a silent-but-violent—you whiff it and gaze into her eyes, relieved it's hers. But when you're in bed, and her one-cheek sneak creeps from under the blanket—all you feel's revulsion. Same stink, different contexts. You never really forgive each other for that, jake. My dad made her pay. Nobody dared tell him he was wrong to. It's called *polite* society. So he cruised through life like a bulldozer.

(Inaudible)

Yah, sure, dude—that's nice of you. Sure—he was lost. But aren't we all? Millionaires, like mandingos, deserve no sympathy. My earliest memory, I think, is me right there, during one of their parties. Watching from upstairs, exactly that spot. Used to hang my limbs through the banister, like a prisoner—my head still fit between, so I must've been really young. Three or something. Even then, I could tell everyone was having an obscene amount of fun. Maybe I'm imagining, but it's as clear as yesterday. My mother wasn't there, so she must've been in rehab again. Women were draped over men. Ice cubes tinkled between songs. And candies and sugar on a silver tray, which I could tell was special, even then—everyone revolving around it like it was the sun. And just as my father's leading an angel down these three steps, just when she squeals in delight at the goodies, endless cops rush through the door. Shouts fill the house. Lights go on. Music zips into silence. I watch my dad get handcuffed. I try to run to help him but my head's stuck. They're leading him away as I start crying and screaming. Everyone looks up and sees me. My pops calls out: "I know how you feel, son." Even the cops laughed.

(Breathing)

That's my earliest recollection of him. Friendly with the fuzz and joking with his friends as he's escorted out. My nanny's hands lifted me up and through the bars. Shhh, shhh, she sang, carrying me to bed. Apparently I cried all night, scared I'd never see him again. But at breakfast, there's my pops, reading the newspaper and criticizing it to his secretary, the way he always did. Like nothing happened. Pays to be the Dictator's golf buddy, no? Till the tide turned and my father turned against him.

(Inaudible)

You know what, jake? That's an excellent question. Maybe he thought enough was enough. Maybe it was self-preservation. I don't know. I only knew him enough to love and hate him. But if he did the right thing in the end, does it matter? Repentance is always selfish. Maybe what eventually happened to him with Estregan was karma. Who the fuck knows, bok. I just know life doesn't teach you much if there aren't any consequences. Come, let's Eiffel Tower this bar. What's your poison? We gots . . . beer, mescal . . . Don Papa rum . . . whisky, Irish whiskey, Armagnac. I'm having a Hibiki. It's 3:00 a.m. somewhere. Dude, come on, it's even got an age statement. Twelve-year-old. If that's good enough for Jalosjos, it's good enough for us.

(Inaudible)

Yah, I always drink my scotch with ice—it's how I get my water. How about the other half of this pot cookie? Can't smoke anymore, so I eat it. Suit yourself. Still or sparkling?

(Inaudible)

You're like my ma. She's so funny: she hates how waiters in Europe won't serve tap, so she picks sparkling, to get her money's worth. Doesn't even like it. Gives her acid reflux.

(Inaudible)

Yah, her relationship with Vita was . . . you know. Effervescent as a belch. I used to tell Vita, Don't be intimidated. My mother's flawless to the eye, but filled with inclusions. Just like her bling. The point of large jewels is their slimming effect. But Vita was always so easily dazzled. She'd get in her own head, her feelings like storms. Flooding her and everyone around her. So intense she'd forget your feelings are just as valid, sometimes even more if she was in the wrong. Vita wants so much to be loved she could never just say sorry—"Sorry *if* my words hurt you," she'd say; never just, "Sorry *I* hurt you." Because apologizing admits fault, and fault makes her too flawed to be loved.

(Breathing)

I know, bud, I'm totally psychomanalyzing—but it's true. To her, it's you, not her. Even when it's totally her and not you. I bet you've already seen her weapons. The way I grew up, words were the worst kind. She promised she'd never deliberately hurt me, but she hurt me pretty fucking deliberately. Shitting on everything we ever had, at the end. Making up these terrible lies, just so she'd be the one who walked away, not me. She'd rather be right than be happy. At the end, she said she loved me too much. But that's not love, jake. That's war. See her now. Any more winning, she'll end up alone and miserable. Ask yourself: Does Vita strike you as happy? So, how's the twelve-year-old, bok? Bratty but smooth, no? Did Vita mention I taught her to appreciate whiskies? Used to be Bailey's was her drink of choice. Baduy. I was so proud to see her at parties, years later, drinking like a man. But you know what she and her gay gang called cocaine? *Fashion.* I shit you not, tsong. I'm like: Fuck off, *fashion*? Call it *coke*. Or *blow*. If you really want, call it *disco*. But never, ever, *fashion*. For fuck's sake.

(Inaudible)

No. Frances doesn't drink anymore. Even Bailey's. Breastfeeding, she says. Shiloh's three. So, this here's the Chinese Room. Obviously. My 'rents loved their celadons and blue-and-whites. This is where crazy Tito Gabe lived till he kicked it, my freshman year at Ateneo. My mother's brother. I transferred from upstairs, for that patio. My next step away from the womb.

(Inaudible)

Yah, Tito Gabe was a hippie who never returned from an Angel's Trumpet trip. My grandfather always told him he was a failure and my uncle had the luxury of believing it. He'd watch you in the garden through those French doors, just staring outside all day. When I was eleven he called me in and brought out his *Penthouse* mags. Eleven, dude! First naked lady I ever saw—well, except for the TV shampoo commercials in Barcelona. So, the first naked woman I could stare at. Which you know is a big deal in a man's development. "Look at her bush!" Tito Gabe would say, rubbing it with his finger like a scratch-and-sniff. His greatest joy was undermining his brother-in-law. Once, at dinner, my pops told me to marry wisely and not make the same mistake he did. Afterward, Tito Gabe took me aside. "Make your own money, hijo," he whispered. "Happiness is a girl who sucks your birdie well. You can always teach her to be cultured. But you can't teach a cultured girl to suck your birdie—because that's not something you know how to do." Oh, that guitar's my son's. Please put it down. Whenever Narcing visits, this is his room.

(Inaudible)

Yah, thanks, it's amazing. He's in college already. Imagine? Great kid. His mother did a great job. Used to hate her for cheating on me and taking him away, but we were so young. I was the weak one—I convinced myself I didn't want to confuse him. That instead of fighting I should become the best man possible for when he was ready to find me. Then I got my diagnosis and reached out. A coward's urgency. Those years without him were the emptiest; I was too stupid to know why. I just . . .

(Breathing)

I want—you know . . . I want to stick around, at least long enough . . . you know, to help him find his way. To teach him: heartbreak sucks, but it's the only way you learn not to hurt those you love.

(Breathing)

Let's get another drink. But first, a funny story. See that wall?—across the garden. One rainy season, the creek behind broke through. Three feet of water burst through these French doors, sweeping into my room and out to the street. I'm wakeboarding at the beach when I get a call, from my friend, Alfredito, who lives down the road. "Cat," he says, "your fucking porn's all over Forbes Park. I recognize your stash." But what could I do? I'm six hours away. Dude, next morning, I get home. Dude, the maids followed my mom's instructions—she had no idea, she never left her room those days. Dude, all my shit from under this bed—books, art supplies, my bong—all of it drying on the front terrace. Everything, including my fine collection of smut—*Hustler, Cheri, Club International*—dutifully laid out, by our virginal maids, under the drying rays of the sun. Joder, hijo de puta, jake. I'm talking close-ups of snatch draped over those lawn tables and chairs. Chicks riding cowgirl, spread on the laps of those bronze Buddhas.

(Inaudible)

Yah, meng, hardcore—money shots, frozen above their pretty smiles, to dry out across that loveseat—the same patio loveseat where my father courted my mother as high school sweethearts. Dude: hassle. Total. My ma threatened rehab—my ma, of all people—if I didn't seek spiritual guidance. From Father Baccante—joder, coño—back then still pastor of San Antonio, and my mother's Church Bitch. That fucking hypocrite convinced me I was broken.

(Breathing)

Nicknamed me Onan the Barbarian. As in, qué barbaridad, no? Literalmente. I promised I'd stop, of course, but you know. The more wrong it feels, the more thrilling. It's like cheating. Or your friend's sister not wearing a bra under her shirt when she comes to borrow his hair dryer. You're rushing to his baño, rifling through magazines by the toilet, making do with Betty and Veronica in bikinis. Tsong, you totally know what I mean. Solo flight is a gentleman's journey. At least do it properly, no? It's healthy anyway. Meditative. Eco-friendly. A victimless crime. So many techniques to master. Edging. Jelqing. The Stranger Effect. Most people can't appreciate self-love. First time Frances caught me, on our honeymoon, after she went to sleep, I'm outside our villa, on the pool lounger, feet flexed like wind flaps, laptop across my knees, and she's standing there with her arms crossed like Richard Nixon— fucking LQ drama for days! Like I was cheating or something. Fucking just join me! Besides, the actress looked like her. At least I never had to hide it with Vita. Come, I'll show you the entertainment room. Used to be my sanctuary, till Franny decreed that video games are a waste of my precious time. I don't argue anymore, jake. So my badass 5K OLED seventy-five-incher now mostly plays *Toy Story* and Baby Shark. With audiophile precision.

(Inaudible)

Yah. Vita and I hung out here a lot. How'd you know? She loved her soaps and telenovelas. *Marimar.* Or *Invitation to Love.* Or *Dallas. Dynasty*, especially, devouring my ma's old Betamax tapes. Vita just loved love. She'd blast her romantic soft-cock rock, belting along to Air Supply. She knew Queen's music, sure, but only from the *Mighty Ducks* soundtrack. So I introduced her to Zeppelin. Bowie. Seona Dancing. Fucking changed her life. Meng, if you find a chick who digs rock and roll, hold on with all you got. The wisdom rock teaches her will see you always forgiven.

(Breathing)

Come, let's sit for a bit—actually, let's not. This couch—wow . . . so gross. Joder. Pablum stains, bloody noses, snacky fingers. My beautiful full-grain leather didn't used to be beige. Come, let's get that drink. I'll have a bottle of anything, and a glazed donut, to go.

(Inaudible)

Yah, what's greatest about Vita—always been—she's like a sponge. And this was way before YouTube tutorials. She took jewelry making. Shiatsu lessons. French courses. I never lived with a woman before,

I didn't know how to provide—so I gave her everything. Even her braces. And my honesty. Never hid a thing from her. Turned out to be the problem. She was the best friend I ever had, meng, but chicks are too muy loca to stay that way. You see how they are with each other. Eventually they use your secrets against you, because they're smart. She's just lucky I rescued her from that One-Mig. Imagine? I fucking whooped his ass when he tried to fight me, with his Tae Bo skills from a Billy Blanks VHS.

(Breathing)

What a total Latka. Still thinks WrestleMania's real. Type who rebels by making his calling cards bigger than standard size. With his Opus Dei education. Fluent in Latin and Vulcan. Chaste till marriage. Like, have some fucking dessert, no? A little corruption's healthy. Isn't that the principle behind homeopathy? Imagine if Vita married that guy, and their wedding night they discover they're physically incompatible. That shit's for eternity, meng! At least take a test drive. If not for yourself, for your future kids' mental health. Divorce is illegal, jake. Adultery's criminalized. And the penalties are much higher for wives. Why even get married these days? Dudes hold all the money, all the power; chicks eat shit their whole lives.

(Breathing)

All for propriety. All for the kiddies. It's not even the Church, it's the congressmen, with their mistresses and second families. They're not going to change the law and pay alimony. Family values, my culo. My ma was done soon as she said, "I do." A year later, she hears about his mistress and runs home to her parents—who lecture her about duty before sending her back. Ten months later, I'm born. A toy to keep her occupied. Dude, imagine sharing your bed with someone who disgusts you. Convincing yourself the gonorrhea he gave you was from a toilet seat. Dude, I get it. I feel for them both. The world's honestly better off without him, but I get it. He had his needs. Both wanted more from life. Sure. All I'm saying, jake . . . I don't want that fate for my daughter. Come, the library's through here.

(Breathing)

My dad smoked his Cavendish and read after dinner, in that chair. A silhouette in the smoke. With the nose and jaw of a man born to be on currency, and knows it. Thought his webbed feet made him a Romanov. When I was fifteen he locked me in here with him for my first marijuana trip. Wanted to be my guide. Yah, meng, that's the word he used. He got stoned and danced like a chicken to "Hooked on a Feeling," that ooga-chakka song. Seriously, tsong. Nearly ruined weed for me. This was actually Vita's favorite room. She wanted to read every book. I taught her how to roll a J at that table. She can make perfect cones, with a wick from the excess paper. Dude, check this . . . pull that book. No, that one. *Alas, Babylon* . . . op, op, step back—the shelves slide away. Watch your step down.

(Breathing)

My dad's bomb shelter. Let me hit that light. The ultimate luxury, thousands of miles from any city worth bombing. Apocalypse in the Third World is redundant. It's a tragedy to lose New York, less so New Guinea. Yah, those instruments—this is where Franny allows us to practice. Sweet, no? I play lead guitar—it's *my* fucking bucket list.

(Inaudible)

Yah, I've had lots. My reggae group used to be Welcome to Jamaica and Have a Nice Day—but that was too long, which was kind of the point. Then we were Sexual Jihad, but got scared of the Abu Sayyad. So we became Feelingero—with a Boston meets ELO vibe. Personnel changes turned us into Chancingero—cocky industrial rock. Then a new guitarist took us pouty honky-tonk and we jammed as Bolero. When he split to get famous we quit fooling ourselves and became the Dilfs. Now we're just DadboD.

(Breathing)

Yah—classic oldies covers, at school reunions, for fun. The first and last *D*'s capitalized, in tribute to the moobs of middle-age. Here, have a CD. Chancingero's *Aural Sex*. Six orig tracks. "Boom-chicka-chicka-bow-wow." "Looking at You Looking at Me Looking at You." "Love Sucks, True Love Swallows." "Spirit of 69." "Belly-Button Cum-Shot." And "Single-Mother Gold-Digger (My Kind of Fidget Spinner)." We're terrible, in a rad way. Sometimes Franny's like, okay already, and comes down so I can sing to her. Sweet, no? She makes fun of me later. I don't care. I just like singing to my wife. A lovestruck Romeo sings the streets a serenade.

(Breathing)

Come, let's go back up. To my favorite room. You sure you don't want some pot cookie? It'll fuck you sideways.

(Plastic crinkling)

Tada! The den. Yah, dude. Totally qué barbaridad. As in, ooga, ooga, chakka, chakka. My dad and his cousins went safari every other year. Those barstools, meng—the size of those feet! African, much bigger than Asian. It's always that way, tsong—but Asians are smarter. That was his cognac-drinking chair—all those antlers were trophies. The Horny Throne. A Salvador always pays his debts. Sipping his VSOP while wheeling and dealing, his superiors becoming peers. If he invited you here, he wanted to impress. That table's where I learned five-card stud. His idea of bonding was winning my allowance. Till I got contact lenses before college and he started losing. Turns out my glasses reflected my hand. When I confronted the fucker he was proud of my anger.

(Inaudible)

Yah, dude, that's a genuine *Dogs Playing Poker*. In 1903, some cigar company commissioned nine versions from a Cassius Marcellus Coolidge. If that ain't cool enough, his nickname was Cash. My pops got it for me when I was a kid, at auction for a few Gs. One recently sold for nearly half a mil. USD. Frances tries, but fat fucking chance. It's the last of our art collection.

(Breathing)

Cash Coolidge, interestingly enough, invented comic foregrounds— those fucking paintings at the fair, with holes where you stick your face in, like a glory hole. To look like a mermaid, or fat baby, or dancing taco wearing a sombrero. That's a fucking legacy, meng.

(Inaudible)

I don't know, dude—*my* legacy? Maybe to be like Cash, nameless but remembered for what you left behind. Sounds fucking refreshing. Come, here's the breakfast room—where I learned about power. Table's round but there's always a head. Rich people love lazy susans because they reinforce hierarchy. My dad, mom, all his yes-men, the secretarial staff, then me. Always last. Now I'm always first, even if it doesn't feel like it. My pops would eat and preach, cajole and berate, make jokes that were all threat and no humor. No one wielded the proverbial stick quite like him. Carrot dangling on one end, other end circling for a whipping. To him, a good deal wasn't one that was fair— fairness was him fucking the other guy. So no, I won't sit at his place. Even if it's still like I'll come down one morning to find him behind his paper, poking at an article and rolling his eyes at me with that smile of his. I tell the helpers to serve from where he sat. Come, here's the greenhouse. That's the powder room, which used to be fucking literal. Through there's the kitchen. Yah, Vita would hang with the staff there. I admired that. Franny thinks they look uncomfortable in their own clothes instead of uniforms.

(Breathing)

I envied Vita, to be honest. Her relationship with the help. I always hated being judged for how you're born. You know how it is, bok. At one point the kitchen was the most dangerous place in the house. After he died. The ones faithful to him, scared and conniving. The ones faithful to my ma, threatened and planning. I saw while watching them pick through his clothes and shoes I let them take, for their families. Even among them my father made a wasteland and called it a kingdom. For fuck all: my ma left and I fired all of them—except the cook, her husband, and her sister, the all-around. The rest knew we had money problems, but didn't pay back a centavo of all we'd lent them. To think we put their kids through school. Come, I'll show you upstairs. After you.

(Breathing)

Watch that loose step. Onwards and upwards.

(Gasping)

No. I'm good. Just pause at the landing. Catch my breath. Oof. Used to toboggan.

(Gasping)

Down these steps. On a tray.

(Wheezing)

I'm peachy, meng. World's my oyster. Rock on. Sure you don't want? Last bit of cookie. Crank it up to eleven.

(Plastic crinkling)

So this is my childhood room—now the Japanese Room, where my ma stays, so we'll just peek.

(Breathing)

My pops used to say the shantung silk walls are perfect for her, because padded. His jokes, dude, after her hysterectomy—he could be fucking cruel.

(Breathing)

His lifetime of women, yet the only time she retaliates, with her Monégasque Reiki instructor, my dad fucks her reputation. So that all she had was us. Come, here's the prayer room.

(Breathing)

Obviously, she believes in everything—which is . . . beautiful . . . I guess. Started with Jesus, with a side of feng shui, then crystals, palm reading, tarot, then hedged with Zen Buddhism, chanting, the Gnostic gospels, then centering prayer, before returning, full circle, to Christ, this time totally—

(Breathing)

. . . as in Opus Dei. It's helped. That's what matters. In there's the Mauve Room; now storage for all our shit. So much shit. There's a leak, so we'll skip it. This is the Sun Room, because it's, well, sunny. Shiloh's room. So yesterday, I go downstairs and my ma's shaking Shiloh. As in, fucking violently—

(Breathing)

. . . for *almost* spilling juice on the white dress she gave her. As in, what the fuck, jake. Then my ma's on her knees, hugging her, going: "Abuela loves you. Don't you love Abuela?" Shiloh's too confused to cry. Then Frances comes in and goes: "Of course you love Abuela. Reina, tell Abuela. No ice cream if you don't." As usual, sucking up to my ma. Shiloh just stands there, aware of the injustice—

(Breathing)

. . . I should've . . . but what can I do? It's not up to me anymore. This morning, I found her here, with a back scratcher, beating that Daisy Duck over there, shouting: "Die! Die!" My little girl. I mean . . . fuck, dude. I just—

(Breathing)

Fuck. I mean . . . this fucking fuckery. Fuck. It makes me—aw, motherfucker. Fuck it. And I can't do shit . . . I—

(Gasping)

I'm fine. It's fine. I'm cool. Like Coolio. Qué barbaridad, is all.

(Breathing)

Come. I'll show you the escritorio. That's what you want to see, no? Where it happened. Before, growing up, it was my favorite room.

(Breathing)

The most mysterious. Reeking of Gotas de Oro and responsibility. No, really, I'm good. I'd peek through these glass doors to watch my grand-pops, in his perfect Windsor and polished wingtips. Signing checks all day, like a general giving orders. So different from my pops, who slouched in his silk robe and babouches, signing like a conductor with a baton. That was my great-grandfather's desk. Chippendale. My dad . . . that's where he—yah.

(Breathing)

People like us, jake, we usually weather storms. That's what makes us powerful. But vulnerable when fuckers like this Estregan see us as cash cows and make us the villain. A page from the Dictator's hand-book: sequester to create fear, distribute to create loyalty. At least Lontok, Glorioso, the rest, they respect the cows they're milking. This stupid boxer might declare martial law, people say, if the December 12 election's not going his daughter's way. Please. Leave us out of it. *We* only get involved when it's self-preservation. That's why the private sector—*we* imported the COVID vaccines. The crooked government always just grabs. And what, we'll let some Johnny-come-lately, still smelling of the canal, take what our great-grandparents, grandparents, parents slaved over, saved for our safety and security, for our kids? Joder, coño. Don't fucking touch my family.

(Breathing)

You get it. That's why Bansamoro can't win, despite his grand princi-ples. You can't jack off and call it making love, no matter much how you love yourself. Even the Ayatollah of Rock 'n' Rolla needs to get into bed with people like us. Look what happened. Somebody in his cam-paign's leaked all that stuff, to torpedo his chances, because they know. That's my reading. At some point Bansamoro has to choose, between politics and his son. Until we know which, why would we back him?

Whoever backs me, I'll back. So that my daughter won't be beholden to some baduy guapito husband who loves her surnames. So that my son won't rely on our shitty healthcare system if he inherits my defective genes.

(Breathing)

Yah, dude, poverty's unjust, but equality won't come through more injustice. Given half a chance, fucking reformers become what they despise. Our country's fucking shameful, meng. It's patriotic to be ashamed of what's shameful. Loy Bonifacio's totalmente loco, but still a fucking hero, driven by shame. Still, they'll bang the gavel and let him fry. Come, I'll top up your glass. I insist. So yah, I was the one who found him. I was downstairs, getting a book in the liraby . . . libery— fuck I'm high. Let's make these ones doubles.

(Liquid pouring)

So I heard the shot. I run up. There he is. Fucking hassle, meng. As in joder fucking coño. Fucking maricón coward. Always leaving a mess for someone else. Wasn't even his last fuck-you, either, jake.

(Breathing)

When I was a kid, he told me this story, proud, from when he was my age. About him and my Tita Lina. My abuela gave them both chocolate bars. Tita Lina eats hers, right away. But my pops, being my pops, he takes just one bite, saves the rest for later. Tita Lina sees he still has and starts bawling. She goes: "Why does Narcisito still have chocolate? It's not fair!" Abuela sees that Lina's right. She tells my dad: "Share with your sister." My dad looked me in the eye, with this proud gleam. "So you know what I did?" he said. "I licked my chocolate. Then I gave it to her." A lifetime later, still fucking pleased with himself. That's exactly what he did to us in the end, jake. Licked the chocolate.

(Breathing)

Fucking all of it. We're there, burying him, trying to squeeze some tears out. Squeeze some optimism out of what's coming—as they say: where there's a will, there's a . . . relative. Rela-thieves, Franny calls them. Circling. Actually, his old notarized will was fair, surprisingly. But his last will, handwritten, which superseded it: divisive as fuck. And his two-page amendment, the writing so shaky it looked suspect: that was designed to hurt. Almost couldn't believe it came from him. Except I could. Even his suicide note—nothing but oration for the historians. Everything as nasty as the blood spatter on the envelopes. His sudden conscience, meng: us paying his dues. Carve-outs for the bodyguard and driver he shat on for decades. Debt and cases for my mother. Illegitimate new siblings for me, jake. Each to get half a share of what I get, without enduring nearly half of what I did. One kid he only heard about, from some woman he called "of communal commodity"—couldn't even remember her name. One mistress, a maid at the hacienda—apparently he let her wear my mom's clothes— this woman fooled him that she was pregnant, but actually she was just fat, and her infant son was her nephew. Imagine? Would've gotten away with it if I didn't insist on DNA testing, like I'm the greedy cunt.

(Breathing)

A guy like my dad, with a maid—what did he get out of that? Yah, so—Oof. I'm feeling a little . . . Let me show you the master suite. Then I'll lie down. Here, outside, I'd sit, fucking hours, scratching at their door, waiting for them to wake up. And this is the bedroom. Where the magic happens. Boom-chicka-chicka-ow-ow-my-sciatica. Yah. Mirrors on the ceiling . . . San Miguel Beer on ice, we're just prisoners here of our own device. I get to look up, watch myself drown in my own fluids. Poor Franny. Didn't sign up for that. I can't resent her resentment. Disappointment in me's our common ground. Frances was an angel who hacked off her wings. She thought that's what I wanted. As if I ever knew what I wanted. But I never cheated on Franny. The only one. She's my wife . . . that means everything. Not that she knows everything about me. Fuck no. Better that way. Relationships should earn honesty, not demand it. When you settle, jake, something happens. The hunger's there, under, eating at you till you're someone else. But she's my Franny.

(Breathing)

My rock. I always adored her opinionated mestiza spirit . . . you know Basques. A smoking Maria Juana Watson—"Go get 'em, Tiger," she'd say, straightening my tie after breakfast, before leaving for her own law practice. Poor thing. Suffers carpal tunnel now, from breast pumping. I wish I could fix everything. Shiloh, our little Plecostomus. With four surnames and three hyphens. Over here my parents had this round bed—rotating Lullaby Due, from 1968. Classic. By Luigi Massoni. Sold it, to get that hospital one. Least the remote's fun.

(Inaudible)

The porn vid? Oh, yah. The round bed. But you know, jake, it wasn't a hidden camera. We shot it together. Vita even joked, "This'll get us famous." When we broke up I gave her the tape. "That's me on there," she said. "You don't get to have me that way anymore." I respected that. She's a decent girl, Vita. Doesn't deserve all the threats. Don't believe the shit about her on Facebook. Red, he hates her because he loved her so much. Treated her as well as he could. I was so jealous I made a ton of shit up. Fuck it—this is *my* deathbed confession. I told them both things. To ruin them.

(Breathing)

He and I used to be close. He'd use my pool all the time, till he got air-con and I hardly saw him. Fucker. Dude, I'm so stoned. Fucking just hit me. That cookie. Honestly, I wish I had a copy. Of that infamous porn. Not for revenge, meng. You think I'm like that? I just want to remember. As in, she's the first girl from out of my dreams. Free, like a wild filly, pretending to be tame to the lucky few. Majesty roaming the great fucking plains of native legends, making gods of horses and priests of horse whisperers. That magnificent mustang and I would talk all night. About who we were. Who we'd become. I said: Just not like my fucking parents. She said I already wasn't. I asked her; she said: President of the Philippines. So sail on, Silver Girl. I really hope she'll be safe. She deserves to be happy. We were always laughing. Always making love. Experimenting. Nothing wrong with that, no? You're not Opus Dei, are you? Because I'm a space cowboy. A toker, a midnight stroker. What's indignation if not just another style of masturbation? I've thought a lot about this. If you're going to do something they'll fucking make you feel guilty about, at least fucking ponder it thoroughly, no? Why can't they just leave me to my past, pot, and porn? No painkiller like a hard-on, meng. Just fucking leave me to my sativa and Astroglide. That too much to ask? Fuck this adulting. Some things hurt more than cars and girls. Let me tug at ecstasy till I slip into oblivion. Fly away with my fapnado. Everyone's sad for me and happy it's not them. It's art, meng—porn, I mean.

(Breathing)

Not dying. Dying, too. It's feminism. Porn, I mean. Everyone deserves equal opportunity to fuck. Orgasm. Surrender. Humiliation . . . if that's your thing. This world needs its dreamers—may they never wake up. Only God can judge us. You understand, no? They let go of so much, how can they not be free? There's power in it. Every one of those girls, I respected, supported in my own way. Till some became Trumptards on their Twitter, then you just gotta fap to them being disrespected. But the rest—mad respect. This porn chick, in an interview, she goes: "I'd rather hate being paid to have sex than hate being paid to sit at a desk all day." You can't fool the children of the revolution. Like, maids—they get exploited. Sorry—"domestic helpers." We export them the world over. Dude, art confronts you, arouses, confuses. Six guys gangbanging a barely legal eighteen-year-old—unappetizing on a videocam, probably, depends. But auteurs, like Mason or Jules Jordan . . . glossy, great cinematography, killer soundtrack, costumes like fucking parodies of fantasies—what was I saying? Dude, I'm so fucked. Oh, yah. Art's pornographic. Uncomfortable. Rare. Beauty. Skill. Play. Authenticity. Lots of fucking Booker Prize novels don't even check those boxes. Used to be precious enough to steal—now porn's all free, jake, no longer intimate. But technically better—no longer the black-sheep sibling of cinema, jake. The stupid cliché story's not the narrative, jake. Just sex, in all its contexts. How do they inhabit their role? How convinced are you? How many boundaries can they break? Look, meng—either exile your perversions, or understand them . . . but exile's a life half lived, jake. How do you appreciate a fucking cliff if you don't look over its edge? Public Disgrace—a website, dude . . . Franceska Jaimes, paraded naked, statuesque, down the ramblas, to the plaza where fucking Columbus presented chocolate, maize, slaves, to fucking Ferdinand and Isabella.

(Breathing)

Show that in a gallery: art. Watch it on Pornhub: porn. Dude, interracial sex sites: fucking racial commentary. Cuckolds. Kink. Stepsiblings. Trannies. A canvas covered in orange. As in, a Campbell's Soup can. Fuck off. If they don't understand, you're a fucking philistine. Don't criticize what you can't . . . the times are a—but fucking people just fucking? . . . Adults, consensual, fucking artistically to some? Porn to everyone else. What about Rothko? Stupid-ass monochromes. Pollock, splooging all over the canvas? Anaïs Nin?—used to be porn, now art? James fucking Joyce! Warhol would've loved Ron Jeremy. Art's honest artifice, meng. Porn people—just more honest than most of us. Stars of the underworld's sky. Their souls for their art. Bodies glittering like gold. And we banish them. Like prophets or bad words.

(Inaudible)

Fuck, no, dude—no way I want Shiloh doing porn. Say that again to my face. I don't want her to be a nun, janitor, or politician, either. Get your fucking morality out of my house. The Vita Nova Sex Vid Scandal. If I released it—which I didn't—but if I did—though I didn't—she's the victim. Or a slut. But what if—fucking just what if Vita was the one? Who released it. What does that make her? Tell me, jake. Should she be buried neck deep, stoned in the village? Or maybe it just—maybe Vita should've been more careful, meng. Always lock away homemade porn. Like any weapon. Aw, Vita. Teenage wasteland. You know, jake, we made a vow. Whatever happened—Lobby of the Manila Hotel, my fortieth birthday. 4:20 p.m. For whatever we needed at that point in life. Maybe one last time. Maybe reconcile and run away. Maybe just stumble down memory lane over poriferols . . . protifero . . . profiter—whatever. Such a hard fucking word. So, let me show you the biggest baño in the world, jake. Vita would lean, just like this, against the door jamb. Sugar in her voice, just for me. Some charming observation. Or trivia. Or singing "More to Lose." Hair still wet, almonds and oranges. The world's most ridiculous baño in the world, I bet. Fucking his and hers excess. Selfishness is a luxury. Or the other way around? My pops would tell me Popeye stories from his toilet. Dropping off the Cosbys at the pool. One time, Grade Two, I brought my classmate here to meet him. It was that fucking normal to me. So much fucked-up normal. That medicine cabinet there overflowed. Into our lives. Got home from fucking kindergarten, jake, my mom here on the floor, burbling drool, barely breathing. Always so trendy: ludes, Mogs, Valium, Dormicum, Rohypnol, Xanax, finally Oxy, like all the cool kids of death.

(Breathing)

Well yeah, life goes on. Long after the thrill of living is gone. But him, he was King Addict—alcohol, blow, alphabet of vitamins and prescription meds. To wake up. Calm down. Lower cholesterol. Relieve gas. Harden stool. Fucking soften stool. Moderate blood pressure. Control mood. Clear sinuses. Maintain potency. Keep thin. Stop balding. Fall asleep. Stay asleep, till the process started all over again. Modern science. Darth fucking Vader, your worshipful. Both fucking worried about my weed. "Denial's the first sign of addiction." In unison. Like they fucking practiced. Now look at this shit. My last chukker. The bronchodilators. Mucus thinners. Antibiotics. Pancreatic enzymes. That fucking vibrating inflatable vest. Sexy! Lungs and pancreas filling with gloop. My inheritance, to match the shortcomings I was born into. I was so much older then, I'm younger than that now. Know what I miss most? Dairy. Fucking ice cream. Not smelling like garlic all the time. Running in the rain. Vita. Fucking shit, even the Care Bears don't care. Poor Franny. Quit law to take care of me. Brings me to the hospital. Wakes to help me cough. Smirks with me when my ma forces the issue with another faith healer. Franny's my One, with a capital O. My ma says it's her pedigree, but no. Love's about timing. Like life's about character. Don't look at me like that, jake. I'm sorry. It won't be so bad. Hell's heaven for the wicked. I got some time yet. A man's got to earn his dying. I'll just sit a bit. Toto Washlet, the Cadillac of shitters. Dude, I'm so fucking high right now. I'm a fuel-injected suicide machine. I'm sorry. Disregard my bullshit. Everything's bullshit. I watch Shiloh sleeping. Envy her. Pity her. The world's her oyster, cruel as it is. Goodbye cruel world—wish I'd seen more of you. Qué barbaridad, this country's so fucked. Who'll take care of my kids? I miss my pops. Maybe he was sick and just didn't tell us. My mind wanders when I pray. Him and me and my ma holding hands every takeoff and landing. Narcing calling me papa again. Shiloh old enough to believe in Santa. Frances and I, honeymoon, skinny-dipping in a secret lagoon, the phosphorescent algae bright as the Milky Way—like standing near the Tannhäuser Gate, crying in the rain and lost in time. I'm not some society-made replicant. I'm human, meng. Animal, vegetable, or mineral? Vegetable: a human bean. So, jake—Manila Hotel. That's what I was saying. Sorry. I get to the lobby, hour early. 4:20 comes. Waited another hour. One more, just in case. So I took what I had left inside and fucking drowned it. Couple a years ago, Vita calls. Out of the fucking blue. I was shocked, jake. She was at a Neil Diamond concert. I said, Does this mean you forgive me? She doesn't say a thing. Holds up the phone so I can hear. "Girl, You'll Be a Woman Soon." In the background, Vita singing along. She's what I listened to. I fucking hope they don't kill her. Dude, I'll just stay here. I'm sorry.

(Breathing)

Yah. On my throne. Long live the king. Fucking Elvis has left the fucking building, fucking señoras y señores. Thankyouverymuch. I'm so sorry. Before the girls get home. I just need time. Time. Here's your recorder—

(Muffled)

. . . your mic. Thanks for listening, meng. I'm so fucking sorry. You know the way, jake. Go on. Have a solid fucking life.

Spoiler alert: we're totally gonna win. Are you seeing those crowds right now? Oh, I got something for you: Moi. Check it—Bobblehead Vita! For your dashboard. Isn't that lit—as in, fire? First thing Boy does as campaign manager is order like thousands. For taxis, buses, jeepneys. With every pothole I'll be Vitaquah from the 'hood, telling it like it is—Vote for me, shawty. The election's exactly a week away, and the support's sudden and fab—donors with billboards, banners, basketballs, plastic fans, all with my face on them. Everyone wanting to invest in a winner. Coz I'm ♪ *never gonna let you down . . . never gonna tell a lie and hurt you . . .* ♪—our campaign remix slaps (and every word of it true). We be Rick-rolling the competition. Boy says all the attacks mean I'm on the right track. "Madam President," says he, "don't forget: Haters hate—that's why they're called haters." Madam President—how hot is that? Bless Boy and his overenthusiasm. He's so pissed at Nur—and I am, too. But I'm loyal and Nur's got my total support. We can hardly blame him for going full macho overcompensating, given what they're making up—the troll armies in full effect, with their storm surge of disinformation, like how he'll change our national flag to a rainbow crescent. I just think it's super unfortunate that he'd named his basketball team the Mythical Fighting Cocks. Right? Madam President—imagine? My first executive orders will bring back the siesta, because productivity, and free the nipple, because equality. I'm kidding—kinda. Maybe we should end our book with crowds in fuchsia, chanting for me to run, while I wave from a balcony, ♪ *through with my wild days, my mad existence.* ♪ I'll keep my promise—for a sequel. But only after a dramatic cliff-hanger in this one, which we can call: *I Was the President's Mistress*—with two exclamation points (coz one's too little, three's too much). Think that title's ironic enough? I say let's just own it. And I want to dedicate it to my fans, my lovers, my haters, but especially to my Mama. Oh, and Proverbs 31:25 as the perfect epi-whatever-it's-called thingy, which is hella fetch. I can't wait to see the book you'll finally write. Just two more interviews with you and I, right? One re: my years shared with Loy; the second, post-election, re: our landmark victory. But like I keep saying, you don't need to trouble Boy or Jojie—beshies may know me besh, but why not hear it straight from the filly's mouth? Don't forget what happened with Furio when he interviewed Jezh. Just saying.

(Inaudible)

Scared? My darling, I've got you telling my story—haters got nothing else to take from me, except maybe my being *this* close to who killed Rita. We'll be fine. We survived Estregan's drug terror, we'll get through his red-tagging. That journalist, the activist couple, their lawyer, those local Opposition leaders—bet you anything they weren't really Commies. Shooting back at cops? Nobody believes that cliché anymore, unless it's convenient. Furio calls this the season of the long knives—power being consolidated, Presidentiables cutting deals. But I eat death threats for breakfast, slathered on my croque mamser. Just promise you'll send these recordings somewhere safe. In case something happens. Maybe even to you—I couldn't live with that. You have a masterpiece to write for us, mister. People finally deserve the truth.

(Inaudible)

Preelection martial law? Another cliché—Estregan's still a showman; he'd be more creative than that for his dramatic third act. Like, maybe use that new flesh-eating disease to declare another EWANQ lockdown (the latest craze for control). Did you hear about that village in the North? People falling into comas so deep they're mistaken for dead, sitting up suddenly at their wakes, alive—to the terror of their inheritors. Guess that's why it's called a wake. Netizens be like: the dead are coming back to life! In time to vote! Rolex's MO, tried and true: whole cemeteries of loyal constituents—so many ghost voters even God's out campaigning to keep heaven. I bet that's what bumps Hope and him up from third place last minute.

(Lighter click. Exhalation)

I'm not worried; I've met so many people who want real change. Nandotards just disqualified the National Citizens' Movement for Free Elections as watchdog—like in last election—but it almost doesn't matter; citizens be out watching voting centers anyway, forming walls against thugs, livestreaming shenanigans, saying nevermore. Did you know, actually, that Edgar Allan Poe died from election violence?—found drunk and beaten on the street, in clothes that weren't his. Cooping, they called it: Thugs forcing alcohol down your throat and cooping you up—locked away till you agreed to vote again and again, in different outfits, for their man. And speaking of men . . . while Nur's on the defensive about his masculinity, Rolex is on the offensive—strong-arming the Abu Sayyad for the release of at least the American triplets. I still can't believe Hope—forced towards the Unity Party, all coz Rolex is now her best chance to do some good in governance; I'd rather lose than pay that price. Meanwhile, poor Nur's walked into his trap: Abiolaville's the only place in the nation with a No Chewing Gum or Sodomy Ordinance—no wonder they dared us to campaign there. Like, Nur with the hunky hotel masseur? Too baduy to be true. In public he's fighting those charges, but in private he's soul-searching about his son, just like Hope did with her daughter. That's between you and me, right? Whatever he decides, I'll stay true to his legacy of national unity.

(Inaudible)

Yeah, Boy's hella upset, but I keep telling him they're just words—what matters is what Nur's actually done for the LGBTQIA-plus community, and will continue once in power. But I get it; Boy's fought all his life. "Tolerance isn't acceptance," he's always saying. "And acceptance isn't equality." He's right. The Philippines *is* tolerant, compared to some neighboring countries—homosexuality's not criminalized, and neither is sodomy (except in Abiolaville)—but the gays, as Rolex calls them, they're mostly accepted only in certain roles: showbiz bading, parlor fag, trans pageanteer, effem assistant you can't live without but always make fun of behind their back (or not even)—like Respeto, Rolex's houseboy. The horrorable Governor Aguirre's such a dinosaur, thanks Goddess. But casual oppression's still so ingrained among us

Pinoys—like assuming your niece is gonna grow up liking boys; or saying someone's handsome son will be such a ladies' man one day. Imagine being a teen questioning your sexuality, hearing such expectations. Watching friends and family mocking homosexuals and transpersons. Sure, most of us may never feel that persecution—but those who do, and speak out, they get branded, as attackers of values, faith, and tradition. Look at Senator Toti Otots saying pride is one of the seven deadly sins, and therefore gay pride parades are sinful. With so-called leaders like that, no wonder people hide. Boy's straight-backed posture was his disguise in front of his father, an air force colonel— pretending out of fear, then out of respect; then he stopped pretending out of fear of not being able to respect himself. And colonel daddy never forgave him. Boy couldn't even see him on his deathbed.

(Sigh)

And Jojie, too—forced to leave the Scouts, an advocacy so central to her childhood. But as a stylist slash interior designer she's had no problem, coz she's *allowed* to be herself in those worlds. Meanwhile, Boy could only marry his husband abroad, even if they're the best parents ever to their nine kids. And Jojie's summited every one of the six highest peaks in the country. Such inspirations, my beshies—so much stronger than the machismosos trying to put baby in a corner. Thing is, not everyone's got it in them to fight—like poor, confused One-Mig, with his good-boy good looks, and skin like a saint statue, always smelling like Japanese erasers. In junior and senior year his best buddies nicknamed him "Badinger-Z," and after a couple of high school reunions he quit hanging with them—his scars so obvious I hoped he'd find acceptance in the world of showbiz, like I was starting to. Unfortunately, that was the late nineties, when your fans were too remote to defend you, and public opinion was still offline and shaped by a few media voices— tough-guy TV hosts and DOM columnists, all nostalgic for lust, their favorite deadly sin. After One-Mig and me moved in together, they said we had to be lying about our chastity. Then they said that if we weren't, it had to be because he wasn't man enough. Wear matching gold virtue necklaces, they call you baduy; take them off, they call you a slut. But I knew the truth and the truth was it didn't matter. One-Mig was sweet, sensitive, as kawaii as a vanilla mochi, with his falsetto

"Somewhere Over the Rainbow" in the shower, and his ability to quote Audrey's best lines from *Breakfast at Tiffany's*, and his never-ending fan-fiction manuscript about a Berlin whirlwind with Liza Minnelli— she fortifying her heart against another swoonable man, he wanting to love her finally properly but admitting she'd be great for his career. (I know, right? Willkommen and bienvenue!)

(Laughter)

With me, One-Mig didn't have to be anything but himself, and me also with him. My purest relationship ever. My only boyfriend who was first and foremost my beshie, and my only beshie who didn't friend me out of pity for my being different. We started on-screen as a teen love-team, and so off-camera we figured, Why not give it a whirl? Boy telling us, with a wink: "If you're gonna be someone you're not, at least let it make you successful." Thing is, One-Mig, with his principles and certainties, he could never lie to the world—like keep a manly porn stash, but secretly for the penises; or ogle girls, but only for their dress sense. The only person he'd ever lie to is himself. Do that all your life, you get good at it—then who you gonna believe?

(Inaudible)

Yeah, maybe it was his religious faith, but I think both me and him knew that God continues to reveal a broader understanding of human sexuality. God wants us to read Her signs, and test them according to Her son's teachings. Besides, if God's all love, as the priests say, and God made sex, how could She not be pansexual? And who knows what feelings Jesus had for the apostles? Just saying. You know what's actually cray? In the Philippines, a gay person who's single can adopt a child, but a gay couple can't—coz the bishops believe homosexuality's a choice, and no lawmaker's man enough to insist otherwise. And don't even get me started on the transphobia—you know I worry when I leave Jojie in the club. I wouldn't dare assume to speak—I mean, trans-people can speak for themselves; but the facts tell us that we should listen, and listen with the intent to hear. Because seventy percent of Pinoys polled say homosexuality should be accepted by society, yet we've got the highest rate of violence against transpeople in Southeast Asia, second highest in Asia—like, Jennifer Laude strangled to death by Scott Pemberton, that American marine who left her naked with her head in the toilet, all coz he flew into "trans-panic," he claimed, fearing he'd be raped.

(Chair scrapes. Footsteps pacing)

I mean, take responsibility for your own illusions! Right? Nobody else should pay for what you believe. One-Mig never accepted the illusions of showbiz, despite all it offered—accusing Boy of exploitation, Boy's heart breaking over being blamed for our romance that was envied by tender hearts across the land. Coz to a dream maker like Boy, nothing's more worthwhile than love—society's best way, he says, to smash the barriers that divide us. Sweet, right? One time even helping a female producer elope with one of the male dancers, and hiding when her brother came around with a knife—till the brother went home and threw acid on his sister's face. All Boy's fault, One-Mig said—even though Boy was just trying to help, and paid for the poor girl's plastic surgery, and made sure the brother was brought to justice. It's so ironic how cynical One-Mig was about the people who just wanted to accept him—though after what happened to his twin, Glendys, guess I can't blame him, even if he and his family blamed me.

(Chair scrapes. Seatback creaks)

But in the beginning, we really were rom-com perfect—our meet-cute so magical, like God smiling down upon us—the music kicking off our *Dance Dance* throw-down, and One-Mig making the sign of the cross, and me thinking to myself: he's handsome, squee, *and* devout? Lord, please! With his moppish Chachi hairdo, enviable chicken legs, and chinky eyes that smiled shut so easily—him laughing, me teasing: Oops! Where'd I go? Till now, a whiff of Safeguard soap or Head & Shoulders brings me back to that exciting time, together forever every step of the way: attending go-sees, doing photo shoots, clipping pages for our portfolios, exchanging smiles at the press-con feeding frenzies prying into our flirtatious rivalry as lead singers in our respective bands—me in the Hell o' Kitties, him in Les Baguettes. *The* It couple— very truly yours, to all our true believers.

(Inaudible)

It did get lonely, yeah—everyone thinking you got it all—but that loneliness brought he and I together. Sneaking up to his bedroom, hand in hand, rescuing me from my pension house—with its claustrophobia, cockroaches, and moral tyranny of Ms. Saavedra. Tiptoeing up the stairs just to listen to his New Wave tapes, or practice our dance routines in the mirror on his closet door—the carpet zapping us when we'd touch, the Holy Spirit our chaperone. One-Mig welcoming me into his refuge from the world—his room, which was just so *him*, feet dragging towards manhood, unwilling to leave the safety of childhood: stickers all over his headboard, the Garfield blanket he once loved, shelves covered with his collections—and moi, his captive audience for his latest acquisitions (like the Witchblade PVC figure he just unboxed; an original Jetfire the Autobot; or a first-gen MG kit of a battle-mecha wielding not just one but *two* lazer swords). One-Mig came to showbiz to fund his hobbies and stayed with showbiz to jumpstart his own businesses—now a small empire of shawarma stalls, bubble tea cafés, house-call computer repairs, and remote-control-toy manufacturing. Always striving for independence, and I learned my work ethic from him—♫ *his mind on his money and his money on his mind.* ♫ Even if he could be so infuriating—our first date at Saisaki, with a free-second-dish-of-equal-or-lesser-value coupon; and our pre anniv and Christmas-slash-birthday break-ups, when he fought me just so he didn't have to buy presents; and how he nagged that my fashion magazines "manufactured desire," quote unquote. And the priciest thing he ever got me: a nonpirated version of Microsoft Excel, for Valentine's—us tumbling into bed after, to make sweet, sweet sums on practice spreadsheets on his laptop, teaching me the pleasures of conditional formatting.

(Laughter)

He even inducted me into the exclusive world of multilevel marketing—Avon, Amway, Herbalife—which is why I could never tell if he was being nice to people or just wanted more recruits. Such weird, so cute—and hella suspicious of the world, always complicating it: JFK had to be killed by the mafia and the CIA, the moon landing had to be a hoax, the *Titanic* had to be an assassination of the Guggenheims, Astors, and Strauses—by Hershey, Vanderbilt, and J. P. Morgan, who all canceled their tickets last minute. I guess being sure of things was just part of being young, especially when you're unsure and searching—me and One-Mig looking into each other's eyes as we shared a mic in the church band, convinced the answers were there somewhere. We'd bundle and click our little grade-school mentees into the church's van, to go for ice cream—playing marriage and practicing parenting, which I assumed I totally wanted. Our religious faith our passion and intimacy—taking turns leading grace in thanks for our meals; and kneeling before bed to speak as one, held hands squeezing through that bit about dying before I wake and praying the Lord my soul to take. With my best friend at my side, nothing frightened me—first time in my life. I still can't believe we had the guts to move in together.

(Lighter click. Exhalation)

Even *that* was just so One-Mig: strong in his conviction, convinced of its purity, never caring what anyone said. And so dedicated to his boy-friend duty that he was the cheesiest Chiz Curl ever, like leaving baduy Post-its on my dressing-room mirrors—JAPAN (as in: Just Always Pray At Night), ITALY (I Trust And Love You), HONGKONG (Hug Only Nice Girls, Kiss Only Naughty Guys)—or cornering me with his power-lines just before I went in front of the camera: "What are the best letters in the alphabet?" (*U* and *I*.) "Did it hurt?" (When you fell from heaven.) I'd smile and he'd smile and his eyes would disappear and together we'd be blind to the rest of the world, so darned in love. He was actually my only boyfriend who in his heart chose me over everyone else. "That's your money, Mommy. Not mine," said he, after they cut off his allow-ance. "Tell Daddy not to worry, I can make my own." Their businesses tilapia farming, prawn crackers, and funeral parlors—but that's not why he wasn't interested; like I said, he would've given up anything for his independence. Except me, I think. And of course his twin sis-ter, Glendys—who I got along super well with, actually. Partly why I tried so hard, playing peacemaker, because family's important, and so that nobody could say I made him choose between them and me. Even learning phrases in Hokkien, and making sure his mother saw me serving him before myself at table. I'd burp after meals. And feng-shuied our condo. And tagged along to temple, helping his grandmother to the car even if she never looked at me, not once, and really smelled like oregano. But the more they rejected me, the more One-Mig stuck with me—which felt almost too good to be true, to this half-breed chick from the province, lost among the big-city crowd, learning how to laugh at the right moments, projecting confidence through canned replies, just as insecure as him. Togetherness gave us certainty—our faith firm enough for us to even tempt temptation, hormones raging, sitting cross-legged, face-to-face on the bed, to momax for eternity— touching, exploring what we each didn't have, before pulling away. "Let's save it," he'd say, gently moving my hand off him. "I love you too much." Which was sweet. Then seemed like an excuse. Then I blamed myself—because that's what you do.

(Pause)

Until what happened to Glendys, I never understood how vulnerable their family always felt—why they never really let me in. I didn't even know till like months later that One-Mig wasn't just Juan Miguel— he's got another name just for their community. Did you know that during Spanish times the Chinese weren't allowed to live with everyone else? A wall literally separating them from the safety of the fortified city. One-Mig's mother's mother came from Hong Kong to work as a nanny—which is so ironic, with all those Filipinas now going the other way—and his father's father was a mortician fleeing the famines of Chairman Mao. His parents were born here, but never shook their accents, their minority once the poorest of the poor, but now richest of the rich—still suffering all the suspicion and racism, like the kidnapping trend that targeted them, and the backlash now against China, which probably shouldn't include them but does. Some deserve it, though, like the Changco brothers—as Pinoy now as you and I, but totally selling us out to our new colonizers—and the taipans, with their real estate and airlines and tuna empires, who supposedly helped launder and retrieve the Dictator's billions hidden in Switzerland, and I bet are now funding his kids' run towards the presidency. Me, I can proudly say my entire shoestring campaign's crowdfunded or given in-kind—average donation: two hundred pesos. Nur and the Liberty Party have large donors, but all that's transparent—I wouldn't stand for anything shady; I don't want office that badly. Seriously. Coz you should see what I've seen, barnstorming like cray—six campaign days left, a third of the country still to visit. They're blowing up my social—the people themselves: student activists, citizen journalists, labor leaders, Filipinx advocates, neighborhood patrols, grassroots rehab initiatives, teachers who bring their own school supplies, fisherfolk organizing against the Chinese maritime militia, tribespersons protecting their lands from resource exploitation, NGOs filling in all the government's gaps, slum residents who I adore for their hospitality and sense of community—hashtag vitasvoters, hashtag theresmoreloveinthephilippines. All sick and tired of our rulers' incompetence demanding our resilience. Election season's the best, honestly: our opportunity to challenge the people in control, to get them doing what they're supposed to be doing—or get them replaced if they don't.

(Inaudible)

I think our problem is we expect our politicians to do everything for us—coz that's exactly what they promise us. But when all those promises are broken, we end up losing faith in the system, instead of the people we trusted to make that system work. And we're like: Fine, it's all so broken, we'll leave it up to you—just drop us a little something something sometimes, even if that something's something we always deserve, like running water, or cops that aren't crooked. That's why my platform's centered on education—the infrastructure of human capital: public schools, continuing ed, skills training, entrepreneurship, and especially civics and rights—so that we can *all* learn how the system works and how to organize ourselves in it, to fix it. My campaign's my crash course in that, learning from everyone I meet. That's why I honestly don't care if I win—

(Inaudible)

... promise! I just want to show people that they, too, can participate—beyond just paying our taxes and doing as we're told. Show them that everyone's a leader, whether of their community, business, basketball team, church group, Zumba club, whatever, but especially of their families (supposedly the most important unit of society, right?). Coz if we're not gonna fight for our families—and teach them the right values and priorities—then who's gonna?

(Chair scrapes. Footsteps pace)

Fernando, and all the others, they promised to free us from politicians exactly like them—promising this time would be different. But it never is. Respeto Reyes's people—like Hope Virdsinsia, Lina La Bina, Fredo Londrey, Julius Pinakalinis, Fay Agud, Aguinaldo Kandura, Baccante and the rest of the conference of Catholic bishops—they were all just replaced by the Estreganettes, Kingsley Belli, Bingo Bobot, Uranus Jupiter Kayatanimo-Uy, Hari Pukeh, Paz Panot, Rusty Batlog, Cantuteh, Angbabat, Rebolvar, and Reverend Laverno Kidohboy. Meanwhile, the usual suspects thrive, no matter who's in charge: the Lontoks, Villas, Toti Otots, Arriola Makapal Glorioso, T. T. Gordion, K. Sisboy Pansen, Bingbong and the brothers Changco, along with Junior's family, and all those others who switch flags according to where the weather blows. We're right to blame them all for all that's wrong with our country— except the fact that we put them in power. The biggest conspiracy is that it's always someone else's fault—I see, says the blind man, even if he doesn't.

(Chair scrapes. Seatback creaks)

One-Mig blamed me for his sister, knowing it would drive me away— even if he refused to admit it, and masked it with his jealousy. So I responded to Cat, at the Metallica concert, because why not do what you're already accused of, even just to see what it feels like? I'm not proud of that, but at nineteen you crave either a touching rom-com or an excruciating dramedy, not unedited reality TV—One-Mig cutting his toenails at the kitchen counter (while I'm cooking soup), or sighing at my problems as if I'm complaining (and not just seeking support). One-Mig, in the end, wasn't so much too little as too much and too late: that fancy dinner at Les Kunishis', my first designer purse that wasn't a Greenhills knockoff, new Post-its with city-name acronyms on my mirror, so many he hid my reflection—a metaphor, if ever there was one. One-Mig super trying hard to be the man he wasn't, till he wound up all macho on the floor in the mall, under a fat kid whose new Air Jordan I was stuffing into a trash can—all coz the kid and his DOM dad had ogled me earlier, in that way that feels like being touched, One-Mig all like: "What's your problem?"—the Dirty Old Man flashing his gun and clapping back so cleverly, "What's *my* problem? What's *your* problem?" One-Mig calling him a squatter, the DOM sputtering like a sprinkler: "Squatter? Squatter?"—pulling back an acid-wash sleeve to screech: "Kiss my Rolex!"—while I'm pulling One-Mig away, hissing, No; hissing, Please; hissing, Let's get some Häagen-Dazs, coz I see where this is going, and where it's going is not who he is: my sweet skinny mega chou, who turns the other cheek, and can't manage stick shift, always chaperoned by his driver like a young samurai with an aging squire teaching him nonviolence in a hostile world. We're half-way through our cones when someone shouts: "There he is!" and my heart sinks, and the fat kid and his fatter brother are charging, and One-Mig's flying against a glass door breaking, then under angry folds on the ground shouting: "You stink, Fatso," his voice as cool as the ice cream on the floor. All while I'm picking up the new shoe that flew and shoving it in the trash can beside me. Afterwards, in the security office, the chief guard's asking if we want to press charges—but One-Mig just wants the baduy, nouveau-riche DOM's name. The guard telling us: "Dominador Laurito." Just some two-bit thug from Carmona, Cavite, who couldn't teach his fugly sons to respect women. I always wanted to get back at them somehow. A lifetime later, I guess I just did.

(Laughter)

Honestly, I appreciated One-Mig's illusion that he was protecting me, but I knew it wasn't really for me. A couple days later, we're on location, for *Touch Me Not*, my first mature role: me, leaving my bucket of laundry, stepping into the river; One-Mig, behind the director, pacing, while the son of the plantation owner—played by Carlo Pizzati—peeps at me from behind palm leaves. And as I wade into the waterfall, right as my dress goes see-through, just as my love interest tears off his shirt and ripples towards me, suddenly there's One-Mig: leaping like a jaguar onto a gorilla—and they're splashing and thrashing, cameras still rolling.

(Clapping)

And the rest, as they say, is tabloid fodder. My career taking off; One-Mig's officially over. Not that he cared, coz he'd never bought into showbiz. From our very first day, on the set of *Ready! Set! Go!*, One-Mig saw only a cramped studio filled with chipped Styrofoam and gluey glitter, moldy plywood and dusty lightbulbs, the grimy masking tape on the floor telling you where to stand. Which to me was all magic—wide-open and sparkling with possibility. And he judged me for that. Like this one time, when our love-team popularity was at its peak—postpremiere of *Spin the Bottle 2: Back to School*—and Boy treated the entire crew to dancing at Faces, then after-party drinks at the Peninsula lobby: I'm trying not to pass out on the damask when the waiter's asking what I want, and everyone's ordered schmancy drinks, but all I want is tea, and the waiter's got me on the spot, coz all I know is Lipton. I'm like, Tea—all eyes on me—then I'm like, Hot tea, and the list the waiter says flies way over my head, and I almost want to cry, till it dawns on me. On second thought, I say, I much prefer champagne. But just as relief floods my lungs, the waiter's asking again what kind, and I don't know what to say—everyone still watching me—about to say pink when I realize: Your finest, of course. From across the table, Boy's looking at me, proud as a mother hen. Beside him was One-Mig, looking like he wanted to vomit.

(Lighter click. Exhalation)

Anyways. Did you know that five bottles of Dom Pérignon contain as many bubbles as there are stars in the Milky Way? That was One-Mig's problem: he never appreciated wonder. Never accepted that make-believe involves believing. Never understood that the second someone in that world says you're beautiful or talented is the moment your hope and insecurity merge, and that some of us grow better that way, coz the catwalk to perfection is paved with imperfections. You're in a gorgeous gown, under floodlights and flashes, wobbling under your disappointing nose and Jell-O thighs, more-stunning girls traipsing around you, a thousand eyes searing from the shadows, with hate or love it's hard to tell—and either you convince yourself you're better than all that (like he did), or you accept that you gotta work harder than everyone else (like I did). Being stared at is so confronting because you know you shouldn't look away—judgment based on how you're perceived, with you at the mercy of your best angles, which you find only through your acceptance of your worst ones. To me, staring back was worth it, just to be, once in a while, part of creation itself. Let there be light; and there was light. If you've ever seen yourself in someone else's art, or held still as a lover took your picture, then you know exactly what I mean—what it's like to feel like you're finally enough.

(Fingers snap)

One-Mig judged me—as if you can blame a gal for starving for a chance to one day wear Balenciaga's summer collection in Milan, or pose for the cover of French *Vogue*. Especially if you were a gangly half-breed tomboy—in a room beside a pungent canal, crackling slowly through crumbling magazines from your Tita Henny's parlor, gazing for the first time at dresses by Ralph Rucci, Halston, Balmain—suddenly waking in the dream, in the deep end of what people think is shallow, while your mochi-faced sexually confused boyfriend's demanding—demanding!—that you choose, just as you're mastering the tricks of the trade and advancing, just as the magic begins to fade and all that seems to surround you is jealousy. Like, are those just her genes, or is it meth, or bulimia? Like, hey babes, what's your secret, cut us a line, how do you do it without staining your teeth? But as Jojie always jokes: "If something's too good to be true . . . enjoy it while you can"—coz one day you'll snap out of wanting everything you once wanted. Like in this book I'm reading, *Dream Lover*—Mica, our heroine, awakening one morning among satin and sunlight off the Mediterranean blue, her wish last week come true, and she's literally living out her dreams—a new one each day, filled with fabulosity and intrigue, chiseled jaws and exhausting finery, till she longs to return to her sweatpants and the food-and-beverage manager who loves her every wrinkle. I still got like forty pages left, but you can totally see the ending: she'll finally find that ancient wishing well again, in the walled Tuscan town of Cortona, and, exhausted from ravagings and raptures, with six competing hunks (Lorenzo, Ignacio, Pip, Alfred, Raj, and Troy) hot on her heels, she'll toss in her last lira—wishing, yes, for normalcy.

(Laughter)

My own choice was tough—no thanks to One-Mig. Coz I for one can tell you nothing's ever normal after you finally get certain wishes. Normal's causing crowds in malls. Normal's people pointing and whispering. Normal's thinking it's all too much to bear, but you can't bear thinking it'll end. Coz you're never the same person after you've walked slo-mo down the street, tossing a Zippo over your shoulder, sliding on shades as your past explodes behind you while a killer soundtrack kicks in and the director shouts cut and the crew cheers. One-Mig returned to *his* normal: his Birkenstocks and socks, his new love handles girdled with gadgets, his illusion of seeing through all the world's illusions. While I stayed in the dream, even after he took my hand and told me: "If you really love me, you'll leave showbiz and finally be yourself." When you talk to him, he'll tell you I'm faking everything. But what if I'm just hopeful for a better world? One where I can actually help.

(Pause)

Help people like Adam, the brave paraplegic boy I met in Baguio, whose parents work so many jobs, and have never taken a weekend off since he was born. They need job security.

(Pause)

Or Shana, mother of eight in Pangasinan, who's my age but looks like a grandmother, always so frightened in bed beside her husband that she only sleeps soundly during her menstruation. She needs access to reproductive healthcare.

(Pause)

Or the old miner in Rosales who walked twenty miles to my rally and waited to talk to me after, even though he couldn't say his name without coughing violently. He needs us to regulate industry and safeguard worker's rights.

(Pause)

Or Noelle, whose husband was shot by police, who claim he was a drug pusher who fought back, though she says he was a devoted father and community activist. Their family and so many others deserve accountability.

(Pause)

Or Lance Corporal Elton John Leonardo, who lost five in his squad along with his right leg, after being ambushed by Communists who were captured along with ammunition bought from one of his superior officers. All those men deserve justice.

(Pause)

Or Ramboy, from Rizal, Palawan, who was charting a course home with his exhausted crew when Chinese militia confiscated their entire catch in exchange for a few bottles of water. They need us to fight for them.

(Pause)

Or Tonio Matanum, the Lumad teacher I visited the other night in a clinic. He didn't have much, but asked me to make sure his family didn't fight over it when he died. I took some paper and sat at his bedside as he listed everything he owned—his books, his kudlung, his grand-father's kampilan, his smartphone, his medal from the Second World War. I told him I'd personally take care of his wishes.

(Pause)

There are so many who need help, while the rest of us doubt and blame, fight and backbite, making everything more complicated than it already is.

(Pause)

Last night, I got a call. Teacher Tonio had died. So I turned my campaign convoy around and drove the seven hours back—to keep my promise.

(Pause)

That's why I don't care what One-Mig says—or Rolex, Baccante, Fernando and his trolls; or the newspapers, or Loy, even, in his trial this week. Why should I? I can close my eyes and make them disappear. Then open my eyes and see what matters.

Juan Miguel "One-Mig" Sontua Transcript.

(49:44.33—One-Mig.M4A)

(Inaudible)

Okay—you want the truth, the whole truth, then buckle up, because it's the truth, and I've got the guts to say it; not your truth, or my truth, but everyone's truth, because there's only one truth—and the truth is: Vits planned all of this, okay?, from the beginning; from her teenage escape to the big city—using Loy Bonifacio's remitted riyals till she got her big break—to her many strategic relationships, because, as she always claimed, falling in love's simply trying for a happier life; at least till it shoots you in the heart, or, in this case, attempts to—like that non-assassination on Sizzle Saturday, just another false flag operation, like the Liberty Party bombing their own rally in Plaza Miranda way back before I was born, evidently, clearly, because it's all so tidy and convenient—the truth only known by that Bonifacio guy, that Everlasting Estregan Supporter turned high-level hitman, okay?, who won't testify for himself; he just sits there in court, shrugging at the prosecutors' questions—because the answers don't matter, not for a slave with a fate like his, not in a world where wealthy people pay rich people to convince middle-class people to blame poor people; Bonifacio doesn't need to say a word, about who put him up to it, or why he didn't pull the trigger—especially not with elections five days away, Vits so close to wielding the power of a presidential pardon, okay?, while Nuredin Bansamoro still believes he's using her, the way he once did to shadazzle his popularity, though she isn't one to ever be used twice, not her, no way—as ambitious as any man whose shoulders she sits on as he climbs toward power, always reaching the next level before he does, till she's the most famous person in a country where fame is next to godliness, a nation that will hand her the presidency—the presidency, okay?—clear as day, when you look beyond the lamestream media and ask the hard questions about who's behind everything—the reason she always called me a cynic, as if I'm not the only one in this book telling the truth, if you look close enough; implying I don't have faith, as if cynicism isn't just faith that the truth will be revealed through our disciplined search for it; finding that the truth's never fair, which is why it hurts, okay?—like how Fernando the Fist would never be accepted by the oligarchs, the old-rich Lupases and Alayas and Salvadors, despite his expansion of our economy for eleven straight quarters, post-pandemic, six-point-five percent last year alone, with exports up to eight-point-two percent, debt-to-GDP lower than ever, Moody's upgrading our outlook from stable to promising, and inflation barely two-point-seven-five percent—never mind all that, because the invisible hand, of the suits with big noses at the IMF and World Bank, prefers a powdered puppet like Respeto Reyes, not a populist disrupter like Papa Nando, the master strategist fighting for what we need: investment from China, panicked respect from America, and communities that are finally safe—costing us only some useless islands, unstatesmanlike F-bombs, and druggies and terrorists who were always dead weight, even when alive; all that now being used as evidence of his supposed treason, material for meme makers and trolls now suddenly pro-Nova—commanded (I suspect, from their familiar style) by the troll king himself, Kingsley Belli—who I predict will be knighted, in three moves, right before the ivory pawn, Vita, outmaneuvers the other Presidentiables to become the black queen, manufacturing consent for her administration, because she knows that victors tell the stories, and stories, when they're convincing, or stubborn, become the truth—like when she and I were props in that kayfabe relationship stage-managed by our talent pimp, Boy Balagtas, who promised fame, for us, and fortune, for himself—true love in a teleserye as real as internet conspiracy theories: like reptilian Anunnaki in disguise across the U.N. and throughout the media, working to enslave humanity—absurd, okay?—though I do wonder about lizardly Vladimir Putin, Victoria Beckham, Silvio Berlusconi, and especially Victorino Otots III, who all look like lizards and have Vs in their names, which people say is a symbol for a forked tongue . . . Vita Nova included, twice over—although shapeshifting lizard people aren't needed to explain what's wrong with this world, where evil's real, commonplace, and straightforward, like Senator Otots's point that reproductive health initiatives give Western governments new markets to reap billions selling their abortifacients; or like Lontok's command of the cops who handled the case of my sister when he was police commissioner, which I'm almost ready to expose, after tracing it through years of evidence linking him to triads, gang rubouts, and even the disappearances of activists back when he was deputy commander of our so-called Dictator's special intelligence police—typical dirt against most politikos, but in Lontok's case doesn't that sound true?—he's either the bumbling referee missing the injustice of a folding chair to your head or a veritable Bobby "The Brain" Heenan, his thick face now masquerading as virtuous and presidentiable—oh how I wish Junior was running with Rolex, instead of Farrah Estregan, because, other than Papa Nando, Rolex is the only politiko I believe; his lies worn on his sleeve, what you see is what you get, his delusions of grandeur only delusional if they fail—which they won't, because he'll sacrifice empty ideals for actual results, that's why iron fists are heavy-handed, they're made of iron, and we Pinoys are so undisciplined we need a firm hand—like how he ended decades of war in the North, forcing Comrade Rubio and Commander Ali to meet him on Abiolaburg mountain, their Communist and Islamist soldiers eyeing each other anxiously from opposite slopes, peace finally because only Rolex had the balls to threaten their families' safety—the leadership we need, not some surgically retouched Muslim with a patriotic stage name who's so weak he compensates with grand displays of humility, as if our country needs another sainted savior of democracy, as if Senator Nuredin "Bansamoro" dela Cruz's piety can save him from being thrown under the bus by Vita—who else but her would have all that black propaganda to leak, okay?—the rest of us still naively idealizing such virtue even while we always ask our leaders to do what we're too virtuous ourselves to do; because a great leader does have to get his hands dirty on our behalf—like our strongman's Martial Law decades ago, only expanding his capacity to address the dire threat of Communism infiltrating universities and the homes of even the well-heeled and powerful; it's true—as citizens our duty's to find that truth among the lies, not be brainwashed by myths manufactured by those who won control of the narrative, spewing the most despicable slander about the strongman's family: that his eldest daughter was conceived in a limousine outside Manila city hall, sired by the mayor with a long chin like hers, after her mother traded her chastity for a beauty-pageant crown; or that Junior died as a child and was replaced by a cousin, who had plastic surgery to look like him, who until today has a taste for cocaine and locked himself in his penthouse after losing his run for the vice presidency years ago, which is why he'll do anything to become president next week, to silence those who say he's the dumbest among his siblings, okay?, clearly not one of their brilliant father's brood—none of those myths true; simply stories told by the victors who did the ousting: opponents, activists, Communists, Fuchsia Liberty Party elitists who gave us nearly four decades of democracy that only proved their illegitimacy—poverty, inequality, crime, corruption on a scale that the strongman never allowed—a lot of people say, my parents even witnessing it when I was too young to remember everything working so well: the proud infrastructure projects, no traffic jams, efficient public transportation (the buses even called Love Buses!), and nightly curfews that kept everyone safe—if you weren't doing anything wrong, then you had nothing to fear under Martial Law; I can show you links, ten times more than you can from the alleged journalists in blamestream media—because we *must* ask the hard questions they don't want us asking—like in Baron Buchokoy's YouTube exposés, based on testimonials from people actually from that era who saw that the first EDSA Revolution's People Power only had a few thousand picketers, only in Manila, only a coup by privileged families and an archbishop with ambitions of becoming pope, or at least cardinal, which he got, okay?—Cardinal Sin; Jaime Lachica Sin, if you can believe that name, because truth is stranger than fiction—but what about the rest of us, the millions of Pinoys across the country who—

(Inaudible)

. . . yeah, that's your point?, your whataboutism?—tu quoque to you, too, you Orion, you—sure, the strongman's family made their share of myths (because that's politics, they're politicians), but nobody truly believes he discovered a cave full of gold bullion abandoned by General Yamashita and the retreating Japanese, explaining the president's wealth—and so what if their family stole?, so long ago, like all politikos; do we blame children for the sins of their parents?—and at least that family gives back, public servants working hard to make their province in the South the most developed in the country—did the Reyes family and the rest of the Fuchsias ever give us that, with their economy that thrived mostly for their cronies?—the victors telling their stories, to serve their own agenda, a pattern evident throughout history; like in the French Revolution, "Let them eat cake," a soundbite Marie Antoinette never actually said, fake news lasting till today, successfully spread by the Jacobins, despite King Louis's steady reforms, lies they made to fuel the mobs' indignation and spiral their country into chaos: eighteen thousand guillotined, three hundred thousand dead; that could happen here, if we're not careful, starting with Vits blown away in Plaza Miranda, okay?—along with you beside her, okay?, if you don't choose wisely—if we don't learn from history, with its patterns showing what happens when entertainers, influencers, showbiz overlords brainwash and infiltrate politics, spoon-feeding 'tards a sucralose of half-truths, which are worse than lies—for example: Rolex stockpiling supplies to create famine in provinces beside his, instead of him simply preparing his constituents for a future possible pandemic; or that Bansamoro must be homosexual, instead of simply a power-hungry perfectionist manicuring his image against prejudices toward his faith; or the media before insisting *I* was gay, instead of accepting my choice to save it for marriage, because Vits was as important to me as my religious conviction—nobody understood that, except my sister, Glendys, Vita's best friend, both so close it was like *they* were the twins, while our parents distrusted showbiz, of course, and people ridiculed our faith—the kind of sheeple who place their faith in quacks and slips of paper with writing they can't even read, swallowing pills with unpronounceable names, ignorant to what's in those tiny pellets costing more than their weight in gold, making Big Pharma billions that's divided among so-called scientists who believe that human knowledge can grasp everything, able to describe an atom or the farthest corners of the universe, but unable to answer what or who created that atom or the universe in the first place, for if God was small enough for us to understand He wouldn't be big enough for us to worship, His creation so immense we're like blind people touching an elephant for the first time, so convinced its trunk is a leg, its tusks are teeth, accepting theories as fact, like the Big Bang, or evolution, or climate change—narratives by secular pagan priests receiving millions to pad global warming evidence so that cohorts across the quadrangle get matching budgets for alternative-energy research—blind to the fact that objective, evidence-based science leads us inevitably to God, which is exactly why thinkers like me, who accept the limits of certainty and embrace our need for faith, we're the last defense against those shoving *their* truthiness down your throats, especially these days, with for-profit storytellers like *Ruffler*, and its alleged journalists, publishing court-proven libel—Papa Nando's opponents, like that Communist Furio Almondo, all tools of Western imperialists, as Paz Panot accurately puts it, traitors against our democracy, cogs in a clickbait machine to monetize our views, evade taxes, enrich their foreign owners, drowning us in biased opinions and cheap punditry instead of actually reporting the facts so that we can decide ourselves—with our own intelligence, as if we're any less smart than they who ooze condescension—because it's more profitable for them to stream disinformation; why else is news now free?—so that you'll be overwhelmed by their lazy lies and surrender your last vestiges of control over our own lives, because a story needs a villain, like Vits claiming at the impeachment that Papa Nando is some Manchurian candidate controlled by China, terminally ill and worried about kompromat against his family, all because her illegal recordings mention meetings with the Chinese diplomatic delegation, as if foreign affairs is not just part of governance, as if suddenly Ambassador Lan Chao Dao is some evil blackmailer holding evidence on Judong Estregan—as if the presidential son really does have a triad dragon tattoo on his back, and is therefore behind that metric ton of shabu smuggled inside a shipment of industrial magnetic lifters, all because some alleged whistleblower at the Ministry of Customs, who I bet you anything is a Fuchsia supporter, testified under pressure—which he recanted anyway—the elite always needing a scapegoat, okay?, either the Jews or, in this case, the Chinese, as if we're some unwashed horde invading like the pirate Limahong—never mind those of us born or raised here, belonging as much as you do, generations migrating for centuries, before the Spanish, before the Americans, but not to colonize, to help build; now they say we Chinoys have dual sympathies, citing as evidence our close community and industriousness—even though the industrial revolution is what liberated the world from monarchies, while immigrants only become fully fledged citizens when our minorities grow powerful enough to dent elections—vilifying our community, attacking our leaders like Bingbong Changco and his family, who started out just like mine, refugees also from Guangdong, my grandfather a mortician only wanting the freedom to benefit from his own sweat, in a culture where his trade would be more socially accepted, in a part of the world we've always been in—it's called the South China Sea for a reason, no matter how some people have renamed it the West Philippine Sea, rewriting even geography because of the politics of politicians—their new victims and villains those Mainlanders finding livelihood in Manila's online gambling industry, living ten to a room, remitting savings to their families, passports confiscated by shady bosses, comfort only found among countrymen who speak their language; they're the latest job stealers and criminals, even if they're just like the millions of Pinoys abroad all these decades, finding livelihood, saving for remittances, seeking comfort among their own in places like Wan Chai or Lucky Plaza or Daly City—that unwelcoming world so familiar to us Chinoys, who've been blamed, hated, kidnapped for ransom in that trend that went on for years, politicians and police profiting from our fear, our bodies, our lives; we've had to learn to survive, just like the Changcos, who are shrewd to hedge their bets, their different newspapers opposing each other ideologically—some call that a monopoly, the brothers call it neutrality; I call it smart, because it's not illegal, it's not wrong, simply a lesson we take from history: you don't survive by taking sides—the Rothschilds bankrolled both North and South during the American Civil War, and both Britain and America in the War of 1812—patterns in history aren't coincidental, because coincidence is the excuse of lazy minds, the patterns actually maps that lead us to the one truth everyone agrees on: that our societies are built to serve those who don't want me and you asking why, okay?—such as why didn't Loy Bonifacio fire his pistol?—and why's the blue of the U.N. flag the same as in Israel's?—and how'd the Liberty Party, our country's most powerful political machinery, come under the control of some sexy-sexy starlet?—and what does it mean that the Masonic pentagram and Star of David share the same pagan roots, the Jewish hexagram's two overlapping triangles totaling six sides, six points, six exterior angles—six, six, six—coincidences, or patterns, or the stitches of the cabal's grand designs?—flaunted, to taunt us, like both Lincoln and Kennedy elected to Congress then the presidency on the same years a century apart, both shot in the head for working to end wars, both assassinated by Southerners, both succeeded by Southerners, with JFK's secretary named Lincoln and Lincoln's secretary named Kennedy; how are such patterns not the architecture of the New World Order?—who enriched themselves selling opium to the Chinese, and used 9/11 to steal poppy fields from the Taliban, and pushed crack to the Blacks, Oxycontin to the rednecks, and shabu onto us brown Pinoys—ruling with such impunity they show off their symbol of the Masonic Hidden Hand, their right one posed inside their jackets, which you should google, really, to trace throughout history: from Salomon Rothschild to George Washington to Napoleon to M. H. del Pilar to Ataturk to Victor Hugo to Lenin to Paul McCartney to Julia Ringo to George Takei to José Rizal to Princess Diana to Tishani Doshi to Kanye West to even Senator Nuredin dela Cruz de Bansamoro, okay?—and Engels was a Mason, who funded Marx, another Mason . . . That blood-red hand of history exactly what Papa Nando's up against, toe to toe on our behalf versus oligarchs like the Lupases, the Alayas, all the world's John D. Rockefellers, that American capitalist who said "competition is a sin" and invested in infrastructure projects in the new Soviet Union while his Standard Oil helped power the Nazi war machine—that's the truth, and the thing about the truth is it's always hiding in plain sight, from the Mock Battle of Manila Bay to Sizzle Saturday to 9/11—don't start me on 9/11, come to think of it; that made-for-TV production supposedly masterminded by a dozen Arab goat fuckers—which isn't racist, because it's true—and not some genius like, I don't know, Bill Gates, formerly the world's richest man who claims to be a philanthropic Catholic but is obviously a Jew, just look at him, with his hardware and software everywhere, and that supposed coincidence that if you type capital *N, Y, C* in Microsoft's Wingdings font you get a skull and crossbones, Star of David, and thumbs-up, which has nothing to do with that perfect, patient, blue-skied, towering false flag attack, of the kind that gives more power to those in power who'll do everything in their power to stay in power, because what's two thousand nine hundred seventy-seven casualties if you believe you're saving millions?—and making millions, too, from each airport X-ray machine priced at forty-five thousand U.S. dollars, plus another hundred fifty thou for those boxes that pretend to check for trace explosives, plus another two hundred grand for those high-tech body scanners that we basically strip down for and put up our hands in surrender, because our safety's worth the shirts on our backs—a small price to pay when our rulers sell their souls on our behalf to the likes of Osama bin Laden, whose Al-Qaeda began in 1979 as a U.S.-backed mujahideen to fight the Soviets, just like MI6 first funding Mussolini, and the CIA backing Franco, and Chiang Kai-shek, and the Shah of Iran, and Selassie, and the Apartheid regime, and Batista, Papa Doc, Pinochet, Trujillo, Suharto, Mubarak, Mobutu, Noriega, Charles Taylor, the Saudis, Saddam, and every Israeli government, and even our own so-called dictator, who wisely made the most of America's support, just like Papa Nando has masterfully done with China and Russia, and just like Junior and Farrah will, too, after they obliterate Nuredin and Vita, so that we Pinoys won't be left out of the New World Order—literally the name given by George Bush Senior in his landmark speech to both houses of the U.S. Congress, eleven years to the day before his son's big moment on September 11, 2001; like I said, don't get me started—how can you possibly not see all those patterns, or admit that Papa Nando's Anti-Terror and National Security laws do in fact keep us safer from the drug personalities, Communist cadres, and other slaves of the globalists who've always benefited from chaos?—how can you not feel for that old fighter, all his progress for our people undermined by the COVID-19 Plandemic of George Soros, that anarchist and secret Nazi who made a mint through his monopoly on hand sanitizer and silly masks, while his fellow deep-state pedophiles in government, business, and media shut down the main thing that empowers us: the economy, which was becoming the best the world had ever seen under President Donald J. Trump—locking us down at home, cowing us, dividing us, because where we go one we go all, making it so not one of us could record the maneuvers of the slaves of the elite, suckering all the normies into rolling up their sleeves for each jab funded by Bill Gates's foundation, their micro, soft nanochip trackers embedded into your deltoid and linked to the 5G network streaming your location and data through Alexa and Siri, web searches and accepted cookies, our fingerprints and secrets and facial IDs out in the clouds while our minds are mapped on browser histories—a vaccine almost everyone was eager to line up for, which I didn't get, did you?; so either I'm coincidentally lucky or actually my faith in God and skeptical awareness keeps me safe, because how could I not have caught a supercontagious killer virus, or known someone who got sicker than just a bad flu, when I rejected the flamestream media's alarmism screeching for us to mask up, stay home, and shut our eyes, while hospitals enjoyed brisk business and received taxpayer funding for every reclassified death of an old person or younger patient with comorbidities, just another cabal profiting off the false flag attack giving sheeple something new to blame— just like blaming Papa Nando for every single murder that happened during his current presidency, as if under Reyes the homicide rate wasn't actually higher; that inconvenient truth ignored while we're distracted by the soap opera of Pinoy politics, with its relatable villains and flawed heroes we sympathize with, the spotlight now pointed right at Vits in the greatest reality show ever, parading in like Macho Man to *Pomp and Circumstance*, her stardom the ultimate weapon, like with the Kabbalah-worshipping West Coast elite recruited by the neo-Illuminati: Madonna; Gaga; Polanski; Weinstein; Oprah; Rihanna, with all her Baphomet imagery in her work—which is why everyone knows about the six million Jews allegedly dead in the Holocaust, but not really the seven million non-Jews killed by Stalin, or eight million non-Jews in the Congo by King Leopold II of Belgium, or fifty million non-Jews under Mao—five zero mil and not a single Hollywood movie, because who controls the studios and therefore our dreams and reality?—like Boy Balagtas, who saw nothing wrong with dreaming up photogenic relationships and compelling biographies—my name's not even One-Mig, okay?—forcing skin whitening and plastic surgery, and ruining the careers of anyone who refused, like me—who endured the falsehoods about my sexuality in our machismo society, okay?, and could never "fake it till you make it," like Boy advised us; but Vits, she could, very readily, innocence written all over her face, like Winnie Cooper meets Rio on that Duran Duran album cover; sweet giggle and tomboyish manners, stinky friendship bracelets around her wrist; not her hungry smile and Manolo Blahniks of today, the world around her finger—"No, no," she says, posing, "I hate having my picture taken," posing, "Please, don't," posing; with her constant humble-bragging virtue signaling, which she spins as hope and inspiration—far cry from the girl who blushed after we kissed and powdery brown patches of Clearasil transferred from her forehead to mine, and she freaked out and wiped my face, blushing till we laughed till we cried . . . She was so real, I hardly recognize her now—don't you be fooled, too, by that star in the sky you wish your greatest hopes upon before realizing it's just an airplane—Vits will betray you, like she did with me, after what happened with Glendys, her best friend, okay?, best friend—and the reason I stayed with Vits so long, the three of us inseparable, knowing how much their sisterhood meant to Glendys—they called themselves the Little Twin Stars; Vita as Lala, because she writes poems, and Glendys as Kiki, even though I should've been Kiki because Kiki is a boy—the two of them so close I'd get pushed aside for their friendship, or stuck in the middle of their rivalry, which I never understood, actually, as strong as everything else they shared, like planning Glendys's debut—two years late, after her Poveda classmates', because of my parents' fears and our Chinoy community's privacy, but she was graduating and our parents couldn't say no—which thrilled Vits, who acted like it was hers because it was so important to my sister; the two of them designing the dresses, bickering over choosing the dancers, the cotillion choreography, and especially which one I'd be dancing with, my sister or my girlfriend—then, that afternoon, taking five from rehearsal, when Vits went downstairs to Foodarama to fetch everyone ice cream, and Glendys answered the phone in our condo, and pretended to be Vits, put on one of her outfits, and left all of us

dancers, taking my car to go to the casting—then disappeared: over-
night, then two days; witnesses saying three men entered the car at
the stoplight, just there, on Shaw Boulevard, in front of Foodarama;
that week, all the waiting: driving at night everywhere, nowhere, trying not to roll down my windows and just shout her name, because
that would mean I wasn't being strong—for my parents, for Vits, who
made a drama of blaming herself, so that the rest of us wouldn't, because my sister wasn't the public one, okay?—Vits crying beside me,
when I'd read out and reply to all the text messages, instructed by the
police negotiator, looking at my parents; when the phone rang my
mommy and daddy held each other while the negotiator spoke into it
like jewing down a knockoff at Virra Mall and could take his business
to the next stall . . . we trusted the authorities, but when we couldn't
complete the ransom money in time—because we only own a funeral
parlor and tilapia farm, only able to pay half, all that we borrowed and
sold—they said they'd see if the kidnappers would accept, and we
begged for two days more; but still my car was found in the morning,
by a cemetery, my subwoofer box moved to the back seat, and Glendys
inside the trunk half wearing Vita's clothes; my mommy unable to
look; my daddy stepping forward; Vits just staring at my sister; the
slo-mo broken by people in uniforms pulling us away as if we were
doing something wrong, as if the evidence mattered to anyone now
that she was gone—imagine, okay?, preparing your daughter for her
wake, because the child you brought into this world . . . because you
want to prepare her for the next one: my mommy washing her body
pure again, my daddy stitching the hole in her head and draining her
fluids to embalm her, doing all they could for their child, refusing to let
anyone but family touch her—and my part, too, dressing her there on
the table, putting her makeup in the light, my twin, my reflection,
never being able to look at myself again the same; leaving her like she
was taking a nap, like everything was normal—like the weeks after,
when Vits acted like nothing had happened, okay?, never crying,
okay?, Miss Emotional not once shedding a tear, even getting angry
when I wouldn't stop investigating if the police delivered our money to
the syndicate, Vits telling me it was just money, as if it was just about
money . . . because the police, okay? . . . Lontok was commissioner at

the time, before being implicated and, yeah, *exonerated*, okay?, in that rubout of that kidnap-for-ransom gang—Vits growing distant when I needed her most, like everything else was wrong except what was wrong, buying me tickets for my birthday for the concert of Metallica, a band I didn't even know, not really, and that Cat guy came over and talked to her, and she moved on—look at her now, moving up, master—mistress—of her own fate; reliable sources saying she orchestrated the assassination attempt, conveniently using that Loy Bonifacio, who only needs to speak at his trial to save himself from dying by revealing the truth: that our so-called Sizzle Saturday was a false flag operation, okay?—someone's made-for-TV cause with a predictable effect, like Marinus van der Lubbe setting fire to the Reichstag, or the shooting of the defense minister's car, or FDR not warning Pearl Harbor about the Japanese attacks—the classic Hegelian dialectic: cultivate a problem you blame on someone else, manage the response, offer a solution that until recently nobody would ever consider; from a girl who rose so deliberately, on pure instinct—first, creating opportunity through a crisis: Loy; then toppling the one in charge: Papa Nando; then removing obstacles: Rajah; then using those who believe in you: Bansamoro, and millions of her followers—presenting herself as the only viable option, claiming destiny, which she doesn't desire but won't reject, because it's her duty for the Motherland, because her victimhood makes us all feel very real emotions, and her defiance gives us a cause that we mistake for our own, fooling us that we're in control, because God gives us the free will that only Satan would work to take away—but when the Antichrist comes, she obviously won't breathe fire or brimstone; she'll have us dancing and believing, because Lucifer was God's most beautiful angel, always already among us, spilling magic into your ears, convincing you her story's yours and tasking you to make her immortal, because on that Saturday, at the very start, in Loy Bonifacio's eyes she glimpsed for herself that truth she'd rather we didn't see, hiding in plain sight—

(Inaudible)

. . . what that is, that's up to you, okay?; your only true choice in life: what you believe—period, full stop.

Vita Nova Transcript: 12 of 13.

(40:12.76—VN12.M4A)

I can explain. I had no choice. Please don't be disappointed—come on, this is our second-to-last interview. How was I supposed to defend Nur?—how could anyone? Homie should've known better. Could've at least told me beforehand—I was most surprised of all. You could see that, last night, at the tag-team debates, me by his side with my jaw on the floor while Rolex read out the juiciest morsels from the cell phone transcripts—meanwhile, Mona Angbabat's spilling the recordings all over social media; nothing's scarier than a well-oiled propaganda machine. Poor Nur—it's terrifying having a loved one addicted to drugs; nobody wants them mummified in packing tape, a sign stabbed into them. But don't use your influence to divert his arrest into a fancy rehab paid for with campaign funds. Due process doesn't really exist anymore in this country, but I would've quit all this to help Nur fight for it. Instead, I was sitting with him alone in the campaign bus, holding his hands, looking into his eyes to promise I'll continue his legacy—but elections are two days away and he's gotta do what's right. He owed it to our team, biting their nails outside for our decision. And to the supporters who put their faith in us. And even to me, coz I can't sacrifice my values just to win. He said it's fake news, but still. You're only as useful as your reputation—isn't that what he said, that time he dumped me by text?

(Whack. Whack. Whack.)

This morning was like jolting from a dream you slowly realize is real.

(Inaudible)

I don't know yet who I'll ask to run as my veep. People will be unhappy, either way.

(Inaudible)

You're right—Boy would be hella great, but then we'd be a showbiz ticket. How about Kingsley?—as a compromise across the divide. (I know, right?) But all the clashes between supporters are breaking my heart—everyone wanting the same good things for our country, just disagreeing which path will get us there. How'd we become such a bloodthirsty people? If someone wrongs you, kill them; if they challenge you, threaten to kill them. That cat crucified on the front desk of my campaign HQ last night—I can't even—and that deepfake porno vid of my face on Eliza Ibarra's body—new technology, age-old tactics (and as disrespectful to her as to me). So many varieties of violence. Last year, Fernando brought back the death penalty—Loy probably the first to die under it, if I don't win. And Rolex got the triplets released—but now their parents are super in danger without them. And the Communists agreed to a ceasefire—but only so NGOs can try to stop the spread of that flesh-eating disease. How can peace and violence both be matters of survival?

(Plastic crinkling)

Tomorrow's the final rallies of all five Presidentiables, and I've got this terrible premonition. One of the mayors who hosted our last town hall was red-tagged and shot the next . . . Hey, stop—I promise I'll wear the bulletproof vest you got me. I'll be fine—I've got to be: there's so much more to tell you, like who killed Rita; I'm almost sure, though I'm no Nando, making fatal accusa . . . Hey, come on—I got you protecting me, right? You'll stand with me tomorrow, as I defend my promises in Plaza Miranda. I super loved last night—as in, quelle surprise. We didn't even let go once, and I slept so well, finally. But please, like you promised, make sure our recordings are secure. I know we still got our final interview together—post–victory celebration . . .

(Lighter click. Exhalation)

—and you're a perfectionist, who'll complete my story perfectly; but just in case, maybe even send them to your publisher? So that come what may, the world can puzzle the pieces together and find the truth for themselves. Coz I still believe most people are good, and good always outweighs evil—which is why evil people convince themselves that the evil they're doing is good. That's what Adolf Hitler did, and the Dictator's family has always done. What Fernando did, and maybe even Loy—who I visited the other day, actually, to let him ignore me. But I had to try—to see if all they're saying is true. I didn't want our last memory to be that morning at the Mustard Seed Foundation—his arm coming out of the crowd, the gun pointing like an accusation. Steel bars, questions, and years separated us, but he was still Loy—with his helmet of thick black hair, which I used to thin in Tita Henny's salon after-hours, and that scar on his cheek, from when he left me to go abroad. A word from him would've felt as solid as the doorknob on my mother's front door. He didn't even look at me. I told him you're going to see him tomorrow, and that I trust you. That if he doesn't tell anyone his own story, the world will tell it for him.

(Silence)

I had to try—he was my first love. That's always the bridge to your childhood, as you get older and wonder where memories end and imagination takes over. Like the bed's sigh and the floor's creak, Mama getting up beside me, dry lips on my forehead three breaths later. Or humming my way down the street to the pump, before the other kids could form a noisy line. And walking to school, the neighborhood swirling, the day warming around me. Or running home through the rain, skipping over snails, my book bag over my head. And my first taste of independence: old enough, finally, to take care of myself, improving my favorite snack—ham and cheese on pan de sal with banana ketchup, and a glass of chocolate milk, growled together in Mama's salvaged Osterizer. (Best, idea, ever. Worst. Milkshake. Ever.) All those memories as if imagined, till I saw Loy sitting in his cell, everything falling back into place, like a piano on my head. I stood there about an hour, sixteen going on thirtysomething—thinking about what Rita once told me: that as soon as you have the answers, the questions change. Loy refusing to look at me, with that brutally honest dignity of people used to bearing indignities. I talked and talked but didn't dare ask why he stitched our lives together again with that invisible thread between pistol and president. I hoped he'd call out to me to stay, but kept walking when he didn't. He was always hella defiant—that's what I fell for, when I was eleven, and all the twelve-year-old boys lined up outside the healer's house, the neighborhood gathering for the fun—the old men mercilessly joking, the boys jostling and boasting till they bubbled over at the thought of what was to come, some making faces, others crossing their legs and whooping. That's when I saw him, surrounded but alone—the way he stood, how he smiled: fearless and ready to grow up. Least that's what I thought, with my precocious wisdom, or maybe envy. Then old Yoseph, the taxi driver— whose cab we stole years later—added his tease above the taunts: "Don't sneeze when the knife comes down!" Loy shouting back: "Your wife already told us what happened!"—

(Laughter)

. . . all the boys laughing, too, suddenly relaxed. All thanks to Basilio Bonifacio—Basi in school, Basiloy to his family, Siso to his mother, and Loy to the world. To his gang he was Boss L, and I was the tagalong runt, the tomboy eager to prove herself and resented for it—except by him, coz I reminded him of his little sister. On my way to school I'd pass his house and hear his uncle shouting from inside as Loy stormed out pulling on a shirt or stuffing his school bag. His father was gone and his mother worked abroad, so Loy was sent to the province to learn to be a mechanic. After dismissal we'd stick around, avoiding the work waiting for us at home—squatting in the shade of the tamarind to grind glass from the trash to mix with rice glue, for the strings of our kites, which we'd fight in the sky above the dry fields. Loy's kites were faster, mine were prettier—at least at first—and he'd whistle the Marlboro Man tune, my lips sputtering only air. Other days, he taught me how to find promising spiders in the branches—orb weavers with slim figures and long legs, which came out at dusk or after dawn, whenever shadows were shifting. "But the beautiful ones," said he, "the colorful, with bright and shiny bodies—those are poison." Loy teaching with the patience of a good student, showing me how to train them, and make stables for my fighters—an old matchbox and a palm leaf folded to keep them apart. Soon my spiders were beating his and every afternoon we couldn't wait to meet up, though he left me behind when he went to derbies; between boy and girl, our friendship ended there—till I . . . well, developed. Till he started looking at me the way I'd looked at him so long. Till the love songs we'd hear at Joe's corner store began to make sense. Till one Friday, on the way to school, he

held my hand—leaving me kilig all Saturday, and guilty through mass
on Sunday. But Monday he was gone, without saying goodbye, to the
city to live with his mother back from abroad—I found out later, from
his uncle's girlfriend, who was sympathetic because she'd seen us blossoming. Two years passed and I stayed angry with him, coz at that age
love's still selfish and nothing's as overwhelming as your own feelings.
Never daring to crush on another boy and even starting to wonder if
I even liked them. Then, a week before my fifteenth birthday, outside
our front window, I heard whistling—the Marlboro Man—and there
was Loy: fully grown, straggly mustache, muscles as big as his smile,
a bleached-blond rat's tail down his back. Me running out into his
arms, and from then on he was my Loy-Loy—but only when I was in a
good mood, which was whenever I saw him. He'd come around, and
we'd watch telenovelas while I helped Mama prepare dinner; always
so proudly formal with her, ducking his head and saying yes ma'am,
and she liked him enough to make him the replica Levi's 501s he'd
always wear—though of course she felt I was too young. When she
had an evening shift, me and Loy would prove ourselves: sitting outside, or leafing through magazines in Tita Henny's salon, or strolling
up and down the street, the whole community our chaperone. Not like
we minded—we loved being seen together. And when his uncle made
him work late, or Mama felt he was visiting too much, we'd whisper
the distance away on the phone—till the party line barged in and
complained, usually just as Loy was saying sweet somethings as rich
as chocolate. In the morning, Mama claimed she could count the hours
we were on by how many turns it took to untwist the phone cord. And
remember brownouts?

(Inaudible)

We loved those, of course—their silence and shadows: the PhilFirst
PowerCorp's nightly gift to young lovers. Me rushing my homework by
candlelight, Loy biking from his uncle's repair shop, us sitting together
on this covered bench outside my house, my body so alive it was
like tuned to the breeze. Mama checking the repellent coils for us—
"Mosquitoes love sweet blood!"—or putting out snacks—"You must be
hungry!"—or bringing out the fluorescent storm lantern—"You'll ruin
your eyes!"—bugs tapping at its last working bulb that would flicker

on its final legs, me longing for it to die. Not that it would've made a diff; Mama always listened—her tinny radio soaps hushing to half volume every few minutes. So me and Loy just talked, or played pusoy dos—the cards crisp and clear, like fairy fingers drumming the table for every five-card finish. Till Mama ran out of excuses and sent us to the corner store, the coins moistening in my hand as we followed Joe's guitar through the darkness. All those love songs: "More Than Words." "Love of a Lifetime." "Patience"—which Loy whistled to, just like Axl Rose. ♫ *Was a time when I wasn't sure but you set my mind at ease, there is no doubt you're in my heart now . . .* ♫ The kerosene light an oasis, and the slouching beer drinkers teasing us, as we arrived to buy my mother's sachet of Creamsilk conditioner, or an assortment of Storck and Choc Nut and White Rabbit candies, or a couple liters of RC Cola. Strolling home, smiling in silence, Loy holding one loop of the plastic bag, me holding the other, the two sweating bottles clinking as they swung between us—our rubber slippers clapping for our love.

(Silence)

When I was older and Boy brought me to my first ballet, or Cat to an awesome concert, I'd close my eyes and pretend the applause was for me—but the sound of my hands would remind me of walking home with Loy, to eat candies and drink soft drinks under the flickering bulb, making up stories about our future—till Mama's voice appeared from nowhere: "Vita, doesn't Loy have a family?" Then one night, just like that, the bulb kicked it, Loy's shadow growing bigger, and I shut my eyes, and for the first time I was kissed. The most important kiss ever, don't you think? The first time, other than your own mother, that you see someone so closely—their pores, wet eyes, breath like warm milk—the first time since you were a kid that you're looking and being looked at with such adoration. Maybe that's the exact distance, right?, between childhood and adulthood: between gazing at your parent and gazing at your first love. Coz learning to love someone like you loved family is the first task of growing up. And just as I gave Loy my second kiss ever, the world erupted in light, TVs and radios blaring, the whole street cheering as fluorescents ticked and hummed around us like paparazzi in slow motion—me and Loy jolting back to stare at opposite corners of the Milky Way, forced awake but forever changed.

The next few months my super happiest ever. Mama knowing something was up—the way I'd sing, or return from school smiling; the way I'd move my textbook over my doodles when she walked by, covering the big bubble letters spelling: "Vita Bonifacio." That's another important milestone: the first time you hide joy—suddenly more thrilling than anything, when you're ashamed of something you feel isn't the least bit shameful. A turning point, realizing your parent can be so wrong. Poor Mama watching like I was a tightrope walker—worried I'd tumble like she did, seventeen years earlier. She doubled her affection and I resented the attention. Thanks Goddess for those rolling brownouts. Privacy's such a luxury in poor neighborhoods and an impossibility when you're young—so our holding hands became as intimate as joining lips, me and Loy outside, just sitting, elbows touching, waiting for the instant darkness as if we could hear it approaching; prepared to claim what was rightfully ours—which we undeniably did, that day, that week before my high school graduation, when Loy climbed desperately through my window from the canal, soaked, out of breath, face tight with fear. "No time to explain," says he. "Will you come?" That's the thing with love, right? Amour fou?—one plus one equals two zillion—and is probably the only reason the world ever forgives our foolishness. "There is always one moment in childhood," Dr. Chopra writes, "when the door opens and lets the future in." And that was my moment, when I clicked my mother's doorknob in place— never thinking for a second it was more than just an adventure, never understanding that what I thought was my dream was just awaking to reality, no more certainties, only consequences, our stolen taxi speeding towards that intersection opening and closing, the two guys with guns on the motorcycle almost beside Loy's window, the police coming fast behind, the headlights ahead like a gate and Loy should have both hands on the wheel but one hand's squeezing mine as the red traffic light gets brighter and bigger and two trucks close in like asteroids coming together and I close my eyes and it's all noise until—

(Pause)

. . . we're through, just us, just Loy shouting I love you, I love you, I love you, as we turn a corner, into the darkness, and lose the past, and all else that was chasing us. The sun rising as the city stood to meet us—

the embrace of buildings, the shouts of graffiti, the hot smog of chaos, the overpasses that seemed too heavy to be safe. Me and Loy ditching the car somewhere in the labyrinth and taking a bus that inched to the bay, so that he could be the one to give me what I'd always wanted and show me the sea for the first time. He said it sounded like the world whispering its secrets. Or promises. I don't remember. Maybe its secrets promised?

(Silence)

You know the rest—every profile on me has mentioned it: the pension-house owners who denied us coz we weren't married; my boyfriend's tireless search for a job; the real ring he somehow bought to fool everyone; and the agony at the airport as he left for the Middle East, vowing to send money for my teaching courses. Then me, alone, the poor fatherless country lass finally done good after being discovered by the soon-to-be-great Boy Balagtas. All the interviewers love to talk about that fairy-tale ending, but don't fairy tales usually start with tragic loss and terrible conflict?—tales of hardship endured by millions, that millions more can never imagine. That ring that scarred us—I loved that beautiful ugly yellow-gold thing, its little diamond like the glass shards we used to grind for our kites. Wearing it reversed in public, to hide it from thieves. Staring at it for hours in private, through the magnifying glass of my mother's old Swiss Army knife, the stone's flaky imperfections proof that it was real. Glitter always promises something, but I kept telling myself it was all for show—even though Loy kept pretending it meant we could finally make love. Not like I didn't want to—I won't lie. But you know how it is here—teenhood's a stormy sea you navigate like a smuggler, while a girl's ultimate role model's supposed to be the most powerful woman ever: the Virgin Mary. Such big sandals to fill—and why I always felt bad doing ads for brands that say youth is all about expressing yourself—coz in reality it's not: it's about being who society says you should be. Like Mama never letting me wear red nail polish—the color of prostis, she said—which is why, tada: Scarlet Hester, our bestseller from Vita Bella, my new low-cost cosmetics line—coz accessible never has to mean cheap, and only you should define what colors mean to you. I always hated that double standard, rich chicks exploring their sexuality as bohemians, while a poor girl's is treated like currency. Loy, of course, not thinking about any of that, as he tried every night, offering promises in exchange, even though I kept telling him we needed to prove my mother wrong. Which proved me right the day he came home, singing the first time in weeks, and I jumped into his arms then wriggled out when he told me—his OFW papers being processed, and how we had to save to pay the recruiter the rest. "I'll do whatever it takes," said he. As if he meant it. Why not do whatever it takes to stay here with me? Then that sweet man—that teenage boy—surprised me like nobody ever has, getting down on a knee (both knees, actually), clasping my hand to turn that cheap ring right-side round, turning that cheap ring priceless by asking: "Will you marry me?" It was everything I dreamt of and everything I feared.

(Inaudible)

Because nobody wants to be another Saudi widow, suffering in silence—helping with his visa, medical exam, community clearance, police check, Ministry of Investigation report, placement permit, facilitation tax, recruiter fees—all just to be left behind. But I said yes— yes, I would. Then I cut his hair for his passport picture, and stood with him in every line, and held his hand and put my head on his shoulder as he daydreamed our plans: send money, return in a year, marry me properly in our hometown church—proving to the world that love's worth believing in. I certainly did. And on his eighteenth birthday, a month before he left, on our bed so narrow I'd often wake as if falling, I gave my fiancé my virginity—crying the whole way through, wanting it to bleed as much as it hurt, needing to feel like I was new. But nothing and everything changed—all my fears replaced by an emptiness that I realized a couple of weeks later was just another kind of fear. Coz if you're gonna sin once by having sex, you're not gonna sin twice by using contraception—coz if God is love, then She'd understand our weakness, as well as our faith that She'd keep us safe. But the fear just sits there, as you count the days. Meanwhile, Loy would go out in the evenings and come back near dawn, with money I never asked about. I just wanted to spend the days together: popsicles in the park, arcade games in the mall, watching ice-skaters hold each other to keep from falling, seeing that fortune-teller again who told us we'd find each other in the end. But right there in the food court, right after buying me a Dilly Bar, that's when Loy asks for my ring back—to pawn, to pay the recruiter, for the remainder before the deadline. And what a scene I make—coz he deserves it. Like how I deserve to have him fight back—so that I can believe he'll fight for me when I need him most. Loy staying silent, the way he does, and I slap him—a long line of red spreading down his face from the stone turned inwards. He touches his cheek, looks at his bloody fingertips, and puts them in his mouth. And there was nothing more I could do. Call it love, call it guilt, but blood stops battles. Like it did that day I met One-Mig, when he won and I ran off, into a store where the shopgirls helped me with sympathy, a sanitary pad, and the floor sample of skorts they didn't make me pay for. To you boys, blood means something different—an ending—but to us, it means life, and its demands. I never told Loy I missed my period—that two days had become two weeks. I didn't want that to be the reason he stayed. My fear strengthening me, when I saw him off at the airport. He looked so hopeful—how could I not pray he'd find everything he dreamed of? "No goodbyes," said he. "Only see you later." I believed him.

(Inaudible)

No, not till a lifetime later—not till like three months ago, at Starbucks of all places, while I'm on my way to the Palace. Loy just walking up, like a ghost, all like, "Hi"—just hi. I gotta be honest, I almost didn't recognize him, even though he looks exactly the same, and I didn't want to talk to him—because shame (I don't know why). But of course we try. Sitting then talking—Loy uncomfortable in his easy chair, arms folded like a thug, ankles crossed like a doll, hair combed like fat Elvis, staring like I'm risen from the dead. But his smile's kinda fragile, like tears waiting for the wrong word. Small talk prevents that—I'm like: You look good. I'm like: How was Jeddah? I'm like: Has our country changed much since you left? Which was, like, a wrong mistake. Loy losing all awkwardness and going off about recruiters, broken promises, the president—scowling like remembering a bite of something bitter. "Why'd you disappear?" says he—like his anger gave him permission. Looking in a way that keeps me silent. Meanwhile, this American mother is at the table beside us, using her outside voice to interview a potential domestic helper. At the table on our other side, her uniformed driver sits with four young women clutching crisp biodatas, everyone watching her two blond boys vroom toy cars across the back of Loy's chair. I tell Loy: The day you left, I went to the cathedral and sat at the last row. I remember this old lady sliding past on her knees, and thinking maybe that's what I should do to be with you. I was still waiting for God's reply when the old lady slid past the other way, covered in sweat. The American mother's voice is shrill and karen-clear, and I lean over but Loy pulls away and frowns at the green-tea Frappuccino I got him. I tell Loy: It was so hard without you. I felt God was too busy for me, and I went out to the plaza where I wasn't alone anymore, and looked through the stalls, at their baby Jesuses and glow-in-the-dark rosaries and candles in all colors for different prayers, searching for something that might bring you back to me. There was a boy selling potions and the third time I walked by he pushed one into my hand, its liquid so bright and cruel it was like fire. People stand around Loy and me—the American mother, her driver, the applicant, and the next one—trading tables so that the driver can explain everything again in Tagalog while the mother tells the next woman the exact same thing. "Thanks so much for applying," says she, the biodata flopping in her hand like a gag prop on *Oh-Em-Gee!* "I see you have, you know, midwife and nanny experience, so how could you, you know, wasn't it hard to, you know, leave those kids?" I tell Loy: I handed the bottle back and this woman appeared, still chewing her lunch, pressing the potion again into my palms. "Guaranteed," said she, gently caressing my arm. "All natural—acacia bark, different plants. I've used it myself, daughter." Then this little girl ran out of the crowd and stopped, eyes all wide, all like: "Are you a movie star?" People stand around Loy and me again, sitting again, another biodata flopping again, questions again that sound like accusations. "So you worked in Jordan—was that for, you know, an Arab family?" Loy's eye sliding over to the mother. "I hope you don't, you know, have anything against Americans. It's just that, you know, sometimes, you know, Arab employers, like, say things. I mean, my husband and I are American, but we're good people. My best friend is Filipino, you know, so I understand your culture more than Arabs would've. Sometimes . . . do you know what prejudices are?

Yeah, they're . . . it's when someone judges someone without—Oh, you already know?" I tell Loy: Remember Mrs. Medroso's pension house, and the CR door without a lock? I sat against it and drank the stuff in the dark and it even tasted like regret, and in the room the pillow still smelled like you and I cried myself to sleep for I don't know how long. I woke up and my guts were crumpling, like paper, like a million paper-cuts, waves and waves, and I changed my mind, I swear I changed my mind, and ran to the CR to throw up, but of course it was too late— blood running down my legs and everything spinned . . . Hey, please don't—that's exactly how Loy looked at me; like you right now. But I want this in my book—because it happens. Because it's true.

(Inaudible)

Yeah—yes, it made the second time so much harder. So much harder.

(Silence)

Anyways. Around Loy and me everyone stands again, sits again, the driver repeating rules, salary, schedule, days off again. But the story I'm whispering to Loy cuts through—I see it in his eyes. "What's your policy on raising children?" the mother says. "What's your philoso-phy?" the mother says. The nanny says, "Kindness?" and the mother goes off about discipline and respect, about her friend's kids bossing their nanny around. "But you won't just be a yaya," the mother says, "you'll be part of the family." I tell Loy: Mrs. Medroso found me and I woke up when the door bumped my head, and I saw between her cankles, in the doorways down the hall, faces peeking, some smirking. Mrs. Medroso was always kind—remember you were sure she knew we weren't really married? The ride with her in the taxi was a blur, but I remember the first two emergency rooms, these bright lights at the end of the road, and Mrs. Medroso throwing curses over her shoulder at the doctors and getting back in the cab. Next thing, I woke up in a hos-pital, babies crying, someone beside me, everything bright, pregnant women in gowns shuffling between the beds, this woman elbowing my ribs and pushing me over the edge—"I'm not Loy," said she. "You kept me up all night."—and I had to stand to keep from falling. My suitcase was there, with sleeves hanging like tentacles, and that's how I knew I was no longer welcome at the pension. Loy stands and everyone looks at him—the mother, the driver, the nannies—like he's an intruder. I chase outside after him with his untouched Frappuccino. His lighter sparks and sparks at the end of his trembling cigarette. He just looks at his drink in my hand—the wet on the cup like the sweat on his face. It's rainy season and humid, another record-breaking day, and I notice his jean jacket—brand-new, with sharp creases from its packaging. His boots shiny and my old rosary hanging around his neck. I tell him I'll give him a ride and I wave at Nando's driver, who's waiting outside the car like a foo dog. Loy shakes his head. Please, I say, Let me take you where you're going. The Expedition pulling up, the bodyguard jumping out to open my door. Loy spits on the ground and walks away. I didn't know what to do.

(Silence)

There was still so much I needed him to know: How all I've ever wanted is to make a world where these stories aren't so predictable. How I saved our money, spending nights at the bus station, too scared to close my eyes. How I slept during the day in Tower Records, in a leather armchair at a listening station in the classical music section. How I carried off leftovers in the food court, coz nobody suspects when you act like you belong. How this recruiter named Stella promised a job in Riyadh, and I took our savings and my new passport to her house and filled her living room with five other girls, waiting for the last woman to arrive, who gave her money to Stella like a sacred offering, and police rushed in, and Stella was caught in the kitchen, and the woman made us sit on the floor—and I answered questions, was told I was lucky, had my money taken for evidence, and never saw it again. How I wandered in the mall and was discovered and worked for Mona, quitting four months later with even less money. How there were still no letters from him, and how Mariclaire, my roommate in my new pension house, told me how she paid rent. How I went alone to her massage parlor and a DOM who waddled like a congressman showed me this room, behind one-way glass—a dozen girls sitting in short dresses and numbers pinned above their hearts, and Mariclaire was there, in her makeup like someone else, staring at her feet like they were useless. How the DOM gave me a tiny advance and told me I'd be very popular and acted as if I should be grateful. How I just wanted to save up for another recruiter. How Mrs. Medroso stood at her gate and told me, with impatient sympathy, that there were still no letters, and I should never wait for a man. How I went to church, that afternoon before starting at the massage parlor, to pray for forgiveness, then went to the mall, to feel close to him, and was losing myself in *Dance Dance Revolution* when this boy steps in and we dance and I bleed and I know I can't do my first shift that night, or the next evening—that evening my prayers got answered, in that same arcade, by God and Boy Balagtas. But Loy kept on walking—the partner I learned about love with— about all it could and couldn't do. And I let him go. Even if I didn't want to. Why does giving up always feel like betrayal? The Loy I once knew, gone forever—even on that very next day, that fateful sizzling afternoon, when his gun cuts through the crowd like a shark's fin and lowers to the stage, and I remember the fortune-teller's words about fire soon as I see Loy staring at me. Another man trying to save me. But why didn't he pull the trigger?

(Silence)

Look who needs saving now. Sorry—I don't mean to be judgy. He . . . they—all of them shared my life and I've tried these past weeks to put myself in their shoes—to understand. To learn from my mistakes. To accept that I don't need to be ashamed or even call them mistakes for them to have served a priceless purpose. I get to choose what to keep. Fernando feeling my face with his fingers. Dancing with Kingsley to old Gardel milongas. That perfect weekend on the mountain with Deepak. Venturing north with Nur. Forgiving but not forgetting what Father Yoda did. Peaking with Red. Letting go of Rolex. Winning with LeTrel. Furio listening when I'd read my poems. Playing "Redemption Song" on Cat's guitar on the beach while he sings. Holding One-Mig's hand in this confusing world. Sharing darkness with Loy. And all the times I was happy alone but didn't know it, surrounded by friends and fans who loved me for everything I am, centered by history and who I can be in it. I admit, I'm scared to go out there tomorrow. To stand before the country in Plaza Miranda. To see another gun in the crowd. Terrifying, but worth it. People are worth the risk. Filipinos are worth dying for—but even more so, living for. Day by day, till everything's better for everyone. Hey. Stop. Come here. Don't worry, baby. I'll be okay. Coz that's not how this story ends. Nobody but me gets to decide.

I'll tell all, during our final interview, about who murdered Rita, and what I saw that moment in Loy's eyes, and the fortune-teller's prediction, and the gazillion things I'm going to do with the rest of my life. It took me forever to realize that I don't have to ask for permission; that I don't have to give it even when I'm asked. That one is not born a woman, one becomes one—as one woman declared to the world; as I've proven to every person who believed in me. I won't be some two-bit part in the background of someone's novel, even if I'll always be a hella flawed protagonist, the product of blind imaginings—even our own, made from fantasies and fears, from misconceptions and misunderstandings. But I know who I am, I'll have you know: I'm all that, and more than you can ever know—a Filipina first, a Filipino second, a leader of one, a follower of many. All yours, baby, at your service; but always all mine, darling—more than everyone thinks, more than anyone can fathom: more than a feed on a screen, or a face on a meme, more than a character in a tell-all, and much more than the president's mistress. I can see you eye to eye. I can look myself in the mirror. I can do all that I'm here for. And I can say, for what it's worth (coz to me it's worth everything)—I am Vita Nova.

(Silence)

Namaste.

(Laughter)

Basilio "Loy" Bonifacio Transcript.

(32:08.14—Bonifacio.M4A)

You got smokes? Alhamdulillah. When these are finished we are also. You should have brought a full pack. I have all the time until they take it from me. Khalas.

(Match flares. Exhalation)

If I tell my story will you make me a legend? The Domestic Helper. I sacrificed everything. Still I sacrifice. I will make the ultimate sacrifice. Don't you know I am a hero? They are always telling that to us. Heroes because we do what they will not. Another name for that is slaves. Willing slaves are not heroes. My uncle taught me how to fix anything but there are things nobody can fix. I still have not learned strength. Maybe before they give me the injection. I am ready. God will welcome me. This jail is nothing. At least you can see the bars. They will not let her win the election tomorrow. I cannot save her anymore. At least we will be together in heaven soon. That is the best thing about forever. If I turned the wheel of the taxi the other way we would not have lost each other. But what can anyone do? That is life. It takes many paths. I left her and my home. I am wandering the world to find my place. I would return to fix what was broken. I had to see with my own eyes which path she took. Did she tell you? In Starbuck. When I saw her even she did not know who she was anymore. We sat and lied to ourselves together. God keeps count. I sinned too many times. I have to win His forgiveness. I would not fail her again. The president betrayed us. He tells us to kill those who deserve it. You see all those thousands he killed. I have always listened. He says lift a gun to save the world from perdition. So I did what I did. I tried. But I could not. I lacked the strength. Someone else will have to pull the trigger. Inshallah.

(Match flares. Exhalation)

Maybe in Starbuck I expected it to be like after we were apart the first time. After my mother went back to Italy to earn livelihood and I went back again to stay with my uncle. When I went to her house and whistled outside her window. When she came out still wearing her school uniform. Holding a pen and notebook. How big her smile was. All grown up but still the annoying girl I knew. The world was ours to take. My uncle promised my mother he would guide me. My father I never saw because he is in America. Probably he has another family there. My mother could not divorce him and start again here. I did not understand what leaving does to you until much later. In Angeles my uncle taught me how to be a mechanic but also how to be a man. His girlfriend worked in a nightclub near the base and he protected her. She went to mass every day and wore short shorts around the house and sometimes asked my help with the chores. That's all I knew about Blessica. It was better that way. She drove me crazy. I listened to them making love. When I was old enough my uncle brought me on his morning rounds. All over the community. It was like he owned it but more like it was his duty. He served as mediator in neighborhood troubles. A valued collector in the numbers games. Very good with the chickababes. Even his enemies enjoyed his company. He ran a cockpit before and knew how to deal with people at their worst. He was more than fair. Kindness or humor or anger he returned double. When they promoted him he convinced them to give me his cell. That was big. I worked under him as a collection agent. We are respected for our ethics. You also can keep fifteen percent of the bets you collect. He was my supervisor. Fourteen supervisors in the sales network report to the table manager. My uncle was in charge of the draw. I always wanted to watch but collectors aren't allowed. Sometimes it is in a safe house. Sometimes in a bus that picks up supervisors as if they're ordinary passengers. I got to know a lot of people. The community was my life. But still my days would revolve around her.

(Match flares. Exhalation)

Even on my collections I would get off my bike and knock at her door. The space of a few words was all we needed. Not really. Sometimes her father shouted from inside. Asking who it is. She and I held hands and

I called back. Asking if he wants to get lucky. He would never answer. It bought us a few more breaths. She was always the one closing the door. But only halfway. I was always the one waiting like a puppy. But only a short time. She'd open it again and we smiled and laughed. "I'm closing it now." She was sad but firm. Closing the door like it weighed a million pounds. Sometimes when I knocked her mother answered. I tried to get her mother to bet so I could visit more regularly. She never did but was always kind. Especially after I inherited my uncle's cell. She offered snacks and enjoyed my guitar and gossip. I knew some tunes and all that happened in our community. Everyone loves songs about misfortune and stories about luck. I'd tell her who was sick. Who got fired. Who became pregnant. Which neighbors won big. What some losers will do to afford one more wager. And the strategies. Some played only on certain days. Christmas. Easter. All Saints'. Others on the birthdays of their children. Some kept the same numbers. Others changed every week. I also helped interpret dreams. A dog means fourteen. A pregnant woman means six. Twelve is a snake. One guy would choose according to the chapter and verse from Sunday's gospel. Maybe it worked. He won a few times. When I had to run away she felt we abandoned her mother. I don't think so. Her mother chose her own life. Sometimes it is stronger to submit. Like the saints. Sometimes I think of how her mother sang when I played my guitar. Something in her voice was like when you first ride a bicycle. But I never got her to bet. Every collector deals with people differently. You can make a bet for those who are afraid to try. Your money but their choice of two numbers from one to thirty-seven. I told them they could pay me back when they hit the jackpot. That's how habits start. When they did not win they felt bad for my lost money and would bet to repay my generosity. Our community was like that. We depended on each other. It was never my wish to leave.

(Match flares. Exhalation)

We can never know God's plan. Today you were blessed. Tomorrow you are smashing the window of a taxi to escape. Next you'll be looking at the wing bending as you fly into the unknown. It started months earlier. First it was good. One night before election season. My uncle picked me up from the house. With him was the table manager with the big mustache he called his pussytickler. They were going to drop off the payola. I did not know why they brought me. Maybe my innocence was a decoy. In the police station they handed over the package. Gave it like returning a VHS tape at Henny's shop. When they introduced me to the precinct captain I saw my uncle's plan. We all went next door to drink and sing. A good strategy. It was my chance. The captain and two of his boys said the sizzling pig face was the best in town. We drank bottles of Negra. They hogged the mic. Nowhere do police abuse more than a videoke bar. The captain's voice was okay. Like a drunk John Wayne. The other cops were terrible. Nobody dared sing "Endless Love" when it came on. Most men are scared by the Diana Ross parts. I took the mic. All the men watching. Karaoke is a great equalizer. Where respect is won. Talent is nothing and creates envy. What matters is bravery. Also personality and humor. If you feel and feel the music then you will command admiration. I sang both the parts of Lionel and Diana. At the end everyone cheered. Even the waitresses. My whole life would be different after that. My uncle paid the chit when our empty bottles covered the table. Captain John Wayne put his arm around my shoulders. Pussytickler said get a room. We all stumbled next door. The captain was a braggart. He showed me the improvements paid by protection money. Fresh GI sheets patching the rusty roof. New tires on two police cars. He was very proud of a cabinet full of office supplies. He unlocked the drawer of his desk and gathered fat envelopes. He saw me looking and winked. "Everyone has someone above them." That's what he told to me. He stuffed his pockets and we piled into the patrol jeep.

(Match flares. Exhalation)

There is nothing like being drunk and driving fast in a police vehicle with the lights flashing. Bon Jovi was on the radio. All of us singing about being halfway there. How free I felt. In the plaza of the next town was a fiesta for the big Estregan fight. When he won his first world championship. Projected on a screen hanging from the branches of a huge acacia. The volume was loud but everyone ignored the undercard. Too busy eating. A whole calf was roasting over coals. My uncle elbowed me and pointed with his chin. At the big table was our boss. The capitalist. That's what you call the gambling lord. Names are important but real names don't matter for a common story like this. He was surrounded by his anointed ones. City councilors. The priest. Some brass from the regional military. Executives from the pharmaceutical factory that donates to the school and community projects. Everyone enjoying the capitalist's generosity. When he's your boss even you walk differently. You smile at girls more confidently. When Nando stepped into the ring everyone stopped eating and always cheered at the same time. When he won in the second round people were crying. There is no feeling in the world like knowing someone will fight for you and win. That was the night my uncle named me his apostle. If he rose so would I. If I became a supervisor my loyalty would reward me forever. If I got sick or injured I could rely on fair loans. When she graduated I would make a good husband and father. Inshallah. Those were the best months of my life. I worked all the time but felt the wind in my face. Especially during the election. That kind of gambling is important in politics. The machinery is oiled well. The capitalist has it all prepared. Lawyers. Officials in his pocket. Men like me sent by the truckload to faraway towns. Violence against strangers is easier. Sometimes I went alone with Pussytickler to drop the payola. Without my uncle. That's how promising things were. I tried to grow my mustache. He teased me and I felt strong. Almost every afternoon I visited after her school. Their house was much nicer than my uncle's. Their street was asphalt. We sat outside and I pretended to help with her homework. She was always tutoring me without saying so. I will never be a reader who enjoys. We wrote our conversations in her notebook. For me to practice and so nobody could hear. The promises we wrote to each other were huge. They cannot ever be erased. One time I tried to shock her with the butterfly knife I started carrying. She touched the wound that became this scar on my hand. She asked me to show her how to unfold the blade. She is never afraid. After my evening collections I always biked to her house and whistled into the darkness. I stopped and made a tok-koh sound like a lizard. I lit a cigarette and waited. The light in the CR window turned on. I made the tok-koh sound again. The light in the CR was offed. I always biked home whistling and fell asleep happy. Friday and Saturday nights we spent the most time together. Usually watching VHS tapes. She liked love stories and I liked action movies about revenge. Sometimes I brought my guitar for sing-along. Once in a while even her father sang. I don't know what she tells you about him. He wasn't so bad. He drank too much but he was a normal man. Like you and me. That was the reason he was so angry. Training his whole life to be elite until one day he was not. There are many men like that around the base. He always pushed her to reach the standard he almost touched. That's why she abandoned them. I gave her that opportunity. She said I was saving her. I promised I always would. Inshallah.

(Match flares. Exhalation)

It was a few weeks after the election when everything changed. Before her final exams. She was studying for teachers' college. The mayor's son stole his father's seat and made big plans. My uncle was now a problem. Even informal organizers are thorns in the feet of politicians. I know it was the new mayor. I couldn't blame him. The world is that way. Nobody can do anything to fix that. I blame the capitalist and his men who made excuses to betray my uncle. He was one of theirs. They did not have enough honor to protect him. They started saying he was greedy. That he was a traitor. None of that was true. He always supported the numbers game. Always believed it made our community stronger. A crime without a victim. That's what he called it. He wasn't loyal to the capitalist out of greed. He was loyal out of wisdom. My uncle needed his protection. But powerful men like them are snakes eating their own tail. Men like my uncle tell them honestly what doesn't work. If pigs and fertilizer reach farmers. If a factory dumps chemicals in the river. If the people who trust you receive what you are sharing. My uncle was only helping our neighbors apply for the new government home loans. That was his mortal sin. When you hear an activist is shot for something like that it is a stupid politician plucking out his own eyes. There are no more matches. The box is empty. Do you have more? Alhamdulillah. That night was when my life began to twist. When I leave everything I know. When I will be lost but would one day find my purpose.

(Match flares. Exhalation)

I was biking home. Our neighbors were on the street. They shouted to me. I ran inside. Blessica was holding him. Blood all over her legs.

She kept wiping her tears. Blood on her face. He was alive. I carried him. I held him in the back of the neighbor's pickup. I told him stay awake. He shouldn't miss such a beautiful night. I told him look at the stars. Feel the cool air. He wanted the radio played. George Michael sang about careless whispers and guilty feet. We got to the hospital. He told me to run. I asked why. So I became NPA. No permanent address. Like millions of us. The cash crop now is not sugar or abaca. It is people exported everywhere. But my story is about how they break you. Destroy everything you are by taking everything you have. This can be done anywhere. I can show you in this room. The man who makes me a killer becomes my friend. I know that is hard to understand. First he tells me about all the violence he experienced. Maybe it is proof of his sympathy. Then he makes me feel it until it burns on its own inside me. I have no pity but I understand him. We kill what we are afraid of. You can pretend all you like but this is happening somewhere right now. Until one day after my work I will see her for the first time in years. On the Filipino channel. Giving a tour of her house from the president. I would see clearly at that moment. I will no longer give them all my life. What little I have left will not be for them anymore. The next week she would not reply to my messages to her fanpage on Facebook. I will watch her Instagram stories. I'll see how far she is from who she wanted to be. Her eyes would speak to me. Telling me. Asking me. When I climbed through her window she was alone. On Thursday nights her parents went to the veteran's club. Her father drank with the men. Her mother danced with the wives and waited to help him home. My pants were soaked from the canal. I scared her but she smiled. She asked why I didn't knock on the front door. When she saw the blood I said there was no time. I asked her to run away. I thought maybe she would panic or cry. Her face had only an expression like calculating bets. She told me yes.

(Match flares. Exhalation)

She said yes. We didn't kiss like in the movies. Time is always too short. The electricity went out and the neighbors shouted curses. Darkness was good but brownouts bring people onto the street. She went to take some of her things and leave a note. I told her I shall return. The street was still clear. I pulled down my cap. A few roads away there was a taxi parked half on the sidewalk. I used to imagine how I would be if I was tested. Always practicing my Bruce Lee moves in the mirror inside the CR. I never thought I would be saved by what my uncle taught me in the garage. I broke the window of the taxi. It started with a spark. She was outside her house. Waiting. That moment never faded from my mind. There were many situations in my life when I wished I had her courage. You hear about an unhappy husband who gets up from the table to buy milk for his family and never returns. I could never do that. Not willingly. That is how I find myself lost the moment I turn away from her. She watches me going to my airplane. That time I am still believing I will see her again and all our dreams will come true. The desert is a prison cell. My passport is taken. The job isn't what I thought. The pay not even a third. I owe thousands of dollars. There are twelve angry stomachs to one room. Not counting the rats and bedbugs. We take turns sleeping on four narrow mattresses. Every day we work hard. I try to call her but she isn't at the pension house anymore. Still I write her letters. I let go of them and they are gone. On Saturday nights we go to mass in someone's house. In secret. Like the disciples in the Bible. Father Joel Pablo helps us. It is the first time I like a priest. Most pretend to care so that you will do as they say. He tells me to contact the consulate but they are not always able to help. I heard many stories. In this country I must hide the rosary she gave me. Their constitution is the Koran. The Bible as illegal as a gun. They know money is a whip. Father Joel speaks my dialect and we pass time together. I know I must go. Your dreams are only as big as the dreams of the people around you.

(Match flares. Exhalation)

After nine months Father Joel helps me. I want to practice my faith freely. To seek my fortune. I don't know where he gets the papers. It is a long journey. From the Red Sea to the Gulf. Do not ask how I make it across the border. I will not say. Others also deserve to follow that destiny. To commit their own mistakes. I would learn that over many years. Until I will be at the airport back home again. Standing at that spot where I told her see you later. If I close my eyes I would almost see her. Even the blind band will be almost the same. Only bald now and gray. Same Beatles and Sérgio Mendes will fill the terminal. The streets will also be the same. Packed with too much of the same. Buses waiting together like a train crash. People piling on and one bus peeling off. The conductor hanging from the doorway like meat on a hook. I will jump on. No matter where it will be going it will take me where I need to go. I will find her and let her see me. Give her the opportunity. Love is always an opportunity. Seldom do we have opportunities. That night when we rushed to escape Angeles we drove slowly. We had to pass through narrow streets. If they were already looking we would be caught. People were outside waiting for the electricity. We passed the store where we used to buy soft drinks and play Famicom. Passed our old school. The police precinct was ahead. They had lights. The noise of their generator made me nervous. I held her hand. Nobody saw us. The last turn was ahead. We looked at each other. I used to believe that love is movement. Love cannot stop or else you die with it. We took the last turn and the dark road unrolled towards the capital. Headlights swung behind us. They grew bigger. The rear window shattered. We heard more shots. I crunched the gears and turned back into town. I had to lose them. The accelerator was flat against the floor. I executed another turn. In the mirror headlights followed and sparks flew against a wall like watusi firecrackers. One headlight disappeared. The other grew bigger. We went up the bridge and our car flew. Our bodies kept rising. I felt we would never come down.

(Match flares. Exhalation)

Up ahead the yellow light turned red. Cars and trucks passed like missiles. She started laughing. I also laughed. We were going to die laughing. For my living I help build an ice-skating rink in the desert. Face my fear high in the skeletons of skyscrapers. Nobody can TIG a tee joint as well as me. I'm the best. I think a lot about my plan. One more year to save enough to pay the loan sharks at home. I wake up one morning and five more years are passed. I see no point. She is gone already. She must be. If only Facebook was invented sooner. I am working at the Mövenpick Beach Club in Al Asimah when another welder tells me about a manpower agency. New Life Enterprises. Probably I am too sentimental. Ten years already I am in the region. I know Arabic already. I know the labor system. All its promises and my worth. It turns out they are people traffickers. This option is a gamble but gambling is buying opportunity. Inshallah. I go with them because the best criminals are professionals. Six Benjamin Franklins gets you across the border and letters of authorization onto the base. The world is there. Servicemen from lucky countries. Americans. Australians. Polish. Ukrainians. Danes. Italians. British. Dutch. Spanish. Canadians. Served by workers from unlucky countries. Fiji. Sri Lanka. Uganda. Nepal. Egypt. Turkey. Macedonia. China. Pakistan. Sudan. The Philippines. Everyone has a purpose. Accountants. Security guards. Butchers. Laundry people. Shopkeepers. Electricians. Beauticians. Technicians. Handymen. I help expand the sewage system. Others put up tents. Clean. Drive. Cook. Serve food. It is like a strange dream of America. Soldiers in uniforms in front of laptops at Seattle's Best. M16A2 rifles on picnic tables beside open Pizza Hut boxes. Iraqis at Burger King with their Coalition colleagues. Indonesians working at Kentucky. Bangladeshis at Cinnabon.

(Match flares. Exhalation)

Indians at Baskin and Robbin. Kenyans at Subway. The restaurants are in shipping containers. Some on the back of special trucks. Not drive-through. Drive-away. That's real fast food. First thing you learn is how to duck for cover. Sometimes it is mortars. Sometimes rockets. Sometimes gunfire. I don't know where other workers get their helmets and vests. I steal mine. We work twelve-hour shifts. On our day off there is nowhere to go. I join our countrymen for mass and videoke. I told you my voice is amazing. It makes people remember lost love. Sometimes there is entertainment for the troops. I see the Undertaker defeat Johnny Nitro. Chuck Norris visits another time. Also Toby Keith. He sings "The Taliban Song." ♫ *I'm just a middle-aged middle-eastern camel herdin' man. I got a little two-bedroom cave here in North Afghanistan . . .* ♫ See what I told you? Amazing. One night we all watch pay-per-view of Estregan fighting a Mexican champion of a higher weight class. But my cheers do not sound proud anymore. You cannot imagine how difficult it is for so many of us. It is a sin how our leaders send us. We have no choice but to believe promises. Our debts become mountains so tall you cannot see the peak anymore. The lucky live in shipping containers with air-con. The unlucky live in warehouses that suck at your skin. Those with bad luck live in shacks of wood scrap with old mattresses for roofs. Contractors like Halliburton use subcontractors like KBR. KBR uses local sub-subcontractors to do dirty work. We have no security. No privacy. Sometimes no food. No medicine. No insurance. Sometimes no soap even. Tens of thousands are killed or injured. Women are abused. I try to change this. Organize people. You never heard on the news about the riots? Hundreds are starving. Workers see what is thrown away by the fast-food outlets every day. They are in line at their mess hall when their rations run out again. Their complaints are ignored. They riot. This happens also in other camps. You know what they receive instead?

(Match flares. Exhalation)

Canceled contracts. Some not even a plane ticket home. They wander around the bases. They beg. Ask help from soldiers. Somebody needs to fix this broken world. Why not me? I would wake on the sidewalk along the bay the morning after I saw her at Starbuck. Every wave like a breath in my ear. I would see in my head what I will have to do. Already it will be the hottest day. My skin burning in the sun. My head hurting from the night. But my mind clear. I will pass by the pawnshop to buy a pistol. I would hail a taxi. We will drive towards the future that never seems to come. The street vendors selling newspapers just like I did. The blueboys and chocoboys still abusing their uniforms. Children begging as always. People in cars pretending. At an intersection I will fold two yellows for a little girl at my window. She wouldn't believe it. Her smile will be beautiful. The driver would hear me and take the Skyway. The city will rise above and below us. Cranes and new buildings. I will remember how I believed the city would give us everything. A broken bone cannot break where it heals. I will no longer be weak. I will follow my plan. I will touch my gun. Familiar buildings passing. I would see her on a billboard. Five stories tall. In her underwear. I will look out the window and think of all her promises. The city would be gone. How dry the countryside had become. The taxi will stop and I'll give the driver the rest of my savings. He would not understand but he'd accept. I will walk in and sit in the middle of the crowd. I would remember the intersection but not how we made it through. The headlight behind us got smaller. I knew who it was but had no power to fight him. He knew I knew him. He was strong enough that justice could not touch him.

(Match flares. Exhalation)

Sometimes you heard stories of a son whose family is murdered. The killer went free. The son learned how society does not do the bloody work of justice for everyone. But he accepts it as life. I was that way. Weakness is why we escaped together. The man who killed my uncle could not wait for me to grow strong. I looked at her in the passenger seat. White as a ghost. Only darkness behind us. The last few houses disappeared. Under the full moon the pineapple fields seemed like piles of broken black glass. We were high above and safe. A shadow screamed around a corner. One light shined in front of us. It became brighter and brighter. Like a train in the cartoons. Wile E. Coyote in a tunnel. I didn't know what Bruce Lee would do. I squeezed her hand and she said go. I asked her left or right. She chose. I tried to push the pedal through the floor. The other car screamed its horn. I swerved left. Left. Left was where our destiny changed. I wish I could say our side-mirrors hit. What a good story that would be. Our car skidded onto the shoulder and back onto the road. His red taillights turned over in a half circle into the black glass. I slowed down to see if he would explode. But that's only in the movies. In real life your pants are wet and your girlfriend is hyperventilating. We drove all night. We made it to the capital. We listened to the sea. All its promises secret. It was the start of a new day. Alhamdulillah. On our base I start to organize the chiefs of the different ethnic groups. I remember what my uncle was doing for others when I was younger. Not always a good man but always doing one more good thing than bad. Many hands make lighter work. That is what Blessica was always saying when asking my help. But the chiefs say people are scared. It is very difficult convincing them. I tell them the Americans don't know our problems. The Americans are not like their subcontractors. Turkish. Qatari. Yemeni. Saudi. The Americans will listen. Their campaign is called Operation Enduring Freedom. We list our complaints. We draft a petition. We call it Operation Enduring Justice. We are not slaves even if we have been treated like slaves. I believe I have nothing more to lose. I am wrong. The day before Ramadan I hitch a ride with a convoy. To go talk to the workers in the first forward-operating base that rioted. Only fifty miles to the west. We are ambushed. There are thirteen of us. Me and twelve Sri Lankan construction workers. A bag is put over my head.

(Match flares. Exhalation)

We are driven for I don't know how long. I know who at the base has betrayed us. I know also what I must do. I call out my nationality. I praise Allah. I speak Arabic and say I am a Muslim from our North. When we stop I am separated from the Sri Lankans. A man questions me in Arabic. He isn't from there. I recognize his accent. I hear the hostages outside reading what they are told. They denounce many things. I hear it all. I am dragged out to witness. If I close my eyes they will kill me also. I cannot remember the name of the young man I was riding with in the front of our truck. His hair combed like a playboy. He was not yet angry at the broken promises and smaller wages. No child or girlfriend. His parents proud of his remittances. I am made to watch. Maybe so that I will be grateful. You can find the video online. The others are just shot. Lying on their stomachs and the gunmen spray bullets on them. Like watering the plants. Google can show you all they do to him. I do not suggest it. But it is there to see. I learn that I am wrong to be grateful. I have another use.

(Match flares. Exhalation)

They take everything from me. What happens when they take even what you believe? What do you believe will happen tomorrow? Believing will not make it true. Believing will only make it matter to you. We believe so that we will matter. I did not matter anymore. The next time I see daylight Ramadan is over. For many years I am useful. All over the region. Faceless among millions of faceless. Feared across kingdoms by those who hear about my capacity. They think I am Hamas or Daesh or Mossad. All wrong. They call me the Domestic Helper. The baby face in a jean jacket who cleans up a mess and takes out the trash. I'm sure you saw my crimes in the news. That is me. I was the one. Netflix can make a series of my life. Maybe you think it is too crazy to be true. You do not know the world. No matter where you run there is someone above you. A public killing is not an ending. It is a beginning. That Saturday would be the hottest we've ever known. I'll practice in my head what I would shout. She will come onto the stage.

The girls would scream. He will come onto the stage beside her. The old women would scream. We will all stand. He would put his arm around her. How could she let him touch her? I will feel the gun. No longer weak. The music will play and he will mambo. The crowd boiling like water. I will wait no more. Dizzy from the steam of sweat and perfume. The whispering sea in my ears. I will wipe my tears. Dry my hands. Take out the revolver. Push to the front. Take a deep breath. Lift my arm. I will aim. If only we swerved right we would already be together forever. Vitalina looking into my eyes. My finger feeling the trigger. But the president danced in the way. Everyone screaming. The world falling. Pulling you with it.

(Match flares. Paper burning)

No more smokes. No more stories. Khalas. The end

I WAS THE PRESIDENT'S MISTRESS!!

I WAS THE PRESIDENT'S MISTRESS!!

I WAS THE PRESIDENT'S MISTRESS!!

I WAS THE PRESIDENT'S MISTRESS!!

I WAS THE PRESIDENT'S MISTRESS!!

!!

Acknowledgments

This part of a novel is conventionally the place where the author breaks the fiction's spell and thanks all those people who in fact helped them. But there are other things which I must acknowledge, as that word is more broadly defined—not just as an expression of gratitude, but as an acceptance of a truth, an action expressing notice, and a confirmation of receipt.

First, I must humbly acknowledge my privilege and limitations, and, ultimately, my awareness that I can never fully understand certain perspectives, ideas, and issues—even though it's my job, as a novelist, to always try. Writing this book taught me just how much there is to know, about which I must constantly expand, deepen, and evolve my understanding. I learned the heavy lesson that there is farther, always, to go.

In the early years of my education, Jesuits similarly taught me that with privileges come responsibilities. It is with that sense of purpose that I've sought to create characters whose experiences are nuanced, complex, and entirely foreign to mine. And whether or not I liked them much, I had to hear each of them out.

For if a writer is to strive to shoulder their role in society—to examine the past, interrogate the present, and imagine possibilities for the future—a writer of fiction, and especially satire, must accept a further one: to be brutally honest, but also hopeful, about what they know to be true about the human condition.

While every novel endeavors to be its own theory of both life and the novel form, inherent to all theories are flaws and fractures that must be tested, by ourselves and others—as *I Was the President's Mistress!!*

will now be, by you readers. My characters, whom I refused to judge on the page so that I could consider all they had to teach from it—the good and especially the bad—will now be judged by you. Rightly so.

For this is also my acknowledgment—indeed, an exhortation—that urgent work needs to be done, by all of us. Because although a novel unpacks the individual (the author, their protagonists), it similarly unpacks their world. And this world, in which we are each complicit, is clearly broken. It teaches too many, too well, how to thrive at the expense of others. Its systems, devised by us humans, are as tentative as any theory and as insufficient as any good intention.

In my native Philippines—for example—Asia's oldest democracy, the mechanisms designed to ensure an equitable share of power over those systems have all been hijacked. The rights and opportunities our Constitution is meant to ensure are lorded over by the very few who claim to lead but in actuality rule. The laws founded upon that Constitution become like bludgeons in their hands, they who seek to maintain their power over the rest of us.

This is no surprise. One of the first things an autocracy works to do is silence then discredit any objections to its ownership and, especially, abuse, of that power. Citing obscenity, morality, honor, security, those in charge all too often govern us obscenely, immorally, without honor, and with little regard for anyone's security except theirs. They cut out dissenters, steamroll checks and balances, demolish organizations that would hold them accountable, recruit legions to shout their justifying propaganda, and thumb their noses with impunity at efforts toward transparency and justice.

They know that to have a voice is to have a vote in the future of our societies; so they seek to ignore, overwhelm, or stifle each of ours. They miscast free speech as a weapon, precisely because it's our most vital tool.

We must acknowledge all that. All of us. And refuse to allow it.

And so I thank, foremost, those who have stood with me in my own efforts toward such refusal—though they here remain anonymous out of respect for their privacy: the many first readers and supporters over the years, from my family, friends, and comrades, to whom I'm indebted for believing in my potential to learn from them.

ACKNOWLEDGMENTS

Here, more conventionally, I must also express my gratitude to the institutions that nourished me and this book—the University of Adelaide; Farrar, Straus and Giroux; Penguin Random House Canada; the Rogers, Coleridge & White Literary Agency; the Melanie Jackson Agency; the Santa Maddalena Foundation; the Civitella Ranieri Foundation; the Radcliffe Institute for Advanced Study at Harvard University; International School Manila; the Canada Council for the Arts; the Conseil des arts et des lettres du Québec; the International Writers' Workshop at Hong Kong Baptist University; Singapore's Nanyang Technological University; and the Spring Workshop in Hong Kong. To neglect to thank these organizations would shortchange the individual human beings who power them—people who are too many and too distant that I'll never get to thank each directly.

Matsalasayois, too, must go to the every all memesters, socmed allies unmet in real life, and undercover satirical geniuses—such as The Professional Heckler and So, What's News?—who informed this novel's jokes and inspired me to laugh bravely together at our country's absurdities and at those people whose selfishness deserves our mockery.

An entire community empowered this book, whose climax must now be written by you in its blank final pages. And beyond.

Miguel Syjuco, September, 2021

A NOTE ABOUT THE AUTHOR

Miguel Syjuco is a Filipino author, journalist, civil society advocate, and professor at New York University Abu Dhabi. His debut novel, *Ilustrado*, was a *New York Times* Notable Book of the Year and won both the Man Asian Literary Prize and the Grand Prize at the Palanca Awards, his country's top literary honor. He has worked as a contributing opinion writer for *The International New York Times*, written for many of the world's most respected publications, and spoken on Philippine politics and culture at the World Forum for Democracy and the World Economic Forum. He serves on the advisory councils of the Civitella Ranieri Foundation, an international arts residency program, and the Resilience Fund, a project of the Global Initiative Against Transnational Organized Crime to empower communities most threatened by criminality.